Praise for *The Girl in His Shadow*

"In *The Girl in His Shadow*, Audrey Blake takes the reader on an exquisitely detailed journey through the harrowing field of medicine in mid-nineteenth-century London. Nora, the ward of the eccentric and brilliant surgeon Horace Croft, learns far more than any woman is allowed. Bravely saving lives while risking her own, she defies the law to pioneer breakthroughs in medicine."

—Tracey Enerson Wood, international bestselling author of *The Engineer's Wife*

"A suspenseful story of a courageous young woman determined to become a surgeon in repressive Victorian England. Fluidly written, impeccably researched, *The Girl in His Shadow* is a memorable literary gift to be read, reread, and treasured."

—Gloria Goldreich, author of *The Paris Children*

THE GIRL

in HIS

SHADOW

a novel

AUDREY BLAKE

sourcebooks
landmark

For Ivy

To Nana, Nancy Runyan, whose gift for healing as a decorated WWII army nurse in the Pacific Theatre brought compassion and hope to the survivors of the Bataan Death March. You inspire me always.

Published by Sourcebooks Landmark, an imprint of Sourcebooks
P.O. Box 4410, Naperville, Illinois 60567-4410
(630) 961-3900
sourcebooks.com

Library of Congress Cataloging-in-Publication Data is on file with the publisher.

Printed and bound in the United States of America.
SB 10 9 8 7

PROLOGUE

H EFTING HIS BLACK BAG, DR. HORACE CROFT STUMPED
down the uneven pavement. Despite the afternoon sun-
shine, the street was silent and the air thick with fear. Shop
doors were shut and bolted, and too many anxious faces watched
from the windows. For fifteen years London had dreaded the
cholera. Now it had come.

Croft had tried to prepare, studying initial reports of the
epidemic from India, Russia, and Japan. An irreligious man,
he gave silent prayers of relief when the outbreak of 1827 died
in the Caucasus before reaching Europe. Foolish of him. Four
years later, the deadly disease advanced from the dark forests
of the East into the shadowy Balkans. The following year it
breached England's rocky shores. Miraculously, the outbreak
was contained in Sunderland, but this was respite, not reprieve.
Three months later, the disease erupted in London.

He'd paid ten calls already today, all within a mile of each
other. He frowned, still troubled by the last.

Jemmy Watt had first sent for him yesterday to tend his
feverish wife. Today, she was dead. So were her children, and
Jemmy was failing rapidly. It would be a miracle if Croft found
him alive tomorrow. This disease was too strong to fight. Even
worse, the lads at the parish were cowards, unwilling to come

for the bodies of Jemmy's family. Croft had shouted and cursed, warning them against leaving corpses harboring contagion until they'd finally cleared them away, but not before binding linen around their faces as a shield against the miasma of disease. All the shouting left Croft's throat dry as pasteboard.

One more stop before he could go home. With this patient, at least, he had some hope. Francis Beady, a stationer, was gone already, buried in quicklime a week ago, but the wife, Margaret, ignored grief with an iron will. Yesterday, though terse and thin-lipped, she'd been determined to keep her ailing mother-in-law alive. Better yet, her child and baby were still healthy. He had left Margaret Beady with a tincture of willow bark for fever and instructions to get help with her mother-in-law's care, though they knew no one would come.

"I'll try, Doctor," Margaret said, spooning water between the dry lips of her mother-in-law, while the little girl—a mere eight or nine—bounced the baby on her knee. The old woman seemed to be turning the corner.

Yes, he expected to see improvements in the Beady house. The shop was closed, naturally, so he knocked loudly on the door. No answer. He checked his watch. Mrs. Beady knew to expect him.

"Mrs. Beady!" Still no sound. Worried now, he rattled the handle. It moved beneath his hand. Unlocked. Horace frowned. It wasn't like Mrs. Beady, but there was little danger of invasion. The neighbors all knew of their affliction. Croft stepped inside, past the dimly lit shelves of notebooks and paper. In only a week, the counters had acquired a film of dust.

It was a small shop, but the Beadys made a better living

than Jemmy Watt. Not that money dissuaded cholera or made it any less lethal. He made his way up the stairs to the family's rooms on the second floor. "Mrs. Beady?" It was too quiet, and the telltale stench hovered on the landing. Resigned to what he would find, Croft walked in, stepping over the toy blocks abandoned on the floor.

He found the mother-in-law's wasted body in the bedroom, but Mrs. Beady had been well enough then to cover her with a sheet. Mrs. Beady was curled up on the sitting room floor, her hair still damp, her lips cracked. The baby lay beside her. It must have died after, for it lay uncovered in a pool of filth, and Croft knew Margaret was not a woman to leave her child untended. He sighed and straightened, tugging at his coat. As for the older child...

Croft looked around. He couldn't see her. "Miss Beady?" He didn't know the girl's name. "Miss Beady!"

He felt more than heard a faint exhalation. She was behind him, huddled deep in a shabby armchair. He tilted back her chin—still alive, her skin hot, her eyes unfocused. He reached to take her pulse, frowning as he counted the slow, thready beats, noting the tremor in her fingers. In her other hand, cradled against her stomach, she clutched a dipper. The basin beside her was empty. Her lips moved, and though she failed to produce any sound, he could almost hear the crackling of her flaked skin.

Water, she mouthed. There was none in the room.

"I'll be right back," he said and went to find the kitchen. There was no water to be had, but in the teapot on the table was an inch of cold brew gone sludgy at the bottom. It would do.

He tried dripping it onto her lips, but the liquid rolled away before she could catch it. Anxious now, he soaked it up with his handkerchief. When he laid the wet cambric on her mouth, she sucked. Her fingers, already skeletally thin—cholera was terrifyingly aggressive—came up to clutch the cloth. He let her work on it, then had to pry it away to soak again. Her grip was stronger than he'd expected, but he warned himself against hope. It was easy, depressingly easy, to imagine patients looking better. Hadn't he thought the old woman would pull through? This child looked as fragile as a dandelion puff.

She couldn't stay here alone. She must be bathed and put into clean clothes. Someone must soak the handkerchief for her and, in all probability, watch until she gave up and died.

Ah. There were curtains. Good enough, and probably the cleanest linen in the house. With two hands, Croft gripped the child's soiled nightdress and tore it down the front. She flinched, but whether it was his hands or the noise that disturbed her, he couldn't say. She was too blue, too thin. With the spare, efficient movements of a battlefield surgeon, he peeled the dirty garment away and pulled at the curtains. The rod broke, and the rings tore and crashed to the floor in a swirl of dust and plaster as sunlight knifed into the room. He squeezed his eyes shut and coughed. The girl made a sound. Leaning close, he cataloged the flicker of her hollowed eyes, the tremor of her lips.

"Hush. We'll get you covered. These curtains will do."

He picked her up and swathed her in the yards of sturdy cloth. Even with the wrapping, she felt no heavier than a good-sized border collie. Croft was sturdy and used to lugging around deadweight, but the extra fabric was a hazard, tangling his arms. He looped it around her slack legs and carried her down the stairs. No one stopped him on the way out, but he made himself knock at the neighbor's door.

"You must send for someone to carry away the bodies," he said to the tired-eyed woman peering suspiciously through the peephole.

She blinked. Croft resisted the urge to blast her. The fool woman must have known the Beadys were ill but hadn't moved an inch to help them. "And that one?" she asked.

"I'll take her."

The woman didn't argue, blind or indifferent to his contempt. In the street, the eyes that found him and his burden swerved away. By the time he got home, he was breathing hard, unable to manage his key. He had to knock and wait for his housekeeper.

"What's this?" she demanded. "You can't bring corpses in the front door." His regular deliveries always came in the dead of night, at the back, because flaunting the fact that he bought stolen bodies was a good way to get his windows smashed.

"This one's alive. You're blocking my way, Mrs. Phipps."

Her face blanched. "You can't bring cholera here!" But she stepped aside. Croft marched upstairs, Mrs. Phipps fretting behind him. "She's sick! What am I supposed to do with her?"

"Get her some water. No, sweet tea. We'll try that. And fetch something for her to wear. One of my shirts will suffice. I'll need your help to bathe her."

No response. He looked back, fixing his housekeeper with a stern look. "Everyone in her family is dead."

Mrs. Phipps sighed with exasperation. "And you think you can save her."

Horace lifted one side of his mouth. With the girl in his arms, it was impossible to shrug. "Probably not. But I'll try." When he reached the next floor, she called after him. "Not the blue guest room! Those are the best sheets!"

———

Unlike her employer, Mrs. Phipps was religious. When she arrived with a sponge and a basin of water, she forgot her desire to safeguard the best household linen. "God in heaven," she murmured. The girl's skin was almost transparent, her eyes sunk in hollows of plum-dark bruise. Her dark-blond hair spilled in a tangled mass against the pillowcase.

"Don't try to speak." Mrs. Phipps advanced with her wet sponge. "Save your strength, child."

The girl improved at first, then weakened for days until she was as thin as an eggshell. The tea and broth spooned into her so laboriously passed through her without even changing color. When she turned as gray as ash and dry as paper, Dr. Croft rubbed his chin and Mrs. Phipps went to the pantry to wring her hands unobserved. Then she set her jaw and marched back upstairs to dose and poultice and bathe, resolute as any soldier facing a hopeless battle. When the fever broke and natural sleep fell upon the girl, Mrs. Phipps wept.

This earned a chiding glance from the doctor. "Don't get sentimental," he said. He finished measuring the child's pulse and went to the chair by the window to record his notes.

Too late. Mrs. Phipps was past forty with no husband. "Mr.

Phipps" was a necessary invention due to her promotion, twenty years ago, from upstairs maid to housekeeper. To Mrs. Phipps, the quiet girl stirring in her sleep was no longer a patient. She was a miracle, a baby brought by a river in a rush basket. And Mrs. Phipps didn't even know the child's Christian name.

As soon as the little one recovered her speech, the housekeeper broached the subject between spoonfuls of broth. "Now you are mending, I should like to call you something besides Miss Beady," she said, watching the girl's throat. "Good. Swallow it down. Take another spoonful." She blotted a drip of broth with a soft napkin. "What did your parents call you?"

The child blinked but a lone tear escaped, leaving behind a glistening silver trail like the snails so injurious to the rosebushes Mrs. Phipps nourished in the patch of earth behind the house.

"Are they gone?" Her dark eyes wheeled around the shadows of the room, searching.

Mrs. Phipps nodded, unable to speak.

"All of them? Peter?"

"All but you." Overcome by her failure with words, Mrs. Phipps pressed the child close, surprised when tiny fingers clung to her.

The child closed her eyes against the pain and whispered, "My name is Eleanor."

"It's a pretty name." Mrs. Phipps caressed the girl's hand, surprised the gesture came without thinking. She had no experience with children.

"They called me Nora."

"And so shall I. Only two more spoonfuls." When she set aside the empty cup, Mrs. Phipps smoothed Nora's hair, then thought better of it and went for a comb. She unpicked the tangles and would have tied the limp strands back with a ribbon, but Nora was asleep.

The first time Nora was well enough to leave her bed and eat gruel in a chair by the fire, Mrs. Phipps shut Nora's bedroom door, tiptoed downstairs, and confronted the doctor in his study. She made certain his door was shut, too.

"Eh?" Dr. Croft looked up.

"Still doing better."

"Good, good." He looked down at his notebook, but Mrs. Phipps ignored this cue of dismissal.

"Sir? I'd like to know what you intend with Nora."

"Who?" He looked up in confusion.

Mrs. Phipps liked and respected her employer. Usually. "Miss Eleanor Beady, the girl you brought home for me to drag back from the grave."

"I suppose we'll have to find out if she has any family."

Mrs. Phipps had already made inquiries and ascertained there were none. Keeping her hands neatly folded (though her nostrils flared), she explained this to the doctor.

"Perhaps the parish—" He caught her stern look and aborted the thought. "I could find a school for her, I suppose."

"She's not a fish. You can't throw her back." She'd never used such a tart voice with him before. "I want to keep her."

"Where?"

"In the blue room, of course. I'm not going to store her away in some cupboard."

"But why?"

The scalpel-sharp question confounded her. She couldn't explain. Mrs. Phipps only knew that she needed the girl, that she would weep for days and days if she lost her. Unable to speak, she mashed her lips together, and Dr. Croft, who regularly had to pick up on what people were helpless to say, suddenly understood this was an emotional matter. He did not like to unduly antagonize his housekeeper. She was the only woman in England who tolerated dusting around severed body parts. He nodded once and returned to his writing. "Never mind. Excellent notion. Might as well keep the girl. In a year or two, when cholera returns to London, I can observe if she's gained any immunity."

Mrs. Phipps was speechless, but decided to overlook his callous words. She'd won.

CHAPTER 1

Thirteen years later. 1845.

NORA PUSHED A WAYWARD CURL OFF HER DAMP FORE-head. The morning fog on the Thames refused to lift, collecting the summer heat like a wet rag spread over the city. Fetid odors lingered in the streets, insinuating their way into the house. Even Nora's tolerant nose wrinkled. She pressed a scented handkerchief to her face and hastened to answer the front door.

Another candidate. They needed a new hallboy, one with rare and expensive qualities: Dr. Croft's household required servants who were quiet and discreet. So far, Nora's interviews had been unsuccessful. Teeth on edge, she tripped over the wrinkled rug in the hall and cursed quietly, half for the rug and half for a boy who didn't know to use the back entrance.

With an annoyed frown, she yanked open the door. "I expected you around back," she announced.

"Pardon?"

Nora's eyes adjusted to the fierce outdoor light. Oh no. Certainly not a hallboy. This was a man, a tall one, wearing a neat beard that failed to hide his youth. He carried an expensive beaver hat in his hands. Nora dusted her hands against her wrinkled skirt and rearranged her face into a flustered smile. "I'm terribly sorry. May I help you?"

He hesitated. "Was I supposed to go to the back? Is that where the clinic is situated?"

Ah. A new patient, a Mayfair one by the looks of him. Nora blushed and wondered why he'd come here instead of sending for Dr. Croft. Perhaps he was suffering from a private complaint, the sort of malady that came from raucous clubs and free women. This one was handsome—handsome enough to get himself into that kind of trouble. People traveled further afield to conceal such things from their neighbors. Or wives.

Nora cleared her throat. "I'm so sorry. I'm afraid Dr. Croft had to go out. They needed him at hospital to cover another doctor's lecture. If you come back in an hour... Or you could come in and wait." *Please don't let him come in and wait.* She'd been too busy this morning with interviews to examine the state of the parlor.

"I'm happy to wait. Perhaps I could look the consulting rooms over?"

Nora blinked. Had she offended him? After coming all the way to Great Queen Street, did he think their clinic inferior? True, the neighborhood was faded and the house shabby, but the clinic was bright and pristine.

"Or if my room is ready, I could unpack my bags," he said.

"Bags?" Only at that moment did Nora see the luggage beside him on the front stoop. *Did he intend to stay?* There were no surgeries scheduled for the day, but that didn't mean Dr. Croft hadn't promised something and forgotten to inform Nora.

"I'm afraid I'm caught out," Nora admitted. "I didn't know

Dr. Croft was expecting an overnight patient, but I'm happy to prepare a room."

"I'm sorry," the man replied, not sounding apologetic at all. "I think we're confused. Let me make a proper introduction. I am Dr. Daniel Gibson, the new under surgeon."

Her mouth fell open. "Under surgeon of what?" she finally managed to ask.

He withdrew the outstretched hand she had failed to notice. "Of this establishment. Dr. Croft hired me. Surely he spoke of me..." Dr. Gibson's voice trailed off as he took in her shocked face.

The day had come—hot and monotonous and like every other morning, except today she found herself staring into the face of her own replacement. He smiled. Was he trying to charm her?

Taking advantage of her surprise, the man picked up his bags and stepped into the hall. His shoes were impossibly shiny after navigating their busy street, as if dust refused to cling to him.

Mrs. Phipps appeared at Nora's elbow. *Good. An ally.* "Is there a problem here?"

"This man says he was hired by the doctor to be an under surgeon. Here!"

"Never!" Mrs. Phipps puffed, squaring her tiny shoulders. She was barely the height of a road pony and spare as the poles they tied them to, but the tall man swallowed uncomfortably under her scrutiny. "Shall we ever learn not to be shocked?" she asked, casting her eyes to the ceiling.

"Well, I freely admit that I am." Nora folded her arms and

planted herself in front of the man to halt further trespassing. "Dr. Croft can't have hired you. Not without consulting
me—the rest of the household, I mean. It's impossible. In the
meantime…"

"In the meantime, perhaps someone could take my coat?
It's unnaturally warm today." He set down both his bags and
went to work unbuttoning his greatcoat.

Nora started to argue, but Mrs. Phipps gave a stern look.
"I'm sure Dr. Croft will explain," she whispered to Nora. "What
did you say your name was, Mr…?"

"Dr. Gibson. Daniel Gibson." He tipped his head. "Thank
you for being so accommodating," he said.

Mrs. Phipps returned his smile and offered, "I'll have Cook
make up a sandwich since you've come all this way."

"That would be lovely. Perhaps after I've seen the clinic."

"Certainly," Mrs. Phipps said.

She led him down the hall, leaving Nora abandoned with
his luggage in the entryway. That wayward curl, sensing Nora's
losing streak, sprang free and landed in the middle of her forehead. Pushing it away, she hastened after them.

She rounded the corner and nearly collided with the man.
He'd stopped to frown at a particularly overwrought painting of
a storm-tossed ship, unfortunately hanging askew. He reached
out and righted it, glancing at her.

Nora suppressed a grunt, painfully aware of the worn hallway carpet, her serviceable dress, the clash of shabby grandeur
and utility in the fixtures. Gibson (she wouldn't think of him as
doctor until he proved his skill) didn't belong here. His impeccable demeanor and Mayfair manners were as abrasive to Nora as

grit on the tongue. Maybe if he got an honest look at the house he'd decide not to stay. Nora quickened her steps, keeping pace with him as he hurried after Mrs. Phipps to the clinic.

———

This was deuced awkward. Daniel frowned, cursing Croft's absentmindedness. Perhaps coming here was a mistake. His family certainly thought so, but he'd insisted. He was lucky, he told them, to have this chance to study with a surgeon as respected as Dr. Croft.

Of course, none of them—Father, Mother, Lillian, Mae—understood why he wanted to study surgery at all. He'd tried to explain: surgery was the vanguard of scientific discovery, a challenge, a test of his mettle, a set of skills that saved lives. Mother had softened at the idea of fame and success, but this contretemps over his arrival made Daniel doubt the wisdom of his choice. *Surgery? Why indeed.*

The housekeeper looked like a true martinet, pacing ahead of him, her skirts swishing with almost mathematical precision. As for the other one… She was peevish, plaintive, and clearly ill-suited for the role of surgeon's wife. No wonder Croft never mentioned her. If he dealt with this at home, perhaps it explained his distracted muttering and long hours at the dissection table. A young wife was a fine catch for a grizzled, middle-aged man, but Croft was paying dearly for this one.

At least you needn't trouble about her. Enduring some female ill-temper—*and eccentricity*, Daniel thought, spying a sheaf of notes weighed down with an enormous skull—was a small price. Horace Croft was a prize surgeon. His lectures at St.

Bartholomew's Hospital were always impossibly crowded, and he hadn't taken an assistant in his private clinic for years. Plenty of men envied Daniel this position.

He would simply have to be patient with Croft's distracted ways and try to nourish a more favorable impression with the women of the house. It wasn't their fault they didn't know to expect him. "I'm sorry my arrival has caused so much inconvenience. A sudden houseguest is quite the surprise."

The housekeeper sighed. "I'm accustomed to surprises after almost twenty years with the doctor." Her mouth snapped shut like a cigar box on tight hinges. The young lady, walking beside him, said nothing.

Well, they didn't have to like him all at once. If it took time to earn his way into their good graces, so be it. At least the housekeeper acknowledged his apology. Whatever people said, in large dwellings, the housekeeper was the woman of the house. Once he won her firmly to his side, he'd make an attempt to get in the good graces of Mrs. Croft, but if that failed, there was always the cook. Daniel had a weakness for toffee trifle.

Names would be nice, though. They had his, and he felt uncomfortable not knowing what to call them.

The housekeeper stopped at the end of the corridor. "The clinic is this way."

The young lady at his side stiffened. "We don't know—"

Daniel spoke up, his thoughts of friendly overtures forgotten. It was time to insist—firmly, but gentlemanly. "I'm here at the invitation of Dr. Croft, madam. I am not a liar."

She stared mulishly at him, practically daring him to pass.

The housekeeper interceded. "I'll show him the clinic." She spoke to the girl, looking past him. "If you'll decide on a room for Dr. Gibson?"

She nodded once, sharply. "Yes, Mrs. Phipps." She left without another word. Daniel decided he would definitely get along better with the housekeeper.

"This way," the older lady beckoned.

Daniel kept pace beside her. "I hope Mrs. Croft will overlook our awkward start."

"Who?" she asked sharply, her insistent steps losing their steady beat.

"The lady, Mrs. Croft." She was probably not a day over twenty, which put her thirty years behind her husband. She had a lovely complexion, completely unmarred by smallpox. Certainly, she'd be one of the inoculated ones. Dr. Croft was an outspoken advocate for the procedure.

"There's no Mrs. Croft." A reluctant smile cut through the frown lines of the housekeeper's cheeks. "Unless he went and grabbed a wife this morning, as well as you. One never knows."

Daniel frowned and paused to quiz out this new puzzle. "But the lady at the door? Forgive me. I thought her the doctor's wife. He told me specifically he had no children."

"Nor has he." The housekeeper's patience was waning. She sniffed as if to say that a stranger appearing from the London streets and announcing he was to live at her house could nearly be tolerated, but a nosy man was insufferable. "You met his ward, Miss Eleanor Beady. She runs the home and helps manage the clinic. The doctor may not have mentioned her, but I suggest you show her the utmost respect." The stern

press of her lips gave notice that it was far more than a suggestion. He wondered if the pretty ward was a bastard child or
a relative's orphan.

"Of course. My apologies." Daniel counted how many
times he'd apologized in the last five minutes and didn't care
for the tally. Especially when his only crime was to arrive at his
appointed time, well presented and punctual.

The housekeeper led him downstairs to a room lined with
bookcases and labeled drawers, as well as a battered desk. "The
doctor consults in here. He has a surgical theater where the
atrium used to be. Best light." She flicked her head toward the
door. "He plans to turn the servants' hall into more convalescing
rooms when he expands, which makes you wonder where the
servants will eat."

Daniel nodded as if vastly interested, though he wondered
no such thing. He was pondering how Dr. Croft kept curious
onlookers from beholding gory surgeries in a glass atrium. Surely
it must be boiling in the summers, and at St. Bartholomew's
Hospital Croft always advocated keeping patients cold.

The housekeeper continued, warming to the subject of her
domestic difficulties. "Of course, there is only me and Cook
that live in, and both of us have rooms upstairs. The other servants live out and come during the day. Odd, but there it is."
She clamped her hands into a knot, daring him to argue.

"I'm sure you manage things admirably." She'd find no
complaints from him so long as there was strong coffee in the
morning and plenty of patients to see. "Where will the doctor
expect me to stay?"

She sighed and rubbed her forehead. "I'm not sure yet.

We've some empty rooms on his side of the house, though that's a grisly prospect as they are full of his specimens. The third floor is nicer, but I can't have you near my or Eleanor's rooms."

"Certainly not," he agreed quickly. The thought of bumping into the housekeeper in her dressing gown on the way to her bath produced an inward shudder. He smiled sheepishly. "I'm afraid I did not catch your name."

"Gracious. What am I thinking? I'm Mrs. Phipps, the housekeeper, and in spite of what you've seen, I'm generally used to commotion." Her eyes narrowed. "Though I hope you are less forgetful than Dr. Croft. One of him is enough. And I don't care for gentlemen who leave bits lying around."

"I spent years at medical school without a valet. I'm used to tidying up after myself," Daniel assured her.

She stared at him a moment, then broke into a laugh. "Lord love you, Doctor, I wasn't thinking about stockings or neckties. I meant bones and things. Just yesterday afternoon I found a handkerchief wrapped around a severed thumb. Dr. Croft had forgotten to put it away."

"How terrible," he mumbled. "I do my best to keep my patients all in one piece."

She gave an approving nod. "Well, that's something. This way, Doctor. I'm sure you'll want to get a look at the surgery." She led him up a half-dozen stairs. They were newer than the rest of the house, and opened into a black cave. "Just give me a moment with the window shades," she said.

He heard her fumbling with something, then he blinked, struck full in the face by a lance of sunlight.

"Let me help." Daniel crossed the room and reached for another cord. He pulled it tight, raising the shade as far as it would go and doubling the light in the glass-enclosed room. He twisted the cord around a cleat so the shade would stay up and stepped back.

The house may be shabby, he thought, *but the surgery is incredible.* The stone walls came only to waist height, with glass panes filling the remaining walls and the entire ceiling. They were covered now by a series of thick window shades, except for the two panels they had lifted, and the light from that segment alone filled the entire room.

"The shades are a little cumbersome," Mrs. Phipps said at his elbow.

"No, they're perfect," Daniel said. Dark and thick on the outside, they shielded the room from the sun's heat when lowered. The slate floor kept the room pleasantly cool. At night or on hot days, with the shades down, the white canvas lining would reflect and amplify any lamplight within.

Scrubbed tabletops shone whiter than the holystoned planks of a navy frigate, and gleaming basins sat upside down to dry in a neat row on the cupboards lining two of the walls. A tray of instruments waited under a layer of bleached linen toweling. Beneath the scent of lye, he detected the smell of blood, but faint enough he couldn't be certain. There was no sign of dust, let alone stains. Four tall mirrors in wooden frames stood along one of the empty walls, and a system of pulleys hung from the metal supports girding the roof—for lamps? Or applying traction? And there, next to the door—

"Why is there an easel?" Daniel asked.

Mrs. Phipps coughed. "Sometimes Dr. Croft has an artist come make drawings of different specimens."

"Of course." Daniel should have realized. Dr. Croft was known for the quality of the illustrations that so often accompanied his reports. "I look forward to meeting the fellow."

"We ought to see about getting you that sandwich," Mrs. Phipps said.

"Of course." He agreed out of politeness, telling himself he'd soon have a chance to look over this marvel of a surgery, inspect the contents of the many fitted drawers, and learn the workings of the pulleys on the ceiling. "This room is fitted up wonderfully. I'm surprised he doesn't offer demonstrations—"

"He lets a few in at times, but the hospital theaters are better equipped for that," Mrs. Phipps said quickly. "This space is far too small."

It wasn't large, but Daniel knew many men who'd be willing to stand shoulder to shoulder and chest to back to see Dr. Croft working in this environment. However, he was not foolish enough to contradict Mrs. Phipps and followed her meekly back into the house, up the stairs, and into the front hallway.

"No, don't worry about your cases," she told him. "I'll have them brought upstairs once the room is ready. You can wait in Dr. Croft's consulting room and I'll send in your tray. I'll let the doctor know you are here as soon as he gets in."

She motioned him into a dimly lit room filled with dancing dust motes and mammoth, threadbare chairs. The heavy door closed behind her. To pass the time, Daniel scanned the books crammed higgledy-piggledy onto the shelves, recoiling at the discovery of a misshapen human ear floating in a glass jar. Of course, Daniel had seen far worse in medical school, but one expected to see specimens there. He gave his jacket a smart tug and settled into Dr. Croft's chair, humming to ward off nerves and wait for his lunch. Hopefully the petulant girl and floating ear hadn't spoiled his appetite. Ten minutes ago, he'd been starving.

CHAPTER 2

NORA STARED OUT THE WINDOW INTO THE STREET, chewing her bottom lip. She was used to problems of all sorts besides the usual domestic wrinkles: broken bones, festering wounds, the doctor's repugnant but necessary trade in dead bodies. But she didn't know how to deal with Dr. Gibson and what he would think of her role in the house. Hadn't Dr. Croft considered that? No. He was careless. He wouldn't think of her, or how he was wounding her by shunting her aside.

She pictured Dr. Gibson inspecting her specimens and tools in the surgical theater and flinched. Surely once she explained… Dr. Croft was often distracted by sudden enthusiasms that were just as quickly forgotten. She'd speak to him and explain why this Gibson fellow couldn't stay. It wasn't her habit to correct the doctor, but she and Mrs. Phipps had ways of governing him.

Nora grabbed her bonnet and an umbrella to shield her from the heat and trundled down the stairs, loudly, so she wouldn't have to hear Dr. Gibson humming to himself in Dr. Croft's consulting room. Somehow he'd inveigled his way there. Not a good sign. Mrs. Phipps didn't usually let visitors wait there, making them sit instead in the more demure sitting room. If she'd let him into the parlor, where Dr. Croft was known to leave some of his more noteworthy and alarming specimens, it

meant she trusted him and felt no need to hide the peculiarities of their household. Nora relaxed her compressed mouth,
schooling her face to untroubled blandness as she hurried down
the street.

It wasn't far to St. Bartholomew's Hospital, less than a
mile, and Nora was familiar enough with the way to exclude
the tumult of the streets from her thoughts. She kept her eyes
demurely down when she arrived, whisking past the porter
engaged in giving directions to a trio of students. Dr. Croft was
in the amphitheater, demonstrating the mechanics of a partially
dissected shoulder. No one saw her enter, so Nora took a seat in
the back. Her errands for Dr. Croft had acclimated the students
and staff to her occasional presence.

"The joint is vulnerable to dislocation anterior and inferi-
orly, but with the proper maneuvers…"

Nora kept her eyes on a freckle on her wrist, just visible
beneath the cuff of her glove. The usual shush and lap of scribbling and turning paper punctuated Dr. Croft's drone. She was
used to these sounds. After she'd spent a late night working
alongside Dr. Croft preparing specimens, they often put her
to sleep. Today her fingers tensed inside her gloves, her pulse
unnaturally fast.

He wasn't alone until a half hour after the conclusion of the
lecture, and even then, the orderly was still at work shrouding
the body, tidying things away. It was a good corpse—little fat to
strip away. She wondered at the manicured fingers, protruding
now beneath the edge of the sheet.

"Dr. Croft?" Her voice was rough from disuse.

"Trouble at home? I saw you come in."

"You could say that." Nora swallowed her surprise. He was always an intense lecturer, so it was unusual he'd noticed. "A…a gentleman came by today."

The doctor frowned, but only for a moment, then his brow cleared. "Of course. I forgot to mention it. Is Phipps in a tizzy, trying to fit up a room?"

"She didn't seem *unduly* put out." Nora tried not to sound bitter, but it leached into her next question: "You did invite this student to stay with us?"

"Oh, he's a full-fledged doctor," Croft replied, gathering up his probes, putting each in its home in the velvet-lined case. "Sadly lacking, though, in surgical experience. He had a failure early on with a mastectomy but he's coming round. Eager to learn from his mistakes and give it another try. Better read than anyone I've talked with in a good long while, and a sincere wish to better his practical skill. Some interesting theories, too, about cauterization. Nice fellow. I think you'll like him."

Nora manufactured a smile. "But sir, you can't have considered. What will he think of—of me being in the surgery?"

"We'll sort it out," he said, buckling the straps on his case. "Phipps is always telling me I push you too hard and—" He peered at her. "You do look a little pale."

"We didn't get back from Lilly Jenkins's confinement until three," Nora said.

"Exactly. And your work with the last specimen—what a wonder. I'd lost hope of ever getting a malformed heart of that size. Miracle the baby lived as long as she did. Your drawing of the atrial septum—"

"You liked it?" Nora asked.

"Of course, of course. But my point is, we could help this fellow."

"Gibson?"

Dr. Croft nodded. "He shows promise. Why else would I take him on?"

"But is he discreet?" Nora asked.

"If it comes up, I'll speak to him." He started up the stairs.

How could it help but come up? She was nearly always in the surgery. Exasperated, Nora picked up her skirts and followed after him. "Sir, it's bound to, unless you intend to banish me." Her eyes pricked, but her voice was level.

"Of course not." He threw a look at her over his shoulder. "But you're right. Does no harm to be prudent. Steer clear of the surgery for a week or two. Let me size him up."

Nora scowled at the worn stone stairs. She should have known that eventually some bright fellow would catch Dr. Croft's attention. He'd only ever wanted *her* because she was convenient. How could she compete with Dr. Gibson, who'd been to medical school, and could accompany Dr. Croft to lectures and work with him in the hospital? Once Gibson made a place for himself on Great Queen Street, she didn't like to think about what would become of hers.

⌒

The state of the house was appalling, Daniel decided, looking into yet another derelict room as he followed Mrs. Phipps to his new bedchamber down the hall. No covers on the furniture, and the pieces that remained in the gaunt space sported flaking gilt and shredded brocade. The consulting room, where he'd consumed a plate of sandwiches while waiting for his room to be prepared, was bad enough with its floating ear and unshelved books. Appearances deteriorated even further on the second floor.

"We'll put you in here," Mrs. Phipps said, as if he were an out-of-season hat. She indicated a tall door with a floral-etched knob and swung it wide. Daniel took three tentative steps after her into the gloom.

"It's very large." Difficult to tell in this light, but it looked like a decent carpet. Whoever cleaned this room must have moved like a whirlwind to ready it so quickly.

"It's unfortunate we didn't have time to give the room a proper airing," Mrs. Phipps said, her tone brisk. Clearly, she had done her best, but when she flung the tatty curtains wide and flooded the room with summer sun, a dozen shortcomings were painfully evident. The high tester bed wore heavy silk hangings of faded seafoam green, and the chairs sat on squat, curled legs, their cushions sagging tiredly. Though the enameled tables that littered the room were clean, years of dust lingered in the air.

"Was this a lady's room?" Daniel stared at what could only be a connecting door.

"It was. Long since. Dr. Croft sleeps next door."

"This room's a trifle big for me," Daniel said. "I'd be content in a smaller one."

"Maybe, if there was any furniture in them. We carried most of it down to the basement for the convalescents. Miss Eleanor's rooms are on the next floor, so I can't put you up there."

Daniel kept in a sigh. He was eager to study with Croft

but hadn't expected this degree of proximity. Unless the door was thick, he and Croft would hear each other snore. Daniel glanced again at the dated, almost grotesquely feminine furnishings. "Perhaps I could have my own things brought over." The furniture at home was straight and soundly made, and didn't make him feel like he'd trespassed into a bordello. Daniel turned around. Mrs. Phipps wore an offended expression. "No, not worth the bother. This is fine," Daniel assured her.

"I quite agree."

Before he could get himself into more trouble, Daniel opened his bag. "I should unpack." Mrs. Phipps withdrew, closing the door behind her, and Daniel began setting out his books. The floorboards creaked with every step, loud enough that he'd consider carefully before moving about after dark. A walk to the washstand might not wake the entire house, but it would be heard from Croft's room. Perhaps even upstairs. Daniel frowned again at the connecting door. The chipped white paint and obsidian knob didn't match the others. Daniel crossed the room, stepping from carpet to carpet. It was quieter this way, but not much.

Croft was still out, and there were no sounds coming through the door. Daniel pulled it open—it stuck at first, then came free with a bump. His mother's attics had more order than this room. It was strewn with medical journals and dominated by a large desk covered in stacks of paper, monuments of disarray in danger of toppling to the floor.

"Saints alive." Daniel retreated quickly but found he couldn't close the connecting door. It must not have been opened for years, and now it didn't fit within the frame. He tried again, more forcefully. *It closed a minute ago*, he thought desperately, wrestling with the handle. He leaned his shoulder into it, his feet slipping against the worn boards, but after five minutes he'd earned nothing but a bruised arm. No luck. He'd have to wedge it closed as best he could with a folded stocking or a slip of paper.

Full of dark grumblings, Daniel searched through his precisely packed trunks for something suitable. How on earth did Croft keep an uncluttered brain amid such a lamentable mess? Daniel folded up an old letter and pushed it under the door. It didn't fall open anymore, but it was only touching the doorframe, not shut.

He went back to the desk and comforted himself by laying out his ink bottle and pens, pleased with his own fastidiousness. He put his correspondence at a straight angle to the edge of the desk. Perhaps while he was here, Mrs. Phipps and Miss Beady might take a lesson in neatness. In the meantime, there was nothing more to do until Croft returned. Daniel had spent enough time in hospitals to know that when you had nothing to do, you slept.

He stretched out on top of the covers, not ready to investigate the quality of the sheets. Disappointment was better in manageable doses.

───

Voices woke him: loud, and not far off. Daniel sat up and tried to guess how much time had passed. The sunlight coming through his windows had matured to a rich gold. It made the ratty seafoam silk look worse than ever. The connecting door had come ajar. Someone—Croft?—was shouting for Miss

Beady, complaining he couldn't find his brown waistcoat. The girl must have been nearby or come running. Though slightly breathless, her voice was calm.

"It's here, Doctor, underneath the box of clavicles. We had to move some of your things to make room for the new doctor's. Would you like me to take them downstairs?"

"No, Gibson probably won't like anyone messing with his things."

"I meant the clavicles," she said.

"No, don't take them. I'm not finished yet. I'm collecting evidence of different types of fractures. I just need to sit down with them—"

"One of these days," she finished. The doctor chuckled.

"Your clean shirts are still on the bureau," she said. "I'll put them away. You don't mind if I take these notes out of the drawer?"

"No, I don't mind. You can put them in— Dash it. And look, there's a problem with the door."

Daniel stilled, realizing he'd unwittingly moved closer. He was only a foot from the door. Creaking floorboards warned of someone approaching. *The girl*, he thought, timing the swooshes of her skirts like he was taking a pulse. No matter. He couldn't be seen. Boxes shifted—Miss Beady was probably trying to clear a space—then something tumbled and struck the door. It swung open and bounced off Daniel's elbow. He squeezed his eyes shut and bit back a curse, but not before Miss Beady saw him. Her eyes narrowed suspiciously.

"I dropped a cuff link," Daniel lied, and clasped his hands behind his back.

"Would you like me to help you look?"

"I'll manage."

"The light in here is bad." She stepped into his room and looked around. She had probably been in it before, to supervise, if not perform the cleaning, but her presence made him uncomfortable. She looked from the windows to his shelf of books.

"I can bring you another lamp."

"Don't trouble yourself. I'm too tired at the end of the day to want any reading," Daniel said, hoping to hurry her away.

She lifted her eyebrows. "We run a busy clinic. Surgeries are scheduled nearly every day, and there are emergencies aplenty on Sundays. You'll need the lamp."

"That you, Gibson?" Croft stuck his head around the door and smiled a welcome. "Glad you're here. We can have a chat before dinner."

Miss Beady stiffened. "Don't be too long, Dr. Croft. It's nearly ready, and you'll want to eat while it's hot."

Daniel looked at her everyday gray linen, adorned with only a narrow white collar that had lost its crispness hours before.

"You aren't going to change?"

"Oh, we don't dress up for—" Dr. Croft began.

Miss Beady interrupted in a voice as hard as flint, her cheeks flaming. "I certainly will. Excuse me."

After she left, Daniel expected Croft to sigh apologetically and make some comment about the sensibilities of ladies. He didn't. "I know we haven't time," Croft said. "But you must see this article by a Dr. Waddy, of Birmingham, who says there is no such thing as puerperal fevers, that they cannot be distinguished from other fevers or inflammatory diseases. An extreme position to take, but he makes one or two good points…"

Daniel hesitated. Should he talk or change clothes? Now that he'd shamed Miss Beady into dressing for dinner, it would be bad form not to do so himself, but Croft was clearly too interested in fevers to bother.

"Tell me about it as I change," Daniel said, and set to work unfastening his cravat. "Why doesn't he think they are different?"

If he'd hoped to deter Dr. Croft, it was a vain attempt. Without any decrease in enthusiasm, he poured the substance of the article through the half-open door. It was an interesting theory, Daniel admitted. Unfortunately, divided attention made him clumsy. He made a mess of his fresh cravat and fumbled with his buttons so long he had to race after Dr. Croft—who was still talking—to the dining room.

"Wonderful," Daniel said. He was panting, but he'd caught up with Dr. Croft at last. "Let's continue our discussion after dinner. I don't want to bore the ladies."

Croft blinked. Then he coughed. "Of course not."

Dinner was depressingly silent. None of Daniel's polite inquiries yielded more than a bland, one-sentence response. So much for his attempt to make a better impression.

CHAPTER 3

For the next three days, Daniel didn't have a thought that wasn't about medicine. His only respite was the few hours when he slept. After yet another long day of seeing to patients—clinic for four hours in the morning, then a mastectomy and rounds at St. Bart's—Daniel was grateful to sit in Croft's consulting room while the older man poured generous amounts of London dry gin into remarkable crystal glasses. "From the Duke of Cambridge for treating his valet's sister during a mild case of erysipelas," he explained when he caught Daniel admiring the vessels. "Which reminds me—"

Croft hastily put down his gin and groped to the back of a crowded shelf for something that interested him more than cut crystal. He handed Daniel the skeleton of a pygmy shrew, hardly bigger than a bumblebee, wired carefully to a wooden base. "Half the size of the common shrew. And eats twice as often." Croft tugged his beard, as he always did when agitated or excited. "But I spent four hours at Dame Bell Tavern with a whaler home for the winter who said his ship followed a cow whale for six days before they were able to take her. He never saw her eat a thing, even when schools of fish rushed right in front of her."

Daniel admired the almost invisible wire tying together the

fragile bones of the shrew. Only Croft possessed a hand precise and tireless enough for such work. He looked into the doctor's impatient face and realized he'd left him waiting.

"Er—" Daniel stalled for something intelligent to say. "Of course, more studies must be done on the rate of digestion. Are you of the opinion that heart rate determines how much and often one must eat?"

The wrinkles on Croft's brow bent into lines of pleasure. "Laënnec thought so. I heard him lecture at the Collège de France twenty years ago. He could hear a diseased heart with nothing more than a wooden tube. Brilliant. I learned to listen from him. It is my dream to auscultate a beached living whale." His face shone like a child's.

Daniel leaned forward in his chair and stirred the fire to combat the chill of the night's cold summer rain. This also allowed him to hide the smile that blossomed as he imagined Croft pushing his stethoscope against the massive wall of a whale's side.

The gin, dying fire, and Croft's low rumble warmed Daniel as he melted into his high-back chair, listening to an impromptu discourse on the multiple chambered stomachs of bovines and how they compared to the sperm whale. How a man so practiced in every particular of the human body made time to study the obscure details of every known plant and animal filled Daniel with astonishment—incredulity, even.

Daniel had just undone his cuffs and accepted Croft's challenge to find the abnormality in the preserved stomach of a house cat when the clinic bell jangled. Daniel replaced the jar with its floating, bloated stomach and sprang to answer, hurrying because the clinic door stood directly below a missing section of gutter, requiring callers to brave a waterfall during a storm. He'd found that out this afternoon waiting for Miss Beady to unbolt the door when he'd returned from St. Bart's.

A boy stood in the pouring rain, his workaday clothes pasted to his small body and his shoulders hunched against the cold. "Me mum sent me to say our neighbor, Mrs. Collins, is doing poorly at a birthing. The midwife needs a doctor."

"How long?"

Before the boy could answer, Dr. Croft pushed past him, his left arm already crammed into his coat. He must have reached for it as soon as the bell rang.

"Grab your bag," he ordered as he stepped into the night, leaving the door swinging behind him. Puddles collected on the floor. Daniel, who'd removed his shoes to wiggle his toes in front of the coals, raced to push them onto his feet, while donning his coat and grabbing the kit bag. He slipped on the wet tiles as he left, catching himself with a bruising blow against the doorframe. On the sidewalk he panicked. Croft and the boy were gone. Daniel caught their black shadows dissolving down Great Queen Street as they turned toward Cheapside. He sprinted after them, cursing Croft for looking like an aged justice and moving like a regimental soldier.

Six wet blocks later, the boy led them into a smart row house on Arthur Street West, where a white-faced woman waited in the kitchen. She sprang from her chair. "Good boy, Jake." She crushed the boy close. Without wasting another breath, she turned to Dr. Croft. "The midwife said there may be a hemorrhage. The husband is a shambles in the front room upstairs."

Croft nodded and went for the stairs. The husband met them on the landing, his haggard face ghoulish in the light of too many lamps. He grabbed Croft's coat as soon as Croft's feet hit the carpet. "Please," he cried. "Please help her. Please hurry."

Croft showed no indignation after being manhandled. He pried the man's hand gently from him and murmured, "I'll see what's about."

Daniel tensed for screams, but as they hurried up the last flight of stairs, they met only ominous quiet. No murmurs of command or encouragement from the midwife. If not for the chaos downstairs, he would think all were abed and sleeping. They followed a tilted rectangle of light along the hallway to a half-open door. Inside, a sweating midwife held a piece of torn linen in her teeth while one hand pressed a bloodied towel between the patient's legs. The other held a needle threaded with catgut.

"I'm glad to see it's you, Mrs. Franklin. How long has she been bleeding?" Croft asked in a voice so low it hardly rose above a whisper. Kneeling by the midwife, he relieved her of the needle so she could use both hands.

The woman dropped the bandage from her mouth. "Took you enough time. I thought I was going to have to suture it myself. The baby doesn't seem especially big but there's hardly room to work. She's been pushing for three hours now."

"Primagravida?" Croft asked.

"Yes. And nearly thirty years old. The head emerged three times but I cannot draw it out."

Daniel hurried around the midwife and Croft to the side of the bed. The patient looked closer to forty, but her face was swollen with exertion, and small blood vessels marred the whites of her eyes. She wasn't a screamer, this one. All of her agony hissed out quietly in her labored breaths.

"You are in the best hands," Daniel said as he pressed her neck for a pulse. Strong and insistent, her blood pushed back against his fingertips. The woman met his eyes for a second but gave no sign of recognition. He needed to make her engage. "I did not catch your name. Can you tell me?"

"Emily," she panted, then screwed her eyes shut and arched her back as another pain took her.

"I don't think it's a rupture," Croft said. "How does she look?"

"Well, pink. Cognizant but exhausted," Daniel said.

The midwife huffed. "There isn't a person who wouldn't be." Daniel didn't mind her scolding. He'd studied with a female midwife in Paris who possessed the hands of a surgeon and the heart of a general. She lambasted him with a string of violent French whenever he moved too slowly or did not anticipate her directions, but she had yanked scores of mothers and babies from the clutches of death by sheer force of will.

"I don't think both shoulders can fit at once," Croft said, struggling to assess the baby's position with his slenderest finger. The midwife backed away and Daniel joined him. "There is too much blood for a normal delivery, but not enough for a hemorrhage. I believe she pushed too soon and lacerated the cervix, but we won't know until after. It's too swollen to tell."

"Emily," Croft said. "If you give me a grand push I will help you with a pull and see if we can get this over with."

With a furious groan, Emily heaved her strength down

onto the baby. A black-haired head emerged up to the nose and Croft took hold, pressing with one hand against the pubic bone while drawing out the fat cheeks with his other. Daniel reached down and took the head, freeing Croft's left hand.

Emily screamed, too weakly to hurt Daniel's ears, but his heart tore at the sound. Her cry was too faint, too forlorn for hope. She was giving up on herself.

"Shoulder," Croft said as if it were a curse. "I'll push down on one to free the other, but there's no room." Just as he spoke, a thrust forced the baby like a lodged cork. It shuddered against Daniel's hand. Below his fingers the perineum split. Fresh blood burst over Croft and Daniel. Another scream took Emily and was answered by a cry from outside the room.

"Emily!" Her husband's frantic voice sliced like a razor inside Daniel's ears. He wanted to shout at the man to shut the bloody hell up. It was essential to focus, and all this screaming transported him to the madness of an asylum.

And then, like a wave, the pressure let up. Daniel staggered backward with the baby in hand. Croft had managed to free the shoulders. The midwife snatched the child into her billowing and bloodied apron, and Daniel fell to his knees beside Croft who was already pulling the jagged skin together to suture.

"Continuous sutures to close the vaginal mucosa," Croft mumbled as he looped the umbilical cord over her leg and pushed the catgut through the broken skin. Emily's flanks quivered. Daniel looked up. The midwife cooed and held out the baby girl, distracting Emily from her pain. The baby let out a shrill cry.

The husband ranted from the hallway, "Emily? I don't hear Emily. Is she safe?"

"Well, you caught a fussy one," the midwife chided Emily. "After I wipe down the baby, I'll go keep him at bay so Doctor can finish up with you. We still have a placenta to deliver."

"Thread a new needle," Croft barked to Daniel. "You should close the perineal muscles separately, but still use continuous sutures." He stepped away and motioned for Daniel to finish.

Clenching the needle to hide the shake in his fingers, Daniel hurried despite Croft's critical stare. The stab of the sharp steel in her inflamed flesh only prolonged the agony of it all. *Not a person. Just a body.* Daniel shut out her whimpers and the way her buttocks flinched away from his fingers. "Almost over," he said more to himself.

Daniel pulled the last stitch tight. A gush of blood rushed over his fingers.

"Placenta," Croft said, shouldering his way back into place. He gave a gentle tug on the umbilical cord. It came easily, and Croft lowered it into a bucket catching some of the fluids falling onto the floor. "You can wash her up while I check the placenta," Croft instructed the midwife.

He carried the bucket to the window and inspected the organ. "No torn edges. I believe you can call that a job well done," he announced to the mother, her head pressed into a wet pillow and her arms almost too weak to hold the baby who squinted against the light and pushed her face from side to side. Croft stepped up to her with a fatherly smile. "I'll let your husband come in a moment."

Emily nodded and managed a smile, and though it was a nurse's job, Daniel couldn't resist sponging her face with cool water. Her bloodshot eyes met his. "Thank you," she sighed. "Does the baby look well?"

Daniel grinned. "Prettiest newborn I've seen all year," he promised.

The midwife draped a sheet over the carnage and mopped up the soiled rags on the floor before she went to the door and called out peevishly, "You aren't very patient, but you can come for a moment and see that all is right."

The father appeared a second later, his drawn face relaxing into doubtful relief. "I thought…" he whispered but felt no need to finish. He kissed his wife's hair. Only after touching her face and arm, reassuring himself she was alive, did he remember the baby.

"A girl," Emily said.

"This is brilliant. You're brilliant," the father said, caressing the baby's plump cheek.

The midwife held out her arms. "She'll look prettier after a proper washing."

He passed her the baby reluctantly, then turned to Croft and Daniel. He took their hands and pumped their arms furiously in turn. "Thank you. Thank you. You must have a drink." Before they could answer he sprang to the door. "I'll be back with some India ale."

Emily laughed quietly as he left but the sound cut off abruptly. "My fingers feel strange. Oh." Her mouth popped into a surprised circle and her eyes widened.

"Emily?" Dr. Croft asked.

She looked up at him, her pupils shrinking like black birds chasing a horizon. "My head," she murmured, her neck going lax.

Croft snatched back the sheet, making it snap like a flag on a line. The windowpane quilt was no longer a patchwork of colors, but one scarlet hue.

"Her hands are cold," the midwife said. She set down the baby and began rubbing Emily's face.

"Palpate the abdomen!" Daniel barked to no one but himself as he pushed his fingers into her soft stomach, feeling his way to her deflated womb.

Croft spread her limp legs apart and inserted his hand. "Uterine atony. It's not contracting. Massage!" Daniel located the uterus and rolled his fist vigorously, her spongy skin giving and collapsing like waves of water beneath the boat of his hand. His first push forced blood to rush out, covering Croft's white sleeve.

The sound of shattering glass alerted them to the father's return. The sharp, spiced scent of spilled ale filled the room. Glistening shards covered the floor.

"Emily?" he cried.

For the first time, Daniel saw Emily's naked body, the fine fuzz of her brown pubic hair caked in blood, Croft's crimson shirt, the white sheet stained and crumpled on the floor. "Get him out," Daniel roared to the midwife. "Take the baby." He heard a scuffle of arms and feet, and then he and Croft were alone.

Croft leaned across her body and put his ear to her chest, simultaneously listening and feeling for a pulse. "Weak and fast. She needs liquids."

"She's not conscious," Daniel pointed out. "Is the massage stimulating the blood flow or halting it?" With every push of his hands an alarming burst of blood spilled from her.

Croft did another internal check. "Damn it! No contraction

at all. Elevate her bottom. Let's try to keep blood near her heart." They each grabbed a leg and hoisted her upward, her arms lifeless at her sides, her red nightgown falling into a heap against her exposed breasts, her face disturbingly unconcerned, as if dozing on a summer afternoon.

"Emily?" Daniel rasped.

Outside the door her husband echoed the word in a panicked cry. "Emily!"

Daniel took both legs so Croft could feel for a pulse again, but blood now saturated the mattress and fell in dark drops on the oak floorboards. His arms shook under the burden of her leaden legs.

Croft met Daniel's eyes and gave a slow shake of his head. He stepped away from the bed. Icy coldness filled Daniel's feet, inching up his legs until it reached his lungs. He lowered her legs and replaced the filthy gown over her battered body. Daniel dropped his face, blinking furiously.

"Why is it so quiet?" the father bleated in the hallway. Whatever words the midwife murmured didn't restrain him. He burst through the door, clawing free of her tenacious hold.

The man looked wildly for Emily. The sight of the white, flaccid shell, heavy and dead, arrested his frantic feet. A thin and pitiful wail rose from the dark earth, through the floor and into his open mouth. The sound pierced the soft spots between Daniel's ribs like a spear thrust into his chest.

The man dropped to his knees and dragged himself forward, smearing beer and his wife's blood across the floorboards. Daniel closed his eyes, trying to erase the picture.

"Emily?" The man took her cold fingers in his. When she

didn't respond, he tried to make her fingers curl around his own, bending the knuckles and pressing her palm to his. "Where did you go, love? Can you come back?" He tugged on her arm, causing her head to wobble. He looked up in desperate hope. "Emily? Are you back, my love?" He kissed her pale fingers and pressed them to his cheek. "I knew you wouldn't leave me."

Daniel pushed his thumb against his eyes, collecting the wetness, ashamed because even the ashen-faced midwife didn't cry. He turned to the window, his face and the horrid scene behind him distorted and wavering in the rain-washed reflection. If only it had been a convenient marriage, loveless and estranged…

Daniel was utterly unprepared when Emily's husband sprang on him, clutching his shirt. "Please? Will you please save her?"

Daniel took a step back, but the man came with him. Croft's strong grip closed over the man's wrists, freeing Daniel. The man was still begging. "Please don't kill her. Please. She is so good. I will pay you anything. Please don't make her die."

"I am so sorry," Croft said, meeting the man's wild stare with somber eyes. "Her uterus hemorrhaged. I want very much to bring her back, but she is too far away now. I cannot reach her."

The man staggered back to the bed, hearing nothing, knowing nothing, weeping over his dead wife while Dr. Croft quietly sent for the undertaker and poured out a dose of laudanum. When the husband had drunk, and voyaged to the brink of fitful unconsciousness, Croft leaned over him and whispered: "I would like to do a surgery to find out what made Emily go away. Would you let me care for her body until she is buried?"

The man gave a confused nod and Croft stepped away, straightening his coat. Incredulous, Daniel found his voice, leaning close so the midwife should not overhear. "You can't do this. He's in no position to decide."

"How many more births like this one would you like to attend? We have a responsibility to science."

"But he—"

"We'll do the dissection in the morning, sew her up for the burial and give her back to the undertaker. He'll know nothing of it."

Such a sensible plan, but Daniel's lips shook at the awfulness of stealing a body from a drugged and devastated man. "I've never dissected someone who just smiled at me."

Croft only shrugged. While he left to make arrangements with the undertaker to bring Emily's body to his clinic, Daniel wiped down their instruments and returned them to the bag. The midwife swept up the broken glass and gathered the soiled linens into a sack. Neither spoke in the choking confines of the room.

"Thank you, Mrs. Franklin," Dr. Croft said, returning with the undertaker's men. "You'll make sure someone stays with him?"

The midwife nodded. "I'll sit here and tend the baby. We'll find a nurse tomorrow."

The undertakers offered to take up Daniel and Dr. Croft in their wagon. Croft accepted, but Daniel shook his head. "I need a moment alone."

Croft didn't remind him of the rain or ask him to reconsider. Perhaps the old man sensed Daniel's disquiet and knew to leave him to it. When Daniel stepped into the black, wet night, he pulled the door closed, relieved to shut the pain behind a piece of wood and walk far away.

The cold rain fell from the brim of his hat onto his shoulders and trickled down his neck. He trudged home, waiting out of sight until the undertaker left. Unable to bear the thought of dissecting the dead mother and stalling for time, he entered the front door and surprised Nora in the hall. She was carrying an armful of linen.

She paused on the marble tiles. "What happened?"

Daniel looked her over, her tired curls falling against her pink cheeks, her dark eyes still full of light, her small breast still full of air, and tried not to contrast her with Emily's shattered body lying downstairs in the dissection room.

He thought of answering. He nearly opened his mouth, but he heard the husband's wail and saw Emily's naked legs covered in blood and could not fit any of it into polite words. "You wouldn't understand," he mumbled. He reached out and took the bundle of linen from her arms. "You shouldn't go down there. I'll take these."

An expression crossed Nora's face that he hadn't time or energy or translate. With wooden feet, he moved toward the clinic stairs thinking only, *I doubt we'll have to drain her. There's no blood left.*

He left the linen in the surgery and gave a silent prayer of thanks when Croft said they would begin in the early morning. With bowed shoulders, he followed the older man back upstairs.

CHAPTER 4

LYING IN BED THAT NIGHT, NORA LISTENED TO THE CLOCK chime two. The house was unusually quiet. The men must be asleep, snatching a few hours' rest after the trauma of a failed delivery. Before morning, they'd be at work again, looking for answers in the corpse. Nora rose up, thumped her pillow, and lay down again.

You wouldn't understand.

Oh, how she longed to fire off the dozen retorts that sprang to mind every time she relived the scene. She knew just as much as Daniel Gibson did—more, even. She knew Emily—her soft voice, shy laugh, and the blossoming wonder in her eyes as Nora had listened to, then described her baby's heartbeat, a happy thrumming, like the purr of a noisy tomcat.

Nora pressed a hand to her eyes in a vain attempt to erase the picture from her mind. These memories were somber now, like watercolors flooded with gray. She was accustomed to death, though prone to lying awake afterward. She had been ever since coming to Great Queen Street.

Years ago, when Nora emerged from the fever dreams and found herself here, orphaned and alone, with nothing to connect her to life with her family, not even herself. The face reflected in the looking glass was wasted and shadowed, not like the round-cheeked girl she'd been.

After weeks of unconscious delirium, loneliness and grief kept her awake. That, and the sound of the screams that echoed through the house. Nora knew Croft was a doctor, but she hadn't understood about the surgery until Mrs. Phipps explained it to her. It seemed too awful to be real, and she shuddered and longed for the cholera-induced nightmares that dissolved on waking. The screams downstairs only got louder when she opened her eyes. By the time Nora was well enough to sit up in bed, she'd collected a dozen gruesome stories from the servants. Still, she needed to see for herself. The savory broth and gentle attentions she received kept a flicker of hope burning. Surely this house could not be as dreadful as she feared.

It was worse. She'd waited until nighttime, when all was quiet. Heart pounding, Nora crept downstairs in her too-large nightdress. Navigating the dark, unfamiliar passageways, her feet shrinking from the cold floorboards, she followed a thread of light from a partially opened door—and discovered Dr. Croft in the surgery sawing through a dead man's ribs as if they were cordwood. She retreated immediately, her hands clapped over her mouth, and sagged against the wall until her legs were strong enough to carry her away. Dr. Croft, focused on carefully lifting out the lungs, never noticed her. She didn't go again. Not for a long time, at least.

She thought about running away, but even an eight-year-old child possesses the sense not to brave the London streets alone. She had food and clean clothes here, and while Mrs. Phipps wasn't precisely affectionate, she spoke more gently to

Nora than to the maids who hurried at her brisk commands. Despite the horror of the surgery, Nora dreaded the day when the doctor would pronounce her cured and dump her on the steps of a charity house to fend for herself.

Though she tried, Nora couldn't stay ill forever. Eventually, Dr. Croft stopped examining her and listening to her chest, though he never said she was better. In fact, he never said anything at all, but no one moved to evict her. *Perhaps*, Nora thought, *if she made herself useful...* After an ironing fiasco that cost two linen napkins and an unfortunate attempt to scuttle coal into a fire that ignited her apron, Nora discovered Mrs. Phipps was in little need of her help, though she seemed to like Nora's company. Nora made herself as agreeable as possible, never complaining about winding Mrs. Phipps's yarn or listening to tales of her many brothers and sisters that only accentuated Nora's own loneliness.

Then came the day when Mrs. Phipps discovered Nora crying over spilled tea, frantically trying to save the finish of the tabletop and wipe up the mess without scalding her hands. As Nora blubbered her apology and begged the housekeeper not to send her away for this mistake, Mrs. Phipps frowned and took the burning rag from Nora's trembling fingers. "You needn't worry over that. You'll be staying on here for good. I've cleaned up far worse than Darjeeling." Grateful but perplexed, Nora accepted the promise.

Dr. Croft showed her to other doctors and explained how she'd recovered from the cholera, but he didn't keep any of his other cholera patients. At least not in their entirety. He had bits of some of them, floating in jars, and he wrote up their cases to print in his books. In a tattered edition of the *Lancet*, Nora discovered her own story with Dr. Croft's prediction that having recovered from cholera, she'd gained immunity to the disease, and realized that she, too, was a specimen.

She had a use, but was she useful *enough*?

Nora wrote a fair hand, having learned from her stationer father. Dr. Croft wrote in a hurried scrawl. Nora didn't ask before she began copying out his reports, and Dr. Croft never acknowledged that she did it. He simply began leaving them stacked on the right-hand corner of his desk and one day at dinner told her he would be obliged if she could correct her spelling of *pharynx*.

Often left alone, she read more, making a game out of matching the case reports to the people she watched come and go. Four years passed as she perfected the knack of making herself simultaneously helpful and invisible. Phipps sent her to school during the day, but the other children wanted little to do with an orphan from a house of horrors. Nora's only reliable friends were the housekeeper, the cook, and the patients she waited on. They were charity cases and didn't complain that she was only a girl of thirteen.

Then, one night while Mrs. Phipps slept and Dr. Croft dined and drank with the head of the Royal College of Surgeons, Nora went down to the surgery with her recently copied description of the painful growth that had necessitated the removal of a coachman's leg. She knew, from overhearing Dr. Croft and the orderly, that the leg was wrapped in linen on the table. Dr. Croft had hoped to have a drawing with the report, but the rendering provided by the orderly was disappointing. Dr. Croft had crumpled it in frustration and tossed it to the library floor.

Nora suspected she could do better.

The smell of blood grew worse the further she went into the surgery, but it was not unexpected. Busying herself with the lamps, Nora flooded the table with light, then gathered her courage and faced the long bundle waiting before her. Steeling herself, she untied the string and the stained wrappings protecting the limb. Sticky damp clung to her hands, not just her own sweat—but she needn't think of that. It wouldn't help her. After she pulled back the wrappings, she repositioned the lamp, bit her lip, then bent the knee to the proper angle. It took more strength than she expected. The shiny, blackening flesh was unnaturally stiff beneath her fingers, and though the joint moved as she wished, the leg was heavy and cold. Suppressing a gag, she pushed her hair off her forehead with the back of her hand.

"There. All ready." Now she realized why the orderlies often muttered to themselves. It was comforting to hear a voice, even if it was just your own. Nora wiped her hands on the apron and picked up the tablet of drawing paper. Charcoals would be better, but she thought she could manage with pen and ink. She sketched the shape of the joint, then retracted the patella with the end of her pen to see the white cartilage beneath. It looked as smooth and hard as the mortar and pestle that rested, dusty with disuse, on Dr. Croft's shelf. He seldom prescribed pills or tinctures and always had them made up by an apothecary.

As Nora drew, she forgot the stink. Her shoulders tightened, and she had to rummage in a drawer for a scalpel and pins after discovering the orderly's incision wasn't long enough to expose the whole joint. The scalpel she reached for was narrow and fit like a pen in her hand. She stroked along the incision, clearing globules of yellow fat and parting a thick band of fascia. Now when she manipulated the knee, the muscles and ligaments spread beautifully. She set aside the first sketch, then began a second, now that she knew how. This time, the leg didn't look so flat on the paper.

She probed the knee joint and moved the light and shaded in her drawing until the only thing it lacked was color and smell. Then Nora wrapped up the limb and washed her hands and tidied her papers. She left the drawing for Dr. Croft on his desk.

Next morning he summoned her to his office. "When did you learn to draw?"

"My mother liked to sketch." Nora hadn't thought of her mother's pictures in years. Her mother had drawn only pretty subjects: portraits of her children, scenes from the windows of their apartment, and views of the Thames. Nora didn't know what had become of them. "And Mrs. Phipps brought in an instructor last year." *Surely he'd noticed the easels and the man painting in the parlor every Wednesday afternoon?*

"Wish I'd known you were this good. Will you make sketches of my collection of skulls?" Dr. Croft asked. He had at least a dozen scattered throughout the house.

"I'd be happy to."

Nora drew the skulls and discovered she was more content when she had meaningful things to do. When she presented the drawings, Dr. Croft exclaimed at the result. Within the week, she found herself standing beside him as he dissected, sketching finished specimens at a side table. He worked long hours, often at night when the corpses were freshly arrived, and cleared them away by morning in case the police came calling. He had a drawer full of forged papers in case of that, "proving" that his bodies were legally acquired.

"As if I'd learn anything from those," he scoffed, dismissing the quality and condition of the bodies sent his way from the workhouses.

Nora was only sixteen when he realized that instead of merely standing at his elbow all night, she'd been passing him tools. He looked at her once and grunted.

"What happened to Jones?"

Nora suppressed a smile. John Jones, the orderly, hadn't been in the house since yesterday. "He didn't come today. His sister's wedding, remember?"

"No wonder we're making such good progress. He's got thick hands." Dr. Croft passed her a pair of forceps, motioning for her to tug on a nerve. "Springy, aren't they?"

Nora nodded.

"It's a good way to tell they are nerves and not fascia or blood vessels. But you must be careful of nerves in the live ones," he said.

It was only a few weeks later that he sent Mrs. Phipps to bring Nora to the basement on a Tuesday afternoon. Jones was gone again, and Croft had a patient with a compound fracture in his left leg.

"Don't be bothered by the screaming," he said as Nora hurried into the room. He passed her an apron. "I need to take the leg off before he bleeds to death." He frowned at her. "Not sure if you're strong enough, but I'll never manage it without help holding him down. If it gets too hard, you can take over the cutting. But I'll be fast."

Nora nodded and braced herself against the table.

You never forget your first surgery.

Nora had attended very few since, only when circumstances were desperate and the patient discreet. She'd never wielded the knife, though sometimes, when she was standing at a fortunate angle, her hand twitched toward the scalpel, longing to feel the difference between saving warm flesh and learning from greasy cadavers. She assisted with deliveries because that required less explanation—people assumed she was a low-paid, uneducated midwife. Some women liked having another female stitch them up again, or having a woman present for a surgery, especially mastectomies. Nora had seen women die often enough.

And Dr. Gibson thought she didn't understand.

Nora kicked away her blanket, listening for movement in the house. All was quiet. The hallboy wouldn't start scrubbing the steps for another three hours. There was no reason to let this newcomer stop her from discovering why Emily had lost her life tonight.

CHAPTER 5

NORA WAS SO INTENT ON THE TWO-INCH TEAR SHE'D found in Emily's uterus that she didn't hear the footsteps outside the surgery door until it was too late. She nearly dropped her scalpel in fright when the door began to open.

It was Dr. Croft, tired-eyed and unshaven, but he brightened at the sight of her behind the table.

"Thank goodness it's you," Nora said. "Is Dr. Gibson—?"

"Awake. Still dressing. Find anything?" He leaned over the body. The head and arms were draped in linen, so it didn't look like Emily anymore.

Nora pointed at the laceration with her scalpel. "Don't forget an apron," she whispered, her eyes on the front of Dr. Croft's coat. It was his newest one, black Bath superfine, and was supposed to be reserved for special occasions.

Someone was moving about upstairs. It could be Mrs. Phipps or the hallboy, but in case it wasn't… "Never mind, take mine." Nora fumbled with the ties of her apron. She passed the stained length of cotton canvas to Croft, who accepted it without looking up. "You did a fine job," he said, and probed at the corpse.

Nora went to the small office where she kept the clinic records. She couldn't make herself stay at the desk. Instead, she stood at the window, fists tight, scowling at the few passersby without seeing any of them. Dr. Croft's reckless decision to haul home another surgeon had forced her into shadows and corners, but if Dr. Croft wasn't worried about her clinic work, why should Dr. Gibson be?

Unfortunately, there were many things Dr. Croft should worry about, and didn't, starting with the state of his coats. His colleagues were another. Croft had no respect for those he considered his intellectual inferiors. Last month he'd shouted at a respected professor of anatomy, and his quarrels with Dr. Silas Vickery, the chair of surgery at St. Bartholomew's Hospital, were the stuff of legend. When Dr. Vickery was appointed chair, their rivalry spilled into the elite drawing rooms and dining halls of London, half the peers of the kingdom cheering for Dr. Croft and his creative successes, and the others passionately touting Vickery's defense of traditional methods.

Despite his brilliance, Dr. Croft was arrogant, and impervious to criticism. If he strayed too far beyond the decrees of the Royal Society of Surgeons, even his unquestionable skill wouldn't save him from trouble. He seemed to have just enough sense of self-preservation not to flaunt Nora's work in public, and when he bothered to call her anything, he called her his "little helper."

Nora understood the secrecy. Women couldn't be surgeons. Henry VIII had made sure of that in 1540 by banning women from the Company of Barber Surgeons. During his bloody rule, Nora might have been whipped or thrown in the stocks. Now the threat of lawsuits was deemed sufficient to deter unlicensed practitioners, and court proceedings were so entangling, so financially ruinous, that it generally was. Henry's statute was still on the books, and the more recent Apothecaries' Act of 1815 didn't explicitly bar women—but only because there was no need—and every month the journals clamored for harsher penalties on unlicensed and incompetent quacks.

The poor who couldn't afford physicians had their midwives and herb women, and no one complained if a wizened grandmother splinted broken bones, but those things arguably fell within a woman's domestic sphere. Amputations and grisly experiments did not. Few looked kindly on a woman venturing outside the narrow pursuits allowed her. It would take only one of Dr. Croft's offended and well-connected colleagues exposing his female assistant for his popular practice to fall out of favor.

Nora rubbed her forehead. Plagued with empty minutes and nebulous anxieties, she reached for the latest *Provincial Medical and Surgical Journal* and sat down to make herself read complaints to the editor against a German-trained surgeon, whose successes had sparked jealously within his Midlands community. Envious doctors had seized upon his lack of a local license to hammer him with lawsuits.

Half an hour later, Daniel Gibson made his unhurried way downstairs. Nora, having discovered that the German doctor, after failing to pay a series of staggering fines was now in prison, did nothing but clench her teeth when Gibson exclaimed in wonder at Dr. Croft's "excellent dissection."

"I wonder you're still standing after so little sleep, sir," he said.

Croft only grunted.

Unable to listen anymore, Nora marched to the convalescent rooms that lined the basement corridor. If the colleges were so severe on a trained foreigner, what would they do to her?

There were far more patients waiting than could be seen in the four-hour span of Dr. Croft's charity clinic that morning: goiters and ingrown toenails and a mother with a feverish child. Daniel hoped it wasn't influenza. By eleven, four of the twenty patients seen had been sent to Miss Beady, who would schedule their surgeries. It was an alarming percentage, but Daniel supposed he shouldn't find it surprising for a man of Croft's skill. The patients certainly didn't come to him for his bedside manner. They might have been cattle for all the consideration Croft showed, but he was careful and exact.

Daniel sent away a rash that was almost certainly a case of syphilis and took a moment to rub his eyes before calling in the next patient, a middle-aged woman with frightened eyes. Exhaustion from the night before made it difficult to focus. His left eye twitched, and the woman in front of him hemmed and hawed so long Daniel knew they'd be here until dinner if he didn't do something to help her along.

"Would you like another woman in the room while I examine you, Mrs. Lobb?" he asked.

"Please." She nodded.

Daniel went to the door and called for Miss Beady. She breezed in from the office, brisk and neat, with a comforting smile for Mrs. Lobb and nary a glance for him.

"Mr. Gibson is a doctor. You needn't be uncomfortable," she said.

But she was. Mrs. Lobb was scorching with embarrassment by the time Daniel convinced her to lift her skirts and spread her legs, and her embarrassment was contagious. Daniel's ears burned as he leaned in and lifted the lamp. "Would you like me to hold the light for you?" Miss Beady asked.

"Yes, please," Daniel said. The exam was easier with both hands free, but it did not help to have Miss Beady breathing over his shoulder. He was sweating.

"Lower the light a little, please," he said with more assurance than he felt, as he thumbed aside the patient's outer labia. He'd done this often enough, but not with a young woman beside him. Miss Beady's presence might make this less taxing to Mrs. Lobb's sensibilities, but what about his?

"Ah, here's our trouble," Daniel said with relief. "A swollen Bartholin's gland."

"Skene's," Miss Beady whispered beside him.

Daniel leaned closer. "Yes, forgive me. A blocked Skene's gland. Easily remedied." He reached for his scalpel, but Miss Beady anticipated him. She placed it in his hand.

"Tell me about your family," Daniel said to distract Mrs. Lobb from the approach of the knife. She couldn't see, and if... "There," Daniel said as she flinched. "All it takes is a small cut. Thank you, Miss Beady. If you could give me a little more room—" Then he might just be able to breathe again. Daniel reached for a piece of gauze. He drained the fluid, then instructed Mrs. Lobb on a regimen of daily baths in salt water while she put her clothes in order again.

"She won't be able to afford the salts," Miss Beady said, once Mrs. Lobb had left. "Not every day. And she'll only come back for a check if the cut festers."

"I know," Daniel said. "But it can't hurt to tell her." He put away the scalpel and turned down the lamp, choosing his words. He didn't like being corrected, not in front of a nervous patient. "Miss Beady?"

"Yes, Dr. Gibson?"

Daniel was not a coward, but the instant her cool glance fell on him, the dignified rebuke he'd planned to give died within him. "Do you often sit in on examinations?"

"Frequently."

Daniel hesitated. He'd speak to her only if she corrected him in public again. She couldn't have meant it maliciously. "Will you bring in the next patient?"

"It's past one. I sent the others away before I came in. The charity clinic is closed now until tomorrow, and you're expected at St. Bart's in half an hour. I didn't like to mention it in front of Mrs. Lobb. You seemed a bit flustered." She glanced down at her hands as she spoke, but it was misguided to assume she was mocking him.

"You're mistaken, but I'd best hurry." Biting back a curse, Daniel checked that all his instruments were in their places and buckled his bag. Doctors acted with dignity, even when denied their lunch.

She nodded. As he passed by, she bit her lip.

"Yes, Miss Beady?"

She looked up.

"Please, speak your mind."

She looked down at her hands again. "Dr. Croft has an excellent book on feminine complaints—"

Daniel resisted the urge to snap at her. *Dignity. Calm.* "I'd like to see it. If you could leave it in my room? On top of the others, perhaps. Next to the lamp."

His barb was probably too subtle for her, which was just as well. He shouldn't be so petty. She was trying to help, and she was right. Mrs. Lobb's exam proved he needed more reading—and the lamp Miss Beady had insisted on providing. Besides, there was no time to spar with her. It was a twenty-minute walk to St. Bart's. If he didn't hurry, he'd be late.

CHAPTER 6

D ANIEL WAS PUFFING HARD BY THE TIME HE ARRIVED AT
the busy drive of St. Bart's, where hackneys and
broughams jockeyed for spots close to the door but out of
the paths of the miserable stragglers making their way nervously inside. Straightening his coat, he slowed his pace and
his breathing, striving for a dignity to match the great north
and south wings that guarded the green square with their massive limestone walls. For more than seven hundred years, the
hospital had seen a parade of the dejected and dying slinking
across the city in search of healing. The chapels on the grounds
and the parade of sisters, students, and priests marked the place
as a charity and teaching hospital. The board surgeons, who
collected generous salaries from lecturing and student fees,
were followed like demigods, while lowlier doctors earned only
scraps and looked forward to the day when they could, if not
earn a lecturer's post, at least open a more lucrative private practice like their mentors.

Dodging the line of patients, Daniel stepped inside but
never made it to the lecture hall. A commotion outside the surgical theater arrested him, and he followed an excited mass of
doctors into the room. Whenever an interesting case or emergency disrupted the usual flow of hospital work, the students

dropped their regular duties and converged like locusts, quickly followed by the physicians and orderlies. Inside, a young man lay on the table, low moans issuing from his mouth, his bloody arm at a grotesque angle. Daniel scanned the pack of men but knew in an instant his favorite colleague, Dr. Harry Trimble, wasn't present. Impossible for him to miss Trimble's fiery Scottish hair. Daniel usually relied on him to help fight to the front row for a better view. Today he settled for the second row and relied on his height.

Peering over the heads of his fellow surgeons, Daniel saw Silas Vickery bend over the boy and listen to his pulse. Daniel checked his disappointment. Though accomplished, Vickery was thick-jowled and thin-skinned, his mouth set in a permanent frown as if anticipating an insult to his skill and intelligence. He examined the patient's arm, but the boy made no sudden movements, just continued his senseless moan.

"Age fourteen, fell from mainmast half an hour ago," Dr. Vickery informed those still rushing to the scene. "Compound comminuted fracture, middle third. Splint this," Vickery directed one of the nearby surgeons before he moved on to the ribs. As the sea of men parted, Daniel caught a glimpse of Croft bent over the boy's head, examining a massive bruise above the left eye.

"Fracture and depression," Vickery announced blandly as he ran his hands up the ribs.

"Fracture of the ribs?" Croft asked as he pressed his fingers into the swollen forehead. A sunken hollow where the brow bone should have been was all the diagnosis needed.

"The skull," Vickery corrected, the words slinking out beneath his black, immaculate mustache. "The skull that you are pressing on. It is fractured and depressed. We may have bone fragments in the brain. I must trepan it."

The men looked from Vickery to Croft, who continued his examination without reply. Rarely had Croft and Vickery ever agreed on a diagnosis. Despite Vickery being appointed chair of surgery five years earlier, Croft pulled in ten times as many students to his lectures and was referred to in journals as the "pioneer surgeon." Silas Vickery was never one to forgive genius when he spent his life doggedly defending the old guard of medicine. And Horace Croft was never one to forgive a lack of imagination.

A young doctor opened a notebook and looked on in anticipation. *Hoping for a fight,* Daniel thought. Croft disappointed them all. He rolled his fingers along the edges of the spongy, swollen forehead, engrossed in his diagnosis. The boy moaned, but never opened his eyes.

"Gibson, come here." Croft hurriedly dropped his coat on the sawdust floor and rolled up his sleeves. Daniel sighed. No wonder Mrs. Phipps complained about him. Daniel abandoned his seat and fought his way to the table. Using his elbow to pry a man aside, he picked the coat up, beating off the mess.

"There is no fracture," Croft announced.

The hurried movements of men taking the patient's pulse, listening to his respirations, wrapping his mutilated bones, halted. Heads swiveled to Croft, dark confusion hanging in the air like lanterns not yet lit.

Vickery's full lips trembled with suppressed emotion. "We can all see the fracture, Dr. Croft. There isn't any skull on earth that could bend at that angle and not break."

Croft looked up at Daniel, his hand still probing the grotesque concave of the boy's brow. "It's not bent."

Daniel handed Croft's jacket to the nearest man, or rather hung it on his arm without asking, and easily made it to Croft as the crowd parted for him. *They're glad it's not them.* How could he possibly advocate Croft's statement while the young man's damaged skull lay two feet in front of him? But to agree with Vickery was unthinkable. The rivalry between the two surgical giants was a popular subject in London medical circles, and Daniel had picked his side when he chose to study with Croft. He caught Croft's stare and tried to communicate his confusion discreetly, wondering if this was a trick or a test.

"Common mistake," Croft reassured the room. "Can you diagnose it?" he asked Daniel.

Daniel pressed the soft skin, his finger sinking into the swollen mass. He pushed farther, encountering pockets of blood, both fluid and coagulated, until he reached the shape of the skull. Probing the bone, he felt no sharp edges of a break, even when pressing into the obvious cavity left by the injury. It made no sense, and he wished he were home where he could let his face fall into the dumbfounded expression that tempted him. He needed a moment to think. Effusion of blood. Depressed skull. Massive ecchymosis. The boy moaned, a primal, unconscious sound. Again Daniel walked his fingers across the yielding skin. The swollen, sinking skin. Unable to hide his smile as realization dawned, he asked Croft in shorthand, "Disguised by the effusion?"

Croft nodded and, ignoring Vickery, turned to the younger, more malleable doctors. "We are witnessing an optical illusion.

The head never caved in. Gathered blood under and in the tissues has swollen the head so considerably that the pocket that did not collect fluid appears depressed. You will feel no edges present in a broken front plate, only the smooth skull."

The men clamored in excitement to feel with their own hands.

"And the involuntary voicing? Erratic pulse, inability to arouse? I've never seen a more obvious case of compression of the brain." Vickery used his height and muscular bulk to displace two doctors and approach Croft. "Bleeding ears," he pointed out. He narrowed his black eyes. "Even you cannot theorize this is anything other than a compressed brain, which requires immediate bleeding and trepanning."

One of Vickery's most loyal colleagues handed him the trepanning kit with a sniff in Croft's direction. Vickery withdrew the brace, challenging Croft to defy him, and ran his fingers over the patient's head to find the best place to drill a one-inch hole in the skull.

Croft shrugged. "One can come to the right result by means of flawed reasoning," he informed the room. "The outer layer of the skull bone is intact, but the inner table may be fractured and causing effusion beneath the skull. This can happen due to the different densities and thicknesses of the inner and outer structures of the skull. I concur with trepanning, but we must not bleed the patient. I believe nature took care of that." Croft gestured to the broken arm, blood seeping through the splint.

"You can *see*," Vickery hissed, his voice low only by the greatest mental effort. "The excess of blood must be drained to relieve swelling—"

"I see we must be quick in addressing the skull. Stertor has begun." A telltale rasping rose from the boy's labored breaths. Croft ran his fingers along the boy's leg and then jabbed him sharply above the knee. "Weak reflexive reactions."

Mumbling to himself, Vickery placed the drill and allowed a student to incise through the integuments and pull back the periosteum. The smooth, unbroken surface of the skull shone white against the bloody wound. Vickery proceeded in testy silence, lifting away a piece of the skull to find no effusion beneath.

Croft humphed in surprise. "Both wrong," he said, strikingly untroubled.

"Close him," Vickery commanded, his chin shaking with rage. As another doctor replaced and sewed the skin, the rattling breathing stopped.

Vickery pushed Daniel aside roughly and searched for a pulse. He gave up in less than a minute. "We had little chance of saving such a case, but did attempt all acceptable means. Perhaps if he'd been bled faster to prevent further compression..." Vickery's sharp glare raked over Daniel before reaching Croft.

All attention, friendly and otherwise, landed on Daniel. He swallowed, but kept his head raised in what he hoped passed for dignified confidence.

"We'll go inform his shipmates," Vickery said, and removed his apron to reveal a finely tailored coat and expertly knotted cravat. He dropped a rag dampened with cerebral fluid into Daniel's hand as he passed. "You can mop up."

Croft hadn't moved from the broken body and continued to run his hands along the neck and head. "It must be the base of the skull," he mused, unaware of the discussion or the receding tide of doctors. "We need to take it apart."

Daniel dropped the rag and wiped off his hands on a dry linen. "It's not a watch," he murmured.

———

Nora left her cupboard office and strode down the clinic corridor, passing two freshly cleaned rooms that smelled of carbolic and lemon. The bedsheets were the way she liked them, pulled tight, as flawless as fields of snow. The other three rooms held patients. Nora had already checked Peter Hugh's bandages. His incision, to treat a bursitis in the elbow, was draining nicely. Dr. Gibson had done well with that one. She should be pleased, if only for Peter's sake.

"Miss Beady?"

She glanced over her shoulder at the unfamiliar voice and saw Geordie Patton, whose eight-year-old daughter, Lucy, was recovering in room four.

He touched his hat to her. "Your orderly, John, let me in."

"I'm glad to see you," Nora said. "Lucy's doing much better." The calomel and saline purges, though unpleasant, seemed to have resolved her stomach pain. "She still has a touch of fever. You know we are happy to keep her."

"It's very good of you, miss, but my wife wants Lucy home."

It had taken all her persuasive power to convince the Pattons to leave Lucy overnight. "You can take her, but send word if there is any change," Nora said. "Watch for pain and redness, and if the fever worsens—"

"Dr. Croft explained."

"Good." Nora nodded. "I'll take you to her."

Lucy, a sturdy girl with a shock of hair so fair it glowed white, was happy to leave and delighted at the prospect of journeying home on her papa's shoulders. She thanked Nora shyly, clinging to her father's hand, and promised to rest and be good for her mama.

Nora waved them on their way, watching Lucy's white head bob over the hurrying crowd before returning to her tasks. She helped John change the linen, then went to the next room, where the last patient, Jane Ellis, lay sleeping.

"Has she stirred?" Nora asked.

John shook his head.

Nora walked to the side of the bed and laid the back of her hand on Jane's forehead. "She's much too warm still. Go home, John. I'll bring down some broth."

His look told her what he thought of that suggestion.

"We must do what we can for her," Nora said. Though there wasn't much they could do for these pitiful girls who came to the clinic, crippled with pain and sweaty with fever after clumsy abortions.

"I'll fetch the broth," John offered.

Nora let him. She went upstairs and saw the post had come: two letters for Dr. Croft, which she would probably answer herself, and one for Dr. Gibson. They hadn't had mail for him before. She turned the letter over, not recognizing the name, M. Edwards, though it didn't surprise her that Daniel's correspondent hailed from an address in Richmond. The fine houses and green spaces of the distinguished suburb mocked the poor of London, who squeezed together and gasped for breath in fetid tenements. Nor should it come as a shock that a letter from Richmond would arrive on such luxurious paper: creamy stuff that felt like velvet and conjured up memories of Nora's father, working behind his shop counter.

Nora set down the letter, gathered up Dr. Croft's, and went to find Mrs. Phipps.

The housekeeper was in her sitting room. This was her sanctuary, a carefully guarded preserve free from anything medical, with braided rugs on the floor, knit cushions, and a collection of china kittens gamboling across the mantel. It was a Tuesday, so Mrs. Phipps was going over the household accounts, paying bills, and compiling lists. "How are things in the clinic?" she asked without setting down the pen.

"Well enough." What else could Nora say?

"How is Dr. Gibson?"

"He believes women belong in a separate sphere." He hadn't said as much, but his treatment of her made it plain, and he was hardly singular. The notion of separate spheres was a common subject of sermons, lectures, and newspaper articles. Women, as the morally superior gender, were made for "sweet ordering," for instilling Christian principles in children and comforting weary men after the trials of the day. The popular refrain filled every conduct book for ladies, young and old. Dr. Croft, who had probably never considered the rules of conduct in his long life, did not own any such books, but Nora had been given one by the rector's concerned wife.

"Don't let it bother you." Mrs. Phipps dipped her pen in the inkwell and resumed writing complacently. "Dr. Croft values your help, and I never contradict the doctor."

"We'll need more lint, catgut, and lamp oil—and I'm reasonably sure Dr. Croft is nearly out of peppermints," Nora said.

Mrs. Phipps nodded and made the necessary additions to her lists in her tight handwriting. Nora watched from behind her shoulder. Butter, beef bones, and cabbages; eggs, onions, and—plums? "Plums will be expensive," Nora said. "So many were killed by that late spring frost."

Mrs. Phipps kept on with her writing. "Dr. Gibson likes plum cake."

He certainly did, though Nora couldn't fathom why that should matter. If plums were dear, there was nothing wrong with spice cake. "Could you order me some more drawing paper?" she asked.

"Certainly." Mrs. Phipps dipped her pen once more, added lemons to the list—were they for Dr. Gibson as well?—and set the sheet aside for the kitchen maid. It was market day.

"Is there anything else you want beside drawing paper?" Mrs. Phipps asked.

"There's nothing else I need," Nora told her, pretending to study a bill from the wine merchant. Consumption of London dry had increased dramatically now that Dr. Croft no longer passed his quiet evenings in her company.

"Not need. Want," Mrs. Phipps said. "You know—"

"What?" Nora looked up.

"You might like some lighter stockings. Or some lace for your gray dress. We always meant to pretty it up a little."

"It's a nice dress," Nora said. "There's nothing wrong with it."

"Of course not. But Dr. Croft never thinks of these things, and—well, you know there is money for you if you want it. I

care nothing for fashion myself, but perhaps you might like—"
She faltered. "Now that Dr. Gibson is here, and you've started
dressing for dinner, we could go to the shops on Oxford Street
together. Perhaps find you a new dress or a new bonnet."

"You think I look bad?"

"Not at all. You always look perfectly neat," Mrs. Phipps
protested. "But you're a young woman, and if you wanted something more colorful—"

"I'm happy the way I am," Nora said too defensively. "I can't
wear whites and pinks in the clinic."

Mrs. Phipps said nothing. Nora's stomach clenched. "I
should go back downstairs. There's a patient."

"I know. My dear?"

Nora stopped in the doorway. "Yes?"

"I hope you know I didn't mean to criticize."

"Of course." But Nora couldn't help thinking, as she walked
along the bare floor of the clinic corridor, that no one had cared
what she looked like before. Was she suddenly expected to be
beautiful? It was hard enough being banished from the surgery, except for the dissections she did at night. The charity
clinic would fail without her. Even if she never treated another
patient, Croft was too busy to manage the day-to-day affairs,
never mind weeding through his mail and making sure he didn't
neglect or offend his wealthy, paying patients. Unfortunately,
managing the clinic didn't seem nearly enough, not when she
could do so much more.

Lace and bonnets indeed.

Nora spent her afternoon spooning broth into Jane and
bathing her with cool water—or the coolest that could be

found today in this resurgence of summer heat. That night at dinner, in her best—but laceless—gray dress, Nora refused a slice of plum cake. Daniel ate his with relish, complimenting Cook and thanking Mrs. Phipps. Nora did her best to hide her resentment. At two in the morning, she bent over yet another corpse in her coarsest frock and a canvas apron, feeling strong because of the scalpel in her hand.

A week later, Jane Ellis died, consumed by fever in spite of all Nora's careful nursing.

"I'm sorry," Daniel said when he saw Nora leaning tiredly against the wall. "No one could have done more. It was a losing battle, in her condition, in this awful heat."

She ought to have smiled, or nodded at least. Instead Nora swept the damp strands of hair off her forehead. She wanted a bath. She wanted a walk in a quiet street muffled with snow, but it was late August, and the heat showed no sign of breaking. "I hate losing." Nora pushed off the wall and walked away.

CHAPTER 7

THE BATH PUT NORA IN A BETTER FRAME OF MIND, BUT A missing button made her late for dinner that evening. She'd had to sew it back on to the gray dress with the white linen collar she now wore as a point of pride. As she hurried down the stairs, confirming the neatness of her hands and her cuffs, she nearly trod on Dr. Gibson, who was examining his cravat in the tall pier glass on the landing, inadvertently barricading the hall.

"Forgive me," he said, stepping aside just a moment too late.

Nora moved back. "You aren't dining at home this evening?" It was a needless question, for he wore his hat and overcoat, but she wanted to know where he was going. He hadn't told her he planned to be absent.

"I'm expected at my parents' home," he told her. "I shall have to miss Cook's plum cake."

Annoyed that she'd wasted time over a button, Nora nodded.

"Enjoy your evening," he told her. "I think this heat is breaking at last."

She smiled. "We can only hope."

⁓

The dining room was empty, so Nora wandered to the window to check the sky while she waited for Dr. Croft. The western expanse was as bright as coral, broken by a single smudge of cloud. The only portent of cooler weather—if there was any—was the heaviness of the air palpable within the house, but that was easily imagined after a week of weary nursing and the loss of a patient. In spite of her wishes and Dr. Gibson's predictions, Nora didn't think they'd be favored with rain.

In the street below, Daniel Gibson hailed a hackney, an umbrella hooked over one arm. Smiling, Nora entered a new wager into her mental ledger. Rain or no rain? She liked her chances against him.

"Nora. There you are." Dr. Croft gusted into the room. "Forgive me, but I'm on my way out. I forgot about this dinner with the board of St. Bart's, and if I miss it, there'll be no one to gainsay Vickery."

"Of course you must go," Nora said. "Will you be late?"

"Not if I hurry."

Nora cast a despairing glance over his ancient waistcoat and limp cravat. No time to do anything for either. "Enjoy the evening." She could pry details of the dinner conversation later from Dr. Croft. There was no point repining or wishing she could be a spider on the dining hall's wall.

He humphed. "It'll go on too long and we'll all drink too much. Except Vickery, that sanctimonious teetotaler."

Nora hid a smile. "It won't be so bad." Tonight she rejoiced at the chance to dissect an enlarged heart Dr. Croft had brought home without stealing through the house in the middle of the night or sacrificing sleep.

"Perhaps you could translate that French case of the boy

with the bleed in his hindbrain? Mr. Wilson said he'd like to read it."

"Of course." Nora hurried him out the door, then went to break the news to Mrs. Phipps. Though Mrs. Phipps decried the waste of a dinner, neither one of them minded eating in quiet style in her sitting room from a pair of trays. As they ate, Mrs. Phipps wandered through reminiscences familiar to both of them. They didn't talk about wardrobes at all, and when they had finished, Nora excused herself to enjoy her hour of freedom in the basement.

Nora woke in the night to the clanging of the bell, clamoring for attention through the drumming rain. She threw back the covers and swung her feet to the floor, which was unexpectedly cold. Her eyes were heavy and gummed with sleep, but she reached for her housecoat and a shawl, stumbled into her slippers, and went for the stairs, expecting Dr. Croft or Dr. Gibson to intercept her. She reached the basement alone.

"I'm coming!" she called to silence the bell. The men must not be at home. Any disturbance at night was reason to hurry in this house, but the bell that had woken her was from the back door. At this hour, it could only be the resurrection men, coming with a body.

Stealing corpses from graveyards was illegal, but a necessary and lucrative business—for the men who dug them up at least. Dr. Croft had specific and exact requirements but was known to pay exceptionally well. Ice in her stomach, Nora opened the door, wondering what they'd brought this time.

It was hard to tell. The men, and the bundle they carried, were all covered in mud. "Bring it in," she instructed, trying not to mind the sludge they tracked onto the floor. The foreman, Sly Tom, as he liked to be called, tugged his cap at her.

"Doctor out tonight?"

"He is." She didn't like the way he looked at her, but she supposed it wasn't harmful. No matter what he was imagining, her robe was thick. Still, it felt better to swathe herself in the thick canvas apron hanging on a peg inside the surgery door. "If you come by tomorrow, he'll pay you. I think," she added, studying the shrouded body dubiously. You could barely see it under the mud, and after days of unrelenting heat... "Just what have you got?"

"Geordie Patton's little girl."

Nora failed to keep her face still, earning a cackling laugh from Sly Tom.

"You hadn't heard?"

"No." It did not help to think of the pretty child with a stomachache and some traces of fever who'd left the clinic riding on her father's shoulders little more than a week before. "She was just here," Nora said. "Why didn't they send for us when she took ill again?"

Sly Tom only shrugged. "Heard it came on quick. Collapsed all of a sudden and gone within the hour. Knew it was the kind of thing our doctor likes to investigate. Would have dug her up two days ago, but there was family guarding the grave. They wouldn't have left but for this rain."

At least three days dead. Nora didn't grimace. "Dr. Croft will have to work quickly. I'd better wash up for him before the rot gets any worse." She glanced behind her. The heart she'd worked on earlier, and a half-finished sketch of a fossa ovalis, took up the entire table. "Let me clear a space."

The heart could wait another day, but there wasn't a minute to spare if she wanted to find out what killed Lucy Patton.

"Put her on the table. Gently."

One of the men gave her a look, but Sly Tom motioned that they should indulge her. Tight-lipped, Nora hurried them out of the house before they could smear any more muck on the floor.

She cut away the muddy, clay-smeared shroud. Thank heaven Lucy Patton was small. There was a good chance she'd be ready before Dr. Croft returned. He'd be eager to discover how they'd failed her, if they could beat the worms to it.

Nora twisted up her braid so it wouldn't swing in the way. Muddy corpses were so much more work. As she peeled away the grave clothes, a bundle of flaxen hair that even mud couldn't disguise fell to the table. Nora caught her breath and fingered the damp strands, remembering the last smiles the girl had given her. Careful as she moved around the sunken-cheeked face and purpling limbs, she bundled the wrappings in a corner so they could be taken and burned. She was always gentler with the children, though of course there was no need.

Once the corpse was naked, Nora started washing, sponging the dirt away, rolling the body so she could reach everywhere— the back of her neck and between the child's toes. Hard to tell what was dirt and what was discoloration, but Nora was thorough, sponging and rinsing every part until she wrung out the sponge and the water was clear. Heavy-eyed, heavy-armed, Nora worked, thinking about the Pattons and little Lucy's stomach pain. She was the second child the Pattons had lost.

Nora positioned the body, then leaned away to knuckle her aching back. There was still more dirt behind the child's elbows. Resigned, she reached for the sponge as the bells of St. George's tolled two. Dr. Croft rarely stayed so late. He must be waiting to see if the rain abated. Or working himself into a rage with Vickery. Whatever the reason for his delay, she sighed and prayed for him to return home swiftly and sober. There was no time to sleep off the effects of club scotch.

Nora looked down at Lucy's face. The mask of death robbed her of plump cheeks and cheerful dimples. Now she wore a demon's disguise, her lips stretched open, revealing her baby teeth and blackening tongue. "I'm so sorry, little one." Nora liked the sound of her whispered voice blended with the drumming rain. It made a soothing lullaby for the child. She laid a linen napkin over Lucy's face. One should not look at a person they knew after death has done its work.

Nora felt the small sternum. The bone was hard, but pitifully small. Children's bones did not offer the same protection from autopsy as adults. Nora could cut through Lucy's ribs with a pair of strong shears. First though, she'd investigate the abdomen, since the child's complaint had been bad digestion and nausea. Nora selected her favorite scalpel, drew a neat line from the clavicle to the belly button, and retracted the skin. The stench of decay bubbled up, engulfing her. Nora turned her head away and pressed a perfumed handkerchief to her mouth as she took a smothered breath of floral air. It took a moment to adjust. The stomach contents had gone foul, the gases distending the bloated organ. Nora carefully avoided it, not wanting the mess it would cause if it burst. She probed the viscera, wondering how much discoloration to attribute to disease and how much to decay. The loops of intestine were in their natural positions but adhered together, like someone had brushed them all with a pot of glue. Working her hands around the sticky mass, she noticed as she neared the right hip bone that the intestines became almost black. Reaching further, she felt a firm lump the size and shape of her little finger, but it was impossible to see. Bent over, she reached for a spoon just as the surgery door swung open.

Nora didn't look up. "About time you're back. I've found something, but I can't see it. Perhaps you can reposition the retractors." No response. That did catch her attention. Too late, Nora realized her mistake. The ungodly hour, her lack of sleep, the sad ache she felt for Lucy and her parents had made her forgetful. It wasn't Dr. Croft at the door of the surgery. It was Daniel Gibson, staring at her in horror, his black bag in his hand.

CHAPTER 8

"GOD IN HEAVEN." DANIEL BIT HIS LIP, SAVING HIMSELF from further profanity. Rain collected on his back as he wavered between the black night and the yellow glare of the lamp where Miss Beady, absurdly small, hovered protectively over a swelling corpse.

Daniel scoured the room for Dr. Croft. *He's asked her to hold a tool. He's stepped into the other room to fetch a new scalpel.* Daniel tested these excuses but the streaks of filth on her apron, the black blood staining her hands, the scalpel gripped in her fingers, refuted every one. He threw down his bag and pulled the door shut.

"What is happening?" His horror echoed off the stone walls.

She spoke again, not so belligerently this time. "The resurrection men brought her. There's always so little time… Where is Dr. Croft? He often asks me to prepare them…"

"Alone?" Daniel stepped closer, searching her dark eyes as his shock melted to sympathy. "Cleaning perhaps," he conceded, "but he can't force you to *open* them. You poor child! You must be terrified."

Miss Beady tilted her chin up, the lamp doing strange things to her rosy complexion in the ghastly room of death. "Terrified? Whatever for? She's not going to hurt me. I hate the suffering that's brought her here, but giving her a bit of dignity is the least I can do…"

"You shouldn't feel the need to *do* at all." Daniel swept on a dissecting apron and meant to touch her shoulder in comfort, but she was prickly and insulted, as usual. "I can finish here. This must never be repeated. I'll speak to Horace."

"You'll do nothing of the sort." She dropped the scalpel onto the table, her steady hands beginning to quiver.

This wasn't impertinence. This was combat. Daniel narrowed his eyes. "What you are doing is worse than foolish. More than indecent. It's illegal."

"Tending the sick is indecent? Discovering the cause of their suffering is indecent?" Her voice rose.

"An untrained girl doing an autopsy? Yes. That is unconscionable." Even as he said it, his eyes studied the incision for the first time. Precise. The skin pinned in place. Hazy disbelief clouded his thoughts, and he forgot everything he planned to say. "How often have you done this?"

He could not read the blaze in her eye, but the gleam of defiance and her silence unnerved him. "Do you know that the slightest scratch could admit the decay into your own blood? A nick is a death sentence."

"Where were you this evening?" she asked quietly, reaching again for the scalpel.

He didn't want to speak of it, but he didn't want her cutting through those greasy intestinal adhesions either, and she seemed dead set on it. He grabbed the retractors first. "I was in Holborn," he admitted grudgingly.

"On a call? I didn't hear the summons."

"There wasn't one. They arrived just as I returned from Richmond and told me a birth was going badly."

"A boy or a girl?"

"Neither. A miscarriage"

She stilled for only a heartbeat. "I'm sorry."

Daniel shook his head. "It's her fourth. It was wretched." He stared down at the corpse. "I'll tend to this. Go upstairs."

Instead of backing away, she leaned forward, blocking his view of the ribs. "Dr. Gibson." The sound of his name cleared a portion of the fog from his heavy mind. He focused his eyes on her determined face. "I know this comes as a shock, but Dr. Croft has trained me for years to assist him. I have been present at hundreds of dissections. I nurse his patients. I am not a child out of her depths. In truth, *you* are the interloper in our household, not me."

He fumbled the retractors, switching them from hand to hand to buy himself an extra moment to process not just her words, but their import. *She cannot mean it as it sounds.* "Miss Beady, I have no doubt you've been forced to adjust to the most gruesome situations through unfortunate exposure. But I say that with sympathy. I think a woman of your delicacy and age should hardly be left to haunt dissecting rooms. It is a disservice done to you."

"Disservice?" she repeated.

"Yes. Dr. Croft has neglected his duty to protect your delicate—"

"If you call me delicate one more time, I will prove you wrong."

Now they were both red in the face, their lips set in the same stubborn frown.

"I certainly won't grace you with that attribute again. You do not belong here," he said.

"This is my home. I belong here as much, if not more than you. You have no right to command me, and as Lucy's body is stolen, dissecting her is just as illegal for you as for me."

This was true, but he wasn't about to admit it. "The law looks aside for physicians. If *you* were caught like this, it would smack of witchcraft. Do you think there would be any mercy? You'd be sent to an asylum if you were lucky, prison if the judge were in a foul mood." He must have finally touched a nerve. Her stiff face wavered and flashed with fear. "This is not a game, Miss Beady. Autopsies are for education and should be done with the utmost care to determine the course of disease and death," he informed her through closed teeth.

"It's her appendix. It's greatly enlarged. I can feel it here. I think there's a stone in it, but I will also examine the lungs and the heart."

She recited the terms with maddening accuracy. Daniel lowered his head and closed his eyes as if praying for strength. "You're not a doctor. I should inspect them," he snapped.

"I treated her as much as Dr. Croft did, and I owe it to her to find what killed her."

Above the dead child's cloaked face, their eyes met, each studying the other like a specimen or new disease. Daniel looked away. "This is ludicrous!" He gestured at the open corpse, at the shining, spoiled organs bulging from the abdomen like overripe fruit. "You shouldn't even be alone with me, let alone here in the middle of the night. My sisters would never dream of such a thing."

"Well, I assure you that Mrs. Phipps will not dream of coming down here to act as chaperone. Nor is it necessary for her to do so. I can scarcely stand to speak with you, and if you are tempted to impose on me, I'm perfectly capable of defending myself." Her eyes trailed over the scalpels, ready and razor sharp. The disgust in her voice pricked him, however silly it was to care what she said.

"You aren't in any danger," he spat back.

"Give me my scissors."

Eloquence deserted him. "No."

"Very well." She reached for a saw. "I was here first. If you intend to stay, you'll have to adjust. It's late. If you aren't going to bed, we'd best get to work." She lifted the saw, and he flinched, recoiling at such an antithesis of femininity. She paused, her hand hovering over the ribs. "I've a better chance of keeping the stomach intact if you—"

He didn't make her finish. He surrendered the shears.

"Thank you." She slipped her fingers into the handles, smoothing her apron with her free hand. He'd thought her unfeminine, but there was womanliness in that gesture, and in the care she used as she draped a cloth across the child's legs. Her white wrist glistened in the light, her fingers finding the junction of bone and cartilage with something like tenderness.

Daniel swallowed in fear. This was a new species altogether.

She snipped through the ribs, as calm as his mother at work in her rose garden. Twice she buried her mouth in her handkerchief, but she never complained about the smell.

Blood fell from the veins like black scabs. Daniel shivered and watched Nora's hands. They were not always steady, but they were stubborn.

With a sponge, she wiped the clots and handed him a large

silver spoon to push away the lungs. Just as he took it from her hand, the door opened unceremoniously, ushering in a violent wind that nearly extinguished the lamps and scattered rain across the threshold.

Dr. Croft's hat was pulled down so far against the rain that he stumbled, hardly able to see anything but the wet floor. He came in hollering. "If the College wastes one more cadaver on that fool… He got the pregnant prostitute that died of syphilis!" Croft unburdened himself of his hat and umbrella by shoving them onto a pile of anatomy books and finally raised his offended eyes to the room.

"Eh? What's this?"

Neither Daniel nor Nora answered. Like children caught in the sweet pantry, they stood suspended, the silent heart just beyond their hands.

Croft's frown deepened, along with the furrows on his brow until he recognized the white hair tangled in the shroud that covered the small face. "What happened?"

"She collapsed suddenly three days ago. Sly Tom assumed you'd want to know why."

"And?"

"There's a stone in the appendix. I haven't gotten it yet. Nothing unusual so far in the thoracic cavity."

Croft picked up a scalpel and began feeling his way through the intestines. "A little more light?"

Nora adjusted one of the mirrors.

Croft made a quick swipe with his knife, then lifted his hands like a conjurer, displaying the inflamed appendix. "A pea-size stone and"—he ran his fingers nimbly across the tissue before stopping and pointing to a jagged edge, stained black with infection—"a perforation to boot. Our calomel purges would never have saved her."

Daniel nodded. He'd seen postmortems like this before, and though informative, they were disheartening. When the trouble was the appendix, there was nothing to be done.

"This is a remarkable specimen." Croft laid the appendix reverently in the basin Daniel held out for him. "We must determine the chemical composition of the stone. Well done, both of you." He grinned. "It'll be so much more efficient now we can all work together."

Daniel caught the satisfied smile that darted over Miss Beady's face. She was smug, this one. He suspected she was keeping score, and that by her count, he was losing.

———

Daniel did not share Dr. Croft's sanguine outlook, not that night or the following day. He should have realized the extent of the situation sooner. Recklessly confident, Croft rejected any scruples that denied him access to competent hands.

And Miss Beady's were competent. It was almost terrifying.

Now Daniel noticed things—like her whispered aside to Croft before he went in to assess a patient she'd interviewed earlier. If Miss Beady wasn't giving a diagnosis—and Daniel doubted she'd hesitate—she was at least simplifying Croft's work. No wonder Croft was able to see so many cases, while Daniel was burdened and struggling to keep up after training two years at the Sorbonne and three more as a wound dresser at University College Hospital. Why, she must have longed to laugh when he'd misdiagnosed Mrs. Lobb. Daniel saw now he was not Croft's only disciple, not even the more experienced one.

Daniel kept his temper in check and saw another half-dozen patients. No matter what Miss Beady thought, he was not an ignorant bumbler. He knew his field, if not so well as Croft. What's more, he knew and respected the law. If word of Miss Beady's involvement here reached anyone unsympathetic, Croft could be dismissed from the hospital and the Royal College of Surgeons. If they decided to fine him for employing an unqualified assistant in individual patient cases instead of collectively, the sum would ruin him. He was a fool to run such a risk when students would line up for Miss Beady's job. There was no lack of men willing to assist.

For half a moment, Daniel wrestled the temptation to set down his stethoscope and go find someone to tell. Not Vickery—Daniel hated him—but there were plenty of sensible men out there who'd agree this must be stopped. Then Daniel thought of the appendix, of the dozens and dozens of beautiful specimens Croft carried from here to the hospital to be pored over and probed by roomfuls of doctors. He saw the packed lecture hall and heard Croft's slow laugh as he admitted his mistakes without ego to a crowd of students. If Daniel searched every corner of the kingdom, he'd find no teacher more effective or honest.

You're an honorable man, Daniel. Not a snitch.

But things couldn't go on this way. He must talk to Dr. Croft, one man to another.

Daniel waited until the clinic closed, when Mrs. Phipps summoned Miss Beady upstairs. He'd mentally rehearsed for an hour, and once he and Croft donned their coats and set out for the hospital—on foot, because Croft liked to walk more than he liked his expensive carriage—Daniel told him what he thought.

Croft listened until they turned onto Cock Lane. "I thought you were an open-minded fellow. That's why I brought you on." He shrugged and shoved his hands deeper into his greatcoat pockets. "If you aren't, if it's too much, you needn't stay."

Daniel's mouth fell open. "You can't mean you'd break our agreement?" Croft merely shrugged as if he'd been asked if he wanted corned beef for dinner. Daniel dodged a man hurrying in the other direction and was tempted to yank Croft's coattails to make him stop. "I infuriated my family by becoming a surgeon at all, and even more so when I passed over a practice in Richmond. I left it all to join you."

"Then I would think it strange if you abandoned ship over Nora. She's a brilliant girl."

"Be that as it may, she is unqualified—"

Croft turned his thunderous scowl on Daniel. "No one trained at my hand is unqualified."

Daniel faltered, his indignation and anger outmatched. They walked to the next corner in silence, the passersby only blurs and smudges of color as they bustled past. He needed a different approach.

"I don't wish to leave Great Queen Street," Daniel said, schooling his anger, "but don't you think—"

"I think a great many things. But I ask no one to believe them blindly. If my work is not evidence enough for you, I don't expect you to endorse it. I'll say only this: fortune favors the bold." Croft's lowered brows made it clear he considered the conversation closed.

They parted when they reached the hospital and avoided each other throughout the day. When Daniel returned to the house, still simmering, he changed his clothes and didn't go to the dining room. Instead, he left a note in the hall.

I'm dining in Richmond this evening. Sorry for not mentioning it.

His belongings could be fetched, should he decide not to return.

———

When Daniel climbed from the hackney and up the steps to his father's front door, he hesitated, his hand poised over the knocker. He'd come on impulse; no one expected him, and his mother was not overfond of surprises, especially ones that might interfere with her seating arrangements.

You're her son. You don't need an invitation. Even if she has guests. He smiled apologetically at Forge, their phlegmatic butler, when he opened the door.

"Welcome home, Dr. Gibson." Forge relieved him of hat, gloves, and coat.

"Are they out? Or already at dinner?"

"We are instructed to serve at eight o'clock this evening."

Good. He had a half hour, then. "You'll let my mother know I've arrived?"

Forge nodded, and if the news would cause consternation,

he didn't say. He held up Daniel's coat, sniffed it, and promised to have it cleaned.

"I'm sure it needs it," Daniel said. "I'm afraid I've gotten out of the habit of noticing."

Forge was too well bred to agree, and he understood Daniel enough to know what he wanted. "Miss Lillian is in the garden."

"Thank you, Forge." Daniel strode off wearing a smile, and it was only a mildly rueful one. He felt better already.

Outside, clipped hedges cast orderly shadows across the terrace in the fading sunlight. Daniel drew a long breath of the sweet, honeysuckle-scented air. He didn't miss the odors of Great Queen Street. It was peaceful here, quiet without the clatter of the streets or the clanging of the bell. Instead of wastewater thrown from the tenements, a gilt cascade of Schubert's Sonata in B-flat Major fell from an upstairs window, the work of his sister Joan. The garden wasn't especially large, but it was cultivated to allow privacy, separated by tall hedges into rooms. Daniel wandered from bench to pond to rose arbor with nothing to do but listen, breathe, and forget. Finally he came to the back of the garden, to a moss-covered Italianate fountain, where he found Lillian at last.

But not alone.

"Daniel!" Lillian sprang to her feet and came to him with outstretched hands and a wide smile. "You've escaped at last."

Daniel kissed her hand, but his eyes went behind her to the shaded spot by the fountain, to a spread of lilac taffeta skirts, slender gloved hands, and a bowed head that any sculptor, Italian or not, would be glad to copy. "Hello, Mae."

Only then did she rise to greet him. "Dr. Gibson."

Well, if she wanted to be formal, he could play along. Daniel bowed. "Miss Edwards."

"How do you do?"

"I'm lucky to find you here. I didn't think—" But Lillian was laughing so gaily there was no need to say more. She brought him into their leafy alcove, sat him next to Mae, and talked for the next quarter of an hour. It was no secret that Mae was shy, or that Lillian liked to rattle. She scolded Daniel for not sending word, told him he should cut his hair, and regaled him with a torrent of gossip. Daniel didn't mind, but nor did he care where the Ashtons took their holiday, who they saw at Tunbridge Wells, or that Laura Evans was engaged to a captain in the Life Guards.

What mattered was that Lillian went ahead of them into the house, leaving him and Mae to follow more sedately. A few moments, given in the gathering dark, were all he needed. Daniel put his hand over Mae's, where she'd slipped it onto his arm for the walk to the house. He leaned in and whispered, "I missed you."

"I missed you, too," she whispered back, a ribbon of satin sound he felt like a touch. "But you never answered my letter."

"I've hardly slept," Daniel said.

"Tell me all about it," she said and squeezed his hand, but of course Daniel didn't.

There was no time, for one thing. Nor would he sully her ears with stories like those. "You look lovely," Daniel said as they went in to dinner.

It was almost two in the morning when Daniel let himself into the house at Great Queen Street. Croft was in the surgery, working wire through a set of bird bones.

"Where's Miss Beady?" Daniel asked.

"I sent her to bed." Croft paused long enough to sweep his eyes along Daniel and analyze the set of his face.

"And she went?"

"She's tired."

Daniel supposed she had reason to be.

"I wasn't sure you'd come back," Croft said as he struggled with the little bones at the tip of the wing, so identical to the bones of human fingers.

"I wasn't certain myself," Daniel said.

Croft worked on implacably. "I like an honest man."

Daniel reached for a stool and sat down beside him. "Would you like help?"

"Why did you come back?"

Daniel wasn't sure of his reasons. *A promise to myself. The urge, near the end of the evening, to quarrel with my mother.* He shrugged. "Curiosity, foolhardiness…"

"A good surgeon needs plenty of both," Croft said, and passed Daniel the bones and the wire.

"So I see."

Croft only grinned.

CHAPTER 9

I N HER BETTER MOMENTS, NORA TOLD HERSELF DR. GIBSON was well intentioned and did not know how his poorly veiled disapproval stung. When she felt less charitable, she bit her tongue and avoided looking at him. So far, this worked. It had been a week since he'd discovered her, and she hadn't thrown any surgical tools at him yet. *Delicacy. Hah!* She wasn't delicate, and until his appearance, the lack of that particular quality had never made her feel inadequate.

Every time Dr. Gibson looked at her, he frowned like she was a faulty clock. Yesterday, when he saw her struggling to roll a corpse alone, he cursed. (It was tricky, especially as she could never stop the foolishness of imagining that rough handling would *hurt*.) At least she thought he swore. It was difficult to decipher his angry muttering. He recovered enough to help her expose the lumbosacral nerves, working beside her in tight-lipped silence. Then, when it was time to clean up, he ordered her out of the surgery.

"You've been working since dawn. You're about to faint from fatigue."

"I don't faint."

"I don't suppose you do." He had made it sound like a failing.

Frowning, Nora went to her room, but the house was too

quiet. She couldn't settle. It was too late in the day to nap and too early to go to bed for the evening. Dr. Croft was in his room, writing. There was no more work waiting in the surgery, and the clinic was closed. Mrs. Phipps was gone until Thursday, making a long-anticipated visit to her sister in Suffolk.

Delicate ladies probably passed their time with needlework or other such purposeless activities. Every time Nora tried to finish a cushion cover, she ended up practicing sutures instead of French knots. Currently, she was perfecting the subcuticular interrupted suture, but Cook had banned her from the kitchens for operating on the poultry. Last week's goose was served looking like a casualty of Waterloo. Dr. Croft had laughed and criticized her technique, but Dr. Gibson hung his head, prodding at his scarred goose wing and taking only tentative bites. In this mood, it was better Nora avoided needlework. She'd only injure her thumbs.

She spent an hour marshaling her emotions into better order while organizing her paint box, then remembered the volume Dr. Croft had just received from a colleague detailing a new Prussian method of cutting tissue flaps during amputation. Dr. Croft thought the technique promising, and Nora wanted to be ready when he attempted it.

She almost tutted aloud when she stepped into the library, but didn't. With Mrs. Phipps away, she supposed it was her fault the room was so neglected. The men certainly couldn't be expected to consider cleaning. The unswept ash of a week-old fire filled the grate, and only a weak light seeped through the cracks of the closed curtains. Nora gathered them back, letting watery sunlight permeate the filmed windows. Glancing back at the table, she discovered she wasn't alone. Dr. Gibson lay asleep on the sofa, an open book on his lap.

For all his assertions that she must be tired, he'd succumbed first. The fact that he hadn't stirred at the light and noise of her pulling back the curtains proved how damaging the long nights had been for him. Langenbeck's book wasn't on the table, so Nora searched the shelves, finally concluding the book she wanted must be in Dr. Gibson's lap or else in the stack resting on the floor beside him. She lowered herself quietly to the thin rug to read the spines. No luck. If she wanted Langenbeck, she'd have to take it from Dr. Gibson's sleeping hands. She hesitated, mapping out the best approach to avoid waking him.

They touched all the time in the bustle of the surgery: shoulders jostling, his legs grazing her skirts, their fingers brushing when they passed scalpels and probes. She'd felt his breath on her neck and reached around his shoulder in half an embrace once to grab a specimen jar from a tray. She had never thought of it until now, when the thought of skimming his hand arrested her.

Nora frowned, trying to decide if he was handsome. He had all his fingers and toes and necessary features. She wasn't going to admit more than that.

She leaned over him. He slept so deeply, she could feel the rhythm of his breathing. His eyelids didn't flutter. His arm was heavy as a corpse's, but softer and warmer when she lifted it off the book. His other hand twitched, reluctant, even in sleep, to allow her such improper reading. Nora eased the book free, then backed away, stepping over the case reports Dr. Gibson had left strewn on the floor.

He was starting to acquire some of Dr. Croft's habits, and Nora couldn't help a small smile. The chaos of number forty-three Great Queen Street would triumph over Dr. Gibson's fastidiousness after all. Truth be told, she was impressed he'd made the attempt to read at all. He probably had to hold his eyes open. Nora curled up in her favorite chair, grateful at least that Dr. Gibson hadn't appropriated it as well. The chair was worn and soft. Sometimes in its embrace, she imagined she smelled sweet tobacco. She didn't know why, for Dr. Croft never smoked. He always said he hadn't time.

She spread open the front cover, looping her ratty shawl around her shoulders. It was a beautiful book, with rice paper protecting the color plates. She always liked the stiff crackling it made and the fragile feel of it beneath her fingers.

She scanned the list of plates and the table of contents, then decided to read it properly and begin with the first chapter, no matter how tempted she was by the middle. She was halfway through the second when she sensed she was no longer alone and glanced, foolishly, at the door. No one. She turned her gaze to the sofa and found Gibson studying her from the couch.

Nora swallowed. Perhaps there was something improper about being alone with him after all. It felt precarious sitting here, with him watching from his temporary bed.

"Do you want your book back?" she asked. Ordinarily, she wouldn't have offered, but she was unsettled.

"Do you remember the cholera?" he asked.

Unaccountably, her fingers trembled.

"You are the child he wrote of, aren't you? The one he called E. B."

Her glance shot to the case reports beside him, and she understood. "Yes." Admitting it shouldn't matter, shouldn't force her to swallow back the bile of shame. He knew the truth now—she'd simply lingered on in this house like a shawl left in a railway cloakroom.

"Dr. Croft kept you because you had no family?"

She nodded. "I think it was mostly an oversight. Once I recovered, he—"

"Forgot." Dr. Gibson shook his head grimly. "No wonder you were so neglected."

"I was sent to school and given everything necessary. That is as close as he comes to affection. And Mrs. Phipps loved me. I soon learned that."

Daniel's eyes narrowed and he shifted against the cushions, provoking Nora into speaking more tartly than she intended. "You disapprove of me."

"Of your upbringing."

"Aren't they the same?"

"I just think you ought to have had a chance to experience a more"—he faltered on his words—"conventional life."

Nora laughed. "I certainly was denied *that*. I'm used to it. I'd be uncomfortable with your kind of people."

"As you are uncomfortable with me?"

He was staring too intently for her to deny it. "Yes." The air seemed to thicken, so she spoke again. "It would be easier for me if you would—couldn't you—be less dismayed that I exist."

"But it is a shock." Dr. Gibson straightened himself to sitting, his mouth neat and serious. "Dr. Croft allows you to practice medicine against the law, and now I am complicit. And you both behave as if that's reasonable." The words lumbered toward her, like a horned cow with its head lowered, both slow and alarming.

Her grip on Langenbeck tightened. "It came about naturally. I have a propensity for nursing. And you are certainly not required to stay here."

"It's far more than nursing, Miss Beady." His dark eyes gleamed, clear and focused.

A breath made her chest rise, and she released the air slowly over her lips. "I can't forget what I know. Am I to let people suffer just to satisfy the charade that I am ignorant?"

Daniel steepled his fingers, his eyes squinted in thought that rushed in conflicting lines across his brow. "I don't know the answer to that."

His honesty sent a jab of pain. Without meaning to, she fingered the ache across her collarbone. "But you will not expose us?" It was the only question that mattered.

"I fear something will, but it won't be me. God help us." Daniel looked her over again, and Nora sensed that he saw only an orphan, drained by cholera and carried through the streets. Her face reddened and she turned to her book.

He got up from the couch. "If you are going to keep reading, you should have more light."

"I'll get a candle." She went to close the pages.

"Not at all. The hallboy can bring it."

The hallboy could have brought it, but when the candle came, Dr. Gibson carried it, depositing it on the table beside her in silence. Nora lifted an eyebrow, but he only nodded tersely and left.

Nora looked a long time at the flame before returning her attention to Dr. Langenbeck's lectures.

Silas Vickery glared over the nodding doctors, his eyes sharpening when they arrived at Daniel's unbowed head. Daniel glanced at the others, saw their furiously scribbling pencils, and realized he'd been noticed because his hands, a notebook in one and a pencil in the other, were at his sides. He jotted something random and illegible, hoping to forestall the remark acidifying on Vickery's tongue.

There was a long pause, in which all the pencils fell still.

"As I was saying," Vickery went on, and Daniel let out a sigh of relief. "The initial swelling reduced when the fluid was drained, but is now followed by a secondary swelling that permeates the muscle and cannot be punctured. This is inevitable when the patient is of weak constitution. He has been bled and kept on a diet of thin wine and boiled oats."

"Close one," Harry Trimble whispered, and jogged Daniel's elbow. His pencil skittered across the page. "You want to watch yourself with this one."

Daniel replied with a quick smile, unwilling to risk words. Vickery was quick to read a slight anywhere, especially from anyone connected to Horace Croft. Because Vickery always led Friday morning rounds, they were fast becoming torture for Daniel.

Whenever Croft published a paper, Vickery spent his next lecture maligning it. This morning, the smells of the hospital were more rancid than usual, and a fly kept tormenting Daniel when he raised his perfumed handkerchief to his face. Daniel endured Vickery's ceaseless droning about his faulty theories of edemas being exacerbated by excess liquid and requiring bleeding until he could bear it no longer.

"Dr. Croft published last week that he finds the patients who are bled and denied fluids show worsening symptoms, instead of improved."

Vickery pressed his lips together so firmly his heavy cheeks trembled, an ominous sign. Daniel had probably just earned himself days of scraping pus from smallpox patients. "There are some men," Vickery began in a low voice, stepping away from the patient's bed and striding down the aisle in the middle of the ward, causing all the doctors to scramble after him, "who believe their hunches and vain imaginations are worth the sum of the acquired knowledge of the whole of the medical profession. Of all men, these are the most dangerous, and the ones who will never receive appointments to hospitals, because they lack the humility to be *taught*."

"Did you hear that? You're dangerous, Gibson," Harry whispered.

Daniel shook his head, watching Vickery lead his flock of doctors to another patient at the end of the ward. "Should we follow them?" Harry asked.

"If I stay behind, Vickery will call it insubordination and have me dismissed."

"You go on, then." Harry tilted his head to where Vickery's acolytes were once again busily scribbling. "You wouldn't want to miss any brilliant recitation of Hippocrates. Make sure you write it down."

CHAPTER 10

AFTER A BUSY AFTERNOON SOAKING OFF CRUSTED BAN-dages and sponging weeping wounds (his prediction that he was destined for pus duty had proved accurate), Daniel escaped to the hospital courtyard with a cup of tea. It was weak but a welcome antidote to the resentment weighing down his shoulders and the lingering smells of the sickroom. He sipped slowly, watching a rail-thin orderly prod a pile of dirty linen, coaxing it into a sulky burn. It was a warm day for October, especially to be tending a fire. Daniel slipped a hand into his waistcoat pocket, hunting for his watch, wondering how much longer until dinner.

Pain blazed along his right thumb as he found a razor-sharp edge of paper first. The scalding tea slopped onto his left leg. Swearing roundly, Daniel set down the cup and shook his right hand, but it didn't ease the sting. An almost invisible slice divided the pad of his thumb. It was barely even bleeding, but the damn thing hurt worse than his scalded leg and he studied it, a small panic welling. Every year Bart's lost more than one doctor to small cuts. Daniel thrust his thumb into his burning tea and dabbed it clean with his handkerchief, certain Croft would have done the same. Working with a needle would be murder for the next few days, his tea was lost and his trousers spoiled.

Gingerly, Daniel reached back into his pocket, drew out the letter that had harmed him, and smoothed it on his dry knee before cracking the seal. Mae would stop writing if he didn't reply.

"Thought I'd find you here."

Daniel looked up from Mae's precisely penned, assiduously conventional greeting—perhaps her *Dr. Gibson* was meant to tease him—and saw Harry. He settled onto the low wooden bench and leaned back against the sun-warmed wall.

"Bad news?"

Daniel rearranged his face into a smile. "Not at all. Just a paper cut." He held out his thumb.

Harry winced. "Terrible place for it. Is it deep?"

"I scalded it with tea."

"Quick thinking," Harry praised him. "Is that a letter from the uppity girl?"

After their two years together at medical school in Paris, Harry certainly knew Mae's name, but he insisted on referring to her this way.

"We are engaged, Harry. If you expect to dine at our wedding, I'd suggest you change your tune." Though Mae's family were as baffled by Daniel's decision to continue his studies as his own, she hadn't broken with him, saying she didn't mind waiting another year. Barely twenty-one and graced with a dowry and a pretty face, she had the luxury of time.

"I just came to sympathize. Not about the uppity girl"— Harry laughed for both of them—"but that devil Vickery."

Daniel shrugged. "I made the mistake of disagreeing with him once." *And throwing in my lot with Horace Croft.*

"Once wouldn't be so bad. You keep at it," Harry said with

a note of praise. Daniel had missed him the last two years while he sailed as a surgeon with the navy. Now Daniel was well ensconced at Bart's and used to Vickery's acrimony, but it was all new to Harry.

"You must approach it all carefully. He wields a great deal of influence," Daniel warned.

"Not against Dr. Croft. Or you, it seems."

"I'm not like Croft," Daniel said, thinking of Miss Beady.

"But you could be. Why else would he take you on of all the students clamoring?"

Daniel shook his head. "I doubt I'll ever have half his skill. You should see—"

"I'd like to," interrupted Harry. "Think you can wrangle me an invitation?"

Daniel stopped.

"Don't be greedy," Harry said. "When you go on about his surgery and his specimens and his pygmy shrew, how can I help wanting to see them? What would it hurt?"

Harry was a good sort. He knew his trade and was quick about it. But Daniel didn't know what he'd make of Miss Beady. *One visit won't endanger her secret*, Daniel thought.

"I'll speak up more during rounds," Harry offered. "Throw out some answers to Vickery's rhetorical questions. It might draw some of his fire."

"All right," Daniel relented. He consulted his watch—without injury, this time. Five o'clock. "We've a little time. But they dine at seven, and I'm still living on sufferance. I can't risk—"

"Riling the housekeeper?"

"She's right enough. I meant Dr. Croft's ward, Miss Beady."

Harry frowned. "Slim little thing? Quiet? Big eyes, blond hair?"

There was no reason to be ruffled by Harry's description. It was all true. "That's her."

"I've seen her come for Croft a time or two. Don't worry. A look at the surgery is all I want." Harry grinned. "But let's hurry."

~

It didn't usually take such a long walk to put Nora in a better frame of mind. Generally, by the time she trekked to the end of Great Queen Street, the lure of the grass, trees, and fresher air in the Temple Gardens was sufficient to clear her mind and quicken her step. Today she wandered through Lincoln's Inn Fields and the Temple Gardens to Blackfriars. She stared at the bridge and the river before weaving through the shouts and stalls of Covent Garden. She must have passed every barrow twice before she noticed that the bells of St. Paul's were tolling six. It was past time to head home.

Luckily, it wasn't far. Once, the houses on Great Queen Street had housed and hosted the crème de la crème, but these days the posh families had moved west to Mayfair. Venerable now, and the worse for wear, many of the cheaper houses were divided into apartments, crowded and shabby, only shades better than the rookery tenements encroaching from Seven Dials, just a few streets away. Dr. Croft's house had witnessed two hundred years of London history, through wars and restoration, when ladies wore panniers and the gentlemen wigs of long curls. Sometimes Nora wondered what the ladies and gentlemen who'd lived here would say about their cellars now holding convalescents instead of smuggled brandy.

Once, the atrium had been for tulips and exotic palms instead of knives and basins, a watercolor of Lucy Patton's appendix, exposed in situ, and Nora's paints, which she had neglected to put away. Nora bypassed the front entrance and walked around to the clinic door, but stopped at the sound of voices filtering through an open window. Dr. Gibson's she recognized at once—quiet and assured—but the lilt and laugh of his companion's was new to her. She opened the door quietly and followed the sound to the surgery.

Two men leaned against the table, their backs to her. She almost didn't recognize Dr. Gibson slouching with his hands in his coat pockets. The other one, laughing in a clear tenor, was copper-haired and broader-shouldered. "Of course, he swears up and down he never went near wee Milly's, but it's plain as day he's got the clap and—"

Nora would have sworn she hadn't made a sound—she hadn't even twitched—but Daniel turned his head and saw her, immediately laying a restraining hand on his companion's arm.

"Who's wee Milly?" Nora asked.

Her presence startled the other man. He must have left the floor to spin so quickly.

"This is Dr. Harry Trimble," Daniel said.

Nora held out her hand. "Eleanor Beady."

The new doctor raised his eyebrows and smiled in amusement at her proffered hand before taking and giving it a hearty shake.

"Dr. Trimble and I studied at the Sorbonne together. He's just come to London to study at St. Bart's. We got to talking, and he expressed a wish to see the surgery."

"It's superb," he said, then caught Nora off guard with a question. "Daniel says this is your drawing?" He tilted his head at her easel and the half-finished drawing of the chambers of a faulty heart.

She nodded.

"Do you do other drawings for the doctor?"

"All of them," she said, but he didn't recoil. "I don't sign them, though." She smiled, and made bold by the admiration in his face, she asked, "So who is wee Milly?"

Dr. Trimble grinned. "Feisty madam out Jamaica way, and the plague of many a sailor." Even when he wasn't laughing, cheery ripples stayed in his eyes. She saw them clearly because he wasn't tall, but on a level with her.

"Are you a navy man?" Nora asked.

"Was. Suppose I still am. No matter how I spruce myself up, folks smell the salt on me." He smelled more like hospital, but Nora liked the roll in his voice and the loose swing of his arms. "You must be Dr. Croft's girl," he said.

"I don't quite belong to anybody, but he keeps me about."

Dr. Trimble laughed, never guessing how true it was.

Daniel didn't even smile. "Miss Beady is the doctor's ward and…helper," he explained hesitantly, nodding at the drawing.

"Is she now?" Dr. Trimble folded his arms. "Miss Beady, what do you know of medicine?"

Nora flicked a glance from him to Dr. Gibson and back again. Trimble seemed interested, not aghast. "I read a great deal. And draw, as you see. Sometimes I also supervise the orderlies. Among other things."

Trimble grunted. "You must run a tight ship. Daniel didn't even want to bring me here, you know." His eyes twinkled. "I must admit I'm curious how such a pretty thing got the running of this place."

"Somebody has to do it," Nora said, trying not to show pleasure at his compliment. His smile was quick and free and his blue eyes startling beneath his colorful hair. "We run out of catgut and carbolic when I leave things to Dr. Croft."

"You don't look frightened at all by the thought of blood and drawing body parts." Trimble's amusement made her narrow her eyes suspiciously.

"I see you've read too much George Eliot and not enough Wollstonecraft, Dr. Trimble. You'll find women are bred to be nervous, not born to it."

Harry's mouth hung in an open smile, as if waiting for the end of a joke. His eyes crinkled in delight. "This is a house of curiosities! If I ask nicely, would you let me observe Dr. Croft on occasion? Daniel here tells me I'd need your permission, and I'm desperate for the chance."

Nora hid a grimace. She didn't need more doctors around the house. Daniel was more than enough—but he was letting her decide the issue, and she appreciated that. "Sometimes an audience is hard on the patients," she equivocated.

"Just once in a while. You can hide me in one of your cupboards. I'll drill myself a peephole."

He'd never fit in a cupboard, but the thought made her smile.

"I'd consider it a favor if Harry could come," Daniel said, catching her eyes. "He isn't... Dr. Croft and he are of like mind."

"About surgery?" Nora asked. Or did Daniel mean about her? It seemed unlikely.

"Surgery, Vickery... I could make a song of the things we agree upon," Dr. Trimble said. "Trickery, bugg—No, that doesn't rhyme," he said, catching Daniel's eye and stopping just in time. "Though when I think of adjectives for that fellow, nothing complimentary comes to mind. He was foul to you today."

Daniel did look drawn.

"I should take myself off. You'll be wanting your dinner," Harry said.

Nora took in his scuffed boots and his lean cheeks, glinting red-gold with evening stubble. "Have you someplace to dine?" she asked, then glanced to Daniel, thinking perhaps she'd over-stepped, but he smiled gratefully.

"I don't want to—" Trimble began.

Daniel snorted. "Of course you do. Don't be daft. Stay to dinner."

"I won't be able to change," Trimble said dubiously.

Nora beamed at him. "Why should we mind, sir? Your dress is no impediment to conversation."

"No, there's very little that impedes my conversation," Trimble admitted. "By dessert you'll be glad to be rid of me."

But Nora wasn't, and neither was Dr. Croft. He'd accepted their guest without a blink and spent the entire soup course quizzing him. Daniel had mellowed after his difficult day, jesting with Croft and Trimble in turn, and even her from time to time. Nora glanced down at her plate and used her fork to flick a raisin out of her pudding. Her cheeks were warm, not merely from the warmth of the candles. She couldn't remember when she'd laughed so easily.

"You must come again, Harry," Dr. Croft said when they rose from the table.

"I should like to." His eyes slewed to Nora and stopped, stealing her breath. She knew it was there, but she couldn't feel the floor. The muzziness in her head wasn't all from her three glasses of wine.

"Please do. Good night, gentlemen." She smiled and escaped upstairs, leaving the men to their port.

CHAPTER 11

"Four more hours to go," Harry said as they strode down the corridor at St. Bart's past a vacant-eyed man on a stretcher and a scullion lugging a heavy pail of water and making for the stairs. "Just keep your lips buttoned tight and try not to use any common sense."

"It's the only way to blend in," Daniel agreed.

A frantic scream interrupted them as it echoed down the corridor. Harry's head whipped up, his expression hard, all traces of humor gone. Harry knew how to diagnose a shriek as expertly as Galen swilling a beaker of urine. When Harry broke into a run, Daniel followed, the roll of bandages he dropped unraveling behind them on the floor. In the entry, they found a woman writhing on a stretcher. The men who carried her were wide-eyed and sweating.

"What happened?" Harry shouted to make himself audible over the screams.

"Her hat blew off into the street. She went to fetch it and—"

"Please be still." Daniel laid a restraining arm across the woman's shoulders. "I can't help you if I can't see."

She shuddered and subsided to a low groan.

"Wagon wheel," one of the stretcher bearers muttered.

Her legs looked sound enough, and she'd never have

survived the crushing injury of a wagon wheel on her abdomen or ribs. But her arms were curled close, like a newborn baby's, and her cupped hands were a mess of blood. Daniel palpated his way down her nearest arm, but at the elbow she jerked away. Keeping the pressure on her shoulders, Daniel reached for the hand. Her fourth finger was crushed beyond repair, the throbbing nerves exposed amid the shattered bones. She screamed hysterically when he moved it the slightest bit.

"Bring her to the surgery. Quickly," Daniel said.

"Please!" she screamed, the volume and pitch like a hot iron on his heart, causing it to gallop wildly in his chest as she flung her body in protest. "Don't!"

The orderlies none too gently muscled her stretcher past other patients and gawkers summoned by her screams. The surgical theater at the end of the corridor was empty, but it hadn't been cleaned since Vickery's last surgery. Daniel let out a hiss of irritation, shoved aside the basins of bloody gauze, and reached for a new roll, grateful he carried his own scalpels with him.

Daniel looked up and saw Vickery striding into the room, his coat flapping. Of course the screams had summoned the one person he least wanted.

Vickery's eyes narrowed. "Proceed." He folded his arms.

Daniel pretended not to see Harry's warning look. "Thank you, sir."

Sweat beading on his brow, he tried to locate sound bone by feeling his way up the metacarpal to the sesamoid bone. It took only his eyes to see the proximal phalanx was lost, but he didn't know how far into the injury bone fragments had been forced.

Daniel had a number of choice words ready to vault off his

tongue, but he kept them in check to deny Vickery the pleasure of his panic. "I need laudanum immediately," he growled, but before he finished asking, Harry appeared with a cup. With a cajoling smile, Daniel began to wheedle the concoction down the woman's throat.

"There now, it looks like hell, I know, but I've seen at least twenty that were worse. Drink up. This will help more than you know."

Her blind stare of pain broke with a glimmer of comprehension. She latched onto Harry's arm with her good hand and gulped from the cup.

"I used to tell the soldiers they were carrying on like women." Harry set aside the empty cup and bent close, until their foreheads were nearly touching. "Let's make a liar of me and see if we can get you to bear up better than them all. What name did they give you?"

"Beth," she whispered, her face wet with sweat.

"You're a brave lass, Beth," Harry said, steadying her, keeping her face firmly turned toward him and away from her injured hand.

Now that she was no longer shrieking, Daniel saw that she was slightly older, perhaps thirty, and well turned out with a delicate nose and white complexion. Daniel took a shuddering breath, completely unaware he had forgotten to inhale. Harry gave him a sideways glance, but Daniel replied with the slightest shake of the head. There was nothing of the finger to salvage, but there was a chance they could save the hand. First he wanted her as drunk and insensible as possible. Harry, bless him, asked questions until her answers slurred and became confused before tipping her back onto a bed. Her limbs still trembled with shock and pain, as if they knew what was coming.

"Disconnect. Make it clean and accurate. Turn off your ears," Harry murmured quietly in Daniel's ear as he tied down her arm. "She's muddled, but I'll give her some absinthe as well."

Despite the drugs, the surgical room rang with Beth's screams as they poured clean water over the wound and began hunting for bone fragments.

"Here." Harry poured some absinthe into the wound, the green liquid spilling into the gaping recesses. Daniel's confused frown intensified as he tried to mop up the rivers of alcohol.

"It helps," Harry said with a shrug. "I don't know if it absorbs into the open flesh as it does in the stomach, but my sailors did better when I put spirits in the wound. Perhaps it numbs it a bit."

The patient didn't look at all numbed. Her eyes bulged from her sweating face as if they meant to escape the horror by jumping out of her head.

"Do not cut off my hand!" she screamed, the fiery words rasping on her throat and climbing the walls like flames that wanted to burn the room down.

Daniel didn't have time to be distracted by Vickery, so he resisted the urge to look up and see the man's reaction. Instead, he positioned the shaking hand, checking one last time for soundness. The words of Croft reciting Snow's philosophy paced from one side of his mind to the other. *Quietly. Treat every wound very quietly.* The lesion gaped, but Daniel looked at the healthy thumb and other fingers. Worth saving. Daniel sliced through the exposed digital nerve and the torn skin until the mangled finger dropped from her hand onto the bleached sheet, which bloomed with the brilliant stain of blood as she blessedly lost consciousness.

When Daniel looked up from his last stitch, his face was white and wet, his eyes stinging from concentration and tears that wanted to make a showing but were forbidden. The first thing he saw was Vickery's smug smirk.

"A surgeon must be stronger and more reasonable than pain," he announced to the surgeons who had filled the room without Daniel noticing. His eyes took in Daniel's white cheeks, his stiff shoulders, and he continued, "Some are not." He flicked open Beth's eyelid to check her pupils and walked away as if the case now bored him. "Cauterize it." The flock of silent surgeons followed him, their notes fluttering like wings through the door.

"Like hell I will," Daniel muttered. Treatise after treatise argued against the trauma of cauterization, and he'd had no luck burning away infection. He would apply leeches daily and pray splints would suffice for the other fingers.

"Are you certain?" Harry asked. "Vickery isn't going to like it."

Daniel looked at Beth, still whimpering in an opium-induced haze, then at Harry again. "Yes."

He bent over her to cover the sutures with fresh bandages, while Harry muttered under his breath every description he'd ever heard given for a man like Vickery. "The best thing I learned in the navy was vocabulary," he confided. When Daniel didn't reward him with a chuckle, he softened his voice. "When they scream like that... I've done it for a hundred men and it's bloody unbearable, but women..."

"She sounded like my sister," Daniel finally replied. Which was only half true. Really, she had sounded more like Mae, whose lips had only ever murmured gentle words and given chaste kisses.

"Well, she'll feel better when she wakes, and I'm sure she'll go on to scream many more things at men, if I know anything about women. Besides, it wasn't her ring finger, so she can still finagle a fine wedding band from someone."

Daniel didn't laugh at this, but he smiled. "You'd better go or Vickery will start aiming at you, too. I'm all right."

Harry sent him a lopsided smile, then went for the door.

It was Nora's habit to tread quietly, and though she stepped ever so softly as she passed the half-open drawing-room door, Dr. Croft heard her.

"Nora? Is that you?"

"Yes."

"Come in. I need you."

Nora stepped inside and folded her hands together, trying not to be aware of Harry Trimble's smile. She'd heard him arrive half an hour ago, but she hadn't wanted to spring at him like an attention-hungry puppy.

Harry Trimble had other ideas. He rose from his chair and held out his hand. "Miss Beady, how nice to see you again."

"You should have come earlier and joined us for supper," she said.

"I don't want to make myself a nuisance," said Trimble.

"You aren't a nuisance," Nora said, waving him back to his seat.

Dr. Croft grunted and resettled himself in his chair. "Dr. Trimble wanted to hear your thoughts," he said.

"Don't look so surprised." Harry laughed.

"I'm not," Nora lied.

"It's Vickery," Dr. Gibson injected with a sigh.

Nora tensed. "What's he done now?"

"Daniel amputated a finger in hospital today but refused to cauterize it," Harry said, leaning forward.

Nora nodded. It was exactly what he should have done. She hadn't seen many cases of cauterizations, simply because Dr. Croft refused to do them, but she knew fewer of his patients died from fever and shock than Vickery's. "How did he take it?"

"If he finds out, he won't take it well," Dr. Gibson put in with a rueful wrinkle to his nose.

"Never does," Dr. Croft mumbled. He raised his glass, realized it was empty, and glanced beseechingly at the bottle of port. Nora, swiftly interpreting, was already halfway to the sideboard. "Vickery's an old crank," Dr. Croft added as she refilled his drink.

Nora resisted the urge to remind him that Vickery was two years younger than his own fifty-four.

"You could try to draw less attention in his lectures," Trimble said with a pointed look at Dr. Gibson.

"Not when he's killing people," Dr. Gibson argued. "I need to gather more cases to prove my point."

"Fine idea," Croft said. "But you'll never convince Vickery. I've written up case after case. He won't see reason."

"There are a few patients I remember," Nora inserted.

"Even if Vickery is blind, it never hurts to have evidence on your side."

Dr. Gibson hesitated and nodded reluctantly. It was a graceful, infuriating dismissal. With narrowed eyes, Nora returned to her tea, regretting her foray into the conversation.

But Dr. Trimble didn't allow her a retreat. "I'd love to see your notes, Miss Beady. As soon as I refresh my glass."

"I've heard about the inexhaustible thirst of navy men," Nora said, going again to the sideboard.

"Completely true," he said with a guilty smile. "Believe every story you hear, and assume that it should be multiplied at least twice. Then you'll understand the navy."

"It sounds like understanding the navy is something ladies shouldn't do," Nora said, hiding a smile and avoiding Daniel Gibson's eye.

"Maybe, but you strike me as a lady who thinks for herself," Trimble said.

"Nora is a great thinker," Croft said. His cheeks were a little pink. "What's more," Dr. Croft went on, "She's possessed of a beautiful pair of hands. You've never seen—"

"I have," Dr. Trimble insisted. "They are beautiful hands. Almost as lovely as the rest of her. There, she is blushing now, so we may turn the subject. I begged a copy of Orfila's *Elements of Medical Chemistry*. Have any of you read it? Yes? You too, Miss Beady? Excellent. His techniques are a trifle grisly, even for me, but the applications—"

It was late, and there was even less port in the bottle when they broke up the discussion. Daniel insisted he must retire to bed if he wanted to see straight tomorrow. Dr. Croft, who'd at one point nodded off in his chair, got to his feet, bid them good night, and vanished.

Dr. Trimble grinned. "He really is as abrupt as they say, isn't he? Still, I'd take him over Vickery any day."

Nora suppressed a yawn. She enjoyed Dr. Trimble's company but the hour was late and she had obligations tomorrow. She rose from her chair, propelling both men to their feet. "Good night, Dr. Trimble." She lowered her voice a degree colder. "Dr. Gibson."

Daniel stepped forward. "Harry, I'll walk you to the door."

"I'd rather go with Miss Beady." He held out his arm and graced her with an entreating smile. "I wanted to ask if I may come again."

"Aren't you expected here in clinic on Tuesday? If you don't show, Dr. Croft will never forgive you." He'd finagled the invitation over one of the many glasses of port.

"Yes, but I'd like to come on Sunday afternoon. To see you. Will you go walking with me, Miss Beady?"

Nora was taken aback. "Dr. Trimble, I—"

"I'd have asked you privately, if I thought there was a chance I could get you alone, but—"

"No chance, Harry," Dr. Gibson said. "I know you have little concern for conventions, but I do."

Dr. Trimble grinned. "That's what I thought."

"I'm not sure I should trust a navy man," Nora teased, though it was a lie. Dr. Croft had once been a navy man and she trusted him implicitly.

"Trust this one, Miss Beady. Trust me...with you." His words stumbled but his drink-dimmed eyes were still fervent.

"I'll think on it," Nora said. He was too charming to refuse, but she faltered with Dr. Gibson watching. She held out her hand in farewell.

"Thank you." Dr. Trimble bowed over it, and Nora took it back, pretending she felt nothing unusual. "Good night."

She hurried away, closing the door behind her, the fluttering in her middle adding haste to her steps. Behind the door, Dr. Gibson muttered something to Dr. Trimble, but she didn't try to hear. She realized, with a sudden, delicious glow, that he was disturbed by her weekend plans, which made the anticipation all the sweeter.

CHAPTER 12

H AVING FAILED TO WARN OFF HARRY TRIMBLE, DANIEL
felt uncomfortably obliged to warn Miss Beady or Dr.
Croft. Speaking to Croft would be easier but, in all likelihood,
profoundly ineffective. Croft had taken a liking to Trimble, and
he allowed Miss Beady to do anything she pleased. No matter
how he cudgeled his brain, Daniel couldn't think of a way to
drop a word of caution in her ear to let her know what sort of
company Harry had kept in Paris.

As it turned out, Daniel's conversational deficiencies didn't
matter. He overslept and missed seeing Miss Beady entirely the
next morning in his dash to the hospital. Daniel flew out the
door, slowing only when he reached the front offices of St. Bart's
where the surgeons assembled for morning business. Harry had
beat him there, but his drawn and white face looked the worse
for wear. His eyelids hung too loose, like crooked sashes hastily
tied above his grim mouth.

Perhaps the navy cannot make a drinker of everyone. Daniel
started to smile as he deliberated what punishments to inflict
on Harry, but another doctor's drawn expression halted him.
The smirk faded from his face as he registered the clues—hands
closed in uncomfortable fists, downward gazes that wouldn't
meet his own. A young Welshman shuffled aside to reveal Dr.

Vickery. His hard blue eyes sparked, but Daniel could not tell from the strange set of his mouth if he suppressed glee or rage. Swallowing in the silence, Daniel narrowed his eyes, wondering why even Harry refused to look at him.

Vickery cleared his throat and spoke in a voice so ominously still it was difficult to hear. "One unpleasant task of the medical profession is observing the pain and suffering brought on by negligent physicians and surgeons. While we all labor to save our patients, you will inevitably be exposed to the sad situation where you, or another doctor, through ignorance and carelessness…" His voice grew rounder and more fervent, causing small pieces of spittle to collect on his bottom lip. It didn't matter what Vickery had to say about him. Daniel wanted only to know who was suffering so he could tend to them. But Vickery went on and on, the force of his gaze and the painfully slow delivery of each scathing word grating on Daniel's restraint, shredding it into painful ribbons.

His patience at an end, Daniel jettisoned manners and decorum. "The patient, sir?" he demanded. When Vickery met him with icy silence he pressed louder. "Where is the patient you speak of?"

"Dying. Of a wound to the finger left to fester."

"A finger?" He couldn't possibly mean Beth. "Miss Carter? She was fine last night. What do you mean she's dying?" Without meaning to he had taken the stance of a fighter, his shoulder braced to take a blow, his head back.

The blow came. "I suggest you see what becomes of a patient when a doctor ignores all rightful procedures. Raging blood infection isn't a pleasant picture."

The room blurred, just a flash of Vickery's narrow eyes and the disappointed faces of his colleagues, as Daniel turned and hastened to the recovery ward. The attendant directed him to a private room where he found Miss Carter, her hand unbandaged and her face white except for the bright-red circles burned onto her cheeks. Her skin was as dry as a desert rock, and just as hot. Daniel refused to believe the woman in front of him was the same one he'd treated only yesterday. She'd been hysterical, yes, but trembling with life. The woman before him now lay limp, inert, her breath skipping feebly like a pebble across a shallow pond. Daniel picked up her injured hand. The stump had swollen to hideous dimensions, the neat, black stitches broken and oozing. Red streaks of infection branched through her palm before making a mad dash up her arm following the median antebrachial vein.

"This isn't right," he whispered, feeling the hot stripe where the poisoned blood was making its way toward her shoulder and heart. Septicemia. He'd never seen it move so fast. He heard someone come into the room behind him. "When I unbandaged her hand this morning, I found the wound uncauterized." Vickery's sad voice held just a hint too much triumph for Daniel to bear. His stomach lurched in warning. He would either vomit or strike a blow, and both would be the last thing he ever did as a doctor.

"I have multiple case histories and treatises..." Daniel's feeble answer hung unfinished.

"And a dead young woman."

Daniel blinked hard to fight the black spots gathering on the periphery of his vision. "She's not dead yet." The fact sharpened his focus. "I need leeches and clean water. Perhaps we could amputate the arm and save her yet." He stripped off his coat and went to unfasten his cuff links.

"You are officially relieved of this case." Vickery interrupted his thoughts.

"You can't…"

"Her parents, who are grieving and awaiting our prognosis, insisted you not be allowed to damage her further." A smile danced in his eyes. Daniel's hand closed into a fist.

"Right now they are grieving a finger, not a daughter. If I could just…"

"Just what? Mutilate her further before you bury her?"

"Stop speaking like her fate is closed!" Daniel cast his eyes around for help, but none of the doctors hovering outside the open door would look at him. "Dr. Croft will see her. She needs immediate amputation, and he's had excellent results with spirits and poultices. For now, she needs clean water and silver nitrate to debride the necrotic flesh. We could flush the vein… She cannot die from a finger injury."

"She *should* not die from a finger injury," Vickery corrected. "It is remarkable what damage pride can inflict." He touched her neck, feeling the feeble pulse. "You may leave now."

"I won't! You left this patient to my care."

"A horrible mistake I will not make twice. I shall apologize to her parents on your behalf."

"Like hell you will!" Daniel threw his bag onto the end of the bed, narrowly missing the other students, and rummaged for a scalpel. The shouts of alarm beside him were muffled by the blood pounding in his ears. He pulled out his instrument case just as a hard pair of arms closed around him. The case clattered to the floor as he lurched in surprise.

"Time to go, Dr. Gibson," Harry announced. In one deft move, he spun Daniel in the direction of the door, his feet sliding across the smooth floor. "He only meant to cut away the stitches and clean the wound," he said as he marched Daniel into the corridor.

He didn't release him until they could see the front doors. "Not here," Harry commanded. "We'll hash it out at the club, bring every evidence before the board, but no one will sympathize with a brawl. Not here. Not like this. It looked like you meant to stab him!"

Daniel spun back toward the corridor. "I wasn't going to touch him, but he'll kill her, Harry. Just to prove me wrong, he will kill that girl!"

"Then God help him," Harry said, his grip bruising Daniel's arm. "And I hope He has time to help you, too."

~

Nora used the satisfying scrape of the whetstone to keep her thoughts sharpened, as well as the scalpel. As she moved the dull instrument across the stone, she watched the minuscule divots in the blade disappear. It wasn't Croft's most expensive scalpel, but it was her particular favorite and she coddled it. As the slow, rhythmic scratch punctuated the quiet of the surgery, she imagined Harry Trimble's arm beneath her own, their boots landing softly on the footpaths in the shady park. She'd contemplated asking Mrs. Phipps for advice, but the older woman had as much experience with such things as Nora.

Despite her lack of feminine refinements, he seemed to like her. A bright sensation rose within Nora's chest as she remembered his smile and his fumbling invitation. Perhaps there was a young doctor in the world more minded like Dr. Croft than she'd dared believe. For the first time in her life, Nora tried on hope like a garment and found it suited her.

She was just replacing the scalpel in its velvet-lined box when the door of the surgery banged open with a cry. "Dr Croft!"

It was Harry Trimble, looking nothing like the smiling picture so recently occupying her mind. His eyes were enormous, his brow glistening, every muscle in his body tense with a need for desperate action.

"He's out on a call. What's happened?" She was halfway across the room already, reaching for her apron. "Can I help?"

Dr. Trimble swore. "There's nothing you can do. It's Daniel, but he's at the club and I can't bring you there."

"Is he hurt?"

Trimble shook his head, easing her dismay only a little. He must have run flat out to the house, the way he was gasping.

"What's wrong?"

"His patient is dying. Blood poisoning. Vickery wants to prove a point and has taken him off the case. Daniel was ready to throttle him. I had to muscle him outside. He was so upset, I gave him a flask of whiskey I keep about me for patients so it's laced with opium. He drank the whole thing neat. I thought we'd find a quiet corner in the club, and he could vent to me until he succumbed to the liquor. The girl will be dead by the time he's sober again, and I hoped this would keep him from doing anything rash. But he's not unconscious yet, and he won't shut up."

"What's he saying?"

"Telling everyone Vickery is killing her intentionally."

"Dear Lord," Nora whispered. "We've got to stop him. He'll ruin Dr. Croft."

CHAPTER 13

S HE WAS BREATHLESS BY THE TIME THEY REACHED PALL
Mall, even though Harry had spared himself a repeated
run by grabbing them a carriage. A five-minute ride never took
so much strength. She and Dr. Trimble both strained their
heads out the windows, as if spotting the destination would
make the sluggish horses go faster.

"There. On the left." He pointed unnecessarily. Nora recognized the place, though women were not admitted to Pall Mall
clubs, and the Athenaeum was no exception. Harry had the
carriage door open before the horses stopped and ordered the
driver to remain there as they sprinted up the steps. The porter,
in one moment passing from surprise to outrage to alarm, tried
to catch her with wide-flung arms.

"Madam, you cannot!"

"It's an emergency," Nora gasped, and pushed past him.

"We won't be long," Dr. Trimble wheezed. "This way," he
said to Nora. "In the coffee room."

A crowd had gathered near the window at the far side of
the room. On tables lay abandoned newspapers and cooling
cups of coffee. Apparently the present show was more enter-
taining than editorials and beverages. Nora's desperate courage
drained away. Her feet slowed.

She heard Daniel's voice, raised in argument, above the laughs. "He must be forced to see!"

"Dr. Gibson." Heads turned. At the first sight of her, the dark suits drew back as if she were a strange animal with fleas. "I've come to fetch him home," Nora said.

"Who are you?" a stiff graybeard asked, swelling as he spoke.

"She is Dr. Croft's ward," Dr. Trimble said behind her. Then added, "A nurse."

Nora bent over Daniel's chair and picked up his hands. "You must come home with me, Dr. Gibson. You are needed."

A man in a brown coat snorted. "For what? Dear girl, you'll find him quite incapable." Snickers from all sides enveloped her, but the man in the brown coat wasn't finished. He surveyed her at length and then drawled, "I'm sure any number of us could satisfy you."

Dr. Trimble snapped, "Watch yourself, Reeves," but Nora was already scarlet. Her arms stiffened at her sides, her tongue a plank of wood. She'd come to help, but that man's comments made everything sordid.

"Jenkins in Edinburgh said cauterization did nothing but torture the tortured." Daniel's words were low and slurred, but the room was so still, they echoed like a barrage of cannon. Nora couldn't breathe. Those who'd been trying to help Dr. Gibson now backed away from Nora with narrowed eyes.

"Enough talk, Dr. Gibson." She raised her voice to be certain the audience overheard. "You've been accidentally drugged. You're not yourself."

He turned his head, bleary eyes fixed on her. "No one will

listen. The girl will die if they don't amputate at the shoulder. I'll show you. Make the incision just there."

Dr. Gibson landed a sloppy grip on her sleeve, making her start.

Dr. Trimble pushed between them. "Time to get you home."

"Is it?" Daniel lifted his hollow eyes to hers. Nora nodded, afraid to speak.

"Come on, there's a good fellow." Trimble hauled Daniel to his feet and tried to slip a supporting arm beneath his shoulders. Wobbling on unsteady feet, Daniel pushed him away, straightening his coat with movements that were a travesty of his usual dignity.

"I'm quite all right." He started for the door, nearly walking into a table.

"Let me," Dr. Trimble said, seizing Daniel. In Daniel's ear he growled, "For God's sake, pull yourself together. We need to get Nora out of here."

That seemed to galvanize Daniel enough to take tottering steps forward.

The caustic stares burned Nora like a hot iron. She wished herself gone from this place far more than the disapproving men surrounding her. Pretending a courage she didn't feel, she steeled her shoulders and ignored the scowl from the porter who'd tried to stop her entering. She wished he had succeeded.

"Well, there are worse establishments for your woman to find you at," one man called out. A chorus of laughter, humorless and menacing, followed them out the door.

Daniel heard his own groan before he managed to pry his eye-lids up and wince against the shaft of late afternoon sun aimed directly at his face. It took a moment to register the sickly, stale taste of his thick saliva, his twisted and wrinkled clothing that looked as if he had fought the bedsheets for every hour of sleep, and finally, the faint touch of death. Daniel knew in the joints between his finger bones, knew in the silence of the house, knew in the dusty darkness of the drapes pulled like funeral coverings, that Miss Carter was dead. The knowledge pulsed like the headache reverberating behind his forehead and reso-nated all the way to his heart as he clumsily sat himself up.

Devil be cursed, it hurt! Daniel rubbed one hand across his aching ribs, exploring the sensation of failure as if it were a bout of angina. He never imagined it would manifest as physical pain. The part of his mind, the corner that had always looked beyond what other people cared to see, considered the thought as well as it could in his sluggish state.

He made slow steps to the window and let in the impa-tient light, ashamed by the bustle in the street from people going about their appointed work. Memories unfolded in his mind like a dark flower opening poisonous petals: a flash of his arm raised as he ranted while Harry implored him to sit, the chuckles of the other physicians, the red, turgid veins in Miss Carter's hand, and another hand. He frowned, search-ing his dark and scattered recollections the way Croft hunted through towers of loose papers to find an elusive note. And there it was. Miss Beady, pulling him out of the club with her smooth and trembling hand. He groaned again as he recalled the way she pressed him into bed and poured him a glass of water while Harry pulled off his shoes. He looked behind him, hoping he was delusional, but the same glass sat untouched on his nightstand, and his favorite black boots sat in a heap on the floor.

All men were destined to end up in the grave. It might be best if he waited here until his day came. Though the wash-basin had been filled and fruit left on a plate with a pale slice of cheese, no one had been merciful enough to leave him a bottle of whiskey. Or better yet, arsenic. Sighs escaped him as he washed his face, scrubbed at his rumpled hair, and dressed himself in fresh clothes. The smell of soap revived him enough to cross the room and press his ear to the door. Hearing noth-ing, he opened it as noiselessly as the old hinges allowed and peeked into the hallway.

In spite of the silence, he was not alone. Nora sat in a chair, a heavy book in her lap. A strangled sound of surprise betrayed him. She looked up and let out a sigh. "You're awake. Harry said the amount of opium in his flask was not excessive, but once you were asleep, we couldn't rouse you."

Daniel tried to readjust his stance to something resembling dignity. "I woke only minutes ago." He could not hold her eyes.

"We've been so worried."

"I'm so sorry," he mumbled. He couldn't trust his memory, but the recollections were mortifying. Because of him, she'd been exposed to innuendo, insult, and public mockery. He scanned her for evidence of fury but her face was smooth.

"Are you well?" Nora asked. "You look flushed."

She got up, set aside the book, and reached toward him but he ducked away. "I'm…" There was nothing to say. "I'm finished," he whispered. Her startled expression mirrored his own grief and embarrassment before he shut the door between them.

———

Halfway down the stairs, Nora crossed paths with Mrs. Phipps, who was clutching a newspaper.

"I couldn't wait," Mrs. Phipps said. "I wasn't sure what to do."

She held out the newspaper, and Nora read it with a growing frown. "It's Vickery's work," Nora said. She bent her head over the sheet of smudged print and forced herself to read past the headline: Scandal at the Athenaeum Club.

...threatening the respected physicians of St. Bartholomew's after his negligence cost the life of twenty-six-year-old Miss Elizabeth Carter...drunkenly defending absurd theories...while the members of the Athenaeum may have enjoyed such a spectacle... hapless failure...a Miss Eleanor Beady, who charged into the club...

She paused and reread the gloating conclusion:

...can only imagine what would drive a young lady to such extraordinary behavior, and what Dr. Gibson has done to encourage her.

One questions the judgment of the so-called "pioneer surgeon," Dr. Horace Croft, in inviting a licentious quack to share both his home and his practice.

The paper crushed under her tight fingers. "It's wrong about everything, but…" Nora appealed to Mrs. Phipps. "You don't believe—"

"Of course I don't." Her forehead creased. "But it sounds ghastly. Dr. Croft is used to such jealous accusations, and he never cares about gossip, but in this case I think he should. And Dr. Gibson—"

"I'm tempted to hide it out of pity," Mrs. Phipps said. "But he needs to know. If he's not strong enough for this life…"

Nora pictured his dismal face as he'd closed the door between them moments before. "If I'm forced to bear this, he can, too." But she wasn't as sure as she'd sounded.

⁓

He spent a half hour pacing and resting his head in his hands. Eventually, though, he had to come out. He'd eaten the food left for him, and it was no use trying to sleep. The air was stale and too cold to open his window. His stomach, that lifelong motivator, finally made him push past the door once again.

This time, the hall was empty. His hair was combed, his shoes on his feet, and though he held himself straight, it was a long, bitter walk to the end of the hall and down the stairs.

Mrs. Phipps was in her sitting room, waiting like a sentinel sphinx, and saw him through the open door. "Dr. Gibson? Miss Beady said you were up." Her knitting needles clicked busily, almost working without her. "She and Dr. Croft are working downstairs. They asked if you would join them once you are ready."

Daniel's throat was rusty with disuse. "I'm not sure—"

"Is it your head? I'll get you some coffee."

"Please don't trouble yourself."

"If Doctor hid every time he lost a patient I'd have not seen him these twenty years." She frowned, an insistent thing that demanded an answer.

"Lost?" Daniel grunted. It was far too gentle a word. "Lost is a lovely problem, easy to solve. I believe the girl is dead."

Mrs. Phipps's mouth pinched until it nearly disappeared. A flash of pity softened her brow before she gathered up a worthy glare and hurled it at him. "Pouting is for children. Get yourself downstairs."

Daniel knew better than to argue with housekeepers, especially Mrs. Phipps. He went.

———

Nora peered through a magnifying glass, comparing the lungs of an Amazonian frog, bought last week from a sea captain of Dr. Croft's acquaintance, to the lungs of a London dormouse which the cook had recently brought to an unfortunate end. With her scalpel, Nora shaved off a rootlike bronchi and transferred it to a glass slide.

"Thank you, my dear." Dr. Croft positioned the slide beneath the microscope. Bent over the eyepiece, he didn't see the laboratory door open, so Nora alerted him with a hand on his arm.

Daniel hovered on the threshold, as gray as the shadows that sagged under his eyes. "Horace—" he began.

The older man motioned him over, urging him to look in the microscope.

Daniel held back.

"No, look," Nora said. "You can see the alveoli in the frog, but there is no diaphragm to move the lungs. There must be another muscle responsible."

Croft beamed at the absurdity. "The lungs are ventral out-pocketings of the gut!" he exclaimed.

Daniel resisted still. "I've come to speak to you about my pressing need to apologize."

"The search for knowledge is pressing. At least, it ought to be." Croft adjusted the slide.

Conveniently, Daniel didn't have to dodge their eyes since they were both too occupied to look at him. "There are things I cannot avoid."

Dr. Croft unbent and pushed away the microscope. "Very well. Let's speak of them." He leaned back against the table and folded his arms.

Daniel swallowed and hesitated, so Croft barreled ahead. "Your patient is dead, and her family have laid a complaint with the hospital board. They've been coached by Vickery—"

Daniel shook his head. "I should have taken the whole hand. I should have cauterized when he insisted."

"Why? Do you honestly think it would have helped her?" Nora's narrowed eyes challenged him.

Daniel turned to her, blood rushing to his cheeks. "No, but I cannot be sure, and—"

"You gave an oath," she reminded him. "Not to harm." She respected that he took the loss of a patient seriously, but this amount of self-flagellation was foolish. He was a man, not a god.

"And according to Vickery—"

"They'll suspend you from St. Bart's," Dr. Croft put in, with exasperating calm. "No official notice has come, but a friend on the board tells me—"

"You see?" Daniel turned from her to Dr. Croft. "I can't tarnish your name by staying here. Or Miss Beady's."

"Harry told me what happened at the Athenaeum," Dr. Croft said evenly. "If Nora doesn't mind their sneers, why should you? They'll forget soon enough."

Nora flashed a doubtful look at Horace.

"Do you mind?" Daniel fixed his eyes on hers, probing.

The set of his shoulders was so brittle that she looked away. "It will pass. I shouldn't have barged in without thinking."

He rubbed the side of his neck. "I don't perfectly recall what I was saying, but—"

"Nothing good." Nora cut him off.

"You see?" He looked at Dr. Croft. "Scurrilous rumors, a lawsuit, suspension from the hospital—"

"No one's suing you yet." Croft shrugged. "It's a pity you'll be released from practicing at St. Bart's, but this means you'll have more time for research. Do something brilliant and they'll beg you back. I give it six months." He bent over the frog on the table, lifting the ribs with a hatpin.

"That's yours, isn't it?" Daniel said. "You wore it last week."

Nora nodded. The hatpin was decorated with three green pearls set in a brass flower, a gift from Mrs. Phipps. "You wouldn't think it, but I find the decorations balance it very well for precision work," she said.

"I thought it looked well in your hair," he said mildly.

Nora had no response for this, so she directed her attention at the frog. "When I electrify the amphibians, the lungs respond more than the mammals, but I can't think why."

"I suppose no one will care if I confine my work to frogs," Daniel said. He leaned over the microscope. "Have you considered the salt content?"

"Frogs and the clinic." Nora straightened and looked at him with such force he didn't dare contradict. "Most of your salary comes from private practice anyway. You cannot let Vickery intimidate you. No matter what he claims, he cannot prove cauterization would have saved her."

"I agree with you wholeheartedly. To cauterize is traumatic and often leads to more infections than it stops. So I didn't do it. But she's dead." Daniel swallowed, suppressing the quaver that lurked in his throat. "And the fact is, her family blames me."

"Pig swill," Dr. Croft said.

Daniel wrinkled his nose in confusion.

"Come again?" Nora asked, as baffled as he.

"It was market day. The road must have been swimming in pig swill. You said the wound was extended all the way from the head of metacarpal IV to the base of metacarpal V, involving both tendons." Croft bent again over the microscope. "When the wheel ripped off her finger, the pig dung from the street would have been driven deep into the hand beyond the reach of your amputation. Should you have cauterized the vessels at the head of metacarpal IV, you still could never burn your way down past the proximal transverse ligament. Perhaps if you had cut off at the elbow, but that is quite drastic when the finger was dangling and it was a tidy job to slice it and bandage her."

"Vickery will still blame it on my technique, no matter the foulness of the street."

Croft's shoulders twitched as he fingered his tweezers. "He has limited ideas. If you can't help figure out these lungs, you should leave."

Nora watched Daniel's face but couldn't detect the thoughts hidden behind his grim expression. She drew in a breath and her pulse quickened with fear that he'd do something hasty— expose her work or leave Dr. Croft's practice. Her fingers flew out, surprising her as they landed lightly on his arm. "You are useful here," she said. "What would you do at home? Give up your work and live a safe life centered on trifles? Here you help people. You do what *matters*."

The hardness softened around his eyes, but nowhere else. She smiled until he rewarded her with a twitch of his mouth. "Very well," he whispered. He held out his hand. "Hand me a magnifying glass."

When they retired to the drawing room that evening, Nora watched surreptitiously as Daniel picked up the paper. When his face went stone gray and his shoulders stiffened, she pretended not to see. But her mouth fell open when he pushed up from his armchair.

"Forgive me. I'm retiring early this evening." He folded the paper and left the room with it tucked beneath his arm.

Nora stared at the closed door, deliberating for a whole minute before finally rising to her feet.

"Nora." Dr. Croft spoke her name like a warning.

She glanced at the doctor, who was reviewing a journal of notes in front of the fire. He'd put his paper down to meet her eyes. "Leave him be."

She stalled, her feet pinned to the floor, even though she was still turned to the door. "You read it?" she asked.

Dr. Croft sighed and went back to his notes.

"Why didn't you talk to him?" she demanded. "He's upset."

"He was a fool," Dr. Croft said, expressing more sympathy with his voice than his words.

"He was insensible with laudanum! It wasn't his fault."

Croft raised a dubious eyebrow. "He was an idiot to fight with Vickery. Trimble wouldn't have dosed him if he'd not tried to stab a doctor."

Nora snorted. "You're one to talk about not fighting with Vickery. You delight in provoking him."

"I have the clout. Daniel doesn't. Nor do you, young lady. You were both idiots." Dr. Croft wet his finger and turned a page.

Nora's mouth hung open. "I was trying to help."

Croft snorted.

"I was trying to save you, as well," she pointed out, her eyes growing hot.

Croft shook his head in what looked like veiled amusement. "Next time, think it through carefully. You must treat every case quietly. Every case, Nora."

Her lashes trembled. "Do you think he blames *me* for the spectacle at the club?"

Dr. Croft gave her a long look, his eyes brilliant in the glow of the oil lamp. "Leave him alone."

"It wasn't my fault," she insisted, her voice rising.

"Daniel isn't the sort to portion out blame," Croft said evenly.

He wasn't, and that made her feel even worse. Nora pressed her lips together. Gathering up her skirts, she swept herself from the room.

Mrs. Phipps was right, Nora thought as she fought her way up the stairs. Either Daniel was strong enough or he wasn't, but only he could decide. She was done trying to help.

CHAPTER 14

WHEN HARRY COLLECTED HER ON SUNDAY AFTERNOON, Nora was ready, an umbrella tucked under her arm. (She'd spent more time than she'd ever admit in front of the glass inspecting everything from the angle of the green pearl pin in her hair, which Dr. Gibson had said suited her, to the drape of her shawl to the buttons on her gloves.) She smoothed her pressed skirts and took Harry's arm.

Harry had on a coat she hadn't seen before, and no umbrella. "Perhaps you should take Daniel's," Nora suggested, glancing doubtfully at the gray sky. "He's working with the microscope just now, so he won't need it."

"Then I will," Harry said, reaching for the jet handle protruding from the umbrella stand. "Though we could always share, you know."

Nora measured the breadth of Harry's shoulders. "We wouldn't fit."

"I don't know," Harry said. "You take no room at all." Then turning to Mrs. Phipps who hovered behind Nora, he promised, "I'll walk her round Lincoln's and bring her straight home to you."

Mrs. Phipps pursed her stern lips. "Mind the pickpockets," she warned them both.

"I'll guard her with my life," Harry said, hiding his grin beneath an almost serious expression.

Nora smiled, because she didn't know what to say, but her silence caused no difficulties. When conversation lagged, Harry always made up the lack. They walked to Lincoln's Inn Fields, where gowned and wigged lawyers and busy clerks walked to and fro beneath barren branches of leafless trees. The wind and the gray sky seemed to have deterred most others.

"May I ask you something?" Nora said, now there was an available silence.

"Of course." He smiled encouragingly.

"You asked my opinion about Miss Carter—"

"Poor woman," Harry interrupted, shaking his head. "I'm sorry for her. And for Daniel. And for you, for that matter. You shouldn't have been caught up in it."

"Neither of us were thinking, but if we hadn't fetched him—"

"You'd never have been exposed to insult and humiliation."

Nora bit the inside of her cheek. "It will pass. There's nothing about me to interest anyone."

Harry's smile returned. "Don't expect me to agree. I think—"

Nora spoke quickly, not wishing to be diverted. "I was hoping you'd share your opinion with me about another case. Dr. Croft recently had a young patient who died of a ruptured appendix."

Harry's smile turned quizzical. "And?"

"I would like to know your experience with this kind of problem," Nora said. "This case frustrates me—like Miss Carter's death frustrates you and Dr. Gibson."

"He takes it harder than me. Daniel hasn't killed as many people as I have yet." His rueful eyes tried to tease, but she saw bleak memories marching across his face. *Navy surgeon.*

"Being raised by Dr. Croft should have accustomed me to death, but some cases..." Nora's voice trailed off. "The child was improving when I saw her last. Her death was unexpected."

He tilted his head. "This is a very serious discussion for an afternoon at the park, Miss Beady."

Miss Beady? "You called me Nora before," she said, sidestepping a muddy crater in the path.

"That was after several glasses of port," Harry admitted.

"Do I have to dose you?" Nora asked. "I'm afraid I didn't come prepared for that."

"If I have your permission, I can do without the port." He laid his hand atop hers, where it rested on his arm. "Go on, tell me about your patient." The wind ruffling Harry's bent head carried the smell of cinnamon soap. He must have scrubbed diligently to lose the scent of the hospital.

She collected her thoughts. "We removed the appendix postmortem and found a perforation about an inch and half down," she said. "There was a stone, about the size of a pea. I haven't analyzed it yet, but I intend to."

Harry peered at her. "You really are a scientist, aren't you?"

"Yes." Nora hesitated, searching for clues in his voice. *Was it patronizing?* "After all that has happened, I was counting that wouldn't bother you."

"Croft's a lucky man. I expect you are invaluable to him," Harry said. "He always sings your praises, but I hadn't realized—"

"No one realizes," Nora said quickly. "And I expect it's better that way."

"Of course, you're right. Well." Harry examined his fingers. "I've seen two cases like this. Both fatal, and I'm only guessing appendicitis was the cause in the second case. There was no post-mortem. But the symptoms were consistent with that disease."

"This child's symptoms were not so clear," Nora said. "At least when Dr. Croft saw her. After a dose of calomel, she improved. Her parents took her home. If it were a hand or a foot, it could be cut away," Nora said. "But even if Dr. Croft had known, nothing could be done."

"No. It's far too dangerous to operate in the abdomen. You know that." Harry frowned at the heavy layer of scudding cloud and shifted so his back would cut the wind. "Although—I'm telling you this only to impress you—I read once of a French doctor who removed an appendix from a living patient. It was only possible because the appendix was protruding through an inguinal hernia and had perforated because the patient had swallowed a pin. Odds of replicating the feat—and the patient's circumstances—are all but impossible."

"One can only hope," Nora said.

Harry laughed. "Yes. Pin swallowing is not generally rec-ommended, even for scientific research."

"We should be going. You'll stay for dinner?"

"I've been hoping you would ask."

⁓

Nora set aside her pencil and yawned. Harry had stayed late again, exchanging navy stories with Dr. Croft and carefully edited Sorbonne stories with Dr. Gibson. Nora could tell they'd omitted the best parts due to her presence, but Harry had given her equal time, examining the appendix with rapt attention and pushing back against her theory that the abdomen could be opened under the proper conditions.

This morning, she'd pried herself from bed early, sketched, measured, and examined the stone taken from Lucy Patton's appendix, preserving its characteristics as best she could. Now it was time to determine its composition—by destroying it.

She rolled up her sleeves and reached for the mortar and pestle.

"Can I help?" It was Daniel, halfway out of his overcoat, halfway inside the laboratory door. Without waiting for an answer, he sidled closer and peered over her shoulder. "Is that Lucy Patton's?"

Nora nodded, angling her shoulder in case he should want to take over. "I'm hoping to determine the chemical composition."

"Distillation is a difficult process," Daniel said.

"I'm familiar with it," Nora said stiffly.

"I've learned not to be surprised," Daniel said with a smile. "You make a point of trying everything." When she made no answer, he continued. "I meant to speak to you about Dr. Trimble."

"He's good company," Nora said with a final note. She didn't want to leave herself open to a lecture on the etiquette of walking out.

Daniel softened his voice. "Thank you for being kind to

him. Harry's a promising doctor, but he lacks connections to help him along. You and Dr. Croft have been good to him."

Nora went still, waiting for a qualifier, but he stopped at the compliment. "We both like him," she said, ashamed of her suspicions. Conceding, she slid the mortar until it lay on the table between them.

Dr. Gibson followed the movement, kept his eyes lowered. "Will you go walking with him again? He is not always—" His words failed. He chuckled at himself as he finished. "Conventional."

Nora laughed. "So that's why he fits in so well." But her smile weakened at her next thought. *And why you do not.*

Is it possible he read her mind? There was something resigned in the way he pressed his lips together and turned back to the mortar, making no attempt to touch it.

"Shall I set up the glassware?"

Taking silence for consent, he gathered retort flasks and bottles of solvents from the cupboard. Scolding herself for hurting his feelings even though she'd held the observation back, Nora brought the pestle down on the stone—too forcefully. It shot out of the bowl, pinged against the window and flew across the room.

"Confound it!" Nora said, dropping to her knees and scanning the floor.

"We'll find it," Daniel said. He was beside her already, unconcerned at being on all fours.

Nora looked away before he could catch the surprise in her face at finding him under the table. "It could be anywhere," Nora grumbled.

"Yes, but you keep this room astonishingly clean. Anywhere

else, I'd give only even odds on finding it, but since we are in your domain…" He reached to a hollow where the slate tiles gaped beneath the skirting board. "It's a certainty." He held out the malformed pebble.

"Thank you," Nora said. "It might have taken me ages to find it." When she would have taken it, he drew his hand back an inch.

"Will you let me grind it for you?" he said. "While you set up the rest? I'm guessing you are as particular with the glassware as you are with the floors."

"More," Nora said.

Daniel picked up the pestle. "I respect that."

Nora had flipped the sign to *Closed* on the clinic door and returned to her desk to update her ledgers when the bell gave a harsh jangle. She rose to answer it, hastily retying the hair she'd only just released from its knot.

"Yes?" Nellie Foster, a repeat patient, stood nervously on the step, cradling her right hand in her left.

"I can't do my sewing anymore," she said, her usually docile voice spiked with panic. "Holding the needle is torture."

Nora led her in and sat her in the examination room, trying not to show her frustration. She'd been battling Nellie's painful thumb for months, and now it looked like the thumb would win. Nellie wasn't married and supported herself as a dressmaker. If she couldn't sew…

"What are the symptoms now?" Nora asked, gently taking Nellie's hand in her own.

"It's stuck. I can't straighten it. I can't sleep, Miss Beady." She watched Nora's every move, her hand twitching.

Nora tutted sympathetically as she examined the stiff thumb. "And the soaks and blisters?" she asked.

Nellie shook her head with desperate eyes.

"Dr. Croft is at hospital today, but I will consult him—" Nora paused when Dr. Gibson appeared at the threshold. "Or perhaps Dr. Gibson has a moment?"

"Certainly," he agreed.

He approached with a tilted head and attentive frown as Nora introduced Nellie and described the case. Daniel listened to the list of failed treatments and took up Nellie's hand as if it were a fragile and priceless artifact. Running his finger along the thumb, he stopped at the base.

"Does it ever pop or crack?" he asked.

She nodded vigorously. "Almost every time I bend it."

"You didn't mention that," Nora said, trying not to sound as defensive as she felt. Not that it mattered. She wasn't familiar with the symptom.

"It's only just started recently," Nellie apologized to Nora. "And I've bothered you with it so much already. I only came today because I can't work at all now."

"You need never apologize for coming," Daniel reassured her. "Miss Beady cares for nothing more than our patients. She is never bothered."

Nora's eyes shot sideways, startled by his smile.

"And she has done an excellent job," Daniel continued. "But in light of this new information, I believe we can solve your difficulty."

Nellie's face lit with hope and her mouth fell open. "Truly?"

"There is a tiny nodule on the flexor tendon," Daniel said to Nora, gesturing her closer. "When it tries to pass through the tendon sheath, it is restricted and creates the popping sensation as it forces its way through the tight passage. The sheath is so inflamed now that the tendon is trapped. That's why she can't straighten it."

"How—" Nora pushed down the feeling of foolishness rising to her face.

"Professor Toulard in Paris let me practice often. The mill workers suffer with it."

Before she could answer, Dr. Gibson turned to Nellie with a level gaze. "How are you with pain, Miss Foster? You've been bearing up with this for months so I assume you're quite brave."

Nellie blanched. "What sort of pain?"

Daniel traced the bottom of her thumb for half an inch. "A very small opening just here. Not very deep and as fast as possible. If you could hold yourself extremely still, I could do it in moments. We nip off the nodule causing the problem and give you three stitches."

Nellie stared down at her thumb in dread. Her chin trembled. Nora opened her mouth to give words of comfort but Dr. Gibson was already speaking.

"Of course, we could leave it as it is," he told Nellie, still supporting her hand in his palm. "With rosy cheeks like yours, I'm sure there are three blokes fighting over you, and you could retire from dressmaking altogether. Perhaps you don't need this thumb after all."

Nellie laughed, even though anxious tears were gathering in her eyes.

Dr. Gibson turned to Nora and lowered his voice. "Would you be willing to send off a note that I am detained? Mr. Collins is expecting me within the hour."

"Emily's husband?" Nora fumbled the fountain pen she'd picked up. Any mention of Emily's violent birthing still shook her. "Is the baby ill?"

Dr. Gibson waved his hand. "No. But he worries. I try to stop by when I can." With his attention on Nellie, he didn't notice Nora's pause, or the thoughtful frown that accompanied her reply.

"Of course. I'll send word at once."

She returned with an instrument tray—scalpel, needles, tourniquet, sponges, and her smallest retractors—balanced on one hip and a basin of ice on the other. Nervous sweat filmed Nellie's face, and her eyes kept darting to the door as if weighing her chances of escape.

Dr. Gibson glanced beneath the towel covering the tray, nodded, and withdrew the tourniquet. He shifted his stool closer. "Miss Adams, how many times have you misaimed that needle of yours and pricked yourself?"

"Thousands," Nellie admitted with a reluctant grin.

"Thousands." He mirrored her smile. "What if I prick you with my scalpel *just once* and give you back your pretty thumb for good?"

Nellie took a steadying breath and gave him a single nod. "But you don't mean right now?" she asked with a rising voice, looking to Nora for help.

"I think you have one minute of courage in you," Dr. Gibson's gaze was piercing. "And one minute is all I need."

It was a risky promise to make, given he had to locate the nodule, avoid the nerve, and free the tendon. Especially when Nellie was the kind who couldn't even stomach the thought of a leech.

"One minute?" Nellie clutched his sleeve with her good hand, wringing the fabric beneath her fingers.

"One," Dr. Gibson promised. "And if we numb your hand in Miss Beady's ice, you'll hardly feel a thing." He flashed Nora a grateful glance, and he carried the hand with its tightly cramped thumb and immersed it in the basin. Ice was expensive, but it would help Nellie bear the pain, besides reducing the bleeding. Maintaining an easy flow of friendly talk, Dr. Gibson tied her arm above the elbow. Nora bit her lip. They'd have to be quick.

"Another minute in the ice, just to be sure," Daniel murmured. "Miss Foster, if you can turn your head and describe to me what you see outside the window."

"There's a hackney with yellow wheels," she began. "And a man in a black hat."

"Go on," Dr. Gibson said, sweeping the ice off her wax-white fingers. Using a linen strip, Nora anchored the hand to the table and took the fingers in a firm hold. Dr. Gibson lifted the towel and picked up a scalpel in his right hand and a pair of narrow, angled scissors in the other. His eyes darted from Nora's to the retractors.

"When I make the incision, are you are able to retract? Have you done it before?"

She picked them up and nodded. She blinked to tell him she was ready.

The blade dove and Nora moved in with the retractors.

"What else do you see outside, Miss Foster?" Dr. Gibson asked as the woman cried out.

Sucking in her breath, she resumed shakily. "A lady…blue jacket…" Her entire body quivered.

The point of his scalpel traced the bottom of the constricting sheath, then scissors moved like lightning, catching the band, cutting and pulling away before Nora had time to blink. "Sponge, please," Dr. Gibson said.

Nora released the retractors and wiped away a smear of blood. He was stitching before she dropped the sponge back onto the tray.

Four sutures, as quick and neat as Nellie could have done them.

"All done," he said with a smile, and released the tourniquet. "I promised three sutures, but it was four. Do you forgive me?"

Nellie laughed shakily as Nora unbuckled the restraints and cradled her wounded hand protectively against her breast.

"Give yourself a minute," Dr. Gibson instructed as he pressed her fingertips, watching as the blood returned to them. "If you can oblige me by moving your thumb, please."

Slowly, Nellie moved it across her palm before pressing it to her smallest finger as if in greeting. "Doctor—" She'd have added more, but her voice broke.

"You'll need to take some drops for pain for a few days. For now, put your hand back in the ice water to cool the burning."

Nellie hardly seemed to notice as he submerged her hand

in freezing water. "Do you mean it won't go back to the way it was?" she pressed.

"This is a permanent fix," he promised as he replaced his scalpel.

After Nellie had gone, Nora paused beside Dr. Gibson, who was drying his hands. But before she could formulate words, he referred to his pocket watch.

"I might not be too late for Mr. Collins after all, if you don't mind finishing cleaning up?"

"Go," she said without meeting his eyes. "I don't mind."

Daniel lingered in the study, his pen poised but hesitant. *Who to write first?* The paper or the board of Bart's? Apologies were painful, and he was in no hurry to remind the board of his drugged tantrum. The paper, however, was another matter. The scathing rebuke formulating in his brain all week brought nothing but savage satisfaction. When Mrs. Phipps appeared in the doorway, he turned away from the desk, grateful for the interruption.

"There's mail for you, Doctor, and I feared you would miss it if I left it in the hall as usual. You've a pile of uncollected post."

Daniel focused on the envelope, registering the black ink of Mae's script instead of the customary green. Did her words look smaller and tighter than usual? He opened the seal and withdrew the single sheet of paper. When had she ever written only one page?

Dear Doctor Gibson,

He paused on the formal name, written square and stiff, and pressed his feet tight to the floor to brace himself.

The most fantastic rumors have reached Richmond. I dismissed them with a loyal heart at first, but confirmation has followed disturbing confirmation. Newspaper reports speak of insubordination, disgrace, and dismissal from the hospital. Perhaps those alone would not sway me, for what do I know of medical ways? But my uncle came from London with tales of a drunken scene at your club followed by you leaving with a brazen woman in broad daylight. The talk is widespread and degrading.

I cried myself to sleep imagining how the man I once cherished could be the topic of such gossip. I've waited these last four days for word from you, praying there was a mistake or at least an explanation. But now I must face facts and follow my parents' counsel and take back the hand I willingly gave you. It pains me, but I ask that you release it as proof you do not wish to embarrass me further.

With deepest regrets,
Mae Edwards

Daniel read the note twice before he moved. His tongue stuck against the roof of his mouth, and his blood moved like sand through his veins. He was drying up. He rose slowly, testing his legs to be certain his bones had not turned to dust. They held him and carried him to the empty fireplace, where he clutched the mantel.

Had it gone so far? Had that mangled hand pointed its bloodied finger at every corner of his life? His gaze discovered the barren grate, swept and black, and he imagined a log glowing with flame. He could have heated the iron and pressed it to Miss Carter's wound and burned out the infection. Perhaps Croft was wrong. Surely fire would have sealed the vessels and prevented poison from entering her vein. For twenty minutes he forgot to mourn Mae as he swam against the tide of time with a live coal in his hand. He would do it now—burn the flesh and burn away Vickery and the club and the letter from Mae.

But when he remembered Mae, he saw the paper in his hand and the cold grate and knew there was no fire. Had never been, would never be. And fire or no, it was not the finger the world thought of now—it was his drunken display in front of notable society.

He made two decisions without thought. They fell and landed noiselessly in his deserted mind: he must leave Croft's practice and he must speak to Mae.

CHAPTER 15

THERE WERE MANY PECULIARITIES ABOUT LIFE AT 43
Great Queen Street, but thumps and bangs coming from
the bedchambers were not among them. After the third jolt,
Nora set aside the latest copy of the *Lancet* and dashed up the
stairs. She skidded to a halt at Dr. Gibson's open door. His
drawers yawned wide, and his once neat rows of books littered
the bed, desk, and floor. Half his things were tossed anyhow
into an open trunk.

"Dr. Gibson?"

All she got was a glance, a temporary pause in his flurried
packing.

"Why are you going?" Nora bit her lip, annoyed with the
stupidity of her question. An ordinary person would ask where.

"My family has heard. They... It's a disaster. I must go to
Richmond."

An open letter lay beside his trunk.

"If I can get to the coaching inn by five, I can take the last
coach," Dr. Gibson said. The purpose of his movements, amid
such disorder, convinced Nora it was best not to argue. She
gathered up three books from the floor and placed them neatly
on the bed.

"Thank you. I don't need any help." He spoke without

looking at her, his voice a cool reproof. Even in his haste, he didn't want her in his bedroom. Nora wanted to protest—why spurn help at such a time, merely to follow convention?—but she couldn't persuade him now.

"Travel safely," she said and returned to the library. He left minutes later, without stopping to say goodbye.

Three days brought no word from him. Finally, Nora asked Dr. Croft about it.

"Is Dr. Gibson not eating with us again tonight?" she asked.

"Hmm?" He looked up, blinking at her, signifying he hadn't heard. He'd also forgotten to remove his blood-spattered apron before coming to the dining table.

"Must you wear that in here?" Mrs. Phipps asked hopelessly.

"Oh. Forgive me." He unfastened it and slung it over one of the new brocade-backed chairs. Mrs. Phipps's eyes bulged.

"I'll run it downstairs," Nora said quietly. She went to the basement and left it on one of the pegs. Daniel's kit bag was still on the chair beside the door. Surely he'd come back for it. He took such loving care of his instruments.

Nora returned to the dining room and helped herself to beef and potatoes, wondering if Mrs. Phipps had lectured Dr. Croft in her absence on the cost of fine upholstery. It was impossible to tell. Both of them chewed in silence. Nora tried again. "I gather he is not returning tonight."

Dr. Croft dabbed his lips with his napkin. "Trying to put things right with his family, and that flibbertigibbet of his."

"Flibbertigibbet?" Nora echoed.

Dr. Croft shrugged. "Some girl he was supposed to marry, but now she's broken it off. She reads the papers, I take it, and assumed the worst, like any woman with no purpose but gossip and a middling talent at the pianoforte."

He snorted and stabbed another slice of brisket. "You know I have no patience for such nonsense. Probably none too pleased about him being dismissed from St. Bart's, either. I imagine his parents are disappointed. Simpletons." He stirred through his peas with his fork. "That man needs to learn to focus on what's important."

Nora watched butter congealing around her uneaten peas. "I knew about Miss Edwards," she said quietly. "I hadn't heard he was engaged to her." She and Daniel had worked together for months in the laboratory and the clinic, but he had given only the most meager glimpses of his life outside Great Queen Street. She'd told him about her parents and the cholera when he'd asked, but he'd not reciprocated with any disclosures of his own.

"In my mind, he's well rid of her. He's got too much potential to be saddled with domestic trifles," Dr. Croft grumbled.

"Such as affection?" Nora murmured at her plate. Dr. Gibson wouldn't engage himself to a woman unless he loved her. She'd been perplexed, even irritated, by his dejection since that scene at the Athenaeum, but suddenly she understood. He loved this girl, and now, because of one mistake, he'd lost her.

Croft shrugged. His mouth was too full of potato to agree.

———

Nora drew a thick line through the row of her ledger, turned the page, and began counting the bottles of quinine remaining in the store cupboard. Checking supplies was routine work, and her thoughts wandered. If she'd behaved like a typical young woman and stayed outside the Athenaeum club, would Daniel's fiancée still have rejected him? The question stalked her as she counted rolls of lint, stacks of sheets, and jugs of lamp oil. The longer Daniel stayed away, the less she believed this fracas would soon pass. Again and again she remembered Daniel's obvious pain when he was packing, his hunched shoulders, the elusive twitch of his eyes. The silence of his prolonged absence. All of it confirmed her fears—he was going to abandon the profession she would give anything to practice.

Harry had explained, earlier that day, that Daniel felt heavily obliged to his family, who had never wanted him to come to Great Queen Street—another thing Daniel had never told her.

Ink dripped into an aggravating blot on her neat page. She was pressing too hard. *Daniel could run away from London and retreat into a life of ease and fortune.* She had no such recourse. But when she imagined their places reversed, pretending she had a love to lose, her stomach flooded with regret. She could not condemn him for a broken heart.

She'd never had romantic love. Since the death of her family, she'd had little love of any kind, besides the stern affection bestowed by Mrs. Phipps and Dr. Croft's distracted approval. Instead of making her fear love, Daniel's pain caused her to long for it—a profound connection to another person, a meeting of minds and sympathies. Perhaps Harry was her chance.

If she could approach him like an experiment it would be easier. Should he pluck up the nerve to kiss her, she could compare her pulse and mental excitement to other experiences and see if her pleasure was heightened. *But,* she wondered, *if the experiment went badly, what then?* Harry was pleasant and amusing and kind, but one stroll and two dinners a week was hardly a way to know someone.

Would he have expectations? The thought nestled raw in the back of her stomach, not entirely unwelcome, despite its discomfort. Perhaps some portion of her craved expectation so long as she didn't disappoint. He was the first man to actively pursue her. There'd been sly looks from orderlies and a few smiles from medical students, but never had one so much as asked her name. She couldn't cling to Harry just because he was her first (and perhaps only) opportunity.

Unless she was wrong? Perhaps he was precisely what she wanted. Never before had she memorized a man's expressions, mentally sketching his crinkled eyes and tilted bottom tooth as she rolled bandages or dressed for bed. She would like to see him more, but Harry was preoccupied with a troublesome case at the hospital. He'd taken on additional duties and would be unable to visit for another week.

Meanwhile, though, there was work. Nora collected her list of compounds to purchase from the apothecary. Nothing she did would solve Daniel's issues with Miss Edwards, but perhaps she could make a case to support his stance against cauterizing. Nora strayed into the library.

She needed an experiment. Something to test Croft's theory of the toxicity of pig dung. She could find a pair of unwanted dogs and give them identical wounds... Nora winced. She was an ardent opponent of vivisection, but how else? If Croft was correct, the risk was too great for any person. She turned to the shelves. She would read everything she could find about blood poisoning, hand amputations, and, if she was lucky enough to find anything helpful, excrement.

———

The fire burned low and Nora fell into a troubled doze, full of nightmare shadows. When her mind was alert and strong, she never succumbed to terrors, but tonight she was tired and dreamed of blood poisoning and the cholera, whimpering and huddling into the corner of her chair.

"Nora." A seismic jolt woke her—no, it was only Mrs. Phipps, shaking her arm. Nora blinked, confused by the brightness of the room. It must be morning.

"I'm sorry. I didn't mean you to wake her," said a familiar voice from the doorway.

"Harry!" Nora exclaimed, and blushed.

"The patient I was supposed to operate on died prematurely. I thought about going home to sleep, but decided to see you instead. I know it's Sunday morning, not Sunday afternoon, and you weren't even expecting me today, but I thought we could walk. I didn't mean to surprise you at an inconvenient time."

He looked woefully apologetic.

Nora leaped to her feet, beating uselessly at her crumpled skirts. "I—"

"Late-night reading does that to me, too." Harry smiled. "Perhaps next week?"

"No." Suddenly she was desperate to escape the house. "If you'll give me a quarter of an hour, I can be ready."

"You haven't eaten, Eleanor." Mrs. Phipps frowned.

"I'll find her something to eat along the way," Harry promised.

Nora hurried from the room, turning back at the door. She knew she looked a fright, but... "Thanks, Harry. I won't be long."

The winter day was unusually clear, a balm after her troubled sleep. Nora drank in the sunlight, untroubled by the chill breeze or the smells of the street that made other pedestrians hunch over and hide their faces.

"You've become pale these days," Harry said.

"I'm worried about Dr. Gibson. Has he said anything more to you?"

"About being dismissed from St. Bart's?"

"Yes. Or...or his family?" She would have added on the name of Miss Mae Edwards, if she were brave enough.

"They're displeased with him. He's doing what he can to appease them."

Nora nodded. She'd feared as much. "I feel his absence in the clinic."

"And do you mind?"

The unexpected question caught her by surprise. Nora blushed and hid her eyes. "He's an excellent doctor. Our patients need him. Besides, I don't want him to suffer." Harry's scrutiny was uncomfortable. He was a doctor, after all—used to holding people's answers up to the light and looking for truth.

"He is suffering, but it's not your doing."

"Isn't it?" Nora didn't believe him. If she hadn't rushed into the club in front of all those men—

Harry shook his head. "He could have backed down in front of Vickery instead of losing his head."

"He's too principled for that," Nora said.

"Holds to his convictions, doesn't he? It won't be easy for him, Nora, but it's his choice to make." He cocked his head at her. "You admire him for that, don't you?"

"Anyone would," Nora mumbled.

"No. Not just anyone." He smiled at her, nudging her to the left, into a bakeshop on the street corner, where he bought a bag of currant buns that steamed as they carried them into Lincoln's Inn Fields. When he saw her picking out the currants and tossing them to the birds, he laughed ruefully. "I should have asked. I wasn't thinking. These are my favorites, and—"

"The bread is delicious," Nora interrupted. "I just don't care for the way currants stick between my teeth." She tossed away another currant as Harry reached into the bag for another warm bun. "Do you live on buns when you don't join us for dinner?" she asked.

"More than I should." He sighed and patted his middle. "The softness of land living doesn't help my figure."

Nora snorted. "I doubt an extra stone or two makes you unattractive to ladies. You must dine with us more often, though."

"I will, thank you." He held out the bag to her.

She took another, pinching off a nibble of bread at a time. "Is he very unhappy?" she asked.

"Daniel?" Harry shrugged. "It will take time."

Nora sighed. "I think it's a mistake to give up. He shouldn't throw his career away."

"Looks like he'll have to, if he wants to win back Miss Edwards." Harry looked at her. "Frightful choice, isn't it?"

"I wouldn't think it is a choice at all. Perhaps she's an irresistible Venus, but I assumed Dr. Gibson would resent throwing away so much knowledge and talent. Wouldn't you?"

Harry laughed. "I've not had a woman try to tame me yet. It would be an interesting experiment."

His choice of words made her face burn, and she kept all of her attention on the pigeons scrambling for crumbs.

"But Daniel isn't the only one affected. How are you taking it?" Harry brought round his head until she had to face him.

"Well, I resent that he left, but—"

"That's not what I meant. I meant the talk about you." He pressed on. "Your name and Daniel's thrown about the club and splashed in that newspaper."

Nora felt her cheeks heat. "I'm sure it will die down. I'm no one important. Besides, I can't complain about notoriety after barging into the club. No one made me do it."

"I didn't stop you. I actually *liked* it, I'm sorry to say. You aren't like other women," Harry said.

"No. I'm not." It came out wistfully, which wasn't what she intended, so Nora covered up with a laugh. "Could you imagine if I were? Dr. Croft would never stand for it. He'd go demented with a *lady* in the house." She added a sarcastic flourish, pursing her lips and raising her eyebrows.

Harry surveyed her as he chewed. Once he'd swallowed,

he spoke. "You are a lady, Nora, an original. You care for him, don't you?"

"Dr. Croft? Yes, I do."

Harry grunted and held out the bag of buns.

"No thanks. I've had enough."

"Feed one to the ravenous birds, then. We can sit for a spell before going back to the house."

They did. Nora confessed her plans to re-create a wound and saturate it with pig dung. "If I can find stray dogs bad-tempered and ugly enough for me to stand to hurt them," she added.

"No distempered dogs for you," Harry demanded with alarm. "I'll find suitable candidates and help you, but I must tell you the navy is full of stories of urine treating wounds, not making them worse. I don't know that anything will come of your troubles."

Nora let her eyes linger on his hands as he flicked a few crumbs to hopeful pigeons. "It's no trouble."

A brazen pigeon cocked its blue-gray head and chortled what sounded like laughter.

⁓

Nora reentered the house humming to herself, her head full of plans, and went at once to tell Dr. Croft about her idea for an experiment. When she found the library and the laboratory empty, she went to Croft's bedchamber. He wasn't there, either.

Neither the hallboy nor Mrs. Phipps had seen or heard from him. A messenger sent to St. Bart's returned without any word of the doctor. "He didn't go to hospital today," said the breathless boy on his return.

"He wasn't summoned by a patient, either," the hallboy reported.

"Where has he gone, then?" Mrs. Phipps asked, flinging out her hands. Of course, neither boy had an answer. Agitated now, she marched upstairs to hunt through his room, Nora trailing in her wake, fending off worry. After a half hour's searching, Mrs. Phipps picked up a bit of paper from the floor. She hissed in exasperation. "He's left us a note. Must have dropped it in his haste."

"Where's he gone?"

"Edinburgh." Mrs. Phipps scowled, then huffed, "That man!"

CHAPTER 16

Two days later, Harry arrived at the house with a pair of puppies in a box. Her hands full of scissors and bandages, Nora looked from the dogs' melting brown eyes into Harry's. "Not puppies," she whispered, fighting to keep her face still.

Harry set the box down. "What's wrong?"

"Have you heard from Daniel?" she asked, her voice tight. Harry and Dr. Croft spoke of him so often by his Christian name that she was forgetting to call him Dr. Gibson in his absence.

"Visiting Mae. I gather she's taken herself off to Bath in high dudgeon. Daniel's gone to win her back."

"He's been gone nearly two weeks now," Nora said, her voice climbing to a perilously high pitch. "I've got half a dozen patients here in clinic, and—"

"Where's Croft?" Harry asked.

"Edinburgh." Nora pronounced it like a curse. "We found a note on Sunday. He must have taken the mail coach in the night. He forgot to mention anything about it." Not even a nudge from the puppy she held against her cheek managed to budge her rueful frown.

"What does he intend to do there?"

"I haven't the faintest idea. Meantime, I've got to stitch up Mr. Hawkins, if I can persuade him to let me, and then I can look forward to infecting these beautiful dogs." Her voice nearly broke. "Did you have to bring such pretty ones?" The silky, wavy coats left no doubt that they had spaniel in their pedigree. Nora fingered the soft ears.

Harry shrugged. "They were abandoned. My landlady found them for me. I thought, since you were in a hurry—" He broke off. "Don't worry about them now. Take me to Hawkins."

She did. Harry looked at his bleeding arm, the result of a collision with a glass pane, and told him that Miss Beady was right, he did require stitches, and that he ought to be glad she had offered to help him as she was very good with her needle.

"She could embroider you a fine flower if you like," Harry teased as he prepared the needle.

Mr. Hawkins, whose considerable belly did not conceal his hulking muscles shifted his arm warily. "I reckon we can just bandage it," he said in the thick accent of a dockworker.

Harry took another look. "Afraid not. The skin is spread too far apart to bind. It'd leave a gaping mess, and I can't stop the bleeding. Your own fault for being built like a cart horse. Your skin can barely fit over your muscles as it is."

Nora smiled. Harry wielded flattery as skillfully as Dr. Croft used his scalpels.

Harry pushed the skin back together and motioned Nora to hold it in place. "You're sure you don't mind?" he asked, studying her face for skittishness.

"Mind a scratch like this? Of course not."

Hawkins flinched as the needle touched him, and when it

pushed through the skin, he jumped, nearly pulling the needle from Harry's fingers.

As the catgut slid through the opening, the man let out a howl. "Can't do it," he said, pushing them both away.

Harry's face transformed into a fierce frown. "You will sit, sir. I've sewn up rowdy sailors and I'll not be bested by you." He shoved the man into a chair hardly large enough to hold him and signaled Nora to return to her post. In a slightly gentler growl, he continued talking as the needle punctured the skin over and over. "You'll be back at work today," he promised the man. "I doubt this hurts as much as the tattoo you'll get to cover the scar."

Nora held her lips together to keep from laughing and covered the neat stitches (sixteen in all) in clean bandages. Hawkins left his coins and hurried from the clinic with wounded pride and a mended arm.

She and Harry emptied the clinic by lunch. Declining his offer to fetch a bag of buns, Nora invited him upstairs for chicken and dumplings. Harry applied himself to his plate with commendable dedication and calmed the anxieties of Mrs. Phipps, who was fretting over the unwelcome dogs and her absentee employer.

"Daniel will send word soon, and Dr. Croft won't be gone too long, or he'd have made better arrangements."

Mrs. Phipps pushed a puppy back onto a towel. "They belong in the shed," she complained. "Not the dining room."

"I wanted to keep an eye on them," Nora apologized and returned to Harry's conversation. "It must have been something important to make him drop everything and hurry off," she said.

"He trusts you to manage things," Harry said. "But I can

help. I'm imagining my own plaque hanging on a town house one day."

She was grateful for his assistance, but not the dogs, who escaped from their box that evening and chewed through a pot of thyme, strewing dirt and leaves across the consulting room. When Mrs. Phipps discovered this, she did not consign them to the shed as she threatened, but brought them upstairs, huffily saying that Nora ought to know better. Puppies were a terrible inconvenience, even if these two, with their shaggy coats, might eventually prove helpful at scaring away rats. "They remind me of a cavalier my sister once had. The dearest little thing."

Nora wasn't brave enough to tell Mrs. Phipps what she intended with them.

It could wait. She had no time for experiments now, not with the clinic. She closed it on the days Harry was unable to come, but she still found herself in a bind with emergencies. Some Harry managed to tend, but when a late summons came on a night when he was working at the hospital, Nora packed up the necessary supplies and attended to the birth herself.

She quashed her fears by reminding herself how often she'd assisted Dr. Croft. She was certainly as skilled as a good number of midwives plying the same trade, so she could deliver a baby without raising too many eyebrows. But what if the next call was for a heart seizure, or a broken leg?

Fortunately, the delivery proved uncomplicated, and Nora returned home in the early dawn, buoyed by the pleasure of ushering a blotchy, mewling human safely into his mortal coil.

It was a relief, when she crossed the dim foyer, to spy the

light of a fire in the library. She hurried into the room. "You're back," she sighed, realizing too late the shorter figure standing in front of the fire wasn't Daniel. It was Dr. Croft.

"Oh, sir," Nora said, releasing her bottom lip from between her teeth. "Thank goodness you're home. I've been looking after things the best I can, but there's still no word from Daniel. Harry Trimble and I—"

He looked at her, not hearing her anxiety or seeing her distress. His face was aglow, not just from the flickering halo of firelight. "Nora." His words entered the room slowly. "This is a strange new world."

"What do you mean?"

He took her hand and pulled her into a chair. He sat across from her, bracing his elbows on his knees. His eyes flashed with excitement. "The line between life and death is blurring. I've seen it myself."

"Do you mean reanimation?" she asked, leaning forward and searching his face.

"No. The opposite. Reanimation is about raising people from the dead. Yesterday I saw a vibrant woman led almost to the grave. Dr. Phelan invited me to see his work with psychiatric patients in Edinburgh." Dr. Croft rubbed his thumb across his fingers making a whisper of dry skin that hissed in the air. "There was an utterly mad woman in a horrific fit and Phelan forced her to breathe his handkerchief and she fell into a stupor. At first I thought he'd killed her. Nonresponsive to any stimuli, even pain."

"A handkerchief?" Nora lowered her eyebrows. Nonsensical speech made her testy, and nothing Dr. Croft said made sense.

They both scoffed at mesmerists and magicians who claimed healing power. "How is it done?"

He grinned. "A gas. Sulfuric ether. All you do is put it on a handkerchief or paper cone and hold it over the patient's nose and mouth. When they breathe the fumes, slumber overpowers them almost instantly."

"A gas?"

"We must tell Daniel."

Nora's spirits dropped like a cooling balloon. "He's not home."

"Eh? Out on a call?"

The doctor didn't approve of mincing words, so Nora came out with it. "Not here in London, sir. He still hasn't returned from his family."

"Young fool," Dr. Croft said tolerantly. "Once he's made a name for himself, he'll find it easier. He won't be answerable to Vickery's circle of warlocks then."

"I'm not so sure. He's... Well, I'm afraid it's very bad, sir. Dr. Trimble says—" Suddenly, it was too heavy to shoulder anymore. Nora's face crumpled. "First he disappeared and then you did, and neither of you bothered to tell me anything."

"We'll sort it out later. I must show you—" He broke off, finally seeing her distress. "Why, what's the matter, my girl? Are you tired?"

Nora nodded, which was easier than speaking through her tight throat. Dr. Croft looked her up and down, taking in her rain-spattered skirts and the heavy satchel she'd left on the floor.

"Where've you been?" he asked.

"Bedford Row. Mrs. Timmin's confinement."

"Oh? On your own?"

Nora nodded. "But it went well. She's an old hand at it, though this one took a little longer."

"You're a good girl." He smiled at her only a moment, and then was looking about restlessly again. "Do we still have a cat?"

Nora shook her head. "I think you took out his lungs a few months ago."

"Confound it."

"There are two puppies just arrived," Nora said cautiously.

"Excellent. Bring them to the laboratory. I want to test my supply of the gas."

"Will it hurt them?"

"Quite the opposite."

Getting the dogs from Mrs. Phipps's room without waking her was impossible. The larger of the two yipped when Nora lifted him out of the box. Mrs. Phipps catapulted upright, setting the rags knotted in her thick gray hair swinging in front of her eyes.

"Why are you taking my dogs?" she demanded.

"Dr. Croft wants them," Nora whispered.

"He will not scalpel them!" Flinging herself out of bed, she hovered over the puppies. "Find him another one. He can't have these."

"I'm not going to harm them," Dr. Croft said, sticking his head through the door.

Mrs. Phipps screamed, and groped desperately for her dressing gown.

"I swear it! No harm will come to them," Dr. Croft said,

flinching under her hail of threats. "Come and see if you don't believe me."

Mrs. Phipps shuddered. "I told you, Doctor, that you would never prevail on me to come in there. If you harm—"

"I won't. Not so much as a needle prick. Come along, Nora."

He tucked one of the dogs under his arm and marched out the door.

"I'll make sure of it," Nora assured Mrs. Phipps, and hurried after.

When she caught up with Dr. Croft in the hall, he was looking the dog over. "Not so singular in appearance. If he comes to grief, we'll find her another."

It did not surprise Nora, once Dr. Croft had successfully sedated and revived the dog—almost magically—that it was her turn to be vaporized. "You'll find the vapor smells quite pleasant," Dr. Croft promised, dampening a fresh handkerchief from the bottle. "I tried some myself. It made the coach journey from Edinburgh pass much more quickly."

He consulted his watch. "I'm curious to see how long you'll be sleeping. Some of Phelan's patients have fantastic dreams when they inhale it, but I've only experienced the sensation of floating on a black ocean. When you wake, I want you to write your experience down. I'll be watching, and I can take notes if you are at first too weak to wield a pen."

Nora nodded. Her heartbeat was fast and her palms were damp, but there was no point in giving in to fear. She climbed onto the table and straightened her skirts. "All right. I'm ready."

Dr. Croft carefully measured out three drops onto a clean handkerchief and held it to her nose. Within seconds, she was swimming into a cloud of darkness that, oddly enough, smelled like apples. Her head tipped several feet below her legs even though she knew she was flat on a solid table. She would have giggled, but she was already gone.

CHAPTER 17

ANIEL SHIVERED IN THE WIND AND DREW HIS CHIN
into the collar of his coat as he passed the blackened
piles of dusty snow that had gathered overnight. He'd returned
to London on the late coach and spent hours nursing a plate of
pork chops and an ale at an inn where no one would recognize
him before finally gathering his resolve to make his way back
to Croft's home. In his breast pocket was an emerald ring that
grew heavier with every passing hour.

Mae had been very gentle, but like every true lady, her gen-
tleness did not entirely mask her aptitude for iciness. Never
a lingering touch or glance. Only practiced words, practiced
smiles, practiced pity. Oh, his embarrassments would pass and
fall out of public consciousness within weeks, but as fate would
have it, Mae's aunt had heard the gruesome tale of his drunken
ravings and then of a young ward who lived in the same house
coming to aid him. The truth hardly mattered when there was
a good story of a trollop and a dead woman and a doctor's
fight for his professional life. Softly, Mae had handed back his
grandmother's ring without a tear. Daniel hardly admitted to
himself that his tears had fallen in the cover of night on the
London street.

In his trouser pocket was Harry's note, meant to make him

smile and rouse him to fight. It did a bit of both, but also intensified the temptation to abandon medicine entirely. He fingered
the letter, half scowling as he remembered the words:

Daniel,

*Chin up! You may board ship at any time and sail on to
America. They have such idiots for doctors there and no
regulations at all. I've been myself and find the women
exceptional and the money free-flowing. In the meantime,
Bart's is dreadful and Dr. Croft has unexpectedly flown
the coop, leaving Nora to manage the clinic alone. I've been
helping her as much as I can, but I expect my extensive fees
to come out of your salary. Come home as soon as you can.*

Harry

The bells of St. Anselm's echoed over the street, informing London's citizens it was time to lay today's sorrows to rest.
Daniel agreed, but he doubted his ability to find comfort in
slumber. Croft's home was only blocks away now. Nora would
be sleeping or perhaps poring over anatomy books by what
was left of the fire. How to enter the house? A brisk hello,
a set jaw? An excuse for bed? A stealthy entrance to avoid
everyone? He decided to sneak in through the back door. So
long as no bodies had been delivered, Croft would likely be
reading in his own rooms. Perhaps Daniel could even sleep
in an empty bed in the patients' rooms. Then he needn't face
anyone until tomorrow.

It wasn't until he opened the side door that he saw the gas lamp burning. Croft was in the dissection room after all—but the corpse in front of him was still fully clothed.

It was the shape of her pert nose and the dull-gold gleam of her hair that registered first.

"Nora!" he cried.

Dr. Croft's arms jerked into the air, causing him to nearly drop his pocket watch.

"What happened?" Daniel demanded, pushing past the old man and thrusting his hands to her neck. Still warm. Her steady pulse under his fingers stopped his frenzied panic so quickly that he felt he'd been thrown from a bolting horse. His breath shuddered. "What's wrong with her? Did she faint?"

Croft's scowl softened into a curious smile. "She's drugged."

"She's not a monkey!" Daniel cried. "Is it opium? Or have you experimented with something more dangerous?" He moved the lamp to get a better look at her color. Not overly pale, but she did have red circles forming on her cheeks.

"Not opium. She breathed ether."

"The dinner-party gas? Why in the world would you give her that ridiculous drug?" Daniel didn't like the lifeless expression of her face. Whenever he caught her sleeping in a chair, she looked only as if she had closed her eyes midthought. Now she looked wholly incapacitated.

"It only makes you silly in small amounts. If you take enough, complete insensibility." Croft held out the bottle to Daniel, who passed it under his nose.

"Smells like old fruit."

"I thought burning pastilles," Croft replied.

Daniel shook the crowding questions from his head to clear room for the one that mattered. "When will she wake up?"

"Phelan in Edinburgh was down for six minutes." He glanced at his watch. "She's going on nine."

"Are there dangers?" He felt her pulse once more.

"Not certain. Perhaps asphyxia." The slightest frown crossed Croft's brow, and he leaned over as Daniel put his hand to her lips to feel breath. It curled warm and reassuring over his fingers.

A movement at his feet startled Daniel, and he looked down to a shaggy creature waddling clumsily over his shoe. "When did you get a dog?"

Without warning, Nora's hand shot up in the air, clutching, and both men jumped as she let out a thin cry. The dog whimpered.

"Nora? Are you hurt?" Daniel placed firm hands on her shoulders. Her eyes opened in fright and she recoiled, making a strangled sound. "What did you do to her?" he growled at Croft.

"I woke up like a dreaming baby," Croft insisted. "Nora? You're at home. With me." Croft lowered his head over hers as she trembled. "You fell asleep. Nothing else."

Almost as quickly as she had woken, her face relaxed and her eyes blinked for the first time. She mumbled unintelligible words and then grew quiet.

Daniel's heart was racing. "Nora?" he asked again when she continued to stare blankly.

"Yes?" She tried to sit up, but Daniel motioned her back.

"Do you know where you are?"

"Yes." Her voice was quite normal now, all trace of terror replaced by confusion.

"Excellent!" Croft said, though the word faltered with relief. "What was your first impression on waking? Why were you frightened?"

Her brow wrinkled as she sat. "Was I frightened?"

"Desperately," Daniel whispered.

She closed her eyes in thought. "I can only... Maybe a dark room. Something on the floor. No, I don't remember. It's entirely gone now." She screwed her eyes shut in concentration before they sprang back open. "So it worked?"

Croft sang a little note of glee. "It worked!"

"Daniel" was her next word. He met her worried eyes as she spoke again. "You're home."

"Quite the homecoming," he murmured. "You looked dead when I walked in." There were a hundred questions demanding answers, but Daniel's body had absorbed all the shocks and disappointments one day could hold. His name on her lips had been the final jolt. She'd only ever called him Dr. Gibson before. He warred between the need for information and the need for rest, and like every true scientist, curiosity burned away the weary walk home and the tug of his bed. "What madness are you two up to? I was hoping to get some sleep tonight."

Horace sniffed. He never did approve of people weak enough to require sleep. "I swear there is something here." He turned back to his work, pen in hand. "Nora, let's check your pulse again. Did you experience any memories or dreams?"

"I must have, but I can't recall a thing now. I'm cold."

Daniel took a clean sheet and swept it around her shoulders. "You needn't make a mouse of yourself and risk experiments."

"Her pulse is fast. Skin a bit pale. Let's check the membranes." Horace didn't have to tell her what to do. She had already opened her mouth and flattened her tongue by the time he went to poke inside her cheeks. "Will you be next, Gibson?"

"Hardly. Why don't you start at the beginning and tell me what this is all about."

"Fair enough." Croft nudged Nora off the table and plopped down the fat puppy. "Easiest to show you." It took some wrestling and sharp whimpers of complaint from the smell before the puppy sank from restless struggles into a stone-cold sleep. Nora prodded the dog, squeezing his paws to check reflexes and blood flow, while Croft timed the puppy's heartbeats. They might reproach him for his absence later, but just now the circulation of a sleeping dog was too fascinating for distraction.

Daniel didn't realize how much he'd missed the bedlam of Great Queen Street until he watched Nora tug on Dr. Croft's sleeve and scold him for pulling on the sleeping dog's tongue. "You'll strain the lingual frenulum." Horace shrugged her off and announced he couldn't inspect the membranes with her dancing about, but she managed to make him loosen the tongue in the tussle.

As warmth spilled over him, Daniel barely resisted the wry laugh building in his chest. After a week of his parents' shame, and a terse exchange of letters culminating in a barren interview with Mae, spending the night reanimating puppies with an orphan girl and a brilliant, mad doctor felt more wonderful than reason permitted. Perhaps it was the effects of the ether,

but he couldn't imagine a better place to be than with this ridiculous pair, drugging themselves and their dog and filling up
notebooks. He flicked open the puppy's eyelid and watched the
pupil shrink in the lamplight as Nora jotted down a note.

CHAPTER 18

L UCKILY NONE OF THE DAY-TO-DAY WORKERS AND TEN-
ants of London gave a moment's notice to the political
or scientific dramas brewing in the hallways of St. Bart's or
the newspapers. Patients appeared with reassuring regularity,
crowding the steps of 43 Great Queen Street, wanting cures
for their boils and burns and bursitis. The first woman who
arrived after Daniel's return thrust out her bandaged hand
that had come to no good end in a grapple with a fishhook
and demanded he "'ave a go at it." If not for the smattering of
rough black hairs adorning her upper lip, Daniel may well have
greeted her with a kiss. With excess care and cleanliness, he put
in two stitches and sent her on her way, free of charge.

After that he maintained a steady flow of patients and distracted himself enough that he only felt the stab of remorse
and humiliation slice through him once an hour or so. Most
often his conscience wielded its knife in the evening when
there were no night calls to attend and the desires to write and
research faded with fatigue. Daniel shut himself into his room
and shuffled papers so any curious ears in the hallway would
imagine him hard at work, instead of mourning over Mae's old
letters. Here, at least, she'd been moved to offer tender words.
Darling, dearest, only, friend, sweetheart... Her letters should

mean nothing to him now. She'd asked him to return them. Good heavens, what he'd give for her to whisper one languid word now.

Daniel looked out his windows at the twisted tree that dominated the back garden and let out a sigh gustier than the wind creaking the branches. Abandoning the letters and heaving himself up from his cold bed, he wandered into the hall and down the stairs with only the vaguest, unformed notion of finding food or company. He noticed a light in the research theater. Horace was out attending to a man with consumption, so he knew it must be Nora. He passed by the door quietly, but halted when a small, persistent cry reached him in the hallway. It was not the squeak of a mouse. He glimpsed inside, but the door blocked his view of the tables. A scrabble and high-pitched peeping convinced him to show himself.

Entering the room as casually as he could, his eyes widened at the sight of Nora with a box of young chicks, chasing some of her uncooperative subjects across the table. "Dare I ask?"

She looked up, her usually tidy hair loose and falling into her face. "Experiment."

"I gleaned as much." Daniel herded one black puff away from the table's edge and almost certain injury. "You've given up on Lucy Patton's appendix?"

"The chemical analysis is complete. I'm still reading reports and looking for cases, but both are in short supply. Nothing I've found is encouraging, so I've acquired these to occupy me for the time being, but they keep jumping out of their box." She managed to press one down before he found freedom. "I need to check them all for health before I begin."

"They look lively to me. Can I help?"

Nora didn't refuse, and they examined each one for signs of illness, injury, or contagion. After that she divided them into two boxes, trying to match the sets as equally in size and temperament as possible.

"What exactly are we researching tonight?"

With a frown, Nora retrieved a soiled bag and dropped it onto the table. Waves of foul odor rose as she opened it, and Daniel hid his nose in the wrinkled linen of his sleeve. She shrugged an apology and said, "Pig swill."

Daniel froze, his dark eyes suspicious over his arm. He'd read everything, but Dr. Croft's paper from thirty years ago was one of the only published cases on the subject. He'd written it after his work for the Royal Navy where he'd treated injured sailors at a Spanish port. Eighteen men had been wounded when a barrel of gunpowder exploded aboard their frigate, and they'd been pulled ashore while the vessel floundered.

Croft had been forced to treat them on the docks where livestock was being loaded. In the haste, one unfortunate young man was laid down in a puddle of pig swill that soaked his open burns, which otherwise were minor enough. Every man eventually recovered, except for that one who died of a raging fever two days later. Croft had theorized that diseased pigs excrete their diseases in their dung, which can contaminate blood.

"Because of Croft's theory about Miss Carter's blood poisoning?" Daniel finally asked when the silence grew too demanding.

"I agree with him. Failure to cauterize didn't kill her. It was the taint of the street."

"So what exactly is your womanly plan?" Daniel tried to tease, but he had little humor in him these days.

"I don't know that it has anything to do with being a woman," she quipped. "But the plan is to make a small laceration on each leg and soak half in pig swill before bandaging."

Daniel's eyes narrowed and he drummed his fingers on the table. One chick cocked his head at the noise and came hunting for food.

"It doesn't help that they are little dears, does it?" Nora murmured as she scooped up the beggar. "I hate experimenting on live ones," she admitted. "But it will just be a nick. I don't suppose you would assist?"

Daniel took a protesting chick in his hand and studied the muscle of the upper leg. "A small transverse cut here wouldn't upset them much but would still give good tissue contact." He stared too long as the chick settled into his warm palm. "Are you trying to save me?"

Nora, most likely expecting medical talk, processed the question twice. "I'm trying to help."

"Whatever we find won't convince Vickery. It may end up hurting more than anything else."

Her cheeks whitened. "Maybe I'm not trying to convince Vickery," she spoke softly before briefly meeting his eyes, and Daniel knew she was searching for the smug man who'd walked through the door five months ago. He wondered how the man in front of her compared.

"So which set is damned?" he asked, looking over the restless birds.

Nora pointed to the ones in the box with the certainty that

always baffled him and handed him her favorite scalpel with a brave set of her chin. "I'll soak the rags," she said, diving into the filthy bag of waste. Daniel would have found that distasteful before. Now it looked like courage.

Nora tended the chicks in her spare moments, but these were few. Four of the six contaminated with pig swill showed signs of infection and two died despite her careful ministrations, but so did one of the chicks that hadn't been touched by excrement.

"Inconclusive," Daniel sighed, once she told him.

"Suggestive. I think we should keep experimenting," Nora said.

But there was no time to find, let alone test another clutch of chicks. Croft's enthusiasm had infected Nora and Daniel, and every afternoon and evening was spent testing ether. The gas was truly a miracle: not only did it consistently usher the three of them, plus an assortment of animals, into anything between a silly stupor and a deathlike sleep, but the excitement of discovery smoothed away any awkwardness that might otherwise have accompanied Daniel's return. There were questions Nora longed to ask, but Daniel gave her no opening. He never spoke of his family or his fiancée, and it seemed kinder to follow his lead and pretend nothing had happened.

In truth, they were too busy conducting tests, recording observations, and theorizing how the vapor worked and the ways it might be used to talk about what had gone before. Dr. Croft insisted on methodical experiments that involved measuring vapor densities in glass tubes for hours. Nora had never seen the two men so excited, or so determined to live without sleep, unless it was induced chemically. Over the course of a month they sedated and successfully revived chickens, dogs, and a sheep. The mice proved more difficult. In spite of lowering the dose again and again, none of the rodents awoke, though their demise was much more pleasant than the end the ratcatcher had in mind.

"Harry told me about ether parties in America," Nora said, returning to the laboratory after carrying out a pail with five little brown corpses. "They hold shows in tents where people go to see others made silly." Harry had walked with her again this afternoon, but in spite of all she'd told him, so far he didn't share their enthusiasm, warning her that in America ether had been dismissed as both a fraud and a failure. They shouldn't risk taking it up.

Nora wondered if it was wrong of her not to warn Daniel of this but decided if Harry felt that way, he'd surely warn Daniel himself. Her own enthusiasm had survived Harry's dampening words. Ether would prove useful, she was sure, even if she wasn't yet certain for what. "I told Harry to come see us test the vapor on the animals, but he couldn't tonight."

"He won't," Daniel said, shaking his head. "He thinks, like mesmerism, the effect is faked."

"Idiot." Dr. Croft prodded the last of the mice. It remained inert, though last time Nora had checked, the heart was still beating. "This isn't faked. But so far we've killed every one. We're giving them too much of it. I want something bigger—"

Nora shook her head. "Mrs. Phipps will never let us have her dogs again." Duchess and Bruno were thoroughly cosseted, and Nora was glad of it. She enjoyed walking the puppies to and from the park and thought it an excellent thing to have two creatures in the household safe from scalpels and experiments, whose only purpose was to make the other occupants laugh.

Dr. Croft tapped his fingers on the table. "If we only use ether to make people faint, all it will ever be is a party trick. I'm convinced it has a greater purpose than that. Perhaps to facilitate childbirth."

Nora set down the empty pail with a clatter. "Are you mad? How will women labor if you make them insensible? The uterus—"

Daniel interrupted her. "It acts on its own, without conscious control. It might carry on perfectly well with the mother asleep."

Nora shook her head. "Without the effort and assistance of the mother—"

"Stop quarreling," Dr. Croft said. "We won't know until we try." Ignoring Nora's gasp, he went on. "Cats first, probably, unless we can find an unlucky whore who might—"

Daniel coughed. "I'll find us a cat."

Nora glared at him. "If I can cut up corpses, I can stand a conversation about whores."

Daniel glanced appealingly to Dr. Croft, but only got a raised eyebrow. Muttering under his breath, he bent over the sleeping mouse.

"It's been nearly three quarters of an hour," Nora said, sure they'd killed another one.

"This one has life in him yet." Daniel nudged a foreleg with his finger, and Nora leaned closer. They peered at the mouse, a bit of fur no bigger than Nora's thumb. Had it twitched?

"This one is female," she said, but Daniel wasn't listening.

"She's still pink in her paws," he whispered. He took Nora's hand and brought her finger to the animal's side. "There. Do you feel that thrumming?"

It was there, though faint—the merest vibration. Nora looked up, catching Daniel's smile. "Let's give it a little longer," she said.

Whatever ether was good for, it wasn't a perfect mouse poison.

The mouse revived, but that did not squelch their argument. It unraveled all through the next week, remaining theoretical: Daniel could not find a gravid-enough cat, and Dr. Croft could not persuade any whores.

"They're happy enough to throw themselves into the hands of butcher abortionists," he fumed, passing Nora a tray of instruments to carry to the washbasin. "But when I offer to help them birth the unwanted child and give it a home, do you think I can convince even one of them?"

Give it a home? "Just what were you offering?" Nora asked, stunned.

"Well, I had to make some incentive," Dr. Croft said. "You turned out all right. If the next one was troublesome, we could always send it to school."

"I was eight," Nora scolded him, through stiff lips, the color rising in blotches along her neck. Daniel had turned away to the basin and was methodically washing his hands. "A baby would be considerably more trouble."

"Phipps didn't mind the puppies."

Nora set down the tray with a clang that rang through the room. The bottles on the shelves swam before her eyes and her cheeks were hot. "You cannot—" She tried again. "I—" It was too much. She turned on her heel and fled from the room.

She was in the park, picking currants from a still-warm bun when Dr. Croft found her. "You forgot your bonnet," he said. It was looped by the ribbons over his arm, but he'd seen that her hands were busy, so he didn't hold it out to her.

"You don't care about bonnets," she told him. "And nor do I, for that matter."

"No. Daniel brought it to my notice." He cleared his throat. "May I join you?"

Nora shifted over on the bench.

Dr. Croft sat down and stretched out his legs. There were scuff marks all over his shoes. "Daniel brought another matter to my attention as well," he said finally. "I was overeager. I spoke without considering your feelings. I'm sorry."

In spite of herself, Nora laughed. "When do you consider feelings?"

"It isn't generally my nature, I'm afraid."

"I know."

His feet shifted. "You've always been easy on me. You probably should have demanded a little more. I didn't mean to imply that you were nothing more than an experiment—" He broke off as Nora flinched. He shook his head. "I'm making it worse."

"I've tried not to be a burden," Nora said, hating the tears brimming in her eyes.

"You aren't! You're more capable than I could have dreamed. I depend on you." He sighed. "And it's more than that. I'd hate to lose you."

"We haven't asphyxiated anything big," Nora reminded him tartly. "And Daniel hasn't let me try the ether more than once."

"I wasn't thinking of death. I was thinking of Dr. Trimble." He frowned, oblivious to her confusion. "He admires you."

"Don't rush to conclusions," Nora told him. "We enjoy each other's company. We take walks." She'd expected Harry to clasp her hand or steal a kiss by now, but so far he seemed content with strolls and conversation.

"The good thing is, he can't afford a wife. I'll have you for a few years yet."

He was trying to distract her, talking silliness like he did while he sutured up patients. "It's all right, sir. I know you only took me because of the cholera."

"Yes. At first. You know the compulsion—to wrestle whatever you can from death." He stopped her from speaking by shaking his head. "No, let me finish. You think you were the lucky one, because you survived. That's true, of course, but—" He cleared his throat. "To me, there's no one who could replace you. I didn't mean for you to think otherwise."

Nora absorbed that, studying the print of her skirt. She smoothed it over her knees and met Dr. Croft's eyes: steady, familiar, and penetrating. His cheek twitched with a half-hidden smile. Nora took a breath, trying not to betray emotion. "You're an awful gambler, you know. You're lucky in my case it paid off."

"Indeed." He took up her hand, stealing her bun in the process. As he chewed, he rubbed his thumb over her calluses. "You must take better care of your fingers."

———

At the end of her day's work, Nora remained in the surgery, staring at the freshly washed basins, the drying towels, at her apron hanging from its peg on the wall. The blinds were drawn and she was alone with her lamp, too flustered to return upstairs. All afternoon, all evening, through a cheerful dinner with Daniel, Harry, and Dr. Croft, Nora had concealed her disquiet. Safely alone now, she could chew her lip and examine the uncertainty prompted by what Dr. Croft had said earlier in the park: *The good thing is, he can't afford a wife.*

Did Harry care that much? Nora wasn't sure, but now she remembered, months ago, how he had looked at her as he'd declared, *I'm imagining my own plaque hanging on a town house one day.*

She pushed away from the cupboard and blindly opened a drawer, counting out needles without paying heed to the total. Harry's aside couldn't have been significant. If he'd meant to court her, he'd have—

Invited her out walking?

Brought her a box of experimental puppies?

She bit her lip and started counting again. The thought shouldn't frighten her. She liked Harry. He was a good doctor.

She could envision him years in the future, prosperous and perhaps a little stout, smiling as he cajoled his more difficult patients.

Her hands stilled, the needle between her fingertips poised
in midair as she realized, in many ways, she'd be an ideal wife for
him. He'd trust her with the management of his clinic and love
her for her clear mind, clean records, and tidy shelves—and there
was no reason why her brow should crease at such a thought.
Harry was a congenial man. He'd make an amusing husband.

Her mind shied away. She finally managed to count out
seventeen needles and returned them to their place in the
drawer. Contrary to instructions, her mind returned to Harry
the moment her hands were empty.

She and Harry worked well enough now, but suppose they
married and he grew to resent her opinions? They didn't agree
on everything, and he wholly disapproved of her interest in
ether. In his own clinic, would he give her the latitude to experiment as she liked? Allow her to assist in his surgeries? Or would
her days be filled with his work and his ideas—or children? She
enjoyed Harry's company, but she didn't feel him as strongly
now when he came into a room, not like she did when—

Don't think it, she told herself. *You can't be such a fool.*

Nora picked up her lamp and left, closing the door firmly
behind her. Upstairs, she selected the thickest book she could
find and lugged it to her bedroom. She read until her eyes
crossed and her head sank onto the pages. When she woke, it
was dark. Her candle had gone out, and she had paper stuck to
her cheek.

He's said nothing of love to me, Nora reminded herself. She lit
a lamp, wrapped herself in another blanket, and resumed reading.

To Nora's relief, Dr. Croft didn't bring up keeping babies again, though the debate over ether still simmered between her and Dr. Croft and Daniel. She couldn't have wished for a more consuming distraction. Would ether-induced sleep help childbirth? Ease the minds of the mad and hysterical? They had as many theories as they had fingers and toes between them, and Dr. Croft was eager to test all of them. They put a melancholic to sleep, and afterward Nora jotted down page after page of the patient's sleep visions, some beautiful, some disturbing. They tried an out-and-out madman next, and he woke within minutes, remembering nothing. Daniel finally found them a pregnant cat, but it hid in the house, and they didn't find it again until it had birthed six kittens in the linen cupboard.

With the abundance of mice and rats available (thanks to an arrangement Dr. Croft made with the local ratcatcher) they'd grown much more precise with their dosages, but Mrs. Phipps still wouldn't give up the honey-colored kittens despite all reassurances.

"I expect that's why this American demonstration failed," Croft said, after finding a report in a Boston newspaper. "No one has considered the effect of temperature on the concentration of the vapor." He sought out a chemist friend and asked him to make him a thermometer.

It arrived nestled within a box full of wood shavings. "We'll try pulling teeth next," Dr. Croft said and went to pay a call on an acquaintance who worked as a dentist. It took three days to convince Mr. Haslett and another week to recruit a willing patient. Fortunately, Daniel had insisted they work without an audience, just in case. The operation went beautifully until the end when the young man grimaced, gagged, and turned an alarming shade of purple. After a frantic moment massaging his limbs and waving smelling salts, Daniel wiped the sweat off his brow and reassured the terrified dentist. The young man remembered none of it, however, and happily sucked his piece of ice after he woke. Mr. Haslett, breathing normally now his patient had safely recovered, said, "All my patients are going to want your vapor, but it's a mite dramatic if you ask me." He began packing up his bag. "Never seen anything like it. It's better for pain than nitrous oxide, but it nearly choked him."

The next day a letter came for Daniel from his father. The emphatic wax seal on the single-sheet missive made Nora think of narrowed brows and a sharp frown. Biting her tongue, she wondered how Daniel bore it, but bear it he did. He said nothing about the letter. That night at dinner, he sat across from her quietly cutting his beef—the only sign he gave that anything was troubling him. Preoccupied by his silence, Nora nearly started when Dr. Croft made an announcement.

"Good news in the mail today," he said.

"Pardon?" Daniel's face reminded her of a cornered fox.

"I said—"

"Did *you* receive good news, sir?" Nora asked, for clearly whatever news had come for Daniel was upsetting.

"Yes. I told you."

Daniel looked up from his laden fork. "What news?"

"I've heard from a doctor in Hampshire who tends a madhouse. He's eager to test my theories that ether will be therapeutic to deranged minds. You aren't running off anywhere again, Daniel?"

"I've nowhere else to be," Daniel said, forcing a smile.

"Good. Then I can set out for Laverstoke tomorrow while you see to things here."

Mrs. Phipps set down her knife with a clatter. "You can't! You haven't enough clean shirts for a journey. They won't be done till tomorrow."

"I don't care about my shirts."

"Don't I know it." Mrs. Phipps wagged her napkin at him as his waving fork dripped gravy down his front.

CHAPTER 19

D ANIEL TRIED TO KEEP HIS MIND ON VOLUME TWO OF Bourgery and Jacob's *Anatomy*, but the wind outside shook the house as he had never felt before. Angry gusts tore across the rooftops as if frantically searching for the rain that refused to fall from the low ceiling of black clouds. The battle between winter and spring was fierce this year. Daniel picked up his scalpel and practiced steadying it against the back of his left hand as the colored plate demonstrated, but his awkward hold looked nothing like the suave illustration. Perhaps if his hands were not so chapped. He'd have to ask Nora for some salve. She knew how to make it so it smelled like fresh greens and not fussy perfumes.

She'd taken to her room early, so Daniel had the library to himself. He tried to use the rare hours alone to study delicate medical issues that he could not bring himself to peruse when she was present. No matter how glibly Horace spoke of labial cysts and lesions from the clap, Daniel could not bear to see Nora exposed to such conversation. In medical school it had taken him months before he stopped squirming during female dissections, and though he hid it by his brisk and bored manner, his heart still seized uncomfortably when he had to examine sensitive areas of either sex. He hated to be the one to strip a patient of what little dignity they had left.

The specimen jars Horace had left on top of the mantel rattled as the wind raked its way down the chimney and scattered ashes from the low fire. Daniel hurried to stomp out the sparks before they burned black circles onto the oak floor, and in all of his trampling almost missed the urgent knock on the front door. Making his way to the hall, he met Nora, her eyes wide.

"A patient?" she asked.

"Perhaps. Let's hope it's something easy like a fever." Daniel did not relish giving up his warm library tonight.

He opened the door and at first glance found no one. It was a moment before he registered the man doubled over almost to the ground. The glow from the gaslight cast the front step into harsh shadows, but when the man raised his face, it was white and covered in dewy sweat.

"John Prescott!" Nora cried. "What happened?"

There was no time for introductions or for Daniel to ask how they knew each other. He stooped down and took the man's arm, unsure where to touch until he knew the nature of the man's injury. The way he clutched his gut, he looked like he'd been stabbed, but Daniel could see no blood in the darkness. "I've got you," he murmured as he heaved the man's cold arm around his shoulder.

The man trembled as he leaned on Daniel and shuffled inside. Nora steadied his back and helped steer him to the nearest sofa. The man would not unfold himself, but curled his knees and hands close around his middle. His speech was labored and husky. "Harry?"

Daniel looked to Nora for answers.

"Harry isn't here," Nora told the man, smoothing wet hair from his forehead. Catching Daniel's eye she said, "He worked with Harry on his last ship. Harry introduced me when we met him in the park."

Putting aside unessential details, Daniel began unbuttoning the man's shirt. "Mr. Prescott, what is your complaint?"

"My stomach. A hernia." He panted with exertion as he straightened himself out. "Harry wasn't at his place so I thought he'd be here."

Daniel opened his shirt and saw a hernia belt cinched low around his abdomen. "Have you had it a while?"

"Aye." Prescott squeezed his eyes shut, the veins blue and raised on his temples. "But never like this. Harry's been treating it. He got it pushed in a week back."

Nora had meanwhile managed to remove his shoes and socks. "We need him in the theater. On the table. You can probably reduce it again."

"How do we get him to the other side of the house?" Daniel bent down where the large man had sunk to the floor, his head on the sofa like a child in bedside prayer. If Horace were there, perhaps the three of them could manage, but Phipps would be no help at all even if they woke her.

"John," Nora spoke clear and loud, the volume masking her fear, "you made it all the way here on this dreadful night, which was exactly right. Dr. Gibson can help you. But we need to get you to the surgical theater where we have a table and better lights and all our equipment. We need a few more steps out of you." She took his hand in a strong grip and helped Daniel pull him to his feet. John bit down so hard on his lip that Daniel feared he'd draw blood, but he kept silent. He didn't cry out until they came to the short stairs that descended into the theater. Prescott's legs shook beneath him.

"I'll take the weight," Daniel promised. "You move your feet and then fall on me every step. There's only six." Despite their best efforts, a strangled scream escaped the man more than once. "Damn it!" Daniel cursed with all the sincerity of his soul. Croft could block out patients' pain, Harry could erect a mental wall and keep agony on the opposite side, but he had no defenses. He'd almost rather let a person die than increase their suffering in a bid to save their life, but this was a coward's way, not a surgeon's. The only thing giving Daniel a modicum of courage was Nora's determined face and quiet murmurs to John, urging him to keep on for a little longer.

While Daniel helped John onto the table, Nora rushed to the lamps, adjusting the reflecting plates to direct the light on John's writhing body. The suffering man took two deep breaths before he wrenched his head to the side and vomited onto the floor. In his agony he'd still had the wherewithal to aim away from his doctor. Daniel's eyes narrowed and his hands moved with greater speed. "Get the truss off," he said to himself as much as Nora. He loosened it and pulled it away as Nora wiped John's face. A small but angry purple bulge protruded from his otherwise normal-looking abdomen.

"Inguinal hernia." Daniel undid the trouser buttons to get a better look and pulled, exposing the man's drawers. "Drape!" he demanded in an angry voice. If it were Harry working with him, he wouldn't have worried at all, but he couldn't have a nude man exposed and screaming in front of Nora. He grabbed the cloth from her hand and threw it over Prescott while his other hand tugged the man's clothing down to his hips. "Perhaps you should go," he mumbled to her.

Nora's movements ceased, and she stared at him over the groaning man. "You must be mad."

"This won't be"—Daniel tempered his language, certain the man was still alert enough to hear and be frightened—"simple."

"I won't make you do it alone. There isn't time for me to find Harry. Look at the color. And he's vomiting." She put her face close to the patient. "John, have you evacuated your bowels in the last twenty-four hours?"

He shook his head. "It hurts like hell." His last word turned into a cry, and a tear joined the beads of sweat at his hairline.

"Hold him," Daniel said in a low voice and waited until Nora got a firm grip on the man's arms before he pressed down on the bulge, trying to push it back through the abdominal wall.

Prescott screamed and wrenched free before he went limp. Daniel and Nora both groped for his neck, their fingers scrambling against each other as they checked his pulse. "He's fainted," Daniel said, alarmed at the speed of the blood thundering through his patient's neck. "But probably not for long. We need restraints."

Nora strapped one strong arm to the table.

Daniel secured the buckle of another restraint and moved to the feet as he answered. "The bowel is strangulated. And black."

"Gangrene? I can try to get Dr. Barnett if you prepare him for surgery."

Daniel's eyes went to the black window groaning against the casement as the wind battered it. "He's six blocks away and half the streetlamps are out. I'd have to get him, but if he's out on call, we'd be too late." It was tempting to run away into the howling night and leave the man alone in his agonies, to wait for another surgeon to cut him open and ignore his screams. Tempting, but impossible. Already Prescott was coming round, small whines escaping with his labored breaths. "It's likely whatever we do will end the same," he warned Nora. "If it has already ruptured, there's nothing to be done."

"And if it hasn't?" Nora's eyes were as large and black as he had ever seen them.

"You know the answer. We've few options. We can attempt to free the bowel with a small incision in the wall, but if the bowel is so much as scratched, he's a dead man." Daniel looked down at his shaking hand. "I've never reduced a bowel obstruction. I've never even done it on a cadaver. I've seen it only once, and I was at the back of the class." He tore a hand through his hair.

"I've done it," Nora said quietly as she probed around the bulging hernia.

"What?"

"Dr. Croft let me do a hernia repair on a cadaver. It was reducible and I just practiced taxis, but he showed me the method after I'd pushed it back through the wall. It wasn't obstructed." A terrible stillness came over her face and then the room. All Daniel could hear was his own breath whistling from his lungs. "And I've been reading..." She hesitated, then finished in a rush. "About a ruptured appendix successfully removed through this kind of hernia. I know where we could cut."

"Such a surgery is madness. Almost certainly fatal." Daniel paused. "Who removed the appendix?"

"A Frenchman. A hundred years ago," Nora admitted.

The rattle of the shaking skylight drowned out Daniel's curse.

"How could we keep him still?" he asked. "This isn't simply finding and tying off an appendix. I may have to resection the dead bowel without letting the intestinal contents leak into the abdomen. Bad enough on a cadaver, but even with restraints, he'll jerk every time we touch him. You're not strong enough. It would take at least three men, and even then..." Daniel studied the truss, trying to decide if they could use it to tie down Prescott's chest and reduce movement. They couldn't get him drunk because he couldn't hold liquids. "Perhaps powdered opium," Daniel said, still frowning.

Nora hurried for the scalpels and instruments, pushing away the bottles of ether they'd left beside the suture needles as Daniel added quietly, "I don't think we should attempt anything, Nora."

Prescott's faint voice surprised them both as it rose from the table. "Please. Please. Harry?" His blue eyes scanned the room in terror as he flexed his hands against the restraints.

Nora froze, her hand suspended in midair. Then she moved decisively. Instead of a knife she pressed a bottle into Daniel's palm. A glass vial of ether.

"Damned if we do..." she whispered. There was a shadow of a mirthless smile on her face and terrible uncertainty in her eyes. "Damned if we don't."

"Do it," Daniel growled, unable to think of anything but the first cut, ligating the artery, probing for healthy pink intestine...

Nora dropped the liquid onto a cloth and held it over John's face. "It's only medicine," she crooned as he sputtered. A minute later she cried out, "Daniel, he's asleep! You need to go now!"

He slid the scalpel across the stretched skin and gingerly sliced through the peritoneum until he touched the dead bowel. Probing as gently as he could in his haste, he announced, "I don't think it's ruptured. There's a chance. But I don't know the proper procedure for removing dead bowel. Do we clamp first?" Daniel watched the pulsing artery, trying to plan his first cut without wasting precious seconds. The black tissue in his hand was too perilous for an ignorant mistake. Behind the dead section, the bowel was turgid with waste that couldn't pass. Daniel looked across the inert body to Nora's anxious face. He could not read her expression, but he saw her hand twitch toward the incision, and he knew what the involuntary movement meant. He cleared his throat, braced his feet, met her eyes. "Can you do it?"

CHAPTER 20

U NABLE TO STOP HERSELF, NORA SEIZED THE KNIFE. SHE didn't realize how winded she was until she heard Daniel's labored breaths across the table. For a moment they breathed in unison, both lungs driven by a single bellows. "I've never held the scalpel on a live person."

Their eyes held, struggled, but his silence won out. Without further hesitation, she parted the outer inguinal ring and leaned close to examine the exposed bowel. Daniel sponged, retracting the muscles that normally held the man together, opening the incision, and tidying it up so she could see. When she shifted or moved her head, he was before her, angling the spoons or the reflectors as if he could hear her thoughts.

"Well?"

It was strange to hear him speaking, but perhaps he couldn't sense what she was trying to detect with her fingers. "There's no pulse in the vessels," Nora said.

Prescott hadn't breathed the ether for long. Soon he would wake, though if she failed, it would be better if he did not. She'd seen this kind of death before, and it was a vicious, ugly one. If it came to that, perhaps they could... No, she could never intentionally give too much ether though she'd loathe herself for every moment the man suffered.

Nora slid her fingers again over the lump of bowel as Daniel went to the drawer where she kept the needles, already threaded. He brought out the box and set it on the table. Nora shook her head. "I need to see how much has gone black." If she tugged gently, they could expose more bowel, hopefully a healthier pink. That was where they'd cut, but—

"I want to open the inner ring," Nora said. The gut in her hand was black but maybe it wasn't gangrenous yet.

She was braced for protest, but Daniel only picked up the spoons. She understood. He would help her do whatever she wanted—only let it be quick.

The dark knot of gut was slick with blood and bits of fat. Nora turned it, peering beneath, but the constriction was too tight. She flicked the scalpel, and a thread of fascia sprang back, but it wasn't enough. The bulging bowel wouldn't turn. "Widen the incision," Nora said. "I need more room." She pushed her hair away from her face with the back of a bloodstained hand while Daniel picked up another knife. A stream of blood slipped from the edge of the table onto the floor, falling with audible drips onto his polished shoe. He slit another inch, then parted the muscles again. Nora leaned forward, scratching at the white bands of tissue with the tip of her scalpel. It spread and stretched, and the bowel dropped like a plum into the palm of her other hand. Breath left them both in a rush.

At her shoulder, Daniel was ready with the string, poised to tie where she directed. The scissors lay on the table, but Nora only gave them a glance.

"Let's untwist it before we try resecting." The words came from her in a whisper.

"That bowel is dead," Daniel warned.

"I want to wait." Without looking at him, Nora picked up his hand with her left and carried it to the intestine coiled inside her right palm. Ever so gently she twisted. "It's looking better since we released it."

Daniel leaned closer, and Nora prayed the inky-hued bowel would lighten. He didn't say it, but she knew they were running out of time. She could feel Daniel's pulse beating at the base of his thumb, and shifted her fingers away, to the patient, where she hoped to detect a similar tremor. Nothing yet, but—

Daniel blinked. "I might be imagining it, but I think we've gone from coal-dust to the color of a well-aged wine." The light in his eyes was breathtaking.

"Let's wait another thirty seconds," Nora said. "If it's not better then, we'll tie and resect."

In a low voice, Daniel began counting, but by fifteen it was plain that they'd prevailed. Daniel stopped counting. "Thank God," he murmured.

"The color of a young merlot now, I think," Nora said, her tight face relaxing enough to allow a grin.

"Don't know how we dodged that," Daniel said. "If we cut out the dead section and tried to stitch it back together…" His haunted eyes spoke volumes. "At least he has a chance now that you untwisted it and got the blood flowing."

They pushed the pink bowel back in the abdomen where it belonged, then Daniel set to work with the needle, tying tight, neat stitches. He was on the first layer of muscle when Mr. Prescott stirred, but Nora was quick with a second dose of ether.

"Will it hurt him?" she asked as she lifted the cloth from his face.

"Not as much as this will," Daniel said, but he studied Prescott's face anxiously. "So long as he doesn't respond like the mice." Still, they watched uneasily as they bandaged the incision and tied the evidence of their work away. Prescott groaned low, miserable pleas, but didn't move enough to interrupt the final sutures. Nora didn't dare drug him again after being reminded of the mice. For now, they'd succeeded, but only time would tell if they had won. Beneath the neat stitches and the remarkably small bandage, the threat of gangrene still lurked. The patient screwed his eyes into knots of pain, beads of sweat doing nothing to enhance the pallor of his face. He muttered insensibly, speaking to a crewmate named Luggins about cannon fire.

"It is all right, Prescott," Daniel said, hoping to interrupt his nightmare. "We reduced it. With rest, a little luck, and the good Lord's grace, you'll recover."

He didn't look at Mr. Prescott as he said it. Watching from the washbasin where she rinsed the equipment, Nora saw that his eyes and his smile were for her.

⌒

Together, they helped Mr. Prescott into an empty bed. When he was stretched out beneath clean sheets and a double layer of blankets, Nora finally asked what she'd been wondering since he'd made the first groan. "Did you suffer during the operation?"

He grinned weakly, his tired eyes fluttering open. "I can feel where you've been, that's certain. Did I pass out? I only remember coming down the stairs. I think it hurt, but I can't remember clear."

A grin flooded her face. She'd hoped, but hadn't believed total insensibility was possible. "So it erased memories that occurred before it took effect?"

Prescott answered with a confused expression.

"Later." Daniel placed a reassuring hand on Nora's shoulder. "He needs rest and time to regain his strength." Turning to Mr. Prescott, he said, "Most of your recovery now depends on you."

Their patient nodded, subsiding into the pillows. As she left the room and closed the door, Nora took a long glance back, reassuring herself that he would soon be sleeping. If not, he had a bell within reach.

"How are you feeling?" Daniel whispered beside her.

"I hardly know." She ought to feel tired, but she was too charged with fear and excitement. "You think we shouldn't tell him?" It hadn't escaped her that Daniel had avoided any mention of the ether.

"Let's make sure he lives first. The first ordeal is over, but—"

"We'll know in a few days," Nora finished.

Daniel nodded absently, preoccupied with the stretching of his shoulders. Nora watched as he worked from neck to wrists to fingers. "Whatever happens, I think we did well," he said.

Nora smiled. "I'll make sure everything's squared away in the surgery."

Daniel shook his head. "We both need something to restore our nerves. Doctor's orders," he insisted.

She was washing down the table when he appeared with a

dusty bottle in hand and two mismatched glasses. "I didn't think Mrs. Phipps would like the good glassware brought in here."

"No, she wouldn't."

"I'm not sure if this is medicinal wine, or celebratory. That was your first surgery, Miss Beady."

"When you say it out loud—" Excitement slid down her neck, the skin rising in goose bumps.

"I'm not sure I *should* say it out loud. We've broken the law. And saved a man's life. At least for tonight." His smile softened the doubt lurking in his eyes.

"I broke the law." She picked up a scrub brush and set to work on the table, unsure if it was fear or thrill that thrummed though her blood, making her light-headed. She couldn't keep still.

"You know, you'd seem more human if you weren't so perfectly indefatigable," Daniel said. He made short work of the cork, poured out two half glasses, and then picked up another scrub brush and began scouring the other side of the table.

"I hate cleaning once it dries. And right now scrubbing is keeping me from thinking. Was I insane? I almost cut open his bowels." Her face whitened, and her bristle brush slowed its strokes.

Daniel placed his hand on top of hers. "You did what you could in an impossible situation."

Nora slipped her hand away and reached around to untie her apron, but discovered herself trapped by a hard little knot.

"Let me," Daniel said.

She bent her head and waited. "Am I stuck?" she asked.

"I may need to bring out the scalpel," Daniel said. "However did you tie it so tight?"

"I hardly remember, I was in such a hurry."

"Keep still."

He must be too intent on unpicking the knot at her back to realize how close they stood, how her skin prickled at the soft touch of his whisper. On the wall in front of her, their shadows fused into a single dark spill. She ought to say something.

"There." She felt his head come up, his breath sweeping the back of her neck.

"Thank you." With clumsy hands, she tugged the heavy canvas away from her gown and left it on the peg. She was too afraid to turn around.

"Nora?"

His hesitancy dissolved her fears into nothing. "Yes?" She faced him, not quite sure how it had happened without bumping his elbows—or his nose. They shared a spot of floor no wider than a hatbox. Wine laced his breath, barely detectable beneath the tang of vinegar and ether that surrounded them both.

He let out a breath and eased a step back, smiling and shaking his head. "Look at us. Do you know what my mother would say if she saw me in my shirtsleeves?"

Nora had theories about his mother, none of them complimentary. "I imagine an exhaustive lecture on propriety?" Her eyes teased.

"More of a nervous attack, actually," he said with a smile.

"Daniel!" she gasped in mock alarm, then added in her normal voice, "Like so?"

"It's as if you've met her," he said, grinning ruefully and reaching for a wineglass. He passed it to her.

Nora leaned against the table and bent her face over the

wine. The plummy scent she'd detected on Daniel was here, but stronger.

"Isn't it lovely?" he asked.

She nodded.

"What shall we toast?"

"Marvelous ether," Nora said, lifting her glass. Daniel echoed her, taking a swallow.

"You were marvelous," he said.

Nora sipped again. "*We* were." Somehow, they'd ended up leaning against the table close enough that their arms touched.

"I like that word better than 'you' or 'I.'" Daniel lifted his glass and drank again. "I want your courage, Nora."

"You're welcome to it, if it's mine to share." She thought of his reckless fight with Vickery. "But I don't think you need it."

He shrugged, not exactly agreeing with her. Nora supposed that was all right for now. She liked the idea of gradually convincing him. "What does your father say when he sees you in your shirtsleeves?" The more she knew of Daniel, the more she thought his family had a great deal to answer for.

Daniel laughed and turned the glass in his hands. "You know, I'm fairly sure none of my family could ever imagine this."

"A hernia repair, or you in your shirtsleeves?" Nora asked.

"Either. Both. Even if they came in now, they'd be appalled by my current state of undress."

"It's a shirt," Nora said. "Everything's covered, but *ladies* have delicate sensibilities, I suppose."

"Very delicate," Daniel said with a smile.

"And Miss Edwards?" Nora asked.

His smile fled, a pained grimace in its place. "She's broken off our engagement, so she'll be spared the sight of me, dressed and otherwise, which—" He set down his glass, his ears coloring. "Forgive me. I spoke without thinking. I didn't mean to twist our conversation to matters...to matters that are..." Daniel's blush spread down his neck. "In poor taste."

Nora gulped from her glass. "I know you meant nothing of the sort. Anyway, I'm not prudish." She set down her empty glass and stood, suddenly conscious of what Mrs. Phipps would think of this tête-à-tête. She'd certainly not approve. And Daniel. Well, she'd told him before she wasn't like other women, but just now, being an aberration annoyed her. Why did ladies fan themselves and blush if someone mentioned the leg and not the *limb* of a table? It was absurd that she, who had just now carefully untangled a hernia from a man's spermatic cord, should let a conversation about shirtsleeves make her feel ridiculous. "I'd better look in on Mr. Prescott."

Daniel set down his cup. "Yes. We've let him alone too long already."

He kept pace with her as she walked down the hall. They stood together, looking over their patient for an awkward moment. "Go ahead," Daniel said, so she leaned in to take his pulse.

"I think it's all right," Nora said, "But after his ordeal—" She passed his wrist to Daniel.

He nodded. "Satisfactory, for now."

She glanced at Daniel, then back at Prescott. "Someone should sit with him overnight."

"Let me. I'm just as afraid as you are about leaving him alone."

Nora hesitated. One of them ought to go. In the surgery, a sudden singleness had been born between them. Focused on John, they'd merged hands and wills like two droplets of water coalescing, natural then, but uncomfortable now. Nora wanted to pull away and reorder her thoughts on her own, but the need to see Prescott through still held them both bound to one room, one bed.

"You're tired," Daniel said. "Sit down on the other bed. That way, if you fall asleep—"

Nora laughed. "I'm too jittery to sleep."

"As if I could, either." He smiled tentatively. "I'll take the chair?"

She lowered herself onto the empty bed, not realizing how much she needed to sit until she felt the quilt beneath her. Daniel disappeared, probably fetching a pillow or a blanket to drape over his knees… No, she'd guessed wrong. He had a notebook and a pencil in his hands.

"I'm just going to record some notes. While it's still fresh. Croft will want to know everything that happened."

"Everyone will," Nora murmured.

The candlelight flickered. Daniel's pencil whispered wordlessly. Nora watched John Prescott's chest rise and fall until she fell asleep.

CHAPTER 21

IT TOOK AN HOUR TO SCRIBBLE DOWN HIS NOTES. DANIEL got up, stretched his legs, measured Prescott's pulse, and listened to his breathing: shallow, but unobstructed. Nora was asleep, propped up awkwardly on the other bed. Daniel fetched a blanket and draped it over her, then sat down to review his notes.

Everything was in order, but his back ached from the long night. He stood up again and took a turn about the room—four strides from one side to the other. He passed Nora and smiled at her slightly open mouth pressed to the pillow. He had no intention of waking her. Better to let her sleep. She'd be sore when she woke, though, with her head at such an angle. Stealthily, Daniel bent over her. Loose strands of hair tumbled over her face. They always did, but just now there were more than usual. A brown smudge—blood, probably—ran across her forehead. He couldn't leave her like this. He put an arm behind her shoulders, trying to ease her to a prone position.

"Shh," he whispered when she stirred. "You'll look like a question mark tomorrow if you stay this way."

Her eyes flew open, dilating wide in the dim light. "Is he—?"

Daniel cursed himself for attempting to move her. He'd not expected her to sleep so lightly. "Prescott's fine. Lie down, Nora. Everything's all right."

She slid down the length of the bed and subsided against the pillows. "Wake me when you get tired."

"Yes, of course," Daniel lied, draping her in a blanket. He stepped back, relieved when her eyes fell shut. He returned to his chair.

Prescott stirred an hour later and drank a little broth that Daniel warmed over a spirit lamp in the next room so the light wouldn't wake Nora. She slept deeply now, not stirring when Daniel whispered reassuringly to Prescott or set down the invalid's spouted cup. When Prescott was sleeping once again, Daniel rose from the bed, knuckled his back, and settled once more into the tortuous chair, swallowing a yawn and sinking under the weight of his eyelids. Dawn wasn't far off. Just a little longer. He'd let her sleep until it was light.

———

When Daniel woke from his doze, he did a careful check of all systems. His heart, though sluggish with sleep, felt light and thready, something electric and uneasy there. He noticed his breathing next, apprehensive. And then the drunken nerves in his head handed him, one severed piece at a time, the memory of hours before. As the picture came into focus, he jolted upright and rummaged the room with his eyes, certain it was a dream. But no, he'd fallen asleep in his chair, sitting in the convalescent room, where he was supposed to be watching John Prescott.

Moving stiffly because of his numb knees, Daniel clambered to his feet. John Prescott lay in uneasy sleep, pain apparent even on his unconscious face. After the surgery, Daniel had draped an unbuttoned nightshirt on him for warmth, but it lay open, revealing the bandages.

"Lord above," he muttered. It was a short and unfocused prayer, but sincere. This man's life was a miracle, but not one Daniel could cheerfully write about this morning. Last night, perhaps in a wine-fueled euphoria—

Idiot, you only had a single glass.

No, wine hadn't incited his mania. He'd been drunk on possibilities, the audacious daring and the panting fear.

Daniel gathered himself. What on earth had he been thinking? He'd lost all discretion. With his reputation in tatters and half the staff at St. Bart's unwilling to take him back, Daniel had dug into a man and performed an operation most experienced surgeons would condemn. Perhaps if he had been able to bear Prescott's screams and restrained him sufficiently he could have maneuvered the muscle apart enough to pry the bowel free of the spermatic cord and push it into place. It was a stretch of the imagination, but he couldn't free himself from the suspicion.

Now, if he wanted to share their discovery and regain his place at St. Bart's, he would have to answer for a surgery that wasn't even his. Nora was the one who saved the bowel.

Nora.

Thoughts of her pooled in the corners of his mind like shadows, no matter how he tried to flex and strain against them. However clever and unconventional, she had no training, no license, and no protection against accusations. But how could he possibly explain how he'd successfully conducted the intricate surgery alone?

Daniel stepped into the office and poured a fresh dose of laudanum. It would be much appreciated when the patient woke. He set it beside Prescott's bed and gingerly undid the bandage. The flesh was angry and red, swollen around his neat stitches.

Prescott's eyes opened, searching Daniel's face for clues. "Am I done for?"

"A sailor doesn't go down that easy," Daniel answered, surprised at the smoothness of his own voice. "I'm just sorry you'll have such a small scar to show for all your trouble." He dosed him and waited for his face to relax, but the clinic bell rang first.

Nora stirred.

"Wait here. I'll answer it," Daniel said, ready to send Sly Tom and his resurrection men to the devil before he allowed them to leave a corpse here this morning.

"Clinic's closed. We don't want any disturbances today," Daniel said as he swung open the door—and found himself staring, not at Sly Tom, but Harry Trimble.

"Do I count?" Harry asked, shaking his coat and ducking away from the rain that had collected on the door casing during last night's storm and was now dripping onto his unfashionable hat.

Daniel's face flooded with relief. "Come inside. I needed to find you."

Harry, usually eager enough, hovered on the step, digging his hands into his coat pockets. "I'm looking for a friend of mine. Served three cruises with me. My landlady said he came looking for me last night, and that he was in a bad way. She told him I might have come here."

"Inside," Daniel insisted, concerned by Harry's haggard face and heavy eyes.

Harry licked his lips, a signal flare of worry from a man normally so unflappable. "I can't. I need to find him. His woman claims he never came back last night. She said he was in agony. If I'd only been at home—"

"He's here," Daniel said.

"Thank God." Harry pushed his way inside. "I brought opium." He glanced back at Daniel, listening to the silence. "Am I too late?"

"He's resting," Daniel said.

Harry frowned.

"Come and see."

Prescott dozed, breathing slowly through an open mouth, transported back to the Land of Nod by his recent dose of laudanum. Nora sat in the other bed, evidently bewildered by the disorder of her hair. She colored at the sight of them and pushed the wild strands back. "Good morning, Harry."

His incredulous eyes swerved from her to Daniel's wrinkled shirt, and then to the blanket dripping off the chair onto the floor. The lines of his face hardened before he fastened his attention on Prescott.

"John!" He crossed quickly to the bed, peeling back the covers before anyone could stop him. At the sight of the bandage he went utterly still.

"Not so bad, is it?" Prescott joked feebly. "Looking at it now, you'd never think... Last night I thought I was a gone man."

Harry grunted. Calmly, he replaced the sheets. "You'll want some broth. Daniel, you and I can see to it." He turned from the bed, sending Daniel such a look of scorching fury that he was compelled to follow him from the room. They stalked to the end of the hall, Daniel bracing himself for a blast of the Scotsman's temper.

"In here," Harry said. "I don't want John overhearing." He stormed into the laboratory. When Daniel turned to close the door, he discovered Nora behind him. He hadn't heard her come down the hall with them.

"I'm part of this," she whispered, slipping past him without giving him a chance to argue.

True enough. And if his thoughts this morning had clarified anything, it was the need to talk. To plan. To do something.

No one sat. A current of suppressed silence passed between them like Volta's electrical experiments. Nora was the first to try to tame the tension. "We had no choice. The bowel came through, black and obstructed. He was vomiting. Nothing was passing and the tissue was black."

"So what in heaven's name have you done to him?" Harry demanded. "Did you cut his *bowel*?"

"No. Only loosed it," Daniel said, trying to calm him. "He'd be dead or expiring in agony if we'd left him alone."

Harry's set jaw loosened a fraction as his eyebrows arched in disbelief. "He was fine a week ago. You never do surgery on the abdomen. The infection!"

"Hush, Harry!" Nora said, reminding him that John Prescott might overhear. "There's a good chance he'll recover. Why are you so angry?"

Harry threw his hands out. "We aren't gods! Playing with

a man's life in a surgery you know next to nothing about... I'm amazed he's still breathing!"

"We weren't playing," Nora said quietly, too intent on Harry to see Daniel's warning look. Harry's face was too hard to be trusted. He was not yet on their side. He might be charmed by her ability to debate theory or run an experiment, but that didn't mean he'd approve of anything else.

"What did you do?" he demanded again. "Mother Mary, have you all gone mad? Where's Croft? He shouldn't—"

"He's not here," Daniel said. "He's in Hampshire."

Harry's eyes drew into slits. "You couldn't have cut into him alone, Dan. John's strong as an ox. Who held him for you?"

"It wasn't as difficult as you think," Daniel said, trying to gauge Harry's color. His mottled cheeks didn't bode well for anyone.

"Harry." Nora laid a hand on his arm. "If you keep on like this, John will hear you."

He subsided at last, muttering darkly.

Daniel ignored his curses and kept talking. "We used ether."

Harry eyes slewed wildly to Daniel. "What do you mean, we? You—and Miss Beady?" His nostrils quivered with the effort of the things he wasn't saying.

"Nora's an experienced anatomist." Daniel's voice rose sharply. "Which you thought very clever just a week ago. I opened and—"

"You let her assist you?" Harry was far too Scottish to let someone else lose their temper without joining in. "You could have given him morphine until he passed out and then reduced it. Poking around the intestines *is* almost certain death, and a painful one!"

"There was no one else!" Daniel spat out, his anger slipping his hold. "You were gone! There was no time to find another. I've never worked on an obstructed bowel, and Croft had walked her through the surgery on a cadaver. She was his best chance. His only chance, really. I opened and found the obstruction, but it was necrotic.

"We couldn't let your friend die in that state. I thought we had to try to resect. Nora had a different idea." Daniel threw her a gentler look. "A better idea."

"I freed it from the spermatic cord and felt for a pulse," she proceeded carefully. "There was none at first. But I waited several minutes, and the veins must have reopened because blood supply returned. The bowel was pink when we put it back. I saved it." Her shoulders were pushed back but her chin trembled. Daniel had never seen a person defiant and pleading at the same time, but Harry showed no signs of softening.

"I sewed up the weak spot in the abdominal wall. It should never trouble him again," Daniel said.

"If he lives." Harry's tone left no doubt about his opinion of Prescott's chances.

"What would you have done?" Nora demanded, her hot voice warming the chilly room. "He was in agony. He crawled here begging for you at the point of death!"

"And I think"—Daniel buttressed his failing self-control with a long breath—"I truly think he has a chance, Harry. Nora did brilliantly. You should have seen her. When we first gave him the ether, he didn't even twitch. It was almost like working on a corpse. There was little danger of an accidental cut because *he didn't move*. If he mends…" Daniel hesitated, thinking of this morning's doubts as much as the long night's eager notes. "I think we could do it again."

"What do you mean?" Harry asked.

"On other patients. You can see my notes. Prescott remembers nothing of the surgery. He showed signs of pain at the end, but it is shut out from memory."

"Don't you see?" Nora cut in, her cheeks flushed. "This could be something tremendous. If Prescott recovers, we can publish a paper on surgical intervention for strangulated hernias and necrosis. The bowel was black but came back to life. That means there is a window of opportunity. I can hardly breathe when I think of what we did."

That made two of them, but Daniel's breathlessness was for wholly separate reasons. Nora hadn't realized, but they'd cast their futures into Harry's hands, and he looked thunderous.

"It could save my reputation, Harry," Daniel argued.

"Not if her involvement gets out," he spat out. "You're already in trouble. If anyone learns an unlicensed, untutored girl was part of this…" Nora flinched, but Harry pressed on, unheeding, "She'll damn you beyond redemption."

Nora stepped back, her eyes black and lost, studying Harry as if she'd never seen him before.

"Nora was brilliant," Daniel retorted, forgetting he'd wrestled with the same worries not even an hour before. "She has a better grasp of anatomy than half the surgeons we know."

"And if you tell any of them that, they'll want nothing to do with you," Harry said flatly. "They'll mock and vilify you both and no one will listen to a thing you say, however credible."

Daniel wished he could deny it. Harry's statement had

stolen the starch from Nora's shoulders. "We'll protect you," Daniel reassured her. If Harry breathed a word…

"But how can you and still publish the case?" Nora's eyes shone, and her voice throbbed.

Daniel licked his lips. It wasn't fair to suggest it, but… "We could keep your name out of it."

"It's not a job for a single surgeon," Harry said. "If you make this claim, you'll be questioned."

Might as well jump for the deep water. "Harry, have you an alibi? Would you be able to say you assisted?"

There was a sound from Nora, only a breath, but it was bitter in his ears.

Harry's closed expression flickered with fury or pain. "I was…not with anyone who would interfere with a lie."

Daniel had never looked a man so squarely in the eyes. "Would you say it?" Now he knew why Harry so often won at cards. His face revealed nothing.

Harry threw a glance at Nora. He shifted his feet, narrowing the angle between him and Daniel and excluding her from his line of sight. "If you publish this case, other doctors will have questions. Lots of them. And John knows I wasn't here last night."

"He's your friend. He doesn't know how much Nora's done. If you asked him to say you were here, why wouldn't he agree to it? If he knows it's to protect the woman who helped save him." Heavily, Daniel turned to Nora. Last night she'd played the hero, and now… "If we frame the case that way, we can publish. Do you mind?"

"Of course I don't." But her face was as blank and mysterious as stones raised by the men of long ago, and every bit as forbidding. "Don't leave John alone any longer. I'll get the broth."

⸻

Daniel tended Prescott and quietly coached Harry on the details of the surgery, despite the images that haunted him—his interview with Dr. Croft, who never advocated abdominal surgery, facing the board of St. Bart's and the gentlemen of the Athenaeum club, blood poisoning or death. And though he tried not to, he couldn't think of Nora without a pang.

"Daniel?" Harry prodded him away from his wandering thoughts. "How many stitches again?"

"Over twenty. In layers." Daniel rubbed at his eyes. "Only ten on the surface."

Harry kept his bitter frown as he had for the past two days.

"We're doing the right thing," Daniel urged him.

"I knew Croft let her work with him, but I never would have guessed how much. But regardless of how foolhardy they've been, no one can know she's done a surgery. They'd crucify her, Daniel. And then they'd destroy Croft."

Daniel gave a sober nod. They at least agreed on that.

"You should sleep," Harry said. "Leave me with John."

Daniel stood, moving like an old man. Harry's voice stopped him before he turned for the door. "The stitches look well, Daniel."

"So did the bowel when she finished with it." He'd never know why the words came out so despondent.

CHAPTER 22

STALKING BLINDLY DOWN THE HALL, NORA VEERED INTO
the surgery. Chest heaving, hands shaking, she looked at
the table where they'd saved Prescott. She remembered their
hands, slicing and stitching, and afterward scrubbing together.
The taste of strong wine was on her tongue.

You little fool.

Knuckling away the salt water stinging her eyes, Nora flung
open the nearest cupboard and heaved down her unwieldy
black notebook. It tumbled from her hands, falling open on the
floor, revealing the rows of her tight script marching across the
overlarge pages. A twenty-year-old case study, the suppositions
of an obscure Dutch physician, a paper written by Dr. Croft
when he was newly licensed: every piece painstakingly gathered
for Daniel's defense. She'd wasted her time. Daniel didn't need
her help. He had Harry. Once John Prescott recovered and they
published the case…

Seizing the book, she tore out one page, and another, then
three at a time. She crumpled the sheets and tossed them into
the corner. It felt like destruction, but later she could smooth
them and retrieve her carefully collected knowledge. No matter
what rage filled her, she could not take it out on truth.

"What in God's name are you doing?"

She didn't turn around. "Leave me alone." Deliberately, she tore out another; paper slashed at an angle as she ripped it in half.

"Stop it, Nora!" He was close now, reaching for her notebook.

"I told you to go away!"

He bent to the floor, gathering up the scattered pages. "Don't be angry. Just let me explain."

"Who's angry? There's no need for a woman to take notes when nobody will read them. I'm *cleaning*." The word hissed out. "I'm *allowed* to do that and it won't shame anyone." He reached out a hand, but she stepped away, bumping into a whitewashed cupboard.

"I am not ashamed. Spare a moment and think. If the board of St. Bart's expelled me for disagreeing with Vickery, what will they do to you? You will be laughed at, censured, mocked—perhaps even sued by the College of Surgeons or charged in court. Wherever you belong—and I freely admit it's hard to know where that is—it's not in a cell. On top of that, Croft would be the laughingstock of London, if they didn't strip him of his license. The miracles we saw will be dismissed as a pack of lies—which we can't afford. Every discovery is a step toward preserving life. You know that."

She looked away. He was right, but she wasn't ready to admit it. She'd never felt as small as she had in that awful scene with him and Harry Trimble.

Daniel wasn't finished. "Even if we had failed, do you imagine I'd let Vickery and his ilk have you? You should be a surgeon, Nora, whether the world knows it or not. I envy your skill and your courage. I'm…" His breath caught. "You may astonish me on almost a daily basis, but I'm certainly not ashamed of you."

The immensity of feeling twisting her mouth was too great to suppress. Desperate, she snatched at the first words that came, since she'd rather argue with him than crumple. "What good is it if I must hide forever?"

"What good? Ask the people who stream into clinic. Ask John Prescott. Ask Croft or the travailing women you assist as a midwife. You do enormous good. Ask any of them."

A muscle twitched in his jaw. He drew a long, reluctant breath. "Ask me."

The wall in front of her blurred as she gathered up her next argument.

"Nora," Daniel's voice slowed to a searching tone. "*Ask me.*"

She turned her head in his direction, understanding at last what he meant by the request. "What good, Daniel?" She couldn't bear to look at him and kept her eyes wandering across the floor, the whitewashed walls, the fluid lines of grain in the wooden cupboards.

He stepped closer until his black shoes came into her view. His laces hung askew, the bow lopsided. "A great deal of good. For my bedside manner, for my research, for my technique, for my heart." Daniel forced out his admission out in a rigidly slow tempo—the last defense of a man schooled to implacable calm.

Her ears hummed with what felt like an attack of vertigo or a lack of air. She flashed her eyes upward just long enough to gather a picture of his anxious face. The crumpled papers lay like twisted bones on the table beside them. "I thought you—"

"You have no idea what I think." He stepped over a quill pen that had fallen to the floor in her fury, closing the space between them. "No idea at all." His fingers slipped up her shoulder, along the back of her neck, and into the untidy twist of her hair. She didn't flinch. A shiver raced down her spine, her eyes shuttered, and her chin lifted all on its own, so that her lips found his as easily as the needle of a compass finds north in darkness, fog, or forest.

By some unexplainable alchemy contained in his touch, her anger transmuted to molten gold, blinding and uncontainable. She lifted onto her toes—

A door shut.

Like magnets whose poles had reversed, they bounced apart, hovering a yard away. Behind Daniel, the surgery door was closed, but she knew when he'd come in, he'd left it open. He always did. It was only proper.

"Harry." Daniel muttered the name like a curse.

Nora went from molten to ashes.

"It could have been the hallboy—" She dashed for the door and flung it open, Daniel at her heels. She glanced down the hall and spied Harry striding away, but he heard them and turned halfway around, still wearing a tight grimace.

Daniel passed her swiftly.

"That wasn't—"

Harry stopped him with a raised hand. "Don't explain. You might want to be a little more careful though, hmm? I can't imagine what Croft would do, were he to walk into that kind of scene. And I advise against using the surgery for your affairs."

"Harry, it's not—" Daniel tried to argue but Harry disappeared into Prescott's room.

Daniel ran a hand through his hair and covered his brow as if it pained him. "That was my fault." He rubbed his forehead, his eyes hidden. Nora cursed herself for not having the right words but embarrassment scorched a hole in her thoughts.

"I apologize if I misbehaved…or took advantage." His agonized words cut through her.

"You are not at any fault." How could she tell him? "I will not mention it or hold you to any…anything. But shouldn't we go after him and explain?" She stepped toward the doorway.

Daniel nodded miserably. "I know his temper. Not yet." He reached out for a crumpled page. "What's this?" he asked as he gently smoothed it.

"Nothing." She woke from her stupor and attempted to snatch the pages away. "Just some notes on my reading."

Daniel didn't return it. "More research on pig swill?" His eyes met hers. "You've done all this to help me?"

She flushed. "And children like Lucy. These poisons that get into the blood…" She stared at her hands.

It took him a moment to speak, and when he did, he spoke softly. "May I see?"

Nora nodded, her eyes skidding to the corridor. She should confront Harry. The longer she waited, the worse it would be, but she couldn't bear to speak of it yet. While her fingers knotted the inside of her pocket, Daniel skimmed her pages, the arguments for and against, the points she'd underlined in red ink, the lines connecting one idea to another.

Daniel's thumb rubbed the edge of the pages. "I doubt anyone could convince Vickery of anything, but—" He looked up. "I'd like to continue this experiment with you."

Nora's breath stilled and she met his eyes, convinced she imagined the double meaning in his gentle words. Impossible to know for certain, but his tender expression left a beautiful doubt. "I'd like that."

—⁓—

As much as his mind demanded he make sense of the last twenty-four hours, Daniel diverted all his attention to the scruffy man recovering in the dim patient's quarters. John Prescott certainly wasn't as satisfying to mull over as Nora, but one cannot say a struggle for life isn't fascinating. With the stitches inflamed and an unpredictable fever striking and mysteriously retreating, Daniel hardly had time to decide whether to hope or despair for John Prescott's life.

Until Dr. Croft responded to their urgent telegram, or better yet, came thundering home, Daniel had to feel his way blindly and try to contain the damage, for his sake and Nora's. Until things resolved, he couldn't force her to examine her feelings or press his own on her. He wasn't even sure what they were. Though tempted to lift the curtain of his mind and examine the puzzle, the lingering smart of Mae's rejection warned him to steer clear.

Instead of deciding what to do, he worked. He had learned at least that much from Dr. Croft. And it kept him from having to speak much to Harry, who hovered in the background, watching Nora with narrowed eyes Daniel couldn't interpret.

He couldn't let her take up with Harry.

Then again, there was precious little he could do. It was like most diagnoses—watch and wait.

—⁓—

Because Horace was a great believer in the stethoscope—Nora had yet to master one—she practiced listening to the inner workings of John's intestines. A few times she heard what she believed was the digestion and movement of food in the afflicted area, but always she passed the earpiece to Daniel or Harry for confirmation, and they looked as doubtful as she.

Only the tension of watching Mr. Prescott ebb and rise with the hours of the day—first better, then sinking into pain and sleep—could distract her from the unrelenting thoughts stalking her. Images replayed of Daniel's low murmurs, the fervent glint in his shadowed eyes, his fingers in her hair. She tried not to let the fierce shivers that took over at her inexplicable moments show.

Harry avoided the subject of what he'd seen altogether, tacitly agreeing to ignore the awkward spaces in their conversation. Sunday afternoon, when she and Harry would normally have walked, the two of them measured John's temperature and drained the wound of pus, speaking only when necessary.

Working with Daniel was easier. Head to head, they bent their eyes to the walls and listened as if blood poisoning had a faint and sinister vibration they could detect if they strained hard enough. Until he gave her some sign or signal that he at least remembered what had passed between them, she would keep her words, her looks, her demeanor as neutral as nature allowed.

"The bowels are moving and the heart is strong. No water in the lungs," Nora announced that evening, after pressing the trumpet to Prescott's belly, back, and chest. It had now been forty-eight hours, and Dr. Croft always warned of the third day of illness. *The body can rally for three days, but don't be fooled...* His counsel rang in her ears as she watched the clock. They should know by tomorrow. In front of John she avoided saying what needed no words: beneath the clean bandage, the small wound was angry and purple. She forced herself not to check it hourly, but not looking only filled her imagination with the dreaded red streaks and black skin that came with a raging fever and then death.

Horace finally returned on Friday, just as John's wound was growing hot. The sound of Horace's cursing among the loud thumps of his baggage being dumped in the entryway traveled down the stairs into the offices. It all sounded like church choirs to Nora. She rushed upstairs, meeting Daniel in the hall.

"Well, I've come home," Horace said, scowling at them. "I had your telegram, and I'd like to know what the deuce is so urgent that I had to race here in such a poorly hung carriage I nearly broke my spine?"

"I'm sorry it was so dreadful, but you'll never guess the takings we've had here," Nora said, easing him out of his greatcoat. "Daniel and I had to perform a nearly impossible surgery alone. The man is still alive, but…"

Horace snapped upright, clearly forgetting he'd just complained of pains in his back. "What sort of surgery? Is the patient here?"

"Let us tell it to you first." Nora hung up the coat, then tugged him into the library. Daniel followed, locking the door. He recounted the story from the beginning, in a hushed voice. Nora knew why he whispered—Mrs. Phipps tolerated much, but finding she had slept through Nora's most perilous night would be her undoing, and they all knew she had a penchant for eavesdropping.

"So the bowel appeared fully necrotic?" Croft tugged at his beard, grown shaggy with neglect. "Was it cold?"

Daniel stopped. "It was hard to tell with warm blood on my fingers," he admitted.

"I don't believe it was cold," Nora interjected, "but there was no pulse whatever, and I knew I couldn't cut the spermatic cord because he would risk losing sexual function."

Daniel's head darted up.

"How thoughtful of you," Croft put in, with a mocking slide of his eyes to Daniel. He got no satisfaction for his joke. Daniel only frowned and pocketed his hands.

Horace turned to her, his mouth half-open and his eyes squinted as he studied her the same way he did before quizzing students at a public dissection. "So how did you free the bowel? Zeus, I wish I'd been here!"

Brightening at his enthusiasm, she hurried on. "Luckily, when I dissected the canal there was just enough room to move aside the cord, but we couldn't reduce the dead bowel. Daniel and I massaged it a bit as we studied it, and after a minute I thought I felt a pulse…"

It took half an hour to satisfy him with the details. "Whether he lives or not, it must be one for the papers," Croft declared. "For the senselessness induced by the ether alone! I had mixed results with it at the asylum. Some patients begged for more, but when they awoke, the effects wore off quickly. I believe it can be used for control and restraint more than for curative properties."

Daniel was the first to inject practical concerns. "We've discussed writing up the case. I'm at work on it now, but we're putting it about that Trimble and I performed the surgery."

Nora stiffened. She knew it was the only way, but perhaps Dr. Croft would see a solution they missed—a way for her to escape the shadows.

Croft frowned, then shuffled some papers on the desk. "I suppose we'll have to. Yes, that will be best."

Her stomach quivered with the blow of his calm dismissal. *At least look at me*, Nora thought.

Daniel cleared his throat. "But I've thought it over and think we should include her as a surgical assistant. No one questions a brilliant nurse, and while it's unconventional for a surgery, it was an emergency. We could simply put her first initial and last name."

Croft waved his hand. "Whatever you like. I want to see the fellow." He hurried from the room, not waiting to see if they followed.

Nora hung back, eyes fixed on the tabletop. She rolled a pencil under her fingers, but it did not keep them from shaking.

"Nora, I'd tell the world if I thought they wouldn't skewer you…"

Daniel did not finish because she closed the space between them and pressed her heavy head into his chest, needing a reprieve, even if just for a moment. Afraid of what he might think, she left before he had a chance to recover.

⁓

That night, alone in his room, Daniel studied his memories of Mae with a doctor's detached and critical eye. Her violet walking-out skirt with the embroidered hem she was secretly so proud of, her purchases of pocket mirrors on market days, the way she laughed through her fingers when she passed on gossip about her servants. He meticulously reviewed the delighted curve of her lips when she gathered lavender from his gardens because it grew so much better there than on her parent's shady estate and her ever-so-subtle hints that she used it to scent her undergarments. Never had she been tented in a billowing apron stained with blood. Never did her fingers soil the dinner napkins with gray smudges of newsprint. Never did she speak comforting words to a pauper woman who trembled in fear while asking for help she could not afford. Never did she risk her good name to protect his.

He'd been casting glances at Nora when she wasn't looking, searching for clues to her feelings or for flaws he hadn't bothered to notice before. To his despair, he found none, only the opposite: a rosy gloss to her hair he'd never observed, a dimple on her chin that only flicked into existence when she used one particular smile, a line between her eyebrows that appeared when she wrestled silently against a bad outcome of an experiment or dissection. This something—if there was anything—between him and Nora was new, and Daniel looked upon anything new with a certain amount of suspicion. It was his habit, inculcated by a demanding father, to prepare for every outcome. Despite his penchant for caution, he smiled in the dark.

CHAPTER 23

NORA RETURNED JOHN PRESCOTT'S EMPTY GRUEL BOWL to the tray. The young man shuffled himself higher on the pillows. "Are you walking with Dr. Trimble tomorrow?"

She hid her surprise by tugging on the sheets and smoothing nonexistent wrinkles. "I'm not expecting him. Drink up your tea."

"No need to hiss at me," John Prescott said. "Dr. Gibson's a handsome one, to be sure."

Nora flicked a scalding look in his direction. For the past week she'd been glad to see him regaining his rather impudent sense of humor along with his appetite, but if he was going to twit her along with the orderlies… "I hadn't noticed," she said curtly.

"I assume he's the reason why Harry doesn't mention you any longer? I've nothing to do in this bed but observe."

"I suggest you give it up. It's not your talent." She felt the heat inch up her cheeks. If even John could see, she had no more excuses. She must speak with—

"Harry," John said. "I was just asking after you."

Nora whipped around.

"Good afternoon, Nora. Afternoon, John." He was just loose enough around the shoulders and tight enough around his eyes that she could discern nothing of his mood.

She forced a weak smile and stood up, smoothing her skirts. "Come to see your patient?"

"Daniel, actually, and Dr. Croft." His eyes grazed hers. "Are they here?"

Her teeth found the soft skin of her cheek. "They're dosing each other with ether. You'll probably find at least one of them conscious." Her joke didn't wring a smile from him.

"If you've a moment?" he gestured to the corridor and she followed him.

"Don't let me interrupt," John hollered after them from his bed.

Harry gave his head an exasperated shake. "The surgeons of St. Bart's know about the case." His blue eyes were fixed and inscrutable.

Nora stiffened. "About John? Do they know—"

"They suspect nothing about you. They've heard that Daniel and I opened an abdomen," he said, sighing heavily. "I've only spoken to one other doctor—Johnson is sympathetic and interested in ether. I thought he'd be good to have on our side—but word got out…"

"How are they taking it?" Nora braced her shoulder against the wall.

"Vickery doesn't believe it. He wants to see Prescott. A number of them do, but they are more generous with their assumptions." Harry folded his arms, barricading his chest. "At least four of them pulled me aside today, asking if we'd demonstrate the ether. They think of it only as a party trick."

"Sounds like someone else I know." She raised her eyebrow at him and he shrugged.

"I do think if you've killed as many rats as you say, Daniel shouldn't be playing with it on a daily basis."

Nora frowned. "Mice, not rats." But the truth stung. Drugs were not toys. Every time Dr. Croft or Daniel went unnaturally still, so did her heart.

"I'm against it," Harry said. "We don't understand enough."

"You haven't seen our latest experiments," Nora said. "You've hardly visited at all." She smiled, trying to let him know she'd missed him.

"I'm surprised you noticed."

The anger in his voice deserved some reply, but approaching footsteps stopped her. "Dr. Croft?" she called.

"No, it's me." Daniel walked into the corridor, still weaving a little from the ether.

Nora jumped toward him. "You shouldn't be walking about so soon." She led him to the parlor, where Mrs. Phipps had left the tea tray, and helped him to the settee. When she let him go, she caught sight of Harry's fleeting scowl.

Daniel grinned at both of them.

"Are you still bosky?" Nora demanded, and Daniel had grace enough to blush. "Drink this." She thrust a teacup at him.

"Mmm. Smells wonderful." Dr. Croft breezed into the room, squeezing onto the settee beside Daniel. "Two sugars in mine. I forgot to eat luncheon."

Nora was well aware and had already added four lumps of sugar and a biscuit onto his saucer. "Harry says they are talking of John Prescott at St. Bart's."

Dr. Croft's eyebrows flew up. "How'd they hear? I've never known such a bunch of gossips—"

"We think someone overheard us talking to Johnson. But Vickery and Thompson have heard of our experiments and they've asked for a demonstration of ether," Harry said.

"Excellent. We'll dose Vickery, and then I can jab him with pins," Daniel said. "No, let's castrate him." He chuckled.

Nora covered her mouth to hide her smile. Dr. Croft lowered his eyes. "Let's give him another ten minutes before discussing serious business."

"Excellent idea." Harry, usually the joker in the bunch, was remarkably crisp.

Harry's persuasions kept the demonstration small. If they failed, better to do it in front of the smallest possible audience. Only Dr. Thompson and two of his assistants, Dr. Corden and Dr. Adams, were invited that Monday evening. Vickery was furious at his exclusion, complaining loudly that doctors who weren't confident enough to endure the scrutiny of their peers shouldn't be allowed to practice.

"We must do it right," Daniel murmured to Croft, nervously tugging at his cuffs.

"We will," Horace said, and handed him a drink. "Stop fussing."

Daniel held his glass without drinking. He'd already downed one brandy and didn't intend to take any more.

The bell rang, and Mrs. Phipps brought the three gentlemen into the parlor.

"Thank you for joining us this evening." Horace welcomed them with a wide smile and poured out three more drinks. They chatted pleasantly for a quarter of an hour. Dr. Corden, handicapped by a Yorkshire accent but blessed with a prodigious memory, cornered Daniel and tried to quiz him about John Prescott.

"I went to see him, you know. Wouldn't say anything to me. Kept his mouth shut tight as a clam. Wouldn't even show me the scar."

Daniel hid a grin. Since John had returned home three days ago, the man had reached near celebrity status with the medical profession. "No one likes to be stared at and prodded," Daniel returned.

Corden grunted. "I've made a study of hernias. I'm interested in the case."

It was a relief to end the conversation there and walk in to dinner. Mrs. Phipps, conscious of her position as housekeeper, had refused to join them, so Nora took the hostess's chair. The gentlemen, unaccustomed to her habits and ignorant of her skills, kept the discussion general, baffling her with unsuccessful forays into fashion, music, and politics.

"I'm afraid I never learned to play the pianoforte," she finally admitted to Dr. Adams. "Dr. Croft never owned one." She took a sip of wine, set down her glass, and said, "But I read your article in the latest *Philosophical Transactions* and was most interested in your predictions about fifth-finger numbness and compression of the lower brachial plexus."

Daniel smiled at his plate. Nora knew only one way to be. Dr. Adams did not hide his shock. "How extraordinary!"

Now that she'd given permission, as it were, for them to talk of the matters that interested them most, conversation flowed easily from routine observation to wild theory: whether fumigation was a practical method of containing cholera, and whether tracheostomy should be used as a last resort against diphtheria. Horace allowed no questions about ether, saying that the gentlemen's patience would soon be rewarded.

Lulled by talk, they idled through dessert. When the pudding was only a memory, Horace laid his hands on the table. "Shall we?"

Thompson had visited the surgery before, though not recently. Adams and Corden, seeing it for the first time, inspected the room, exclaiming over the size and the excellence of the fittings. Corden, the youngest of the trio, seemed to have a particularly hard time keeping his hands at his sides as he stared admiringly at the pristine floors and tabletop, the mirrors, the heavy white blinds, drawn now for privacy and to keep in the warmth. Croft was always extravagant with lamp oil, but the room seemed even brighter than usual tonight.

Daniel cleared his throat and loosened his cravat. "If you do not mind me removing my dinner jacket, I can take my place on the table as soon as Dr. Croft has the inhaler situated." Horace had already signaled for the hot water to be brought up from the kitchen and was placing the thermometer below the glass bulb that would hold the ether.

Turning to the other doctors with a winning grin, Daniel was surprised to see their eyes narrow.

"It's unusual to demonstrate yourself," Dr. Thompson pointed out. "You are highly motivated to exaggerate the outcome. Feigning sleep or senselessness is not difficult."

Dr. Adams and Corden did not look as suspicious as Thompson, but lines of doubt framed their frowns.

"Gentlemen, I have no intention of deceiving you—"

"You do have much to gain," Dr. Adams pointed out. "With your career on the line."

Daniel fumbled for words and ran his anxious glance over the room. Harry could do it but his face was still stiff enough that Daniel couldn't be certain he'd be willing. Croft always woke well, but he had as much to prove as Daniel. "We don't have a patient at present. If one of you wanted to volunteer…" His voice trailed off at their dubious expressions.

"Miss Beady." Horace spoke up and all eyes snapped to the corner where she stood, the shadows puddling beneath her dark skirt. She raised her startled face to the small crowd. "She would be willing to demonstrate."

"Well, now, we didn't mean—" Dr. Corden hedged. He'd spent the best part of dinner discussing anatomy with her and didn't look at all anxious to see her experimented upon.

"Nonsense." Croft waved his hand. "I brought you here to prove that this method is reliable and safe. What better way to convince you of my certainty than to demonstrate on my ward?"

Daniel flinched at the memory of Nora lying still on the dissecting table. She hadn't woken peacefully, gasping and crying out in terror, but it was the recollection of her deathly stillness and the sad toll of expired mice that spurred his protests. "Dr. Croft, I hardly think the doctors would forgive us for using a young lady. I think you'll find if I demonstrate—"

"I don't mind." Nora stepped forward, calmly confronting their eyes and resolutely avoiding his.

Daniel opened his mouth, but how could he protest when he'd
asked the doctors here to witness how safe it was. He clamped it
shut again, begging his mind to invent some alternative.

Dr. Thompson had a hungry look about the eyes, and
Harry's disapproval leaked out of his stoic facade. Croft, irre-
pressible as ever, rushed forward to take Nora's hand.

"Nora has observed several of our experiments and has
already sampled the ether." He led her to the surgical table.
"You will see the ease and safety of the insensibility."

"But to what end?" Thompson demanded. "Making
girls faint on demand is more the work of a magician than a
physician."

Daniel sighed with relief. "See, Horace. Let us convince
them ourselves and leave Miss Beady out of it."

"I insist," Nora said with infuriating finality as she lifted
herself onto the table. "Ether has a good many uses, sirs. It is
not a party trick. How often during a surgery have you wished
you could induce a faint and spare your patient the consciousness of pain?"

In spite of her calm words, Daniel saw the minute quaking
of her chin and the flex of muscles between her eyebrows. She
was probably more worried about waking badly again and bun-
gling the demonstration than about her safety. The set faces of
the doctors made further protest impossible. Daniel clasped his
hands behind his back and throttled his own knuckles to stop
himself from seizing her and carrying her away.

"You will put your worries to rest once you observe,"
Horace promised the doctors. "Dr. Gibson, if you would like to
administer?"

She smiled at him as he fitted the inhaler Horace had fashioned over her nose and mouth. Daniel kept his face impassive, though his fingers were white as he watched her nose wrinkle with the odor. She gave him the most imperceptible shrug as if she knew exactly what lecture he was planning for her when they were alone again. He could scarcely hear Horace lecturing on the percentages of vapor to air and the stages of senselessness.

Nora wheezed hard after one minute and twenty seconds and Daniel removed the mask, but Horace's hand was instantly there, securing it back in place.

"Coughing begins in the second stage and quickly passes. She should be nearly there," Horace pronounced as Nora's eyes trembled to a close and her fingers went limp on the table.

Daniel saw nothing but Nora's fallen eyelashes, lax lips, and the undulations of her ribs, telling him she still breathed. He could scarcely breathe himself, counting out the seconds.

Horace pinched the tender skin of her forearm and turned to the doctors as he produced a needle from his pocket. "Now is the time to still all doubt." He took the needle and pricked her white skin, leaving a crimson drop of blood behind. Nora lay like stone.

Thompson came forward. "It is easy to resist a needle prick, Dr. Croft."

"Choose your test, Dr. Thompson," Horace replied, handing over the needle to the black-eyed, balding surgeon.

As the calculating doctor stepped forward, surveying Nora's helpless form, Daniel stiffened. The doctor's eyes lingered too long on her figure.

"I find the lips particularly vulnerable, as well as the eyes." Dr. Thompson took Nora's soft lip between his roughened fingers and without warning probed the needle deep into her gum.

The men all gasped—Daniel with rage. Nora did not register the wound despite the small pool of blood swimming across her bottom teeth.

"She didn't move a muscle," Dr. Corden murmured as he drew near and examined the puncture in her mouth.

Croft snatched the needle back from Thompson. "I'd rather not cause her any lasting discomfort," he scolded. While he answered the torrent of questions that spilled from the doctors, Harry stepped forward and mopped the blood from her mouth.

Daniel thanked him silently and returned his focus to her breathing. It distracted him from what he'd like to do to Dr. Thompson for his sadistic stunt. When she finally awoke, filling him with weak relief, the astonishment and congratulations of the other doctors hardly registered in his numb mind.

CHAPTER 24

A WEEK AFTER THE DEMONSTRATION, ONCE DR. CORDEN'S enthusiastic praise had percolated through the wards and surgeries of London, Nora watched Daniel playing with the scalpel he was supposed to be sharpening after a busy day in the clinic. It didn't surprise her when he set down the knife and cleared his throat.

"I've had a letter from my parents," he said in an off-hand voice that was dismally unconvincing. He was the most deliberate man Nora knew. She wondered how many times he'd silently rehearsed this casual introduction of a painful topic.

"Oh?" Nora set down her sponge. Dr. Croft, in suds up to his elbows, merely grunted.

"They're making a visit to London."

"When?" She couldn't tell if this was happy news or not. Daniel's face gave nothing away.

"They arrived on Monday. My mother wished to do some shopping, and—"

"They're already here? Daniel, you should have told me. They're welcome to visit here, you know." When she and Mrs. Phipps exerted themselves, they could make the house respectable enough for an afternoon call, and it would be worth the effort if it helped Daniel make peace with his family. If they saw the value of his work, perhaps then—

"They always put up at Grillon's Hotel," he said.

Nora swallowed and waited. Daniel didn't say more, and to her surprise, Dr. Croft was also silent, drying his hands on a linen towel with painstaking care.

"What's wrong?" Nora asked.

"I am to join them tomorrow for dinner," Daniel admitted. "And I insisted you both come. It will be good for them to meet my associates."

Nora blushed with pleasure. How funny which words made her blush and which did not. A conversation on the clap had nearly bored her this morning, but when Daniel called her his associate... *He wishes to introduce me to his family.* Nora ducked her chin, repacking the clean knives, forceps, and saws in Dr. Croft's traveling case.

"I hope you don't mind," Daniel went on. "I felt they need to accept the reality of my life, now that this is the path I've chosen."

Nora could hear the smile in his voice, which meant he knew she was blushing. She clicked the latches of the case shut and spun away, depositing it on the bench by the door, afraid Dr. Croft might also see.

"I'm glad to come," Dr. Croft said.

Composed now, Nora turned around. Dr. Croft was still meticulously drying his hands, but Daniel looked at her sideways in that electrifying way.

"I thought it might be easier... I thought the evening would go better if we had more to occupy ourselves with than food, though I think you'll like dinner at Grillon's." He flashed a smile at her, then went back to staring at the traffic rolling past the basement window. It was a bright morning, and he had to squint through the sun's glare. "There's an exhibition of mesmerism at the Drury Lane Theater tomorrow night. I wouldn't mind comparing the powers of mesmerism against those of ether—and I'm afraid my mother is ghoulishly fascinated by the subject."

"Something for everyone, eh?" Horace chuckled. "Sounds like you've given it a great deal of thought." He glanced behind his shoulder at the surgery. For now, it was spare and sparkling. "Don't worry. Nora and I can put on a show as good as the rest of them when we need to, can't we?"

They could, but… Nora felt a surge of panic.

Dr. Croft chuckled. "No need to be alarmed, Eleanor." He dug under his apron and into his pockets, drawing out a roll of bills tied with the catgut they used for suturing. He slipped the bills out, peeled off two and pressed them into Nora's hand. "Take Mrs. Phipps with you to Oxford Street. Find yourself something to wear. But nothing too silly and brainless. I detest costumes. What time tomorrow?"

"Dinner is at seven," Daniel said.

Dr. Croft gave a pleased nod and strode from the room, whistling.

Nora folded the bills carefully, trying to imagine herself in something stiff with crinolines and ruffles. "I won't know how to choose," she said carefully. "If I don't come home with something drearily plain, I'll end up with something gauche and vulgar."

Daniel brushed a loose bit of hair back from her cheek, his laugh rumbling through his ribs and into her own. "Impossible, but I should like to see you try."

CHAPTER 25

WELL, MESMERISM CLEARLY DOESN'T WORK BY MAKING them insensible," Daniel said as they filed from their seats during the show's interval. "He made them feel cold, even though the room is warm."

Nora nodded, her eyes on Mrs. Gibson's beaded shawl. They were pressed in the crowd, waiting to exit the theater (if it were possible) to catch a breath of air. "They shivered like they were truly caught in a rainstorm."

"What we don't know," Daniel said, "is if mesmerism is effective at erasing a physical sensation. We've seen how it can create one without actual stimuli, but—"

"If it's the same to you, Daniel, I'd rather not speak of physical sensations in mixed company," Mrs. Gibson said, contradicting herself by adding, "It's insufferably hot."

"Are you enjoying the show, madam?" Dr. Croft asked. "I'm finding the demonstration stimulating, even if I suspect it is disingenuous." He'd labored at small talk all evening, which was most unlike him.

Though he'd won few replies, he was faring better than Nora. Hiding her frustration, she smoothed the skirts of her green taffeta gown. The expensive confection had been purchased in haste under the commanding eye of Mrs. Phipps.

It was a lovely dress, cut in puritan lines in a fabric that was not puritan at all. Wearing it, Nora felt like a duchess in a painting, her back straight and steadied by the ballast of wide silk skirts. In this gown—only in this gown, Nora silently amended—she was indistinguishable among the extravagantly clad theatergoers.

Unfortunately, the moment she'd entered Grillon's Hotel, Mrs. Gibson, resplendent in diamonds and fussy French tailoring, had frosted over, responding to conversational sallies with sniffs and pursed lips. Daniel's attempts—addressing Nora and his mother in turn at dinner and then the theater—were hardly more productive. The sumptuous meal had turned to sawdust in Nora's mouth beneath Mrs. Gibson's disapproving stare, and the excitement of attending the theater and wearing such a beautiful gown was now as sour as vinegar.

"The show is compelling, but I do not approve," Mrs. Gibson said.

"Oh?" Dr. Croft lifted an eyebrow.

"After what we've seen, how could any person of character submit themselves to such a thing? To render one's will to anyone, no matter how upright, destroys one's claim to character. The professor might have asked them to do anything!"

"Surely there are limits," her husband said.

The lady sniffed. "They didn't remember what they'd done when they woke. What if, in private, a mesmerist, ordered a person—a lady—to do something *objectionable?*"

Nora held back a smile at such pronounced italics. "You think a man could impose on women through mesmerism?" she asked.

"I do not doubt it," Mrs. Gibson said darkly. "It's wrong for a lady to allow a stranger such extraordinary power."

Nora edged past the door. It was only slightly less crowded along the mezzanine. Mrs. Gibson's objections had come as a surprise, as she'd appeared to enjoy watching the mesmerism in progress. Yet it was troubling. If women like Mrs. Gibson condemned mesmerism for separating a person from their will, what would they think of ether? Claims that surgeons could be trusted would never allay such fears or persuade reluctant patients to surrender themselves to the gas if they thought doing so would compromise their reputation.

"But what if the trance were useful?" Nora asked. "Suppose a woman were mesmerized during childbirth—"

Mrs. Gibson blanched. "What?"

"She would be calm, she could be reassured, perhaps even persuaded that she was sitting in her own garden, resting in the sun—"

"Some subjects are not fit for polite company," Mrs. Gibson said, looking Nora up and down. "Clearly, you've had a most *eccentric* upbringing."

Before Nora could gather herself sufficiently to make a reply, Dr. Croft broke in, a steely ring in his voice. "I do not permit anyone to scoff at Nora's upbringing."

Mrs. Gibson bristled. "I certainly did not scoff—"

Heartened by the heat in Horace's blue eyes, Nora found it possible to be charitable. She spoke in placating tones for Daniel's sake. "My upbringing is unusual, but fortunate. Dr. Croft took me in when my entire family died in the cholera epidemic. Few orphans have ever been so lucky."

"Fortunate indeed," Mrs. Gibson said over arched eyebrows. "But surely you must agree that you would have benefited from an education."

"I have been educated." She might have stopped there and defused the situation, but a spark had lit in her middle, urging her to press on. "Dr. Croft has not been so small-minded as to deny me opportunities to learn. Perhaps *you* don't care to discuss these topics because a lady's traditional education is so limited."

Mrs. Gibson's cheeks purpled.

"Mother, I would appreciate if you did not take it upon yourself to—"

She ignored Daniel's objection. "I will not endure the insults of this guttersnipe!"

"Mother!" Daniel placed a hand on her arm as if he meant to escort her away.

Dr. Croft stiffened. "You're mistaken, madam," he drawled. "Miss Beady's family was successful and respectable."

Daniel's father snorted. Dr. Croft turned to him. "I had a humble start myself, you know. A farmer's son. My beginnings propelled me to success."

Mr. Gibson rearranged his expression to something more polite, though still streaked with doubt.

"My ward may hold her head up in any company. Not only has she an excellent mind, but Miss Beady is my sole heir. I generally pay little mind to such things, but my solicitor informs me she will inherit a handsome independence."

The tumult of the surrounding crowd couldn't touch the unnatural silence that distilled on them. Daniel's mother's lips fell open, but she seemed to have lost the power of speech, and Daniel was as immobile as if he'd been stuffed.

Nora had always assumed Dr. Croft would leave her enough to keep her off the streets, but his entire fortune? The truth landed heavily on her breast, pushing the air from her lungs.

Mr. Gibson broke the silence, saying with false heartiness. "How very good of you, Dr. Croft. But I dare say you consider yourself the fortunate one." His gaze, formerly so dismissive, now held a gleam of appraisal.

"Well put," Dr. Croft answered, offering Nora his arm. "Shall we take our seats again?"

Nora swallowed. She wasn't sure which was worse: Daniel's stricken face, his father's ghastly smile, or his mother's gray-tinged cheeks. It was too much, coming after hours of Mrs. Gibson's thinly veiled scorn and the theater's stuffy air and stifling heat. Gathering the strands of her fraying temper, Nora forced a rigid smile. "I've had enough for one evening. I should like to go home."

Daniel had stayed behind with his parents, his face miserable and apologetic, as Dr. Croft led Nora away to his carriage. They were silent most of the way home, Nora's tears escaping down her cheeks, until Dr. Croft felt moved to pat her reassuringly on the arm.

"Pair of troglodytes," he said, fumbling in his pockets. Instead of a handkerchief, he retrieved the end of a roll of lint and passed it to her. "What a disaster."

Nora sobbed a laugh. "It certainly was." Outside the gas-lights threw the muddy streets into bleak shadows.

"One of these days that woman will die of apoplexy," Dr. Croft said.

"Only if dyspepsia doesn't finish her first."

He cast a secret smile out the window, thoughts crossing his face that he didn't share. "Don't give them a thought. You behaved yourself becomingly."

The lace cuffs of Nora's dress blurred as she looked at them. "I understand your aversion to London society now."

They parted inside the house, on the stairs. As Nora made her way to her room, she wondered how much of her feelings he perceived. She hardly understood the dragging wretched-ness herself. Most individuals would be happy to discover they stood to inherit a fortune.

But she couldn't forget Daniel's appalled stare, or cease worrying about what it might mean. Once he'd escorted his parents back to their hotel, he would come home and tell her.

She hoped.

Daniel gazed at the front of the house, once fine, now presiding over a rather down-at-heel street. Often over the past months, when his eyes snagged on flaking paint or fraying upholstery, he'd held in a sigh of irritation, wondering what Croft spent his money on—for it certainly wasn't appearances. He had none of the common vices and positively flaunted his disdain for luxuries. Aside from stocking his clinic, and a generous allowance for pur-chasing specimens and books, Croft spent hardly anything at all.

Over the course of his career, the fees amassed from his wealthy patients, from teaching—even from his lowly clinic, for the volume of patients treated there was astounding—would be sizable.

Daniel hadn't considered that, but he should have. *Idiot*, he scolded, staring at the windows burning yellow against the warm night. Inside, somewhere, was a working-class orphan turned heiress. A girl turned scientist. A woman who'd impressed him beyond measure tonight. She had taken the worst of his parents as quietly as a lamb, enduring much more than he had any right to expect of her. Daniel clutched the iron rails girding the house and tried to think of how to apologize.

Horace's ill-timed declaration tonight had complicated everything. How would it look if Daniel confessed his feelings now, moments after discovering she stood to inherit every last farthing? His earlier caution would look like reluctance outweighed now by the sums in pounds sterling. Not only would Nora suspect his motivations, but Horace would as well.

He wanted to walk inside, take her hand, and apologize for his parents' shameful treatment of her, to groan aloud, like he'd wanted to at dinner, and lay his head in her lap. It looked blessedly tempting in his mind's eye, with Nora sweeping his hair away with her smooth fingers as he pressed his ear against her leg, cushioned by her soft green skirts. His breath hitched, but he steadied it as he climbed the stairs.

He opened the door, his ears pricked, bracing himself for tears. Though he fled the watery storms of his sisters and mother, he would stay and comfort Nora's. If, in contrast, he found her giddy with joy for the wealth she stood to gain, he would press a glass of brandy into her hand and toast her like a queen. And if he found another scene like the night of the surgery—torn notes and scalding words—he would take the heat of her anger as patiently as she had taken his parents' scorn.

It was worse than he feared—silence and empty rooms.

The only person about was Mrs. Phipps, rocking in her favorite chair and watching him as he entered. Her frown was a walled city, fierce in its stony stillness.

"Nora has retired to bed."

"I'd hoped to speak with her." He fell with a defeated sigh onto the sofa. So no duel tonight, no resolution. His heart thudded uncomfortably. What to do with his nerves now that he'd braced for a scene?

"What would you have said to her?" Horace's shadow filled the doorframe.

Daniel flinched in surprise, but he returned his gaze to his feet and removed his shoes. They were making a blister on the side of his arch. "I don't know. I was going to see how she felt first. I was certainly going to apologize for my parents. I know they were frightful. My break from Miss Edwards hit their pride and their pocketbook more than I realized. They had plans for Mae's inheritance."

Mrs. Phipps sniffed and rolled her frown into a low grumble of words not meant to be understood.

Croft stomped into the room and stood before the empty fireplace, his evening clothes stripped off except for his shirt and trousers. His sleeves hung loose without the gold cuff links gifted him by the Earl of Liverpool. "Do you have intentions?"

The rocking chair creaked as Phipps leaned forward.

"Even if I did, I couldn't declare them now," Daniel snapped, his cheeks reddening. "The timing is terrible. What would she think of me? What would you?"

Croft pursed his lips and waited in silence until Daniel met his eyes. The clock on the mantel should have beat out the long seconds, but in the excitement of the day Mrs. Phipps had neglected to wind it, and it was stalled at fourteen minutes past six. If only he could return to that moment, before this evening's debacle.

"You know I have the greatest respect for Miss Beady. She is brilliant and charming." Daniel's voice caught on a briar of emotion and tore, so he closed his mouth before anyone detected the wound. He blinked furiously, trying to clear his thoughts of the sudden image that had arrested him. It was simply her face. Her intelligent eyes and expressive mouth turned up into a warm smile.

Croft growled impatiently, so Daniel cleared his throat and went on. "You cannot blame me for their rudeness. I've risked everything to work with you. You know I don't feel as they do."

Croft assented with a brisk nod. "I suggest you make that clear to Nora before there is a misunderstanding."

Daniel looked up and saw Mrs. Phipps's mouth open, but she snapped it closed and glared when she saw him looking.

Was Croft warning him off? Daniel closed his eyes. Horace didn't know there was anything between him and Nora. But his voice blazed with rebuke.

"I will," Daniel said woodenly, stupidly, unsure if he had just agreed to declare his love or leave her alone.

He walked to his room like a man wandering a foreign street, hoping to catch a familiar face in the crowd.

CHAPTER 26

MRS. PHIPPS CAME TO HER ROOM EARLY THE NEXT morning. Nora half expected Daniel, with words of contrition and consoling promises, so Mrs. Phipps was a disappointment.

Of course, she knew better. Daniel would never come alone to her bedchamber, which was why she'd retreated here. Only now she regretted it, wishing she'd stayed and spoken with him last night. As Mrs. Phipps let in the morning light, Nora sat up, mentally inspecting the hollow spot under her ribs where her doubts had pooled into a nauseating collection of disappointments. Even that made no sense. The list of triumphs was long: the extravagant dinner, opulent theater, news of her future inheritance. The list of defeats was small: the Gibsons' sneers, and the unreadable but unpleasant expression that crossed Daniel's face when Croft pronounced her his heir.

Did he think her unworthy of the doctor's generosity? Perhaps he found it unpalatable that a girl who did nothing more than recover from cholera should rise so high.

She flung off the covers, her temper expanding. *He's a snob born to snobs.*

Mrs. Phipps turned her head. "Tetchy this morning?"

"Perhaps," Nora snapped.

Normally that would earn a sharp reproof, but the old woman smiled. "Good. I hate being stormy all alone. Those people!"

Nora accepted her dressing gown from Mrs. Phipps and swept her hair off her face. "Did Dr. Croft tell you, then?"

"I gathered enough. Dr. Gibson is drifting around in a fog. I think he is embarrassed by them." Mrs. Phipps studied Nora as if rummaging for any clue of her feelings but Nora had only one emotion to share—confusion.

"Perhaps you should speak to him," Mrs. Phipps offered as she stepped up to Nora with a brush in hand.

"Why?" Nora asked, submitting her hair to be stroked and smoothed.

"Because you are both baffled. I suppose it would be better to know what you're about."

Mrs. Phipps found a pin that had hidden in Nora's hair, making a tangle as she slept on it. She eased it out while Nora thought in silence.

Her eyes closed in pain. "I think I will stay in my room until he leaves for the day."

"You can't hide forever." Mrs. Phipps pulled Nora's chin round to peer into her severe and wrinkled face. "But you can torture him for a morning. I believe he deserves it."

Nora leaned her head into the woman's weathered hand. "Thank you."

It worried Daniel that he got no glimpse of Nora the next morning. He needed to speak with her, to map out the miles of distance he now knew lay between them.

"You can't dawdle," Horace said, shoveling in another mouthful of eggs, his eyes scanning the latest issue of the *Boston Medical and Surgical Journal.* "Corden's sticking his neck out, inviting you back. Won't do to be late."

Daniel forced down his coffee, then he and Croft picked up their bags and went.

Though overjoyed to be back, it was damned uncomfortable for Daniel at St. Bartholomew's Hospital, and it had nothing to do with the heat collecting on the stones and bricks of the congested city. It was not the crush of jealous elbows vying for spots in the demonstrations, where lives hung by catgut threads, and grandstanding surgeons competed for praise and recognition. All that he had adjusted to years ago as a student at the Sorbonne, and then as a wound dresser at University College Hospital. The crush and noise and smell were only vague inconveniences. The problem was the black-eyed, black-haired giant of a man who grimaced whenever he crossed Daniel's path: Silas Vickery.

Last week, Vickery had demonstrated an amputation midway along the femur, completing the grueling procedure (for patient and surgeon) in an astonishing eighty-two seconds. The buzz over Daniel's surgery was diminishing Vickery's acclaim. Hatred glittered in his eyes, so Daniel stuck close to Croft, shielded in part by his indifference.

Right now, Croft was as untroubled as ever, listening to the chest of a young man, barely more than a child, who had gone to the copper works to earn his living and returned home sick and wheezing, the weight falling off of his spindly body.

Harry bent his red head close to Daniel and murmured, "I

had a young shipmate with a breathing disorder, but I could never sort it out. He was fine if we didn't run him too fast. Weak constitution."

Daniel nodded, grateful to have Harry volunteer any comment, especially a natural and friendly one.

Croft pressed his ear to the wooden tube and then moved it down to the fifth rib. Before Daniel could ask if the symptoms were perhaps the beginning of consumption, Vickery strutted into the room.

Horace glanced up as if a fly had buzzed too close and went back to work. "Perhaps Doctor Vickery can enlighten us?"

Silas Vickery's smile was a horrible thing to behold, slippery and cruel. "I've come only to deliver this morning's paper."

He extended the rolled sheets to Daniel and deposited them graciously into his surprised hand. "Good day to you," Vickery said and bowed himself out.

Daniel stood in stunned quiet, looking to Horace for direction, but Croft was equally perplexed.

"Oh, hell," Harry cursed and took the paper. "What will it be?" It was only then that Daniel put the pieces together. There must be wretched news for him or Horace. A fire? Slander? A lawsuit?

The young man in the bed tried to continue describing his symptoms but Horace hushed him. "It's hysteria from the dark and confined spaces, most likely. Your lungs sound robust," he murmured and turned away from the boy's stunned face. Every doctor in the pack scrutinized Harry's expression for a clue as he scanned the lines.

"Here it is." Harry swore again and pushed his face closer to the words. "Third page."

"There has recently been circulating a fantastic account of surgery on the inner vitals of the stomach of a shipman docked in London. Disgraced doctor Daniel Gibson of the surgical practice at 43 Great Queen Street boasts of the unprecedented accomplishment of repairing a deadly hernia while his patient slept peacefully and recovered fully. Fearing the scientific community is being duped by the ego of a man eager to regain his good name, renowned surgeon Silas Vickery of St. Bartholomew's invites Doctor Gibson and his mentor, Doctor Horace Croft, to a public meeting to defend their scientific claims."

There was more but Daniel only heard the echo of his own disbelief, filling his ears and blocking the sound of the other doctors' protests. He'd attended many such symposiums, from dull recitations of treatments to raucous debates that ended as vicious shouting matches.

"When?" he asked quietly, but no one heard.

Croft laughed, muttering a few choice words for Vickery that broke through Daniel's fog and made him smile in spite of himself. "We'll make him eat crow in front of every doctor in London," Horace promised, and the doctors surrounding him perked up like boys invited to a cockfight.

Daniel's dark frown returned. Vickery was a calculating and careful man. Something twisted inside his stomach, and he looked to Harry to see his worry mirrored—perhaps even multiplied.

Vickery knew something they didn't.

⁓

"Forget about your parents," Nora said, brushing aside his apology as she broke into her soft boiled egg. "I never expected them to like me."

Daniel studied her face doubtfully. "I'm ashamed of them," he added.

Her eyes lifted to his, but he could not read the thoughts in them. The morning sun played through the tall parlor windows and landed on her shoulder like a tame song bird. "Let's forget it," she suggested. "We've too many other problems to borrow a new one."

Daniel swallowed, then gave a reluctant nod.

"You still look worried. Is that on my account, or Vickery's?" she asked.

"Both," he admitted.

"Every medical detail of your paper was true. Vickery cannot prove any of it wrong." She glanced down at the newest copy of the *Provincial Medical and Surgical Journal* spread out before her.

"Only it wasn't my surgery." Daniel gave her a rueful grin and set his toast down on the tray only half buttered.

"I'd rather wipe the floor with that slippery man than have all the accolades in England," she pronounced.

"Would you?"

The certainty drained from her face like water sliding down a grate.

Daniel steadied his voice. What he said must be given in the most factual terms, void of all pathos. He didn't realize he was still clutching the butter knife. "I fear someday you will hate me." When her head snapped up he continued, certain of her attention. "I worry time will cloud the memories and you will somehow remember me as the man who stole your work instead of the man trying to shield you." He silenced her protest by speaking over her. "Time does cruel things."

Something churned behind her eyes. A worried crease cut into the smooth skin between her eyebrows as the truth of his words marched across her face. She dipped her head and pinched the tablecloth between her fingers, twisting it methodically as the seconds passed. At last her voice ventured out. "You say 'remember' as if one day you will only be a memory."

The breath Daniel had been holding released, leaving behind a bemused grin. "*That* worries you? More than this mock trial and public scrutiny and the fact you cannot tell the world what you accomplished that night?"

She caught the grin hiding in his eyes and drew back. "Don't laugh! It's all terrible enough without that. I hate Silas Vickery. I hate that I cannot face our accusers and explain exactly what we did." Her fervent words slowed and she turned away. "But yes, I also hate you speaking of being only an irksome memory."

Daniel rose and took the empty cushion on the sofa beside her. "I'm sorry." His voice was as sincere as the touch he placed on the fists held tight in her lap. Her hands loosened, but only fractionally. "I wasn't mocking you. I just find you a wonderful mystery." More words came to his mind, ready formed, automatic, but he pressed his lips together, fully aware of what it would mean if he let them loose. Her fist tightened again and she turned to him, so close he could count every golden fleck lurking in her fawn-colored eyes. A harsh shout from outside made her draw back and glance to the window.

A loud woman trundling a cart down the street passed by, hollering about her sore feet to a companion who was either nearly deaf or soon would be from such volume. Nora's eyes crinkled and she released a buoyant laugh. "Should we invite her inside? Offer to help her?"

Grinning, Daniel put one hand at the top of her neck, cradling the back of her head in the empty cup of his palm. Her eyes registered no reluctance, not even surprise. Not once did he think of the fine shape of her occipital bone, nor the curve of the cervical vertebrae as his finger trailed along them. "The clinic's closed. Bunions and corns can wait until later." So could his worries over Silas Vickery.

He bent her head up, thinking only of the softness of her lips as he gently explored them in the warm morning light.

Nora had been too busy with the clinic, ether, and her research to visit St. Bart's. Or so she told herself. The truth was, full days were a convenient excuse. She'd avoided the place since barging into the Athenaeum club, but if she meant to show her face at Vickery's so-called symposium, she'd have to rediscover her courage. If she couldn't pass these men in a hospital corridor, knowing what they'd said of her, how would she ever sit through the debate tomorrow evening?

She wouldn't, so she'd talked herself into putting on her

new hat and an unobtrusive walking dress and marched herself to the hospital, carrying a basket with Horace's forgotten
notebooks and his left-behind lunch. He was always forgetting
things, and she used to relish errands like this that offered the
chance to watch a demonstration or listen to the end of a lecture from outside the theater door. She'd wander about, peering
into the wards and watching the doctors as she pretended to
look for Dr. Croft. It was easy to do when no one bothered to
take notice of her.

She certainly would be taken notice of now, and it made
her uncomfortable. The porter at the door admitted her, but he
spared no extra civilities. "I expect you'll find Dr. Croft in the
upstairs wards," he told her.

Nora thanked him and walked away as fast as she could,
telling herself it was foolish to imagine everyone was watching her. These men—and the nuns bearing trays and scrubbing
stairs—all had work to do.

A young doctor passed her on the landing, then jumped
back a step. "Miss Beady."

"Good afternoon, Doctor." She recognized him, but couldn't
for the life of her remember his name. She'd never needed it
before. She'd passed him countless times—once, standing next
to him at the back of a lecture, he'd silently offered to sharpen
her pencil, assuming she was taking notes for Dr. Croft—but
he'd never addressed her by name before.

He glanced at her basket. "Smells good." He smiled. "Who's
the lucky man? Dr. Gibson or Dr. Croft?"

Nora narrowed her eyes. "Dr. Gibson never forgets his
meals," she said. "Nor would he expect me to bring them to

him. Have you seen Dr. Croft?" she asked, anxious to deliver her burden and be gone.

"In the surgical ward." He jerked his head, but Nora was already walking past him. She found Horace in a second-floor corridor, scribbling a note to himself on his shirt cuff.

"Ah. Excellent," he said when she passed him an open notebook.

"Mrs. Phipps said to remind you to eat your pie," Nora said, frowning at his ruined shirt.

"Of course." He reached into the basket absently. "I'd show you some of the patients, but I have a surgery on an ingrown toenail to start."

Nora winced. That was one she didn't mind missing. The method was easy—the pain insufferable. Horace had a dread of fingernails and toenails because his own were so sensitive.

"You've hacked off limbs on a battleship so don't look so cowed by a toenail. I'll see you at dinner," she said. "You can tell me how it goes."

On her way out, she practiced her calm face and confident air, until stopped by a whispered argument hissing from the shadows near the back exit. She could not recognize either man and paused, wondering if it was better to retreat to another door or to walk past them, pretending deafness as a nun or nurse might. Before she could decide, the quarrel ended, the two men breaking apart like splintered ice. One vanished outside. The other, marching furiously toward her, was Harry.

"Nora!" He twitched with something almost like fright, his feet freezing in place.

"Are you in trouble? Who was that?" she asked.

He passed a hand over his forehead, then glanced swiftly over his shoulder. "This way," he said, taking her by the arm. He steered her around the corner and into a dingy courtyard. "Sorry. That was Vickery. Just giving me another dressing-down."

Nora's brows pinched together. "He'll have to let up after tomorrow evening," she said. "All the doctors will be on your side soon."

"Of course," Harry said with a mechanical smile. "The meeting." He pressed his lips together. "I've been meaning to speak to Daniel and Dr. Croft about tomorrow. I don't think I can join them onstage. They are both eloquent men, and I'm—"

Nora stopped him with a hand on his arm. "What do you mean?"

He squirmed under her gaze. "It will be better for them if I don't go."

Nora stared, appreciating for the first time how much Harry had changed in the last two months. His usually cheerful face was now worn and harassed. "You can't back out now. You're critical. And since the paper was published naming you as the other surgeon, your career depends on it as much as Daniel's."

Harry shook his head. "I should never have agreed. I'm a liability."

Nora dropped her voice to a whisper. "Harry, it's nothing more than describing the surgery, and you know every detail." She took a bracing breath. "Everyone expects to hear from you."

He looked away, scrubbing a hand through his untidy hair. "I know what they all expect." He raked his eyes across the empty courtyard, unable to hide the fear of being overheard. "I just… If I were to lose my place at St. Bart's—"

"You won't." Nora squeezed his arm. "And if you did, Horace would find work for you."

"He's a great doctor, but he can't hold the entire profession at bay, Nora." Harry's misery faded into a comfortless smile. "Though if anyone could, I'd bet on him."

Nora colored and brought her hand back to her side, hiding it behind her skirts. Perhaps Harry no longer wanted to work from Great Queen Street. After all, until recently, he'd been—to borrow a phrase from the kitchen maids—walking out with her. Now they were civil, barely even friends. "I'm sorry, Harry. I shouldn't keep you. I'm sure you have things to do," she said.

"Yes. Vickery will flay me alive if I don't…" His voice trailed off, and Nora's stomach spasmed with guilt.

"Will you dine with us tonight?" she asked. "You can speak with Daniel then. You might feel better if you practice what you'll say together."

Harry winced. "I'm expected at dinner with an old ship-mate, I'm afraid," he said.

Nora tilted her head. His words felt like a lie, but it would be unkind to insist on the truth. "Rum and tobacco and who knows what else?" she asked.

He relaxed into something almost like his usual smile. "Don't make me admit it."

"Don't be up too late," she scolded teasingly.

"Certainly not." He gave her a mock salute, not quite himself, but close enough.

CHAPTER 27

DANIEL EXPECTED VICKERY'S ENTOURAGE AT THE PUB-
licly advertised meeting—grim old doctors posted like
guardians over the knowledge they'd collected and hoarded
for decades. He expected the lively young pack from medical
school who had no notions of loyalty, relishing a bloodbath
of scientific ideas as eagerly as they sliced into cadavers. He
expected a few old men who found the topic of research and
medicine ghoulishly attractive to slide out of their London
town houses and take in a free evening of entertainment.

But when he entered the lecture hall, he did not expect
the good number of women, leaning on the arms of their
escorts and talking in bright tones. There were no poor
here, as there would be at a public trial, but a good number
of the middle class had answered the call to spectate this
public brawl of words. It was an altogether festive affair,
with a subtle undercurrent of hunger. They had come to see
someone humiliated and would not be satiated without a
disgrace.

Daniel swore quietly. All this, and no sign of Harry.

Twice yesterday he'd cornered Daniel and explained with
increasing frustration why it would be better for all parties if
Daniel answered the questions alone.

"I wasn't there, Daniel. Do you realize how easily I could be tripped up on a question, or get a detail wrong?"

"You've read the paper."

"A hundred times, but—"

"I'm counting on you," Daniel said, losing patience at last. "I'll see you tonight at eight o' clock."

And it was already half past seven.

Daniel pushed through the crowd, set a hand on Horace's arm, and leaned in to whisper, "I don't see Harry."

Horace glanced about the room and frowned. "I'll nip over to his lodging. He can't desert now."

The comment surprised Daniel. "Did he speak to you, too?"

"Said he wasn't feeling up to it. I'll fetch him." And with that, Horace was off, leaving Daniel beside a surprised-looking young student, with nothing to say and a compelling urge to consult his watch.

"Good evening." Daniel nodded at the student, then made a quick circuit of the room until he caught sight of Carl and Myrtle Denwitten, Mae's cousin and his wife, all the way from Richmond. He stopped, unable to hide his surprise, but the moment he gathered himself to approach them, they turned pointedly away. Sweat collected in his palms. What he hoped was a localized feud had spread farther than he realized, and no doubt whatever happened tonight would be reported to his parents by dinner tomorrow. Meanwhile, Horace's chair stood empty and Vickery sat enthroned next to the empty place onstage, making a show of studying notes.

Daniel heard a burst of laughter and turned to see a plumed society matron smiling at Horace Croft, who must have returned without Daniel noticing. He'd brought Harry—praise God—unsmiling and pale as wax, but present with a good five minutes to spare. Heaving a sigh of relief, Daniel went forward to shake his friend by the hand. "I was starting to think you weren't coming," he whispered.

"Didn't want to," Harry began. "I feel terrible. My head is ringing, my throat feels like it's been scratched to ribbons by a feral cat—"

"Stave it off for an hour," Horace interrupted, passing Harry his flask.

"You'll be fine," Daniel whispered under his breath as Harry took a long gulp, wiped his lips, then gave a pained smile.

Croft made another witticism, one Daniel had heard many times before, but it was new to the lady beside him, and she rewarded Croft with another laugh. With Harry this nervy, it was as well Croft was at his best tonight, smiling jovially and looking almost as distinguished as he ought. Phipps or Nora must have harangued him into the fine black vest and heavy gold watch chain. Croft possessed a limited reserve of expansive manners that he usually reserved for deep-pocketed patients, but they were on display for all tonight.

Daniel cocked his head at Harry and motioned to the stage. "Shall we?"

"I can't," Harry said. "Daniel—"

"Just come," Daniel said, slipping an arm around his shoulder. "I need you beside me. You needn't say much."

A few onlookers smiled at them as they wove their way across the room, and two strangers wished them well, but most watched them like a pair of racehorses, as if deciding to bet for or against them. Daniel thanked the random well-wishers as Harry followed with a stiff jaw.

"Here are the men of honor now!" Dr. Corden called as they neared the stage. He swept a hand in their direction. "Doctors Gibson and Trimble." Applause fluttered through the crowd, and Daniel felt his face go pink as the audience filtered into their seats. He spared a glance at Harry, who still did not wear any of his natural charm. Daniel's anxiety intensified to a faint echo of alarm—until Nora looked up from smoothing her gloves in a chair in the front row.

He could see as he approached that she wore the burgundy dress that she wore to church, simple, but well fitted and becoming. Next to her sat John Prescott.

"Excellent! Look who she brought," Daniel whispered to Harry.

Harry's eyes tightened. "John didn't tell me he was coming," he murmured, anxiety tinting his words.

Daniel eyed him carefully, trying to diagnose his strange demeanor. "Don't you think it will help? The best evidence of all is the living patient."

Harry adjusted his voice to more careless tones. "I was only thinking he'll show the crowd every scar he's got, and before the night is over, they'll care more about his run-in with pirates than they do about surgery."

"That is the best scenario I can imagine," Daniel murmured, smiling at the crowd through stiff lips. The vague worry gathering in his spine sharpened and raised the freshly cut hairs on the back of his neck, but there was no time to heed it now. Everyone was watching as he paused beside her.

"Miss Eleanor Beady, the finest nurse in England," Daniel said, introducing her for the benefit of the nearby crowd. "And our patient with an amazing will to survive, John Prescott."

A woman beside Prescott blushed as if she'd been introduced to a celebrity, and no wonder, for Prescott was handsome now that he wasn't fevered or gray with pain.

"Miss Beady's much comelier than our ship's doctor," John said to those standing nearby. "He's got a black tooth and a fierce hand, so you can see why I prefer help of the female variety."

Nora moved purposely to Daniel's side. Before he could speak, she tilted her head and whispered, "Is Harry all right?"

Daniel glanced to his left and saw that Harry had drifted away again.

"He's anxious," Daniel admitted. "Perhaps we're asking too much of him."

Nora pressed her lips together. "He'll feel better once we get Vickery off our backs. Be brilliant tonight. He needs it."

"It was a brilliant move to bring John," Daniel whispered, adding because he couldn't help it, "You put all the other ladies to shame tonight."

She raised her eyebrows, checking that no one was paying them any mind, saw they were still watched, then pitched her voice even lower so no one would overhear. "Are you trying to flirt with me at a scientific meeting?"

"'Try' is the correct word. I never seem to succeed."

Nora's laugh was for him alone, but the moment was too short for his liking. A slight woman, young and well dressed, advanced to where they lingered at the bottom of the stairs to the stage. She held out her hand to Nora. "Miss Beady? You are the surgeon's girl I read about?" She went on, certain of the answer. "Georgina Carmichael. I'm determined to have you to my ladies' circle. We are all bored to tears with poetry and needlepoint."

Daniel grinned, imagining Nora sharing her theories about pig swill over tea.

Harry nudged his arm. "We should take our places."

With Horace bringing up the rear, they mounted the three steps to the stage, Harry shuffling as reluctantly as if it were a scaffold. Croft took the seat next to Vickery, looking more like St. Nicholas awaiting Christmas than a man who'd been summoned here to have his reputation torn like a carcass in the street, but Vickery did not appear troubled by Croft's popular reception in the crowd. A smug and dangerous tilt to his lips was almost obscured by his neat beard. He seemed unusually pleased with himself. Daniel's stomach plummeted, and he tightened his fingers around the arms of his chair as Nora settled into her seat.

Dr. Adams had agreed to moderate the evening. Though Daniel found him cautious and uncreative, he'd been friendlier since visiting their ether demonstration. He would not tolerate too much innovation from Daniel, Harry, and Croft, nor too much hostility from Vickery. He was a fair choice.

Adams introduced the case, his paunchy stomach piping in and out like an organ as he attempted to speak loud enough for the people at the back of the hall. "It is a long-standing tradition in our community of physicians to be given the chance to explain and defend our findings, as well as refute the doubtful claims of others. Doctor Daniel Gibson and Doctor Harry Trimble have made fantastic claims about a recent procedure they performed, though both are novices of less than three years in the noble profession of surgery."

Daniel winced as Vickery straightened, a stern schoolmaster about to deliver his blows for the good of discipline and order. Croft, however, kept his easy posture and wide grin.

"If their case has been honestly presented, it is a proud feat for them and Doctor Gibson's mentor, the distinguished doctor Horace Croft. If it has been exaggerated or fabricated in any way, it is the duty of Doctor Silas Vickery and his colleagues to expose the falsehood. We will hear first from Doctors Gibson and Trimble as they acquaint us with the particulars."

Nora's stomach tightened when Harry stood to speak. She smiled, hoping to convey encouragement, but he avoided her eyes. He cleared his throat and began, his deep voice traveling around the room as he described John Prescott's symptoms, and how, two days before the surgery, he had reduced the hernia using the standard method of applying external pressure. He kept his descriptions terse and clinical and then yielded the rostrum to Daniel.

Daniel looked less burly than Harry behind the wooden stand, but more confident. He rested one hand on the surface and paused to take a sip of water. She knew how he must be trembling, but he betrayed no sign of nerves. He described John's symptoms when he arrived at the surgery, detailing a circumstance with which any experienced surgeon was familiar.

"Mr. Prescott was at a point of certain death, and I weighed whether intervention would reduce or increase his chances of survival. It was difficult to know." Sympathetic heads nodded in the audience.

"When you considered an open reduction, had you ever heard of any successful attempts?" Dr. Adams asked.

"I had never witnessed one," Daniel said, and a gust of murmur swirled up to the ceiling. "But I was aware Dr. Croft had experimented with cadavers."

Dr. Adams's frown lessened, but Dr. Vickery interjected before Nora could exhale her breath of relief. "You had seen this experiment? Tried it yourself?"

An affirmative would have been easy. Nora saw Harry plead silently for the lie, knowing Daniel would never give it.

"I had once seen it at the Sorbonne, but never attempted it."

"And the outcome of this surgery you observed as a student?" Vickery leaned forward.

Daniel's eyes were hard above the lectern. "The patient died."

The audible reaction of the crowd made Vickery raise his voice. "Yet you felt emboldened to try."

"Not trying was a guarantee of death. Mr. Prescott asked me to try."

"So we are to let patients choose their own treatments and surgery?" Vickery's voice was cold and quiet but most of the audience caught the words.

"I take it under consideration when my patient knows the risks and wishes to attempt a cure," Daniel answered.

"And you believe your patient, with no medical background

and on the point of collapse, knew the full risk?" Just the arch
of an eyebrow and Vickery could twist a question into a chill-
ing accusation. Nora's breaths turned into prayers, inhaled and
exhaled.

"Let's not labor under false pretenses." Beside her, John
Prescott rose to his feet, his right hand clenching shut as a hundred eyes swiveled to him. He raised his chin. "I knew enough. I
was a dead man without help. As a lad I served almost ten years
as a loblolly boy. I've watched more surgeries than most men
in this room. I know when a rupture means death." Nora felt a
rush of gratitude and a chill of apprehension as Vickery's gaze
narrowed on him.

"Are you a surgeon, Mr. Prescott?" Vickery asked.

"No, sir."

"Then it's possible you were mistaken." Vickery's eyes
flashed.

Prescott's temper was getting the better of him. His face
flushed. "Excuse me, Doctor, but I believe mistakes are possible for surgeons as well as mere mortals. Seeing I'm alive and
well today, I don't see as Dr. Gibson made any. He and Miss
Beady—"

"Miss Beady? Was a lady present?"

"She was in the house when I arrived. She helped me inside,
with Dr. Gibson."

Daniel cleared his throat. "Dr. Croft's ward, Miss Beady,
keeps the surgical records and cares for the patients. She is a
competent nurse and helps run the charity clinic."

Vickery's face turned calculating. "But what of Dr. Trimble?
Where was he?"

"He arrived later, after I'd administered the ether," Daniel said before John Prescott could speak.

"You began this procedure without consulting another surgeon? Alone?"

"Mr. Prescott was in the greatest distress," Daniel began. "I gave him ether to save him from pain. I could not administer laudanum because he was unable to swallow anything. I hadn't yet decided—"

"When did you decide? And what about Dr. Trimble?" Vickery said. "You were remarkably lucky he turned up in such opportune fashion."

Seated behind Daniel, Harry opened his mouth to speak, but closed it again. A violent crimson overtook his throat and spread like a rash, mottling his cheeks.

"What day was the surgery, again?" Vickery continued.

"It was the twenty-second of May," Daniel affirmed.

"I'm afraid that can't be," Vickery said. Shaking his head, he rose from his chair. "It pains me to discredit a colleague who might once have shown promise, but deceit cannot be allowed to stand." Filling his lungs, he pointed dramatically at Daniel. "This man's claims are nothing but lies, dangerous lies to a hopeful public who must be protected from charlatans and amateurs. Patients who are forced by necessity to submit to the knife must know they will be treated by men who are trustworthy and professional, not radicals trying to redeem their reputations by hopeless and unlawful experiments. Dr. Gibson was alone that night, and I have proof."

The hall went still. Nora watched, sick, as Vickery turned his head and waited, as if some truth were about to burst onto the stage. In the audience, eyes swiveled across the room, looking for the promised evidence. A reluctant voice croaked behind Daniel.

"I wasn't there."

Nora didn't mean to gasp. The sound tore out of her involuntarily, but was lost in the reaction of the crowd. Daniel spun as though struck and stared at Harry, but Harry refused to meet his eyes. "I had treated John before, but I wasn't present for the surgery."

Daniel's face went as white as Harry's was red. Alone and exposed at the rostrum, he resembled a martyr facing a hungry lion.

"So this alleged surgery has no witness." Vickery's tone softened to a sad confusion that made his words all the more terrible. "And Dr. Gibson pressed you to lie for him out of friendship?"

Harry responded only with a clenched jaw and miserable expression.

What had Vickery done to turn him? Fury coursed through Nora, warmer and thicker than blood.

"The patient's alive, Silas," Horace growled, leaning forward in his chair. "You can't argue with that."

"Wait, Horace." Dr. Adams silenced him with a hand. "I'm interested in these questions. Spectacular claims must be verified."

Vickery preened. "Every surgeon knows that opening the bowels is exquisitely dangerous and impossible to perform without assistance. Seasoned surgeons rarely attempt it."

Nora glanced from Daniel to Dr. Croft. Even in the middle

of the most desperate surgeries, she'd never seen his knuckles go white. He couldn't defend Daniel after Harry's confession, and losing to Vickery would ruin him and Daniel both. There was no witness to save them—no one but her.

Onstage, Vickery continued, Nora's fright blurring his words. She only caught his final, dramatic flourish. "Who is to say you did not reduce the hernia in the conventional way while your patient was unconscious with your parlor gas and then cut open and sew the skin to give the illusion of a groundbreaking surgery?"

Ears ringing, Nora rose to her feet, her voice foundering under a wave of noise from the crowd. Daniel flinched, his mouth moving in warning, and though she couldn't hear him, the message was clear. *Don't, Nora.* The last time she'd tried to help, it had only hurt.

"Sir." She tried again. "Sir, I insist you let me speak." The hall quieted. She sped on, before her courage failed. "The details of the surgery are accurate. Dr. Gibson was not without assistance. He had mine. I witnessed everything."

CHAPTER 28

FOR A MOMENT, VICKERY STOOD MUTE, A GHASTLY EFFIGY.
Nora fought the impulse to quail and shrink. The narrowed eyes of the crowd struck her, but she remained on her feet. Perhaps Vickery was too confounded to address her directly, but in disbelief, his sharp eyes darted from her slender fingers, steady despite her trembling legs, to her eyes. Vickery's mouth opened a fraction as he breathed out a sigh of both shock and victory. "I would love to hear what you have to say, Miss—?"

"Beady. Eleanor Beady. As you very well know." She sensed the stir her name caused among the doctors, but this wasn't the Athenaeum club or the halls of St. Bart's. It was worse.

"Go on, Miss Beady." Vickery's slick words spilled across the stage. Daniel clutched the rostrum as if losing his balance.

Dr. Croft stepped forward, his stern face reminding Vickery that his unusual path to renown had led him through ten fierce years in the navy. "We are here to discuss a surgery, not harass innocent young ladies."

Vickery folded his arms. "She is the one who insisted we hear her, Horace. For years you've let us believe this charity case in your classes was keeping your notes and running your errands. I'm vastly interested to know what she witnessed in your home when she was left alone with a disreputable surgeon."

Nora fought the urge to melt back into her seat. She was not sure if the voices were garbling or growing louder. A bit of both.

"You've kept this poor orphan as your pet," Vickery sneered at Croft, "an experiment you concluded and decided to keep. Tell me, do you use her when dogs and mice do not suffice?"

The crowd gasped. Croft and Daniel moved toward Vickery just as Dr. Adams rose, waving his hands. "Gentlemen, please! I cannot allow insults to any lady," he cried. Dr. Croft's clenched hands spurred encouraging yells from a handful of medical students who had long dreamed of fisticuffs with Silas Vickery.

"And there will be no violence!" Dr. Adams barked. He took over the rostrum, glaring at the doctors on the stage until all returned to their seats. "We will remember our position as men of science! And we will remember the sensibilities of the people in attendance this evening." Dr. Adams's voice shook. He was too mild a man to moderate a brawl. "Dr. Croft, you may answer the charges."

It was a loaded word, fizzing like a fuse through the audience.

"Dr. Vickery." Nora pitched her voice louder. "Dr. Vickery. You leveled a charge at me. I'm perfectly capable of speaking."

The crowd tittered. Vickery, thrown off balance, snapped, "You are not a surgeon. You have no standing here."

"You demanded a witness," she replied evenly. "There is only me."

Vickery snorted. He scanned the crowd, refusing to meet her eyes. "Dr. Croft is responsible for her. He must explain."

Observing the reaction of the crowd with the same critical stare he gave his experiments, Dr. Croft started in measured words. "From her early years, Miss Beady has shown a keen mind. Living in my home, she has naturally been surrounded by research and experiments. She moved from helping me clean up afterward to assisting me in them. It helps to have an assistant with smaller hands. She's capable."

"Capable of what?" Dr. Vickery asked. "Have you made a woman into a loblolly boy?"

"You seem to forget the sisters who pass by you every day in hospital, doing the skilled work of healers and nurses. Miss Beady continues their tradition of mercy."

Nora thanked God there was an audience. Dr. Croft might have murdered Vickery already without it.

"First a foundling, then a scientist, now a saint!" Vickery thundered.

"I make no claim to the last." Nora glanced from Daniel to Dr. Croft, wishing for the first time she had never allowed her curiosity to turn into proficiency. Never had it felt like a detriment until this moment when those she loved were floundering to protect her. "Now, may I speak?"

If she hoped courage and dignity would temper Vickery's ferocity, she fooled herself.

"Caution, Croft. Whatever she says now is witnessed by a host of professionals." Vickery threw his arm toward the audience. "Such things can have a person committed—"

Dr. Croft's eyes crackled with fury and he steeled his chin. "She is my ward, and I'll not allow any asylum to seize her. Let her speak or accept Dr. Gibson's word."

"That seems reasonable enough, so long as she is willing," Dr. Adams said.

He gestured to Nora who firmed her lips and made her way to the stage, acutely aware of the strange numbness in the tops of her arms and the backs of her legs.

Dr. Adams offered her his hand on the stairs. Vickery simply glared from behind his folded arms and demanded, "Miss Beady, what role did you play in this farce?"

"If you consider successful surgery a farce, then I don't know what you are doing in the profession," Nora replied, emboldened by Dr. Croft's snort of laughter. "I agreed to be extra hands during the surgery. Someone must hold clamps and pass tools."

You are not a medical student, Nora reminded herself. *Or a hospital dresser.* And she'd done considerably more than hold clamps and pass tools. She licked her lips, trying to gauge the sentiment of the crowd. "I could not let a man die for the sake of convention. It may not be common for a woman to be present during procedures, but desperate times…"

"Miss Beady," Vickery bellowed, "I accuse you of practicing medicine without a license." He turned to the crowd, gesturing like a preacher warning of the apocalypse. "And all along, she has been encouraged by Dr. Croft. He must be fined. He must be subjected to the college's discipline. The work of this woman—untutored, unlicensed—cannot be permitted. The risk to the public—"

"You forget, Silas, that the patient is alive," Dr. Croft put in. "How many of yours have survived such a surgery?"

"Here, here!" Someone lobbed a shout from the back.

"I would never attempt such a thing," Vickery hissed. "No sound man would."

"Then Mr. Prescott must be grateful he didn't come to you,"

Nora said. "It is true I have no license, but who would grant me one? And I am not untutored. I have observed the practice of a renowned physician and surgeon for ten years. Most surgeons of the world would envy my education with Horace Croft. It is far more advanced than many of your surgeons in hospital."

"And so you made the formidable leap from watching to assisting with the surgery of John Prescott's hernia?" Vickery demanded.

"I did. As I said before, necessity compelled me." Blood pounded in her ears, muffling the stirring crowd, and though tempted to glance their way, she kept her eyes on Vickery.

He stroked his beard with manicured fingers. "If you are as learned as you claim, I assume you will understand my terminology, but you may stop me when I confuse you. When the bowel appeared necrotic, why did Dr. Gibson proceed with a dangerous and hopeless surgery?"

The crowd was silent. Nora licked her lips. "Because it was impossible to tell the source of the discoloration. It could have been black with necrosis, which would have been an agonizing death, but it also could have been a small impaction or bruising, or clotted blood."

Vickery's eyes narrowed. "If the bowel was truly strangulated and dead as you say, John Prescott would not be sitting behind me today."

"It was strangulated, but it was not dead, though at first it appeared so, which was why we couldn't simply reduce it. Mr. Prescott's hernia was dangerously trapped against…" Nora glanced at the audience, realizing she'd stumbled into a trap. Everyone waited for her next word, including a lady in the second row, busily applying her fan. Admitting the hernia was trapped against the spermatic cord in front of these devouring eyes was impossible.

"Against what, exactly?" Vickery's smile chilled her. "Do you know where an inguinal hernia is located?" He turned to the audience as though gravely concerned. "In the interests of scientific inquiry, I must proceed, but I am afraid some of the details we uncover will be far from polite. Any ladies present may wish to leave rather than hear such unpleasantness."

No one dared retreat after such a tantalizing promise. The fans moved faster. Nora blanched, but she kept her voice even. "Of course I know."

"Did you *see* this hernia?" he asked.

Anger raced like a fire under her skin, consuming her. She did not mean to glance at Daniel but could not stop the impulse. His steely eyes only confused her. When she didn't answer, Vickery repeated the question.

"Did you see the hernia?"

"I did. I'd hardly present myself as a witness otherwise."

"In such close proximity to this man's reproductive organs? Forgive me, ladies and gentleman, but for the sake of science, we must be clear." At least two of the ladies in the audience pretended to faint.

"It's not so scandalous as you say." John Prescott stood, his mouth in a handsome smile. "I could show you the scar. It's a good six inches from anything delicate." He sauntered up to the stage, and a lady in the front row gasped while the rowdy medical students roared in laughter. "I trust they covered my dignity during the procedure." He pulled a chair from backstage and settled into it beside Dr. Croft. John didn't look at Harry, whose own eyes seemed fastened to the floor.

A war of words had broken out in the back of the room between supporters and detractors, giving Nora a moment to gather her courage. She said evenly, "Modesty seemed less important in the moment than Mr. Prescott's life. If I hadn't assisted, Dr. Gibson could not have saved him. Such a surgery is impossible to conduct alone, even with restraints. It was my idea to use the ether."

"Your idea?" Vickery's eyes glittered and he turned to Daniel. "The most fantastical element of the surgery was not your doing, Dr. Gibson?"

"You've made a circus of this proceeding," Daniel spat out in disgust.

"*I?* When you speak of a woman performing parlor tricks and surgery?" Vickery gestured for the crowd to scoff with him. They did not disappoint.

Nora allowed her eyes to focus just long enough to assess the circle of men surrounding her. At her left side, Horace hovered, a lethal desperation in his eyes, while Daniel froze on her other side, gray tinged and lock jawed. Harry hung his miserable face, his wish to disappear as tangible as the shock in the room. Before her, Vickery towered, his beard trembling with triumph, and behind her, John's eyes were wide and bemused. She felt herself suspended inside a storm cloud, the electric charges crackling dangerously around her and her only retreat a fatal fall.

"Saving a man's life involves no trickery," Nora declared. "But you are motivated by jealousy because you lack the skill, knowledge, and courage to do what Dr. Gibson did."

"You mean what *you* did?" Vickery watched her closely, daring her to contradict him.

She swallowed. Her chin rose despite the nauseating blur of the riled audience. "Yes."

———

Daniel tried to make sense of the shouts thrown from the audience, but his ears refused to organize the angry hum into language. His friends were all casualties to these grenade-like revelations. Harry was lost to him, inexplicably turned witness for a man they both hated. Horace was bleeding dignity in silence like a bull with a slit throat. And Nora—the audience had moved to the edges of their seats, vying for a look at her as if she were on trial for her life. Daniel took a fast inventory of his lungs, the way his breath seared on intake and rushed away as if it did not want to sustain him. He was mortally wounded as well, but he must make an appeal for his friends.

"I'd like to say something."

He spoke at the volume of one speaking to a friend only a few feet away instead of to a packed hall, yet people caught the movement of his lips, and a hush fell as they leaned forward. Daniel moved toward the front of the stage but did not hide behind the lectern. "There seems to be rather a carnival atmosphere to these scientific proceedings. But we are here to discuss medicine." Daniel's quiet voice marched steadily, like a drummer advancing despite a hail of bullets.

"If one sets aside the curiosities, there is one thing left—a successful surgery. John Prescott was a dead man walking—his bowels strangulated, nothing ahead of him save the agonies of a slow death. He arrived on Dr. Croft's porch pleading for Harry Trimble," Daniel's voice caught on the name of his former friend, the loss washing fresh over him. "Dr. Trimble was not to be found. I was wrong to ask him to lie about his involvement, but I was thinking only of protecting Miss Beady from scrutiny."

"You were thinking of your career," Vickery scoffed. "It was the perfect opportunity to salvage your reputation since the only witness was a girl who couldn't reveal your deceits without revealing her own. I'd like to know if this is the only occasion you've been so criminally negligent."

Daniel's jaw tightened at the rising chorus from the crowd. If Vickery kept on stoking their fear, he'd win.

"I might not have been at the surgery, but I never said there wasn't one." Harry's Scottish burr broke over the tumult. "I didn't perform it. Even if I had been there, I probably wouldn't have attempted anything so bold, but Gibson did and it saved John Prescott's life. Prescott would not have stumbled in for help if it were not a matter of life and death. I've seen him with bleeding wounds, working under cannon fire. He does not fuss over nothing."

Vickery snarled. "You cannot be sure. You weren't there. Shall I enlighten them, Dr. Trimble?"

Hatred distorted Harry's face and Daniel waited for a flood of insults to pour forth, but Harry clenched his teeth, damming the flow, so Daniel spoke quickly, before Vickery launched his next retort. "I give my word as a gentleman, not a sentence describing the surgery was exaggerated or fabricated. Three other doctors have verified our claims about ether. We wrote our paper with complete accuracy. The only dishonesty was to exchange Eleanor Beady's name for Harry Trimble's, and that was done to avoid just this sort of persecution. I did not want such a courageous and intelligent woman harassed unjustly."

With relief, Daniel noted a few faces in the audience who looked more intrigued than scandalized. "Attempting the surgery was mad, as Dr. Vickery claims. That may be his only claim with any truth. But without intervention, Prescott's fate was death. Was I to watch him expire without attempting any relief? Miss Beady, having observed our many experiments with ether, suggested the gas could put him to sleep and release him from pain since he could not swallow opium. Our first priority was to provide relief."

"After Prescott fell insensible—that is what ether does, and I welcome another meeting to discuss its properties—his affliction looked much more manageable. In his complete stillness, he looked much like a cadaver, and I knew the surgery had been successfully performed on these. Miss Beady has been researching appendix surgeries, which are just as rare and just as dangerous. That is why her presence was so valuable."

He found Nora's face, two yards and yet a world away, her shoulders straight, ready for another lashing. He would help her if he could.

"Miss Beady is a rare species of woman. She cannot help her native intelligence. She never set out to become a scientist. Dr. Croft made no secret of his professional pursuits, and before she knew what she was about, she knew more than most medical students. She was certainly a shock to me when I came to Dr. Croft's practice nine months ago." His unsteady laugh was repeated by several people who had been holding their breath.

"But I've observed her work for many months. She's well read. She has a masterful recall. It was her suspicion the blackness in Mr. Prescott's bowel was from clotted blood and not dead tissue."

Dr. Adams interrupted. "What made you suspect a clot, Miss Beady?"

His eyes were interested, not mocking, and Nora advanced to the front of the stage, close to Daniel.

"The bowel was black but only in one spot and something about it… I—" Nora paused, her mouth half open, a smile so small only Daniel could see it playing at the corners of her lips. "It was intuition."

Several women in the audience had curious expressions, their faces agleam and puzzled.

Dr. Adams chuckled. "A feminine answer, indeed."

Nora's half-formed smile fled and she pointed to John. "You see tonight the final result of our experiment. John Prescott has years of life ahead to get himself into trouble for king and crown."

"I second that!" Prescott hollered, and the sight of him, tall and hale, pushed the spellbound hands of the audience into applause. It was not raucous, but it was sincere.

Horace slapped his hands together, like a prizefighter after a victorious bout. "Well, I hope that satisfies—"

Dr. Adams stilled him with a raised hand. "Don't rush me, Horace." He heaved a sigh and slowly found his feet. "Well." He glanced at the ceiling, then at Nora, then at the crowd. "Well. We are not assembled tonight as a disciplinary board. We have met to discuss scientific advances, and we certainly leave with much to ponder. There is evidence that this surgery, whilst not performed by Dr. Trimble, did indeed happen as described."

He rubbed his jaw. "John Prescott's survival bears witness to an exceptional surgery. Dr. Gibson admits to deceit, albeit to protect a reputation. And Miss Beady," he said, pausing before he finished, "is a most unusual addition to the discussion."

He shook his head. "Horace, it appears those who associate with you turn into first-rate surgeons. Accidentally, even." He looked over the audience and gave a small, bemused shrug. "There's much to ponder. But I believe that's enough said for one evening."

For a moment, no one moved. Like the newly woken subjects of a mesmerist, the audience hung between two realities until Dr. Adams's words asserted themselves. People shuffled to their feet, turning back to the silent stage as if hoping for an encore performance. Vickery rose, his chest bursting with anger he refused to exhale. He glared at Nora, but she didn't shrink.

Harry lifted hollow eyes to Daniel. "I can explain—"

Daniel shook his head, almost invisibly, and passed his friend like a ghost. He went to Nora and drew her away from Vickery, who was evaluating her the way a cat does a wounded mouse. A dark-haired, impeccably dressed man pushed his way up to the stage. "Miss Beady," he called anxiously, holding up his handkerchief to catch her eye. "A moment, *per favore.*"

Her feet slowed. Daniel, judging the man as an impertinent dilettante—or worse, a reporter—shielded her with his arm and hurried her down the stairs and out the rear exit. "We'd best get away," he murmured.

Unusually for her, Nora kept silent. They hadn't lost exactly, but this wasn't a clear victory, and as for what lay ahead...no one ventured a prognosis.

CHAPTER 29

"COWARD," DR. CROFT SPAT OUT AS THE THREE OF THEM climbed into the carriage to return to Great Queen Street. They all knew who he meant. Angry as he was with Vickery, Harry's wavering had won him the role of villain-in-chief. "I'll never forgive him."

He wouldn't, Nora knew. To Dr. Croft, the smart of betrayal, intellectual or otherwise, never lessened. He relished contradictions and disagreements, but disloyal sellouts were excised from his acquaintance like tumors and denounced in his writings, public and private. The heat of his anger had softened Nora's, leaving her with doubts instead.

"It makes no sense," Daniel murmured, and Nora looked at him, wondering if he'd read her thoughts. "Harry hates Vickery."

"Do you think it was a matter of his integrity?" Nora asked, remembering yesterday's encounter in the hospital corridor. "We forced him to lie."

Croft snorted. "What we saw tonight was the opposite of integrity. If Vickery doesn't ruin him, I will."

To prove the point, he marched upstairs as soon as they arrived home and slammed his bedroom door loud enough to rattle the window glass in the hall. Daniel laid his hat carefully on the console table. "Do you think you should go to him?"

"He'll feel better after ruining the points of a few pens," Nora said, and Daniel nodded.

She forced a smile. "It could have been worse."

Before he could reply, the door flew open. Daniel took a protective step in front of her before realizing the intruder was only Mrs. Phipps, red-faced and breathless.

"What—" Nora had never seen her so outraged.

"I went," Mrs. Phipps announced, pressing her hand to her tightly laced middle and leaning over to capture more air. "I saw it all. I tried to catch you after but you raced from the stage, and I was in the back."

Daniel helped her to the couch.

"So you know?" Nora asked, her face growing warm, but Mrs. Phipps didn't hear her question.

"That man! I nearly liked him! You walked with him!" Her words puffed out in a fury, and she rounded on Nora. "What were you thinking, Eleanor Beady? Now they all know!"

Daniel found words before she did. "I expect it was for me and Horace. We were floundering after Harry..." All eyes fell at the mention of his name. "How did the crowd take it where you were sitting?" Daniel asked.

Mrs. Phipps wrinkled her nose and sniffed.

"Ah," Daniel said, his hope fading.

Nora lowered herself into Croft's armchair. "I suppose Georgina Carmichael will no longer be interested in hearing from me at her ladies' circle," she murmured. A paltry loss, all things considered. Her mind veered back to the question dominating every thought. "Why did Harry do it? Whatever you say, I know he loves you like a brother, Daniel."

Daniel shook his head as if to dislodge the question from his ears.

She ventured deeper into the painful subject nonetheless. "What did Vickery mean when he said he'd enlighten us about Harry? He must be in trouble."

"Wouldn't he have told us?"

Nora tapped her fingers on the arm of her chair, but her thoughts were too disordered to formulate answers. All she had were questions, and each one bred more. Daniel scratched the back of his neck. "Let's not forget Adams accepts our account of the surgery. Since we've few other contenders, I think we should count that as a cause for celebration."

Mrs. Phipps sniffed again, a scoffing, angry sound. "I'd hardly call it a victory, but I do feel the need for wine."

"Shall I bring up a bottle of burgundy?" Nora managed a smile.

"I will," Mrs. Phipps insisted. She left the room, her shoulders uncharacteristically stooped.

"Truthfully..." Daniel studied Nora carefully. "It's generally understood these situations require something stronger."

"Stronger sounds wonderful," Nora said.

They walked into the library, where Daniel poured out two measures of whiskey.

Nora coughed. Her eyes watered. And she forced down another swallow. Blinking, she said, "Once it's inside, the warmth is rather nice."

"Just don't be in a hurry with it," Daniel said. "Especially as you haven't eaten."

They drank in silence, aware of the occasional thumps

from Horace's bedroom. He was doubtless venting his temper by stomping about or searching for some long-forgotten specimen, but—"Sounds like he's rearranging his furniture," Nora said.

Daniel grimaced. "Vickery crossed a line tonight and Horace couldn't protect you. I believe he feels it deeply." The way he looked at her suggested Horace was not the only one. When the doorbell rang, she at first mistook it for the clock and rose to her feet slowly, unsteadily.

Daniel beat her to the door. As soon as he opened it, he attempted to shut it on the worn brown shoe that pushed inside.

"Not tonight, Harry."

"I can't believe you have the nerve to show your face here," Horace stormed, passing Nora as he rushed down the stairs, his fury releasing in a flood now that he could direct it where he wanted. "Spying for Vickery with no warning—!"

"You have it wrong," Harry called as he unsuccessfully tried to force his way into the house. "Let me explain."

Daniel cut Horace short. "I can accept you turning on me, but how could you expose Nora and Horace after all they did to welcome you?" He leaned into the door. "And for God's sake, give Horace a little time."

Clutching the stair rail, Nora stepped toward them, but it was too late to reason with any of them. The shoe vanished, the door thudded shut, and Horace shouted, "I've had all the time I need!" through the thick wooden panels. He turned away from the door and lifted his eyes to Nora, blunting his sharp tirade. "My dear..." She'd never seen him so gray and wretched, or Daniel so tense and drawn.

"It's past midnight," Nora said. "Regardless of whether we can sleep, it's time we were all in bed."

⌒

She woke with a headache, long past breakfast. Mrs. Phipps had left her a tray. For a while Nora lay in bed, contemplating the prospect of cold chocolate and toast. She wasn't up to either. The fears that rose up for her own future could not eclipse the troubling worry in her stomach for Harry. He'd tried to fight his way inside last night, and that was something. He deserved to have his say, to her if to no one else. She rose, washed, put on her hat—and went out alone.

Harry was sitting on their bench, clutching a bag of uneaten buns. When she approached, he hastened to his feet.

"I didn't know how to find a way to speak to you, but I hoped you'd come walking," he said.

"I came looking for you. If you weren't here, I was going to try your lodgings." Nora sat down, took the bag from him, and bit into a bun—no longer hot, but still tasty despite the currants. "I spent most of the night lying awake thinking. I couldn't see any reason why you'd do it, save one—" Carefully, she advanced the hypothesis that had formed in the night. "Vickery must have offered you a great deal of money, or you're in a great deal of trouble."

"Three hundred pounds," Harry said flatly.

Staggered by the sum, Nora had no response.

"Might as well have been thirty pieces of silver," Harry said.

She flattened her hands against her skirts to keep them still. Though such an amount was difficult to resist, she was disappointed. "I know how it feels to long for a place in the world," she said quietly.

His head jerked sideways. For the first time he looked at her. "I turned him down. More than once, Nora. It wasn't the money. You're right about the trouble. I—" He broke off and shook his head. "I'm ashamed to tell you."

She laid her hand atop his fingers, lying on the bench beside her. They were taut and jumped at her touch, but she kept the contact, hoping to draw him out.

Harry closed his eyes. "The sailing master from my first ship lives in London. He's retired now, enjoying his family and his remaining eye."

Nora said nothing, using the silence to prod him. He continued reluctantly. "I have the greatest respect for him. He has a daughter, only seventeen. She was with child. Not her fault. She went to Tunbridge Wells with friends of the family, and some bastard forced himself on her. I'd kill him if I could." He swallowed. "Her father brought her to me late one night when I was working in hospital. Asked to see me alone. She was in a ghastly condition. She'd tried to kill herself. If you'd seen the mess she'd made of her arms…"

"Of course you helped her," Nora said.

Harry pulled away and dropped his head in his hands. "Anyone could have stitched her up, but her father asked… God help me, she was so wretched and desperate, I couldn't refuse… I relieved her of the baby. I told myself she'd kill herself otherwise, and I honestly believe she would have. I used an empty theater and took care of everything myself. But I kept her in hospital overnight, and even though I only noted the injuries to her arms on the chart, Vickery examined her and was suspicious due to the bleeding. He couldn't prove it, but he knew what I did."

"He threatened you?" Nora asked.

"It was worse than that," Harry said. "It took him a while, but he eventually remembered the date and confirmed it in the chart. The night I tended her was the same night as John's surgery."

Nora drew in a long breath.

"He knew I couldn't have been there, and so the hounding began—threats to discredit me, to investigate the girl. He said he'd protect me, give me money if I retracted the paper and discredited Daniel. I refused, but he wouldn't let up."

Harry dropped his hands and turned to Nora. "I'm all alone, you know. I can't lose my place at St. Bart's." He sighed. "Finally, I thought I saw a way out. The next time Vickery cornered me, I told him I'd agree to his terms, but only if he signed his name to my friend's daughter's chart. I needed some assurance that he wouldn't always have a hold on me. He signed happily enough. He even gave me the money. In return, I told him all he was getting from me was the truth. In his eagerness, he assumed I'd expose Daniel, but I told myself it would be all right. The truth was only that I wasn't there, which hardly disproves Daniel's testimony. But I worried, so decided it would be better if I simply failed to appear and returned the money. I tried everything I could think of to get out of it."

"I didn't listen," Nora said, remembering Harry's protests.

"No one did," Harry said bitterly, "and Daniel and Horace all but dragged me onto the stage. I was sick with worry, but I never thought what my admission might do to you."

He stared at his feet. "I don't know what to do."

Nora swallowed. It would be torture to try to continue at St. Bart's having made enemies of both Dr. Croft and Dr. Vickery, but there were other places: port cities with views of the sea, pretty inland towns.

"You could leave London," she said. "Take Vickery's money and settle someplace else. Rent a house, start your own clinic."

He grimaced. "My own life."

He'd never had one, Nora realized. He'd always been at the beck and call of His Majesty's navy, and then the board of St. Bart's. Harry straightened his shoulders. "I know a doctor in Truro looking to retire."

"Cornwall's very far," Nora said, and Harry smiled ruefully. "Far enough?"

"They'll forget eventually," Nora said, though she was by no means sure.

"It's not what I imagined, but it could be a good life."

Nora nodded.

"I imagined once I could do it as other men—a city practice worthy of acclaim and a place on the board of a hospital. I'd have a house and all the conventionalities. A wife. Children." He sighed. "For a time, I thought that wife might be you."

She stiffened.

"Of course, once Mae cut off Daniel, I suspected I was in the way."

"Harry, I—"

He waved her to silence. "It hardly matters now. I just wanted you to know."

Nora squeezed her fingers and looked at the vague space

above his shoulder. Harry looked beaten down today, and rightfully so, but he'd recover. His general air of confidence had always made her suspect he was good at pleasing women. And that he liked doing so. The thought didn't stir her; it was a clinical observation, no more.

Inevitably, unfailingly, her pulse quickened at the mention of Daniel. He had none of Harry's promise of adventure and drama, but his quiet smile and skilled fingers promised other things—loyalty and brilliance and *work*. The kind of work that filled her mind long after she finished because she could relive the moments repeatedly, committing every nuance to memory.

Harry broke his bun in half and gave part to her, so they could each have more bread to crumble and throw to the birds. "I'm sorry, Nora."

"I understand," she said as the smug pigeons pecked at their crumbs. "You were in a terrible position. I'm sure Daniel will come around as well." She paused, meeting his blue eyes and seeing true regret. "Is the girl recovering?"

Harry sighed and blew his frustration up to the sky. "Her body is sound. Her soul carries scars. She's only a child."

"It's Vickery I blame, not you."

Harry nodded, his thoughts private.

They tossed crumbs for half an hour, aiming for the shy ones, until their hands were empty and Nora brushed off her skirts.

"Good luck, Harry."

"And you. I'm—"

"I know you are," Nora said. She smiled at him.

He wrestled with words before settling on a plea. "Will you

tell Dr. Croft and Daniel why I did it? They'll hear it better from you."

Nora nodded, then watched him walk away, his step hurried, the sun bright on his hair.

Dr. Croft was pacing the hall when she returned.

"Where were you?" he demanded.

"Out for a walk," Nora told him, and nothing more.

Daniel's expression was veiled. "We were ready to summon the hounds. Are you all right?"

Nora nodded.

"I'll tell Phipps to go ahead with luncheon," Croft said. He hurried off. Daniel offered her his arm to walk into the dining room.

"You shouldn't have worried for me," Nora said. "I just needed some air." It was a thin excuse after absenting herself much of the day. She didn't think Horace would know who she had seen, but she wondered, watching Daniel as he escorted her to a chair and seated himself across the table, if he might have guessed—and what he thought about it.

CHAPTER 30

THERE WERE GAWKERS OUTSIDE THE HOUSE THE NEXT morning, a good half dozen, and the newspapers were conspicuously absent at breakfast.

"Am I in trouble?" Nora finally asked, setting aside her last half-eaten corner of toast. The bread was tasteless, and the thought of forcing down another mouthful—

"It will pass," Dr. Croft said calmly.

"Give it time," Daniel said, spreading marmalade onto his toast. He hated marmalade.

"I'll stay out of the clinic today," Nora said, half hoping they'd contradict her.

"Probably a good idea. It won't last long," Dr. Croft assured her.

She rejoined the men at luncheon, before they departed for the hospital. "It was a quieter morning," Daniel confessed, answering her worried glance.

"Billy Epsom was in to have his stitches removed and asked that we give you his best," Dr. Croft put in, trying and failing to console her.

Nora watched them walk away to St. Bart's from the drawing room window. There was no one watching the house. She donned her cloak and bonnet, intending to take a short walk, just to stretch her legs and air her worries before they turned sour. The instant she slipped out the door, she heard shouting and spun around. A flock of men rushed from the street corner, their jackets flapping.

"There she is!"

"Out of my way!"

"A moment, Miss Beady!"

Reporters.

Nora ducked inside and bolted the door, waiting until her heart slowed and the knocking ceased before moving away.

Mrs. Phipps, summoned by the commotion, watched with pity in her eyes.

"I'll stay in today," Nora told her and hurried upstairs.

That evening a letter came by messenger addressed to Dr. Horace Croft. Mrs. Phipps carried it upstairs and brought it into the library. "It's from the Royal College of Surgeons." She hesitated on the threshold, turning the letter over in her hands.

"Give it here," Horace said. Abandoning his fireside chair, he crossed the room in an eyeblink and tore open the seal. He read it through twice, grunted, and passed it to Nora.

"I don't think they know what to do with you," he said. "But as you can see, I've been fined and ordered to cease and desist from allowing unlicensed amateurs to practice in my surgery."

"Amateur?" Daniel snorted. "If they could see her—"

"The point is, they won't," Nora said, and swallowed to quiet the ringing in her ears. "Or they'd have written to me."

"They're being ludicrous." Dr. Croft tossed the letter onto

the empty grate where it rolled to a lopsided stop. He said nothing more, but Nora knew he'd noticed the careful wording. The five pound fine was particular to "Miss Beady's unlicensed treatment of one John Prescott." Five pounds here and there wouldn't hurt Dr. Croft, but if the college fined him every time she treated a patient… Nora looked away from the wad of paper, wishing for a wreath of flame to devour it.

The minute Nora left the drawing room, Croft headed straight for the whiskey and spilled out two copious glasses. Daniel accepted his dose warily, wondering what Horace meant to say that required so much liquid fortification.

Horace tipped the amber liquid down his throat and grimaced. "What do we do with her now?"

"Pardon?"

"I cannot foresee how this coin falls." Horace paced heavily before pausing at the mantel. Phipps had left the windows open to combat the stifling heat of the day, but the old man was still forced to remove his coat and loosen his sleeves as he spoke. "Perhaps the public will treat her like a curiosity, or some society favorite will think her novel and tuck her under her wing. It's possible."

The words rang hollow to Daniel. He took a seat on the leather sofa, his eyes catching the small scratches left months ago by the American scorpion who had not appreciated Croft's attempt to relieve it of its tail to study its venom. The arachnid had scrambled across the armrest, trying to sting the upholstery as Daniel ran for a specimen jar to contain it. For once, Nora had made no move to assist. Daniel grinned at the memory, but sobered quickly as his thoughts returned to the present. "You are describing the best possible outcome." He spoke more calmly than he felt. "What is the worst?"

Horace took another sip, keeping his face turned away. "They make her a public example, call her a threat to her sex. No one can institutionalize her without my consent, but if a patient sues her, I can't save her from trial or prison. Nor can I shield her from becoming a pariah. If Vickery has his way with the board of St. Bart's, that's what she'll be, and you and I tainted by association." Slowly he swung around, his shoulders sagging. Daniel read sadness in the sharp, blue eyes. "Did I do wrong by her?" Horace asked.

"Not at all," Daniel argued, reminding the man he had saved Nora's life, not only from cholera, but from the poorhouse or a home for foundlings. No, the bright woman laying her head on clean linens and dreaming of experiments she would conduct tomorrow could never say he'd done wrong by her. Daniel talked until he ran out of words, but Horace made no indication he heard any of it.

"We sent her to finishing school for a year when she was sixteen, just as Mrs. Phipps wanted. She made friends there. She does not seem unwomanly to me." Memories marched across Horace's baffled face as he searched for his mistakes.

"Because she is not unwomanly. Not in the least. Her manners are impeccable." Daniel felt for a moment the ghost of her bottom lip between his own and suppressed a smile. "She is accomplished and beautiful and intelligent."

"I didn't think there was any harm in letting her follow her natural inclinations. But now I've marked her like a fox in the hunt." A scowl crossed his miserable face.

"Perhaps it will come to nothing," Daniel suggested.

Horace's eyes sharpened like a flint throwing sparks, and he focused his steady gaze on Daniel. "I wonder if more than that will come to nothing."

Daniel rinsed his mouth with the burning liquor and swallowed. That was a sharp turn in direction, but he tried to take the curve smoothly. "I would never drop her because some see scandal where there is none."

"Do you intend marriage?"

Never had Daniel heard that sentence used with such accusation. "I hardly know myself. We have not spoken of it."

Horace's frown deepened and Daniel turned his eyes to the tabletop without seeing the inlaid carvings that scattered the India wood with gold flowers—a token of appreciation from the Duchess of Ashbury for an operation Horace had performed on her prize greyhound. Daniel could not muster full volume when he spoke. "I hardly know the rules with her."

Horace only grunted, but it somehow conveyed agreement.

"I do not know yet if we are well suited." Daniel picked up a pipe just to have something to hold, and a memory intruded rudely on his thoughts. It was Nora sketching out a dissection while Daniel worked methodically on the vein structure of the thigh, losing hours to the task. Only when he had looked up and met her dark eyes did he remember fully where he was. Horace waited silently as Daniel turned the rosewood pipe in his fingers. Finally his gravelly voice rolled out like the crunch of horse hooves across a rutted path. "We don't know yet what will happen. For her sake, I suggest you decide promptly and live by the decision."

The liquor was gone now. No longer glistening in the crystal glasses, it burned against Daniel's ribs. He could not tell if the heat was a fire of courage or cowardice. He set the pipe down, the soft clunk of wood on wood the only sound in the overwarm room. "I suspect you're right. But remember—I can only decide for me, not her."

Horace grunted again. This time it was in sympathy.

CHAPTER 31

THREE DAYS AFTER THE SYMPOSIUM, NORA REALIZED someone was hiding the newspapers. She couldn't find any in the house. Daniel and Dr. Croft were out—Dr. Snow was holding a special meeting on his experience with ether—so Nora confronted Mrs. Phipps with it. "Why don't we have any newspapers?"

"They must be about somewhere. One of the gentlemen must have mislaid them." Mrs. Phipps spoke calmly, but there was a rosy tint to her ears.

Nora folded her arms. "Tell me the truth, please."

"They don't want you to see them. Dr. Gibson's been hiding them in his room."

"The medical journals?"

"And the *Times*." Answering the lift of Nora's brows, Mrs. Phipps continued, choosing her words like a child hopping a bridge of stepping-stones over a rushing stream. "There were some letters to the editor about the morality of ladies practicing surgery. And some complaints, I'm afraid, because it is illegal."

"Because of a technicality," Nora scoffed.

Mrs. Phipps corrected her. "Because you aren't registered with the General Medical Council. It was mentioned in several of the letters."

"The regulations are a tangle. Everyone knows that. Dr. Croft is only licensed to practice in London, but no one cared when he traveled to Devon last month to attend to Lady Highbury. No doctor spends the money to register everywhere."

"But he is registered somewhere. You, on the other hand—"

"Well, if that's the only problem, let's put on our bonnets and go register!" Nora's voice rose sharply.

Mrs. Phipps ignored her outburst. "Dr. Croft says this will pass, like any nine-day wonder. He suggested you and I go to the country, as he fears you will be bored."

Nora's nose wrinkled. A holiday in some quaint town would exacerbate her boredom, not cure it. As a result of the inquiry, several physicians had come forward with their own experiments and findings on the properties of ether, and Daniel and Horace were thick in the middle of discovery while she lurked behind, berated and humiliated. They pitied her predicament, but pity was cheap when it did not infringe on their work or exact any sacrifice. Nora did not expect them to petition Parliament or pick up cudgels on her behalf, but some show of unity seemed fitting. It was as if she were stranded on a raft, alone and drifting away, with no pole or paddle to keep her own course. A chilly resentment gathered in her stomach, threatening to swim up her veins to her heart.

After luncheon, she asked Mrs. Phipps to join her for a walk. She wore a deep bonnet, and they took a turn around the park. She remembered sitting with Harry, feeding the ducks, and turned from a sad thought to a bitter one—how unfair it was that she was a byword, while Daniel and Horace were sought after and admired. With a pang, she realized her thoughts of Daniel were colored with a gray haze, a tint that felt sick and lifeless.

Only if you allow it, she told herself. This would pass, and then they could return to the way things were. She would be careful, the unobtrusive assistant who helped with dissections and tidied up notes, who jotted down findings about cases and cures. If she didn't treat people, but confined herself to research, there were no laws against that. And her anatomical drawings earned praise instead of disdain. There were ways to stay close to the work she loved.

Bolstering her spirits with weak half measures helped—some. She returned home in more hopeful spirits, only deflating when Mrs. Phipps gave her a searching look in the hall. "My dear, are you all right? We were out for an hour and you never said a word."

"I'm sorry. You know there's too much on my mind. I didn't mean to be such trying company."

Mrs. Phipps untied the ribbons of her bonnet more slowly than usual. "Dr. Croft is right. You need a change of scene."

Nora shook her head. "This is my home."

When daylight staggered over the jagged rooftops of Great Queen Street, Nora rose and ordered herself to work in front of her drawing board. Every event since that horrible night—drinking whiskey with Daniel, Harry's confession, the insistent reporters—was obscured in a dreamlike fog. It was as if she'd been picked up from the lecture hall and dropped in the drawing room on Great Queen Street by a whirlwind, the days between obliterated.

She mixed her colors absently, losing herself to the pools of pigment. When the latch clicked, her heart leaped with reflexive joy, too innate to be sensibly apprehensive. She knew from the footfalls this was Daniel.

He picked up a book and settled into one of the more comfortable chairs, but he didn't read. Nora kept drawing, pretending she didn't notice.

"You've spoken to Harry, haven't you?" His voice traveled over her shoulder and broke her concentration.

She faltered before carefully pacing her words. "I have. How did you know?"

"Whenever Horace insults him, you change the topic. And you went somewhere when you disappeared for hours the morning after the meeting."

Nora placed her pencil down, blocking it with a handkerchief so it didn't roll to the floor. "I know you're not ready to speak to him, but I needed to know why he turned on us."

Daniel winced, and the book in his hand fell closed. "You sympathized from the start. Even after he—"

A sharpness in his voice warned Nora to proceed cautiously. "I wanted to tell you. Vickery blackmailed him. He promised him secrecy and three hundred pounds."

"He *bought* him?" Fury tinged Daniel's words. "Secrecy for what?"

It took Nora many long minutes to relay the story, because he kept spouting questions and oaths. By the end, the truth quieted him as his anger cooled into despair.

"What real choice did he have, Daniel?" Nora leaned forward as she finished, daring him to see a solution she and Harry had missed. "It was expose me or the poor girl. She could still be prosecuted."

Daniel gave a miserable shake of his head. "As can you! And what would you have me do with the man who sold me out? Shake hands and share a pint?"

Nora resumed drawing. "Not today." By the way the air rushed from his nose intermittently, she knew Daniel was still fuming, but eventually, as she added a pink wash to the flesh of the arm, she noticed all was silent again except for the slow turn of his pages and the occasional passing of Mrs. Phipps in the hall. She was so absorbed that his sudden words startled her.

"I know why you spoke in the auditorium," Daniel said.

"I'd have thought it obvious," Nora answered. "Vickery is a monster who shouldn't have his way."

"That's part of it." He tapped the book against the side of his shoe.

"What more is there?" Nora rubbed a charcoal line with the pad of her thumb, shading beneath a malformed ear.

"You're a surgeon," he stated. Nora's thumb went still.

"It was your surgery, and you couldn't let it be discredited by a fool. I didn't realize how alike we are until I saw you at that podium."

Daniel's words expanded inside her mind, like light stretching over the horizon and pushing away the dark. But he didn't know everything. "That's true," she admitted. "But"—she lowered her brush and waited until his darting eyes landed on hers—"I also couldn't bear to see Vickery strike you down."

Daniel rose from the sofa and advanced, only stopping when he lowered himself to sit on the floor beside her chair. "That's what I believed, but afterward I remembered I wasn't the only man in danger. Horace was, and still is. And Harry..." He swallowed. "I thought it was me, but now I'm not sure who you were trying to save." Nora's mouth fell into a small frown, tight at the corners. A nebulous complaint hummed at the edges of her mind. Before she could examine it, Daniel picked up her hand.

He turned his eyes to her fingers. "I realized there could still be feelings between you and Harry. And if there are—"

"Daniel!"

"You ran straight to him at your first chance. I watched you go. I thought his betrayal may have awoken something in you." He let her pull her hand away. "I wanted to ask but you've been deep in thought, and I hardly liked to trouble you, with everything else you are facing."

Words fell like fragile wares from a tipped shelf, shattering into useless pieces in her mind. She could not find any shard large enough for a sensible thought.

"Harry warmed to you first and I was so stubborn," Daniel added, sinking away from his place at her elbow.

She stopped him with a touch of her fingers: light, almost undetectable. "I'm stubborn, too," she reminded him, and wrapped her hand around his arm to pull him close.

"Thank heaven you are." Daniel drew level, hesitated until she smiled, and gathered her in a warm kiss.

Nora thought the kiss was a sign things were changing for the better, but Sunday came and went, and Daniel didn't find her alone again. He was harried, almost single-handedly managing the clinic and working to redeem himself in the eyes of the remaining skeptics at St. Bart's. Dr. Croft remained vexed and tired, and though Nora was used to his ways, these days it was easier away from his presence than with him. Perhaps it was the letter from the Royal College of Surgeons, but he held himself back, seldom speaking freely with her. Isolation echoed in her chest as in an empty cavern.

Monday morning, Nora waited until Daniel and Dr. Croft left for St. Bart's, reporters hounding them and following in their wake. She watched until they passed beyond the potted yew tree before she fled down the stairs and escaped in the opposite direction, cloaked, bonneted, her eyes fixed on the ground. Never had anonymity felt so sweet. No one stared as she stepped through the brisk morning, her sharp footfalls matching the fierce bursts of wind. She'd brought only a small basket, so she couldn't do much shopping, but she could fill it with herbs. The smell of mint on her fingertips always cheered her.

The man at the onion cart accepted her coin with bored eyes, and for a moment she wanted to kiss him, despite the aroma of his wares, for seeing her as nothing more than another customer. She walked on to Mrs. Peeke's stall to look over her bundles of herbs. They were a bit smaller than other sellers' but the most pungent. "Good morning," Nora said, fingering the soft leaves of the lemon balm.

When Mrs. Peeke paused too long, Nora glanced up, catching the woman's frown and the way she angled her shoulders. Nora mustered a smile, convinced she was imagining things.

After all, only last month she'd used Mrs. Peeke's herbs to concoct a salve for the woman's dry, cracked knuckles. "These look fine," she said, picking up a bundle of parsley.

Mrs. Peeke cleared her throat and pretended to brush something off her skirt. It reminded Nora of moments at school when she'd overheard girls whispering about the orphan who lived with a body snatcher. She kept her voice low and clear. "Is something the matter, Mrs. Peeke?"

The woman shifted under Nora's direct gaze. "I don't like my herbs going to a house of disrepute."

Nora laughed. "Since when is hollandaise sauce disreputable?"

Mrs. Peeke glared and held out her hand. "It's the same price as always. Take your herbs and be gone."

Nora replaced the bundle on the table, feigning a dignity she did not feel. "I'll buy elsewhere." She spun on her heel and fled, blindly navigating the stalls as tears blurred the faces she didn't want to see. She had known there would be doctors who scorned her, but market women with whom she'd chatted easily for years? Her hands shook as her mind replayed the scene. Nora hurried to an out-of-the-way bench where she dropped her head, grateful for the bonnet's protection, and pressed her fingers together as she tried to slow her trembling breaths.

"What happened?" Mrs. Phipps said, when Nora came into the kitchen with her almost empty basket.

Mumbling like a child caught misbehaving, Nora told her. When she finished, Mrs. Phipps untied her apron. "Come upstairs." She led Nora into her sitting room and all but pushed her into a chair. "I've held my tongue long enough. You cannot remain a prisoner in this house."

Nora looked away instead of answering. Of course Mrs. Phipps had discerned her red-rimmed eyes. She'd probably noticed the way Nora had taken to peering at the edges of the curtains, checking for reporters and slipping into the back rooms whenever the bell rang. "Are you here to tell me it will pass in another week or two?" Nora's voice came out more tired than angry.

"I am not." Mrs. Phipps's stiff chin indicated a coming battle. "I'm here to tell you that you are not allowed to stay here any longer."

For a half second, childish fears of being sent to the streets flared in Nora's mind, but they burned out in the next instant. "Not allowed?" she scoffed.

"I'm sending you on holiday. To Suffolk. My sister is fond of you. You can stay for the summer. It's nicer than summer in the city."

"All summer? Dr. Croft will destroy the house without us here, even with Daniel to temper him." Nora allowed herself a relieved laugh. Mrs. Phipps would never leave the men entirely alone.

Mrs. Phipps straightened her shoulders, trying to appear bigger. "You're right, of course. That is why I will stay here." She had the decency to drop the volume of her last words and look away.

Nora pressed herself against the back of her desk chair, letting the wooden slats take her weight. "You're sending me away?"

"You needn't look like that!" Mrs. Phipps scolded. "It's for the best. There's no peace for you here." She stepped forward, her face softening. "Felicia is tough as a guard dog. She'll let no one pester you."

"But my research? I can't do anything in Suffolk." Felicia Phipps was a kind woman, but easily shocked. Nora's days would be spent sketching landscapes, tending the garden, and sewing shirts for the poor.

Mrs. Phipps smiled pityingly. "You can't do any good here either until all the gossip dies down. I managed this house alone before you and I can do it again. Their shirts will be ironed, and I'll make sure Dr. Croft doesn't forget anything important."

"But Daniel…"

Mrs. Phipps cleared her throat. "He agrees it's best. He and Dr. Croft both want you removed for a span. They can sort through the matter themselves."

Nora's voice rose like a hurricane gust. "They arranged it without asking me? How considerate to spare me the trouble of deciding."

Mrs. Phipps lowered her brows, dampening Nora's fury as effectively as she had since her childhood. "Shouting never fixes anything. You'll enjoy the summer. You can spend a week at Southwold Lighthouse and take in the sea air." She gave Nora's hand a firm pat. "I've told Felicia you'll arrive next week. I've already begun packing your things."

Nora had no interest in lighthouses or the sea, but Mrs. Phipps gave her no chance to object. She kissed Nora's head and retreated, leaving her frozen in her seat. They'd all known for days she was leaving, and only Mrs. Phipps had seen fit to tell her.

It was like one of Croft's dissections—breathtakingly fast, thorough, and devastating.

CHAPTER 32

FOR NEARLY AN HOUR, NORA STARED WITH DISSATISFAC-
tion at her drawings of Horace's collection of clavicles—
precise, detailed, and accurate, but there was little point to all
her trouble. Paper and ink, even in skilled hands, remained
lifeless things and the resulting drawings made no immediate
difference to anyone. It was useless to draw; they still had no
parsley for tonight's sauce, and the idea of fetching any from
the market heated her cheeks and spurred her pulse to a shallow flutter. If she kept on this way, she'd hyperventilate.

Nora packed away her charcoals, then her books. Then she
left the drawing room, either to confess the truth about the
parsley, free her collection of chickens, or throw her months'
worth of notes into the fire. She wasn't decided yet. Deaf and
blind with her preoccupation, she was almost at the foot of
the stairs before she noticed Mrs. Phipps arguing, her feet
planted on the front-door threshold as firmly as any warrior at
Thermopylae, and refusing to yield. "Dr. Croft's not here. You
can't see him." Mrs. Phipps's voice was sharp and insistent, and
until now, Nora hadn't heard a word.

"I'm happy to wait." The answering voice hummed rich
and accented, but Nora couldn't see around the door as Mrs.
Phipps was closing it on the gentleman's foot.

"We don't want company," she grunted.

"I'm not a journalist. Let me see Miss Beady, at least. I know she's here."

Grimacing, Nora retreated, but the man must have spied her through the gap in the door. His voice reached out and caught her before her third step. "Miss Beady! A moment, please!"

"She doesn't want to see you," Mrs. Phipps said. "She doesn't want to see anyone. She's leaving shortly for Suffolk."

"Then I must see her before she goes." The certainty in the man's voice made Nora turn around, just as he thrust past the door.

"Miss Beady. There you are." Two feet or so above Mrs. Phipps, a smile widened. His eyes, dark beneath black brows, crinkled, and his thin face relayed intelligence and experience. She recognized him as the man who'd attempted to stop her after the symposium. "I can't leave England without paying my respects."

Nora stiffened.

"My name is Salvio Perra. I teach anatomy at Bologna University. I wanted to congratulate you on your remarkable surgery." His words rose and fell with the musical cadences of his people—the rich waves of Italian trespassing on his practiced English.

Nora narrowed her eyes. "I'm in no mood for jokes, sir." At her nod, Mrs. Phipps reached for his arm.

He sidled away, ignoring the housekeeper. "My God, what is the matter with you English? I'm perfectly serious." Reading Nora's suspicious frown, he laughed. "I suppose no one has congratulated you at all, and I have so many questions to ask."

"The details are in Dr. Gibson's paper," Nora said.

"Details." He snorted expansively. "I've read the thing half a dozen times. It is not the same as hearing from you." His gaze was friendly. Admiring, even.

Behind him, Mrs. Phipps hovered, her eyes asking Nora for instructions. Still not trusting the stranger, Nora was just curious enough to give him a chance to speak. She drew herself up another inch. "May we have some tea, Mrs. Phipps? Dr. Perra—"

"Professor, if you don't mind—"

"Professor Perra. Will you join me in the drawing room?"

The smile, impossibly white and wide, grew even larger. He bowed. "Thank you, Miss Beady. I should be delighted."

Nora knew it took only a moment to take boiling water from the kitchen stove, pour it into a pot, and send it up with the necessary implements to make tea. A mere two minutes, perhaps three, had passed since she'd invited Professor Perra into the drawing room, yet it felt like an age. She perched on the settee, hoping she looked more composed than she felt. Professor Perra was walking around the room, admiring the titles and specimens on the shelves.

"You have a wonderful collection," he murmured.

Mrs. Phipps gusted into the room before Nora could reply. "I've brought the tea," she said unnecessarily, and set it down next to Nora as forcefully as an earthquake.

Nora busied herself with the cups. "What brings you to London, Professor?"

He waved a hand. "Curiosity, business, a visit to my married sister—ah, you have the lectures of Anna Manzolini!" He took down the volume lovingly.

"If you are from Bologna, you must have seen her anatomical models," Nora said. "I've heard how remarkable she was, but I've never seen—"

"Seen them? I pass them every day. She is a product of our university," Perra reminded her. "She taught my grandfather, you know. He told me she was the most brilliant anatomist he'd ever known."

Nora froze. Somehow Manzolini had always felt like a long-ago foreign fable, but here was someone speaking of her in the flesh.

"A lady anatomist?" Mrs. Phipps asked.

"Don't look so alarmed, madam. You have one of your own right here," Perra pointed out. He smiled at Nora. "Aren't you?" he asked when she failed to respond.

"Well, you see—"

"I think I do. This reaction to your discoveries must be very trying. And so absurd. Your Royal Medical and Chirurgical Society admitted Professor Manzolini, you know."

"I didn't." Nora licked her lips. "I didn't know that, I mean."

He came to the chair opposite and sat down, careful of his coattails. "I understand you're being pestered by the press."

"They're shameless," Mrs. Phipps said.

As Professor Perra reached for his tea, a wedding band gleamed on his lean, brown finger. Nora's eyes darted from the plain gold ring to the lines around his mouth and eyes. They told her nothing, and when he raised his eyes from his cup, her own shied away. He must be over forty. Of course he was married. Most men found a way to keep both a wife and a career, but after living with Horace, it seemed a novel idea.

"What will you do now?" he asked, startling her with the question.

Nora hesitated over her answer, and Mrs. Phipps stepped into the breach. "Miss Beady is taking a holiday. My sister has a cottage in Suffolk."

"I see." He glanced back at Nora and must have seen her drooping, because his eyes narrowed and he rubbed a thumb along his jaw. "That is what you want?"

The visit to Suffolk was necessary, but she couldn't muster any enthusiasm at the prospect of living amid strangers for an indeterminate length of time, with nothing but books for company—books she'd lost interest in reading, at that. "It's best I leave London," Nora said listlessly, remembering Mrs. Peeke. She lifted a shoulder and sipped from her cup, hiding a wince when she scalded her tongue. "A change of scene…"

Professor Perra chuckled. "I'm glad we agree." His eyes flashed merriment at her puzzled expression. "My dear child, there's no need to martyr yourself on the altar of English convention. I understand why you're determined to quit London, but why not travel to Bologna? You can study anatomy and medicine, while acquainting our Italian doctors with the properties of ether."

"She could not travel so far. Not alone," Mrs. Phipps said, as breathless as if she'd sprinted up a flight of stairs.

Professor Perra smiled without opening his lips. "I would be honored to count her among my students."

Mrs. Phipps set down her unsteady cup. "She can't travel with you." Her eyes, as sharp as Nora's in this case, flicked to the wedding ring.

"No, not alone, but Miss Beady and whatever companions are necessary for her safety and comfort could journey most comfortably with my party. I'm here with my family. We sail in two weeks from London."

"Nora's needed here," Mrs. Phipps said, aghast.

"I thought she was needed in Suffolk," the professor said quietly.

In the pause that followed, Nora came alive, breaking the invisible crust that held her still and silent. Her voice was rough, her pulse febrile and shallow. "Stop discussing travel plans." If they kept on like this, Mrs. Phipps would soon chuck the teapot at him. "It's an impossible idea."

Why, the expense alone… Nora stopped, remembering Croft's liberal resources. But, of course, it wasn't her money to spend as she liked. Besides, she couldn't journey without a companion, and Mrs. Phipps would never agree to go.

"I quite agree," Mrs. Phipps said, tightening her lips and nodding decisively.

"There are difficulties, of course, but I suspect"—Professor Perra's smile widened as he reached for the sugar—"you have overcome greater before, Miss Beady." He eyed her while stirring his tea, but Nora kept her face expressionless, sipped her tea, and said nothing.

"Of course, if you and Dr. Gibson have an understanding, you may not wish to journey so far as Italy," Perra said.

Nora set down her cup. "What do you mean, sir?"

He shrugged. "I only thought... At the symposium, the way he spoke to you...and the chatter at the clubs..." His voice broke off, and he spread his hands apologetically. "It seems I was wrong. Forgive me."

"We have no understanding," Nora said, and the words echoed forlornly in her head. Quickly, she silenced Mrs. Phipps with a scalpel-sharp glance. "Tell me about your city."

Professor Perra relaxed into his chair. "The university is the oldest in Europe, probably in the world. The best of our wax anatomical models are displayed in the Palazzo Poggi, beneath an array of frescoes..."

Daniel's stomach rumbled as he stepped off the curb, making Horace glance up at him. "Hungry, lad?" he asked.

Daniel nodded. They'd both missed luncheon, and Daniel was looking forward to his dinner. If he wasn't mistaken, Mrs. Phipps had ordered cutlets of beef tonight. His mouth watered, in spite of the worry that creased his forehead, growing as they neared Great Queen Street. All day he'd wondered. "Do you think Nora knows yet?" he asked, relieved to finally say it out loud.

Horace shrugged. "Today or tomorrow, I expect."

If Nora was to journey to Suffolk as planned, Mrs. Phipps would have to tell her soon, and no amount of scowling at the cobbles could lessen Daniel's dread of it. They all did, which was why Mrs. Phipps had volunteered, patting Daniel's shoulder and telling them to leave things to her. "She'll take it best from me, I think."

But he wasn't sure, so for the past week, except when he hadn't been able to stop himself from asking her about Harry, then kissing her—fool that he was—Daniel kept his face rigid, forcing himself to focus on the task at hand. With dogged determination he avoided imagining the house without her: no one straightening Horace's collars or greeting the paperboys with candy and exclamations of delight. No pleasant profile bent over drawing papers in the evening.

Horace sulked over the coming parting in his own way, of course, glowering more than usual at the students of St. Bart's. Today he'd elbowed a nervous American lad away from a patient so harshly he upset a box of leeches onto the floor. In the evenings, instead of lingering over dessert and arguing cheerfully over difficult cases, Horace now retreated to his study, generally with a box of bones to wire together or a sheaf of scribblings under his arm.

As much as Daniel wanted his dinner he recoiled at the thought of another silent hour at the table. "She'll be bored in Suffolk," he murmured.

"The rest will be good for her," Horace said. "She's too quiet these days. And pale." He frowned accusingly at Daniel, then softened. "If she thinks we want her to stay, she'll never go. Make it easy for her."

Daniel only partly agreed, but since the part of him that didn't agree also wanted to kiss her until blood glowed again in her cheeks and the words caught inside her rushed free or evaporated, it seemed better, for the time being, to listen to Horace. Nora was dejected just now, and best left to the care of a woman, or so Mrs. Phipps claimed.

As if summoned by his thoughts, Mrs. Phipps arrived as they entered the hall. She was agitated, almost hovering on her toes. Daniel's anxious stomach plummeted in a solid lump to the floor. "You told her, then?"

For half a breath, Mrs. Phipps looked puzzled. "Oh. Yes, I did, and... Well, we can talk of it later." Her mouth ironed flat. "Right now, there's an Italian in the drawing room. He's been here almost three hours. Wanted to see her notes on etherizing, and then he started in with questions about those infernal chickens."

"Who?" Horace asked.

"An Italian?" Daniel said at the same time, pausing in the act of removing his gloves.

The housekeeper sniffed. "Professor Perra. Says he's from Baloney."

A frown gathered on Horace's forehead, then melted from the warmth of a broadening smile. "University of Bologna," he corrected. "He sent me a note last week. Afraid I forgot." He strode to the drawing room, forgetting to remove his coat and hat. Daniel followed, but the sight of Nora and a black-haired man seated closely on the sofa stopped him at the threshold. Their heads were bent, their attention fixed on the notebook spread on her lap. The man nodded as Nora's finger traveled across a row of figures.

"Professor Perra! What an honor!" Horace's walk and the welcoming spread of his hands were unexpectedly grand. Both heads snapped up, and in an instant, Professor Perra was on his feet, advancing with an outstretched hand and a genial smile, avoiding the low table that was cluttered with empty cups and a cake plate holding a sprinkling of crumbs.

Three hours, Mrs. Phipps had said.

"I've been acquainting the professor with my work," Nora told them.

Perra seized Croft's hand and pumped it energetically. "I've been consumed by curiosity since the symposium. I had to see you. Your work—and Miss Beady's—such a triumph."

The effect of his praise was as telltale as whiskey shine in Nora's eyes. Daniel crossed the carpet, manufacturing a smile through the resulting tangle of introductions, in which Horace grinned and blundered, Perra paid compliments with satin dexterity, and Nora blushed, failing to meet Daniel's eyes. A knot of unease tightened between his shoulders. "What brings you here?" he asked, once they had all settled onto the sofa and chairs.

"To London?" Perra asked.

"To Great Queen Street." Daniel gave the man a level look.

"I wished to offer my congratulations and sympathies to Miss Beady. What a shame that she must be driven from London. In my country, we're more practically minded."

Daniel hid a grimace. Of all things Italians were known for, practicality was not one of them.

"Professor Perra's grandfather studied under Professor Anna Manzolini," Nora announced, breathless worship in her words.

"Did he?" Horace leaned forward. "I don't suppose—"

"A brilliant woman. A legend in her own time. Her influence at the university is incalculable," Perra said.

"Ladies are allowed to study in Bologna," Nora added.

Horace turned to her, his head jerking like it was fixed on a rusty cog. "Are they really? I thought, during the occupation by the French—"

"That was many years ago, Dr. Croft," Perra explained. "While it is true there are few female students, I count myself fortunate to have influenced the careers of two notable doctors, marvelously skilled in the art of forceps delivery."

"What style of instrument do they prefer?" Horace asked, distracted.

"Levret's. They are so much better at accommodating the curve of the maternal pelvis."

"Professor Perra has offered me a place," Nora said, returning the conversation to more immediate matters. Her spine was straight, the knuckles of her clasped hands as white as Daniel's own. She was too far away to reach.

"Nora—" he began.

"A place?" Horace asked, frowning at the cushions of the sofa as if he was searching for an extra seat.

"At the university," Perra put in quietly. "Since she is denied all real opportunity here."

Horace chuckled. "She has plenty of opportunity. She knows as much as—"

"One always has the opportunity to *know*," Perra broke in with a delving gaze, "but what good is knowing, Dr. Croft, if one is not allowed to *act*?"

"The chance is too generous to dismiss out of hand," Nora said.

"But—"

Daniel interrupted Horace before things grew any worse.

There was a light in Nora's eyes that made him uneasy. "Bologna would be a dream come true for any of us." He cast a smile about the room. "But I haven't eaten since breakfast, and this is far too serious a topic for empty stomachs. I see you've finished all the plum cake."

"Perra, you'll stay for dinner?" Horace asked, hurdling the change in topic with his usual enthusiasm.

"I would be honored, if it is not too great an imposition," Perra said.

"Not at all!" Horace waved airily and stood. By the time Nora rose, Daniel was at her side, walking alongside her to the dining room.

In spite of Daniel's misgivings, the conversation flowed. No one mentioned Suffolk or Nora's coming departure. Perra was full of questions for them all, but especially Nora.

He's a new acquaintance and interested in her work, Daniel reminded himself. *Let her enjoy the praise.* It took some doing, but he managed to squeeze in mentions of cases he and Nora had treated together, and tried not to notice the eager glow on her cheeks when she spoke with Perra.

After dinner ended and the party scattered, Daniel passed the drawing room on his way to bed and caught a glimpse of Mrs. Phipps fluffing the drawing-room cushions rather savagely.

"That man's trouble," she grumbled.

Daniel rescued a fringed tapestry pillow, shook it, and returned it to the armchair with a thump, unwilling to admit in words that he agreed with her.

CHAPTER 33

U PSTAIRS IN HER ROOM, NORA PACED THE FLOOR, CHEW-
ing a thumbnail, a habit she'd not indulged for a decade
or more. Professor Perra appeared in every sense a mild and
patient man, yet his words dogged her with the insistent ferocity of a half-starved mongrel. As quickly as she kicked them
away, they returned, nipping at her. She sat down at her dressing
table, extracted five precisely placed pins and set to work comb-
ing out her hair, but the task couldn't prevent her from drifting
into an imagined surgical theater, where she stood pressed in
the midst of a crowd of students, jotting down English notes
from the stream of lectured Italian. Even in her mind, it was
difficult. Passing muster in French and Latin taxed her to her
limit. Believing she could muddle through in Italian...but
human bodies were the same everywhere, and other students
would share notes. If she went to Bologna, she would study like
she never had before.

Her heart raced, forcing her to place a hand atop her breast.
Professor Perra had made it plain female students were
the exception in Bologna, but his calm assurance that they
were not freaks of society thrilled her. In Bologna, she could
walk from a sun-drenched, sweltering Italian street into quiet,
high-ceilinged university halls, a doctor's satchel clasped in

her hand, the forceps, scalpels, and retractors inside sharpened, polished, and gleaming. Perhaps in class, she would glance up from her notes and catch the eyes of a student of her own sex. The stranger might be bashful and frightfully bright, or bold, brilliant, and flirtatious. She might be any number of things, but she would be female, and that alone would make her sympathetic and easy to understand. Whoever that other woman was, Nora saw herself in her—the version she might and most longed to be.

———

Nora sought Daniel in the surgery just before sunrise. She knew the sounds of a body arriving, even up in her room. The clinic was closed, and if anyone came, she could escape into one of the empty convalescent rooms without being seen.

"You've been very busy," she said quietly as she slipped into the surgery. Before Daniel's bent form lay Mr. Wilhems, a frequent patient, his forceful face already falling into unfamiliar hollows, though his color told her he'd not been dead very long. *How quickly they lose all trace of themselves.* But Daniel hadn't opened his chest cavity at all. The only place he'd parted skin was the back of the cadaver's right hand, from the middle finger to the wrist.

Daniel sent her a tired smile. "I'm not doing a true dissection. I pleaded with Mrs. Wilhelms to let me take a small look at his hand. I promised to dress him and return him as good as new in a few hours." He frowned at his choice of words but didn't correct himself.

"May I help?"

He glanced at the glass walls, but she'd already made sure the shades were down. "I believe I'd like to replace the bones of his middle finger with a few wax sticks. That way I can keep them without horrifying his wife. Do you mind cutting some to the right size?"

"What do you want his bones for?" Nora wrinkled her brow. Unlike Horace, she'd never known Daniel to hoard bones as curiosities and specimens.

"His arthritis. It's been dreadful for decades, and his fingers are deformed completely. We'll have to make sure we reconstruct the hand to look bent and unusable."

Her fingers twitched to touch the open hand, to feel the tension of the tendons.

"I want to know what does it. It is one of the worst ailments for pain, and I can offer no relief beyond warm poultices," Daniel explained. "I thought if I could make a more thorough study…"

Nora stepped up to Daniel and slid her clean fingers along his bloodied ones, pausing atop the dead man's mangled bones. Their fingers waited together, touching both life and death, and a thrill went through Nora, slipping down her shoulders and pooling at her feet, not simply from being at the dissecting table again. She was here with him, and to her, the smell of his skin was stronger than the scents of blood or soap.

She closed her eyes lest distraction sway her. She hadn't come here for sympathy, or to re-create finger bones.

"Nora?"

Shaking her head, she pulled her hand away and rummaged in a drawer for wax. "Pass me that larger scalpel." He laid the knife in her hand. She allowed herself several minutes of silent work, her back to Daniel, before she inhaled and prepared herself to speak.

"What would you say if I told you I don't want to go to Suffolk?" The shaded glass walls of the room batted her voice across the stone floor, returning it to her ears louder than she intended.

"I'd say I don't want to lose you to Suffolk, either, but we have no choice."

The wax fell in ugly chunks onto the side table where she worked. Nora stared at it until it blurred. "Professor Perra believes I do have a choice." She forced herself to face Daniel, almost undone by his suspicious squint. "His invitation is sincere. He's very insistent."

Daniel's expression was too schooled to display disdain, but she detected it in the tightening of his cheeks and neck. "I'm more than aware."

She waited in stillness, absorbing the unexpected hostility lurking in his words. "Is that all you have to say?" she finally asked, barely above a whisper.

"I don't like him trying to convince you to travel away from your family."

The piece of wax toppled from her fingers onto the table. "You are worried for Horace and Mrs. Phipps?" The bite in her words made him look up from his dissection.

"I'm worried for you. You'd have no one to protect you from men who would take advantage."

Nora retrieved the wax and handed the piece to him, none too softly. "Protect me from Professor Perra, you mean? He's married, Daniel. He offered me a place as a student. He would be one of my instructors. His interests are solely academic."

Daniel stared hard at her until her cheeks burned. He needn't voice what he thought of the professor's interests.

"You wanted me to go to Suffolk," she reminded him as her tears brimmed, making her even more angry. "You planned it with them without even telling me."

"Bologna's a site farther than Suffolk," he mumbled as he bent back over Mr. Wilhelms. In the following silence he managed to free the damaged middle phalanx. It fell with a clatter into a metal collecting bowl. Just when Nora despaired that he would say no more, his low voice traveled across the room to her waiting ear. "How long?"

"I've barely thought beyond the leaving. Perhaps a year?" Her stomach trembled as if it wanted to expel tension the same way drunkards expel their liquor.

"You can't finish medical studies in a year," he argued, his body closed and bent as if to keep her out as he worked.

"But I'm not starting from the beginning." She made sure he was absorbed in placing the piece of wax before she wiped her eye and rubbed the tears off on her skirt.

He stopped working and hung his head. "You would truly leave us?"

The ache hidden in his accusation stung enough to make her fingers tremble. "You are the ones sending me away."

"To the country with relatives. Not across the world." He put down his scalpel and let her see the hurt in his eyes. She did not know if he could see hers.

"There's nothing for me in Suffolk." Her voice rose. "I

cannot work there, and I cannot live if I cannot work. Would you exchange sutures for needlepoint? Tend flowers instead of patients? There's nothing for me at the seashore or the lighthouse. There's nothing for me anymore in London!"

Daniel flinched. She'd never seen that expression. Not when Harry betrayed them or when he lost his spot at Bart's, not when a surgery failed or his reputation hung in tatters. "Nothing?"

"Daniel. I didn't mean you. Or Horace or Mrs. Phipps. You have to know how I love…" The words died in the air, quelled by his darkening expression.

"Do I?" Daniel ripped a length of catgut free and spoke in broken sentences as he threaded it. "Yesterday a stranger from Italy shows his face. Now you're setting sail with him?"

"Not with him! Not because of him. Because of me. I cannot spend my life pretending I know nothing. I cannot bear how the people in London look at me. In Bologna, that won't happen."

He didn't answer until he'd finished several sutures, and when he did, his voice was cold.

"Horace is growing older. You know his heart is not what it should be. Would you abandon him here after all he's done for you?" His distress didn't affect his needlework. The stitches marching up the back of Mr. Wilhelms's hand were meticulous.

"Horace wants me to leave London! What does it matter if I take a train to Suffolk or a boat to the Continent?" In her agitation, her carelessly tied knot of hair slipped, a heavy lock falling against the side of her face. She shoved it aside with the back of her wrist and bent over her work, muttering, "Don't pretend indignation for Horace's sake. A few days ago, you thought I loved Harry. Now you are jealous of Professor Perra. If I were half as fickle as you seem to believe—"

Daniel dropped the dead man's hand onto the table. "You are too innocent, and it makes you easy prey. Did you even think to consult me?"

"That's what I meant this to be," she threw back at him. "A consultation."

"By informing me you want to cross the Mediterranean and live in Italy? I thought we had a future together. I'm to have no say? No choice in the matter?" His voice steadied, the anger slipping into something she didn't recognize.

"Choice?" Nora's eyes blazed. "You and Dr. Croft and Mrs. Phipps gave me no choice about Suffolk. Harry gave me no say when he exposed me. The Royal College gave me no choice when they barred me and wrote instead to Dr. Croft! How dare you complain to me about a lack of choices. We have no agreement, no understanding." She expected him to shout a rebuttal but instead of giving her a reason to rail further, he dropped his head and studied the stained floor between them. Silence crashed against the stark walls, shaking the air like a cathedral bell. The corpse lay in mute sympathy between them.

When Daniel spoke, his words sounded like a scaffolding of sentences, each one nailed rhythmically in place, one solid syllable at a time, unforgivably calm. "I don't want you to think the professor is the only man to make you an offer. Would you like to hear my alternative to Bologna?" He turned to her, all the fury washed from his expression, but none of the fight.

"If I asked you to marry me, would you stay here in

London? Forget Bologna? In a few months, once you returned from Suffolk and the worst of the storm had died down, we could marry, so long as you don't mind continuing to share a household with Horace. Eventually, once I've a clinic of my own, we'll buy our own home."

Her chest collapsed, her ribs caving in as if her lungs had disappeared. He took advantage of her breathlessness, closing one hand over her arm and pulling himself closer, bending his head so his whisper slid into her ear and raised the hairs of her neck. "I would never ask you to stop working. You could nurse in my clinic and help me with dissections and research, Royal Surgeons be damned."

He ran his hand from her waist, along her spine, until he grasped the back of her neck in the gentle curve of his fingers. "Don't go to Italy. Choose a life with me," he whispered, then closed his mouth over hers. His hands roamed over her back and across her waist, making her forget his question entirely until he freed his lips long enough to ask, "Is that a yes?"

His ragged breathing made her ache, almost as much as the hesitation that paralyzed her tongue, stopping the answer that would have flown from her so lightly and easily just a short time ago. She licked her lips. "I want to." Wanted it painfully, but still she was compelled to ask, "Can I have both?"

———

Daniel went numb, like he'd been plunged into an ice bath, his nerves, for the moment, overwhelmed by paralyzing cold. He waited for her to recant but all she did was wet her lips again.

"You want to go that badly?" Daniel asked. "Isn't this"—he

gestured at the lamps, reflectors, and orderly cupboards, but of course he meant himself more than his surroundings—"isn't it enough?"

Her eyes grew more anguished. "Why didn't you ask me before?"

Conscience pricked him. "I thought we had time. I didn't know how you felt, and I didn't want to antagonize Horace."

She shook her head, only a fraction of an inch, but still contradicting him. "You knew how I felt. I'm not like other women, trained to flirt and dissemble. I don't smile and touch and kiss without giving my affection."

Daniel released an exasperated sigh. He'd known, but knowing wasn't the obstacle. Images of his parents and Mae and Harry spun across the darkened shadows of his mind. "It's not that simple," he argued. "Until recently, I was attached elsewhere. Even after Mae freed me, you were preoccupied with Harry. Then when we were both free, Horace had to go and announce your inheritance. A hasty marriage would have made me look like the worst kind of fortune hunter. I didn't want us to begin like that, but now—"

"Now we're worse off than before!" Her eyes narrowed. "I don't wish you to marry me only to save me from the shame of my unwomanly pursuits. Or perhaps the greater shame of being ignorantly seduced by some Italian doctor? Which is it—am I too removed from my sex or too weakened by it?"

"You know that's not why—"

"No, Daniel. I don't." She dropped her eyes, hiding behind lids stained violet by lack of sleep, and turned toward the door.

"Wait."

She glanced back, and he fumbled desperately to translate feelings—ragged, tearing—into words. "Maybe we could marry now. Go to Italy together."

Breath left her in a rush, fluttered, petal-like, across the room. "How could you leave everything here?"

"Because I'd be with you." His face flushed as he tried to swipe away her objections.

"And Horace?"

"If we married, Mrs. Phipps could stay and keep the wheels on his wagon for a year."

Nora's glance darted, scanning the space between them. For a reckless moment her eyes lit with the possibility and Daniel tightened his grip on her fingers. He was ready to press her further when a shadow engulfed her.

"Mrs. Phipps can mend his clothes and tidy his house. She cannot take on the experiments, the patients. She cannot persuade doctors to listen to him or help him write papers that will save lives."

Daniel's empty mouth refused to fill with words to contradict her. "But surely he could—"

"He can't, Daniel." The tear at the corner of her eye reassured him she was swallowing the same bitter disappointment. "And how could I ever study if my every thought was guilt for abandoning him and taking the one doctor he trusts to work beside him? Guilt for distracting you from the practice when you're just making a place for yourself?"

Daniel slowly admitted it to himself, letting the truth inch over him painfully. Because of the discovery of ether, Croft would not merely work himself to death. He'd kill himself or a patient with overly ambitious tests, make new enemies, and alienate the fence-sitters who, for now, were curious enough to listen.

Nora drew up a reluctant breath and Daniel braced, knowing he would hate whatever she said.

"If you stay..." Her fingers twisted together, then her eyes found his, at once calm and troubled. "I would never worry for Horace, knowing you are at his side, and I would never blame myself for limiting you—heavy burdens, and you can spare me both."

He felt his proposal tumble into the void between them and shatter. "But I—"

"You are meant to be a great surgeon. Horace saw it. I see it. There is love between us, but it doesn't erase our difficulties. I have to go to Bologna and you have to stay. If your affection lasts—" She stopped, licked her lips, then forced herself on. "Ask me again."

She was gone before he summoned a reply, gliding out the door saying, "I'm going to speak to Horace."

He moved to stop her, but halted at the petulant clanging at the clinic door. A moment's indecision expired when the bell rang again. He'd handled it wrong, but there was still time, and it would be better to try again once he'd had more time for thinking. Stunned, numb, Daniel stepped heavily to the door, praying that the bell ringer's urgency might overcome his fog of misery, if only for a few minutes.

His hopes were dashed when he admitted a young boy, accompanied by a younger sister, scratching her red and swollen face. The boy explained both of their parents worked all day in the mills, and his sister had begun breaking out in spots after her morning porridge. Holding up a precious shilling, the proud boy set his chin and silently dared Daniel to refuse services.

The children looked to be five and eight, but Daniel was a terrible guesser. Childhood seemed a nebulous thing to him, broken only into infants, children, and adolescents. Daniel lifted the girl onto the table, her large brown eyes serious and her pouting lips mute. A quick inspection revealed a clear case of urticaria, spreading out under her armpits and even inching into her pink ears. "Gracious, I bet that itches," Daniel said.

She nodded, misery and discomfort threatening a tear. Her brother pushed himself closer to have a look and with clenched hands asked in his most grieved and dignified voice, "Is it the plague?"

Daniel suppressed a laugh, and the boy glowered at being mocked in his distress. Daniel remade his face grim and serious and looked the boy in the eye. "I thought so at first, but I've had a closer look and I believe it is a condition known as urticaria. You can see from the many weals on her skin and the way it itches." The boy nodded gravely as Daniel pointed, as if confirming the diagnosis. "It may have been nettles or something her skin is sensitive to. It's a dreadful thing to itch all over, but I believe it will be gone in a few days and she'll be no worse for it. I'll give you a bag of oats and you can wash her in cold oat water to relieve the itch." And then for good measure, "She is very lucky you brought her here in time. I do have a bit of salve we can try."

As Daniel applied the liniment, he tried to pry a few words from the stricken girl. She watched his every move, and a few times her fingers hovered near the salve until Daniel invited her to take a bit. She gingerly collected a tiny amount on her finger and sniffed it, a curious and calculating look on her face. Her wide dark eyes and smooth hair reminded him of only one person. Perhaps he and Nora, one day... "What will you do when you're all grown?" he asked as they anointed her arm together.

She weighed his question, tried silence for a few moments, and finally answered, "I'll work in the mill."

Daniel smiled and helped her off the table. When the door closed behind them, he leaned against it and sighed. He pictured Nora upstairs, arguing with Horace, or walking her fingers over their dusty globe around the Iberian Peninsula and into the bright Mediterranean Sea, her eyes growing wide with possibility. For her to stay and keep house and launder his linens seemed as sad an answer as the little girl's. Daniel's mind flashed back to his years at the Sorbonne, the late nights and French girls and his drunken antics with the American students. Nora would have her own adventure in the hills of Italy, wine flowing, her pale skin a wonder to the olive-toned Italians. He shook the cruel image away and crossed the room to close the jar of salve and return it to the dispensary. He'd already begged. He'd kissed and proposed. He'd lost.

Daniel pressed his hand against his temple. There was no salve for this. And no one to blame but himself. He let himself feel the sting of regret, the venom of it spreading through him, but he quieted it with another sigh and took the broom to sweep away the dried mud that had fallen off the children's shoes.

CHAPTER 34

AFTER HER DISASTROUS CONFERENCE WITH DANIEL, Nora cherished little hope that Horace would hear her request calmly. Reluctant and taut-nerved, she cornered him in the library and attempted a briskness she did not feel. Planting herself several feet from his direct line of sight, she dared to utter her practiced line. "I've decided to travel to Bologna to see for myself if it is as favorable as the professor reports."

Horace tapped his page and grunted. She had to repeat herself before he looked up, then wait until his own thoughts emptied out of his mind to make room for her declaration. When at last they did, he frowned and wrinkled his nose in distaste. "I haven't time at present. Perhaps in a few years."

"You?" she asked in confusion. "No. I didn't mean to imply you would leave your work. I'll go on my own to attend university there."

He let one unkind laugh burst out before answering, "Unthinkable."

A cold deluge of disappointment broke over her. "But you said it was a brilliant idea to Professor Perra!"

Horace clenched his pipe in his back teeth. "Eventually brilliant." He waved a dismissive hand. "How will I run clinic without you? A few months is possible to manage, but a year? Two? You're needed here."

"Am I a prisoner?" Nora asked softly.

Horace's slack mouth allowed the unlit pipe to drop to his lap. If she hadn't lived with his towering tempers all her life, she would have trembled when he rose to face her, his papers slicing through the air and landing in a chaotic flutter on the floor.

"I should lambast you for that."

"I wouldn't blame you," she answered. "But you know it takes a great shock to get you to leave your articles." They both looked down at the abandoned sheets. "I have decided to go. Would you hold me here where I am made a criminal or hide me away in Suffolk where there is nothing for me but banal distractions? Which do you wish for me?"

Croft narrowed his eyes and advanced with roaring voice. "I wish you to get back to work!"

"Sir, I wish the same but we have lost that option! I am banned. I am barred. I am watched. I am maligned." Tears were never the way to move him, but hers erupted and fell without restraint.

"It will pass," he mumbled, but Nora did not know if he meant her notion to go or her infamy. She shook her head in wordless dissent.

"I'm due at the club." He shuffled the papers together and brushed past her, but she sidestepped, staying between him and the door.

"The only thing that will pass is my chance, and if it does, I will never forgive you."

His eyebrows lowered and drew together, and for a

moment Nora forgot to breathe. She swallowed. "If I were a man, you'd allow it."

"I've spent more than a decade training you, and to hand you over now—"

"Would be another of your many kindnesses to me."

He flinched. "Dr. Thompson is expecting me."

Whether this was true or merely an excuse, Nora couldn't say. She didn't move until the front door closed, not with Horace's customary heedless force, but with an ominous, quiet click. Sometime later—Nora couldn't say if seconds or minutes had passed—Mrs. Phipps startled her by laying a hand on her arm. "Would you care to join me for a cup of tea?"

Nora focused on her slowly, as if she was reviving from an ether dream. "No, thank you. I've cleaning I'd like to finish alone."

Tight-jawed, tight-lipped, she went up to the attics where she threw together a great pile of rubbish without anyone observing the heavings of her heart. Then, as daylight faded, with Horace and Daniel still playing least-in-sight, Nora hauled the rubbish to the back garden with the help of the hallboy and set it alight. Arms folded, she watched the bonfire flare and scorch, then returned inside, dusty and stinking of smoke. She sent for a tub of hot water and shut herself in her room, sitting in the steaming water as soap bubbles popped and vanished, and her fingertips turned white and wrinkled. When the water was cold, she was relaxed and composed. Yet she hadn't changed her mind.

Daniel returned home in the early morning, intent on changing his clothes and returning to St. Bart's before Nora awakened. Horace's story, grumbled out over glasses of scotch at a secluded table at the club—Daniel made sure of that, since Horace was too vexed to remember decorum—worried him. Her plan to gallivant to Italy was no passing whim.

His hand on the knob of the clinic door, Daniel noticed the hallboy, swathed in a grimy smock, raking the remains of a fire into Mrs. Phipps's rose beds. "What's all this, Peter?"

The boy shook his head. "I'd steer clear of Miss Beady if I was you, sir. She's in a rare taking."

Yes, she was, and—Daniel forced himself to admit it—he would be, too, in her place. What would he have done, had his parents not finally been persuaded to send him to the Sorbonne? He'd threatened to enlist, and the thought of their only son toiling as a lowly surgeon's apprentice had made them relent. From there, given the little they understood of medicine—and perhaps some willful ignorance—he'd gotten his way with less trouble.

But Nora couldn't enlist. She had few options of any kind. If Horace denied her this one… Daniel went up to his room, but instead of changing his shirt, he tapped on the dressing-room door.

"Horace?"

No answer. Daniel pushed open the door. Horace sat at his desk, writing feverishly amid the jumble. "What is it?" he asked, surprising Daniel, who was used to speaking once, twice, three times before catching Horace's attention.

"She is unhappy."

Horace grunted.

Daniel sat at the edge of the desk. "We can't send her to Suffolk like putting a coat in summer storage."

"It isn't like that," Horace said, ceasing the angry scratching of his pen.

"She thinks so," Daniel said. "And perhaps I understand. I would do anything to keep her here, but I would do as much—more, even—to make her happy." *Even if I lose her*, he added silently.

"You are a damned fool, Gibson. We could not ensure her safety or oversee her education."

"True. And she is in your care, sir. It is your money and your decision, but I think you know you must let her go." As fools went, Horace was a prince of the species, scared, stubborn, so blinded by his own brilliance that he often stumbled on the smallest specks of reason. Still. Daniel had said his piece and meant it. Too late to take the words back.

The house vibrated with furious silence. Nora couldn't bear to see Daniel, though he twice sought her out in the library. "Don't make it harder for me," she told him the second time, escaping out the door, her book held to her chest. Up in her room, she was unable to read, so she set the volume aside until half past seven. Breakfast. Better to face Dr. Croft when he was full of sleep—hopefully—and strong coffee.

He didn't seem particularly flush with either when she found him in the breakfast parlor, but he was alone, and Nora was grateful not to face both men at once. Dr. Croft was gray-faced, though so far as she knew, he'd spent the night at home, not summoned to St. Bart's or attending a confinement. He preferred to approach things directly, so Nora felt no need to shepherd him gradually to the subject. "Why won't you let me go?" she asked, staring fixedly at her toast as she applied an even layer of plum preserve.

"It would be negligent."

"Negligent to whom? You answer to no one for my care."

"I answer to reason. Sending an English girl halfway around the world is unreasonable."

"America is halfway around the world. Italy is—"

"I am acquainted with geography," Dr. Croft said tersely. "Why are you so determined to leave us?"

"You decided to send me away. If I'm not needed—"

He set down his coffee cup and heaved an exasperated sigh. "Eleanor Beady, that is the worst logic I've ever heard from you. You are needed!" He banged the table for emphasis, rattling the cups. "But it's miserable here for you, and until this infernal fuss dies down, I want you to be happy."

"Did you for a moment think I would be happy in Suffolk? You were right that I need to leave, but at least this option provides some hope for me."

"Does it?"

She studied his skeptical eyebrows. "Yes. You can hire me a companion. I needn't travel alone. I can journey out with Professor Perra, and it won't be that hard to join another trustworthy party when it's time to come home." Dr. Croft had traveled any number of places, and Daniel had spent more than a year in France. "I'm not asking to explore the mountains of Patagonia."

Horace crumbled bread onto his plate. "What about Daniel?"

"What of him?" Nora countered, and took a large bite of toast.

"Won't you miss him? I thought—"

His careful question and crafty glance were the end of enough. Nora gulped her dry mouthful and set down her toast. "Was it you?"

"I don't understand," Horace said, with the same artful indifference he used when she confronted him for spoiling his shirts.

"Did you tell him to propose?"

"He did what?" Horace half rose from his chair.

Taken aback, Nora needed a moment before answering. "He asked me to stay and marry him."

"Well, why don't you? You suit perfectly!"

Nora glared at him.

"My dear—"

"A marriage license is not a medical license, Dr. Croft. I am still hopeful I may obtain both."

Horace shoved the crumbs from his shirtfront, catapulting them across the table.

Nora pressed on. "I'm confident other scandals will eclipse ours while I am away in Italy. When I return, there may be a chance for redemption. Think of it! The lectures I will write home about. The articles I will translate and send."

Horace resisted her enthusiasm with a growl. "And if I don't give you the allowance?"

Nora slipped a lock of hair behind her ear and met his

hard eyes. "Then I will sit beside a lighthouse in Suffolk and discuss dress patterns with old women until I am called home."

Horace did not shrink from her stare, his expression masked in consternation. She knew she'd struck a fatal blow when he muttered one word. "Damn." He laced his fingers together, stared at them a while, then cocked a look at her. "Are you sure you and Daniel can't—"

"I have nothing to offer him right now but scandal. Let me go and make something of myself first." Her voice was level, but the inaudible tremors beneath made her try to slow her breaths. He was softening, but if she failed—

"I don't understand why you insist on this," he said, running a hand through his hair. "If you'd just—"

Nora pushed to her feet, holding back an unexpected sob. "That is the great benefit of being a man, with every opportunity in the world before you. You cannot understand."

But he understood enough not to interrupt her as she retreated from the room.

It was past two in the morning when Daniel hung up his cloak, but there was still light coming from beneath the library door. He let himself in and found Horace scowling at an assortment of bones, his wire abandoned on the table. "I'm not finished with the owl yet," he said.

"She's still determined to go, then?" Daniel's question was hardly necessary. If Nora had given up, Horace would not still be scowling over an assembly that should have been as easy as a child's block tower for him.

Horace sighed. Daniel took a chair.

"This is your fault," Horace grumbled. "If you'd managed better, we'd not be in this mess, not that I'm sure marriage at her age is especially desirable."

They were used to each other, so Daniel neither laughed nor winced. "I would like nothing better than to marry her. But if I had the money to send her, I would."

Horace quirked an eyebrow at him.

"She's right," Daniel went on. "She should have choices."

"Even if she chooses that Italian?" Horace asked. Daniel hesitated. He was by no means sure, but bleak acceptance had come over him these last days as he'd tried and failed to work himself to shreds. He could go to Nora and grovel, kiss her senseless, or wait until she bowed to the inevitable so long as Horace held firm, but none of these paths offered any satisfaction, not when he recalled the exhilaration they had felt the night of Prescott's surgery—the wash of fevered determination, the forced bravado, the incredible synchronicity. If he married her now, they might be happy enough. But that wasn't enough, not when he'd caught a glimpse of what might be.

"I've asked about him. He's known and respected," Daniel said.

"Yes. But can we trust him?" Horace asked.

"I'm certain we can trust Mrs. Phipps," Daniel answered.

Horace almost choked. "You want me to send both of them?"

"Nora needs her more than you do," Daniel said quietly. She would require a friend in Italy, someone to care for her in ways she couldn't herself. "Would you want Nora to go without her?"

Horace chewed his lip.

"We can hire a temporary housekeeper," Daniel said. "My mother has recommended some names." In fact, his mother had been thrilled to learn Miss Beady might soon travel to Italy.

"Anyone we hire will resign within the week," Horace argued. "Phipps is the only one I've ever convinced to stay."

"We might need to change our ways of doing things," Daniel said.

"Do you think Phipps will agree to go?" Horace asked skeptically.

The library door swung open without a click—it hadn't been latched. Mrs. Phipps stormed into the room, swiping at her cheeks. "Dunderhead! You can't think I could bear seeing her sail off on her own." She tugged at her lace cuffs with such ferocity that it was a miracle they didn't tear. "And I can handle any presuming Italians."

For the first time in days, Daniel chuckled.

⸻

"Are you coming down for dinner?"

Nora looked up from her Italian grammar to where Mrs. Phipps stood at her bedroom door. "I'm not especially hungry." She nudged an empty plate under her bed with her foot, so Mrs. Phipps wouldn't know she'd been munching biscuits and green apples while studying. Letting them think she was starving herself could only help her cause. Mrs. Phipps sent her a pleading look, so Nora set the book aside and shook out her skirts. "I'll come, but I may not eat anything," she warned.

Halfway down the stairs, she caught the scent of roast

goose. Her mouth watered. Apples and biscuits were all very well, but they couldn't be considered a meal and—she slowed on the last few steps and looked back at Mrs. Phipps. She was smiling complacently, undoubtably happy she'd coaxed Nora to the table, but that wasn't all. The same keen sense that allowed Nora to perceive the slightest changes in patients now told her something was afoot.

Nora advanced to the table, her ears pricked, her eyes squinted in suspicion. Daniel's civilizing influence showed after all these months. New crisp, white linen—Mrs. Phipps had been granted her wish—set off a dazzling display of candlelight and perfectly polished silver. There was not a bone or specimen in sight. Horace and Daniel had already arrived, standing behind their chairs: solemn and wary perhaps, but not stiff or angry. The door opened again before she could ask.

"Forgive me. There was an overturned wagon blocking the end of the street." Professor Perra, escorted by the hallboy, breezed inside, straightening his cuffs, flipping his coattails back and taking the seat across from her as Daniel helped her into her chair.

Nora darted a startled glance at Daniel, but he only flashed a brief smile, not holding her eyes, and the talk fastened on a new case in the hospital before the covers were even lifted.

Conversation flowed around her until midway through the first course, when Professor Perra set down his fork. "Well, that is all very interesting, but, of course, it's not why I've come." He smiled at Nora. "Miss Beady, I believe you've decided?"

She swallowed a mouthful of peas, then found her tongue.

"My studies deserve serious attention," she said. "I should like to go to Bologna, but—"

"But she worries she will be gravely missed," Daniel said. "She is right. She will be." He spoke smoothly, but it was the voice he used to comfort his suffering patients.

"It is a wrench, losing her for even a little while," Dr. Croft said from the head of the table. "My dear, are you certain you wish to go?"

She stared at Horace, her wide eyes disbelieving. "Yes, if I may."

He frowned at his plate, sawing with uncharacteristic clumsiness at the very tender goose. "You may go. Only because Phipps says she'll go with you, mind."

She clutched the edge of the table, looked from Horace to the professor, to Mrs. Phipps, fondly smiling, to Daniel. It was his face, so careful and brave that convinced her this wasn't a joke.

"A year or two passes quickly," he said.

"I'll count on hearing from you often," Nora replied, feeling winded. "Long letters," she added a touch severely, with a look at Dr. Croft.

"It was Daniel's suggestion that Mrs. Phipps join you," Horace grunted. "He's taken it upon himself to find a temporary housekeeper."

"Mrs. Phipps is irreplaceable, of course, but we shall find someone adequate," Daniel said.

"How will you manage in Italy?" she asked Mrs. Phipps, whose straight back and stiff chin did nothing to convey enthusiasm at the prospect.

"How could I manage here if all I did was worry about you?" Mrs. Phipps said with a sniff.

"But—"

Grinning broadly, Professor Perra raised his glass. "Wonderful. To your new life, Miss Beady!"

Nora sipped, too flustered to do more than stammer general thanks. She turned away from the others, holding Daniel in her sights. "I expect a letter at least every fortnight," she repeated, this time more commanding.

"I'll report all our tiresome details," Daniel said.

"They won't be tiresome." Beneath the table, she reached out and brushed his hand, catching his thumb with her little finger.

Horace cleared his throat, but Daniel didn't take his hand away. He smoothed her skin, roughened by lye soap, with his thumb.

"There's much to plan," Mrs. Phipps assured her. "I know we've little time, so I've already ordered us lighter clothes."

Nora swallowed a gasp. "You've been conspiring against me. Again."

"For you," Daniel corrected. "I hope you don't mind, but this is a sight more difficult than Suffolk."

A funeral procession, Daniel thought glumly as their steps threaded the crowds of St. Katharine's Way. He tightened his arm and pulled Nora closer as a group of sailors hurried past, followed by a woman using her apron to carry loaves of bread that left curls of white steam drifting behind her. Even Horace was silent as he guided Mrs. Phipps through the fragrant, noisy throng. An eruption of laughter came from one of the countless sea-themed pubs, and Daniel fought the impulse to turn on his heel and pull Nora home with him.

Instead, he studied Mrs. Phipps's bony hand, its clenched fingers implying all the strength of an eagle's claw. There'd be no harm to Nora with the old lady near. Before he could smile in relief, his face fell into a deeper frown. Daniel tried not to imagine the whispers of Italian medical students, inviting Nora into their practices, into marriage, into bed... A fast shake of his head did little to clear the image, but it made Nora glance up in concern.

"I will study quickly," she said, softly enough that the rowdy conversations around them hid her words from all but Daniel.

He nodded. It was no use arguing. She would see soon enough the gravitational pull of the lectures—knowledge coming in from every corner of the globe, discoveries and humbug thrown together so carelessly one scarcely had time for an experiment before there was something else to pursue. The yank in his chest surprised him. He longed for the lecture hall of the Sorbonne, the shouting matches between his instructors in furious, insulting French, the flushed faces of men fighting for a view of a dissection. What he would give to join her in Italy! But he was no fresh student. He was twenty-six now, with a practice that needed building and a reputation in need of mending. Rushing to Italy with Nora would do nothing to secure his tenuous future, and it would be a poor show of thanks for Horace who, without his women, would need someone to civilize him.

They built this street too short, Daniel thought when their feet reached the water. He could have sworn it was longer, could have sworn he should have more steps with her beside him. Nora raised her face, her eyes wide, and swung her glance from Daniel to Horace as if looking for rescue.

"Very well," Horace grunted. "Your trunks are loaded. Mrs. Phipps has every baked good imaginable in her ponderous bag." Mrs. Phipps smiled in spite of herself and clutched her carpet bag closer. "There is only the loathsome business of goodbye and we can all get back to work."

His voice hitched and a gloss in his eyes betrayed him despite his bored, gruff words. Daniel had no defense for an old man threatening to cry. Croft cleared his throat and gave his jacket such a smart straightening Daniel feared for the seams. Nora stepped up to Horace. She did not give the embrace Daniel expected. Instead she laid her hands on the old man's whiskered face and kissed each cheek.

"You dear, dear man. God bless you."

He sniffed in surprise and looked down until she continued. "And check your buttons on your vest before you leave home. It is ridiculous that a grown man can look so askew."

Horace humphed and brushed her hand off his shoulder. "Don't argue with your professors, you pernicious little imp. Unless they are wrong."

Nora turned from Horace and met Daniel's eyes. Understanding, Horace led Mrs. Phipps several steps away to give her a private goodbye and assurances about the state of the silver and the plaster in her absence.

Now that they were alone, Nora took Daniel's hand in hers. "Are you certain?"

A great many answers flooded his brain, flashed to the surface like silver fish displaying their shining fins and disappearing beneath the ripples.

"Certain enough," he answered. "But it is loathsome."

"Hideous," she agreed.

"Are you frightened?"

She looked up to the maze of ropes on the ship, paused for the shouts of sailors arguing how to load a stained-glass window, and a smile triumphed. "Yes. Also grateful."

"It won't be easy, but you wouldn't want it if it was." He smiled. "You are made for this. You've been preparing all your life." The sunlight did delightful things to her brown eyes. He cast his eyes over her dress, the tight, flat lines of her back and ribs, and could not keep his hands from pressing to her waist. He ran his fingers along the stiff planes of her corset, wishing he could squeeze her as tightly as he wanted. "I don't expect any promises. I leave you utterly to your heart's desires."

Confusion crossed her face as her eyebrows lowered. She stammered, "Of course. Nor do I expect from you..."

Daniel cut her off with a kiss, not at all polite. With one hand, he tugged her closer until he felt the press of her body against his chest, and with the other he enclosed her fragile neck, supporting it while he pushed her head backward with the force of his lips. He could not speak his hopes or intentions, but nothing would stop him showing her.

She met him fully, and though it lasted only seconds, when he released her, the weight of fear was lighter, as if he'd set down a heavy pack after miles of bearing it. "I'll be here when you return," he said, running his hands behind her ears, resisting another kiss long enough for words they both needed.

"I'll see you then," she promised, and leaned forward to meet his lips softly, surprising him by the passion in a touch so light and fleeting.

As they parted, he took her gloved hand in his. "It has been a pleasure working with you."

She caught the mischievous tone and smiled. "I admire your work, Dr. Gibson."

"And I, yours. Perhaps I will soon call you Dr. Beady."

Horace stepped closer, his pocket watch gripped in his hand.

Nora laughed. "I hope so."

The ship was lined with waving passengers, waiting for the dawdlers to hurry. It was time.

"I love you both," she said as Phipps pushed her toward the ship.

Both men raised their hands to their chests, quite unaware the other had done the same thing. With equal amounts of pleasure and embarrassment, they absorbed the words.

Daniel turned around, as if the blow of parting would blind him if he didn't shield his face. He waited until the cry of the sailors and the creak of the rowboats told him the ship was moving before he turned back and found her, waving with one hand, the other pressed firmly to her heart. Daniel copied her, felt the pain leak through his fingers as he held it over his left breast.

"You didn't like her much at first." Horace's voice surprised him out of his reverie.

"Perhaps if you'd warned me," Daniel countered. "She came as a shock."

Horace laughed as he waved to her, and Phipps shook a crisp handkerchief at them.

"I do believe in good shocks."

The sun in front of them silhouetted the clipper ship and shot blinding rays as they tried to keep their eyes on her.

"Have Pastor Merrill's stitches been removed yet?" Horace asked, shuffling his feet impatiently.

"Scheduled for this afternoon." Daniel sighed. Hemorrhoid stitches were the last thing he wanted to think about as Nora slipped farther away.

"I believe we'll need to schedule a surgery for the Jenkins girl with the bone cyst. I think it will cripple her if we let it grow any bigger. We can get it done in less than two minutes with the ether to quiet her. We can use the bone drill."

Horace turned and began his walk back to the carriage, Daniel following with heavy feet. The old man stopped talking of the surgery and softened his voice to a more tender tone. "The only thing for it is work."

Daniel looked up the bright, crowded street as a beggar thumped past on a wooden leg. A city full of bodies to mend that wouldn't wait for his complaining heart to stop aching. "I have better luck with the chisel than the drill."

Horace frowned and pressed his lips together in thought. "I've a femur bone at home. You can show me."

CHAPTER 35

Nora watched until Daniel and Horace were gone, until London vanished behind them, and Mrs. Phipps had given up and let Professor Perra escort her to their cabin. Towns and factories and villages slipped by in a blur as they sailed downriver.

"Left your heart behind you?"

Nora turned. A gentleman stood a few paces away, leaning his arms on the rail. He smiled at her, so she responded as she knew how—literally, raising a hand to her chest. "No, it's here, pumping just as it ought. But I left someone behind, and I'm missing him already."

"He's a lucky fellow."

Nora moved her head ambivalently, a twitch that was neither a shake or a nod, and only passably polite. She didn't feel like speaking. She turned away and heard the man leave. Her lips trembled. In her hurry to avoid him, she'd at last turned away from London. From Daniel.

Of course, it was ridiculous to stare so long, imagining the love in her eyes winging westward to find him. He knew how she felt, no matter which way she faced.

A gust of wind tossed her skirts, flattening them against her stiff new petticoat. Above her, the signal flags snapped. Her loose hair whipped into her eyes. She tucked it firmly behind her ear, bracing against the currents of air and the sway of the ship. The wind was at her back, and the way to look was forward.

AUTHORS' NOTE

In the usual division of labor between Regina and me, I tackle the beginnings and she the majority of the research. She rescues me from drowning in a book's middle, and I sweep away the extra commas. So I will begin explaining how we wrote this book, and when I mire myself in words she will extricate me. Be grateful.

This book began as an experiment after years of friendship and consulting with each other on our individual work. Regina had lost herself down a rabbit hole of medical history and, in an effort to pull me in, left a copy of Steven Johnson's *The Ghost Map* on the bedside table of her guest room when I came to visit from Canada. As she predicted, I plunged in alongside her. We couldn't get out! We took the thrilling challenge to record together a story of medicine as it evolved in the 1840s. For writers, this time of scientific inquiry is incredibly fertile. But we wanted to write about a woman, and that's where it became both easier and harder.

In the late eighteenth and early nineteenth centuries, women healers and midwives were being edged out by licensed physicians and surgeons. As medical practice became increasingly scientific, it also became a protected male preserve—but not everywhere. Anna Manzolini (1714–1774), referred to in our story, was indeed a teacher of anatomy at the University of Bologna. Famed for her wax anatomical models, she was celebrated throughout Europe and appointed as a lecturer in her own name after the death of her husband. (Previously, they had worked together.) Such was also the case with physicist Laura Bassi (1711–1778), also of Bologna.

This "family model" of participation in medicine or science was used by other notable women, including Caroline Herschel (1750–1848), the German astronomer, living in England, who began her studies and her work in collaboration with her brother.

Studying the careers and imagining the internal conflicts of these women was compelling: they worked, succeeded, and undoubtedly understood their own brilliance. But they could seldom claim by right the positions that could have been theirs. If there was an Eleanor Beady in London, she was a secret. The heartbreaking truth is that thinking women were forced by convention to work anonymously or in the shadow of husbands, brothers, and fathers, and not merely in the field of medicine. English political hostesses drafted letters and speeches for their menfolk, but were never credited in newspapers or on the floor of Parliament. Immortal novelists hid behind the names of George Eliot and Ellis, Acton, and Currer Bell. Yet there were many great women in this time, and they should be celebrated.

James Miranda Barry (1789–1865) lived as a man so she could train and work as a surgeon in the British Army. Florence Nightingale began her training in Germany in 1850, five years after our story. Under her own name, she revolutionized nursing and became one of the most famous figures in England. There was no qualified female doctor in England until Elizabeth Garrett Anderson (1836–1917), who trained in Paris. After she was admitted by the Society of Apothecaries in 1865, twenty years after our story, the society changed their rules to explicitly bar women from the profession. Undeterred, Dr. Anderson went on to establish the first medical college in England for women.

Eleanor is our creation, but we hope she is a fitting tribute to the women who inspired us, bright lights on a path that was—and can still be—dim and daunting.

Students of history will search in vain for a man named Horace Croft, but they may recognize in him the genius, passion, and recklessness of John Hunter (1728–1793), who inspired us. Dr. Hunter was a fearless scientist. He could conduct a surgery (without anesthesia) in minutes. He dissected stolen bodies, was famed for his remarkable specimens, and filled his home with them until it became such a house of horrors that people paid admission. He was hot-tempered and died of a stroke brought on by an angry quarrel with his colleagues at the hospital. Both Regina and I read and reread his incredible biography, *The Knife Man*, written by Wendy Moore. It is a riveting book.

We were also inspired by John Snow (1813–1858). His investigations of the 1854 London cholera epidemic led him to the source of infection—a contaminated pump. He removed the handle, and the epidemic stopped. This faith in scientific deduction was remarkable, because the bacilli that cause cholera were still years away from discovery. Most physicians of the time—as well as the brilliant nurse and statistician Florence

Nightingale—were miasma theorists and believed the disease was spread by bad air.

Dr. Snow was also an early adopter of ether. He developed a device to regulate vapor temperature, allowing doctors to administer controlled doses, which greatly improved the safety and success of surgical anesthesia. Incidentally, he was anesthesiologist to Queen Victoria.

Most of the cases and surgeries we describe in our story are factual, taken from the *Provincial Medical and Surgical Journal of 1840–1842*.

The history of surgical anesthesia is magnificently chronicled in *Blessed Days of Anaesthesia* by Stephanie J. Snow and proved so fascinating it had to become part of our story. In October 1846, a dentist, William Morton, used ether to sedate a patient for a tumor removal at Massachusetts General Hospital, sparking numerous experiments. Within weeks, a letter carrying the news reached a member of the Athenaeum club in London, who promptly informed the dentist who lived down the street and Robert Liston, professor of surgery at University College Hospital. Both men immediately began their own clinical trials and could have shared this discovery with our relentlessly curious Horace Croft.

Unfortunately, we wanted our characters to experience the mystery of ether anesthesia, so our story takes place in 1845 and 1846, when ether was still a party drug, not a revolutionary experimental treatment with an identified purpose. "Gas therapy" was not new, but it was not well understood. Beginning in the late 1700s, chemists, philosophers, and doctors inhaled oxygen, nitrous oxide, carbon dioxide, and other gases to treat conditions as diverse as consumption and venereal disease. At the same time, surgeons and dentists throughout the world were experimenting with different pain relievers including opioids, nitrous oxide, and hypnotism. It took longer than expected, but these two inquiries began intersecting well before William Morton's world-changing demonstration.

Humphry Davy, the famed chemist, investigated the effects of nitrous oxide on the nervous system, inducing lifeless states in lizards, rabbits, and snails. In 1824, Henry Hickman, a Shropshire surgeon, published a pamphlet describing the amputations he conducted on animals made "torpid" by the inhalation of carbon dioxide. His work was met with disinterest. Dr. Crawford Long, an American surgeon living in rural Georgia, quietly and successfully used ether as a surgical anesthesia in the early 1840s, but he never published his findings, largely because he couldn't explain the effects of the gas.

To Regina and me, given this history of reckless and unpublicized early experimentation, it seemed permissible—even probable—for a London surgeon's apprentice to accidentally stumble on the surgical possibilities of ether. The fear, confusion, and fascination we imagined such a discovery would provoke were impossible to resist.

If you found yourself swept away in the drama, anxiety, and frenzy of the Victorian medical world—as we hoped—know that you are in good company. We sympathize.

Jaima Fixsen
Alberta, Canada
February 2019

I am generally asked two questions about this work of fiction—why and how.

The first question—why I chose to write about the medical world of the 1840s—is the easier to answer. Simply put, I could not resist! After reading David McCullough's chapter on medical students in his fascinating work, *The Greater Journey*, it was impossible to find enough history books to whet my thirst for knowledge. My degree is in history, and it has been one of the greatest passions of my life since childhood, but never has one narrow field of study so seduced me. What pathos! What egos! What terrible courage and heartbreaking ignorance!

I hunted down the digitized catalogs of medical journals of the day—an online microfiche of sorts—and lost myself for hours in the vividly recorded cases. Can I express the true wonder of discovering I knew the color and texture of the tongue of a woman who suffered from seizures? I watched consumption patients unexpectedly improve for three hours before falling into a stertorous decline. I read breathlessly, sometimes tearfully, hoping for outcomes already decided by fate nearly two hundred years ago. I came to love the strangers I found—their boils and blisters, their cancers and cures.

My motivation to write this narrative was strictly emotional. For five years I researched and read, every new morsel of curious truth so compelling that I had to share this intoxicating story with others. But I felt the scope of the history too grand, too intricate, too demanding to tackle alone. That brings me to the second question—how.

Many have asked me how one work of fiction came to have two authors. How is it done? Which chapters are *hers* and which are *mine*? Let me be emphatic in saying none of it is mine. All of it is mine. Let me explain.

Jaima is a writer of immense talent and intelligence. She is the one and only person I ever would have collaborated with in this endeavor, and not only because I love and trust her; I defer to her knowledge and skill. She has written several historical novels, is uncannily familiar with Victorian England, and is trained in human anatomy. But more than that, she believes in and encourages my voice, just as I love hers. There is no ego when we write. The object is the story and only the story—to do justice to the men and women who inspired us to try.

This was a work of intense unity and single-minded collaboration. I do not suggest any writer attempt it unless he or she has a Jaima. In general, we divide labor by assigning ourselves scenes and writing a first draft. Together, through countless hours, we edit and add until the sentence I began ends with her flourish; the house she builds is adorned with my gas lamps and soaring windows. There is not a sentence we both haven't carefully nurtured, weighed, discussed, and polished.

Please know that every page was written with the ghosts of long-departed patients and doctors as close as our next word, our next heartbeats. To them we bow our heads and pay all our respects.

Regina Sirois
Kansas, United States
2020

READING
GROUP GUIDE

1. Though she's more qualified, Nora worries about being replaced by Daniel. Have you ever found yourself in a similar situation? What did you do about it?

2. Dr. Croft often resorts to disreputable methods of getting subjects, such as paying grave robbers or taking advantage of grieving family members. For him, the ends justify the means. Do you agree with him? To what extent?

3. Throughout the story, Nora conducts a series of experiments and independent studies. What was she hoping to learn?

4. We get to see nineteenth century medical techniques through Nora's eyes. Which treatments surprised you the most? Are there any techniques that carried over into modern medicine?

5. Nora is one of only a few women in a field dominated by men. Do you see any parallels between her situation in the nineteenth century and today?

6. Dr. Harry Trimble finds himself in a difficult situation when Dr. Silas Vickery blackmails him into speaking at the trial. Do you think Harry really had a choice in betraying Nora? What would you have done?

7. Compare Daniel's relationship with Mae and his relationship with Nora. How are they different? Are they similar in any way?

8. Daniel comes from an upper-class family while Nora and Harry come from the working class. How does socioeconomic background affect how they are treated by other people?

9. While Nora originally disliked Daniel, the two eventually grow to love each other. What brought them together, and why?

10. What did you think about Nora's decision to speak up for herself, though it results in public disgrace and punishment?

A CONVERSATION
WITH THE AUTHORS

You did extensive research before writing this story. What were the most surprising details you uncovered in your research process? Was there anything you found particularly interesting that didn't make it into the final book?

R: We won't live long enough to be able to write every fascinating thing we came across. The most surprising thing for me—how attached I became to the cases I studied. It became an addiction to browse through medical journals that are almost two centuries old, hoping the patients would recover. Another interesting fact for me was how many times something had to be "discovered." You would think once one doctor or scientist made a discovery, it would revolutionize the way doctors treated patients, but that is not at all how it worked. Information was slow and unreliable. There were language barriers and so many fraudulent cures and medical claims that it made the legitimate ones difficult to find or trust. For example, Ignaz Semmelweis discovered washing hands saved women from postpartum fevers and infection. He was so maligned for his theory (even though it worked!) that he died disgraced in an asylum!

J: So many innovators were reckless, unscrupulous cowboys! Some practices were absolutely hair-raising, and we ended up toning down the animal experiments in our book significantly.

I wish we could have worked in a detail from the life of Dr. John Hunter, who infected his own genitals using material from a sick patient in an attempt to determine if syphilis and gonorrhea are different diseases. Unfortunately for Hunter, the patient had both, so his conclusion that they were a single disease was wrong.

As coauthors, what does your brainstorming look like? Do you ever disagree on which direction to take?

R: We talk frequently, and sometimes exhaustively. Whenever we have a new idea, we walk through it on FaceTime so we can see each other's expressions and reactions. A few times, we seemed to have divergent opinions, but the longer we discussed, the more we realized we wanted the same thing. We have never had an argument about the direction of the story. We are both so in tune with the characters that we know when something is right for them and genuine to their personalities. Coauthoring is a high-level exercise in communication and cooperation.

J: When we are lucky enough to brainstorm in person, we tend to walk in the woods or sprawl out on the carpet, but most brainstorming and revising happens via FaceTime. It's rare for us to disagree. We both trust each other a lot—especially when either of us has a "Nope, don't like that" feeling. More often, I think we get a "Yes! And then—" feeling from each other's work.

What are some of your favorite books or authors? Do you have similar reading lists?

R: I think our reading list is actually pretty diverse, which is why we bring such different strengths to the table. I tend to be an extremely introspective reader. I love stories told in first person (*Jane Eyre, Moby Dick, All Quiet on the Western Front*) that delve into character more than plot. I am a huge fan of the classics. I usually read more nonfiction than fiction and am always working my way through a history book of one kind or another. David McCullough is a favorite of mine.

J: Our reading lists are actually pretty different. Regina is much more literary than me. I don't have the stamina to read *Moby Dick*, and I'm addicted to genre fiction, especially thrillers and comic romance. I have at least one going on my e-reader at any given time. One of my all-time favorite reads is Eva Ibbotson's *A Company of Swans*. Also, though it is not for the faint of heart, Dorothy Dunnett's plot-snarly Francis Lymond series. We both love reading history, and I'm especially drawn to the nineteenth century and the history of science.

Throughout Nora's journey, she juggles societal expectations of femininity while trying to build a career. Do you think this is still a conflict women face today?

R: I think it depends on the woman because situations vary widely. I believe there are women who shatter all ceilings and are celebrated for it. I also think there are women belittled and forced to conform to others' expectations. I have been fortunate enough in my life to never feel limited by my gender but empowered by it.

J: Yes, I do, though Nora reminds me that many groups have been and are unfairly disadvantaged by social power brokers. Women continue to face challenges, but I am inspired by the hard-won successes of nineteenth and twentieth century women. Their victories can and should be models for further change.

What advice would you offer aspiring historical fiction writers?

R: Dive deep and be ready. Writing a historical fiction requires discipline and patience because you will be on a creative roll and have to stop because you don't know the correct term for the strap that goes around a horse's tail (it's a crupper) or who sculpted the statues on the facade of the basilica of San Petronio (it was the female Renaissance artist Properzia de' Rossi). Every time you try to write, you will find yourself researching. It is why it takes so much longer. It is why it is so satisfying.

J: Write about people you care about, because you'll spend a lot of time with these imaginary friends. Don't let your people and their problems become secondary to the history, even when it is tempting. Oh, and if you can, find a best friend to write with. You'll have way more fun.

ACKNOWLEDGMENTS

Our heartfelt and everlasting thanks to Jennifer Weltz, advocate and agent, and the tireless team at JVNLA. To Anna Michels, Jenna Jankowski, and Sourcebooks for embracing and improving our vision. To Justin and Jeff, who encourage us through late-night writing sprints, join us on working trips to Canada or Kansas, and cheer us on in this creative journey. And to our children for the burned dinners, and the discussions of dissections and amputations over the same.

For a list of the authors and publications we gratefully turned to time and again for reference and inspiration, please see our authors' note.

ABOUT THE AUTHORS

Audrey Blake has a split personality—because she is the creative alter ego of writing duo Jaima Fixsen and Regina Sirois, two authors who met as finalists of a writing contest and have been writing together happily ever since. They share a love of history, nature, literature, and stories of redoubtable women. Both are inseparable friends and prairie girls despite living thousands of miles apart. Jaima hails from Alberta, Canada, and Regina calls the wheatfields of Kansas home. Though they have each authored several novels, this is their first joint venture, and hence, Audrey's first book.